The Bowmaker Girls

Elizabeth Lord

PIATKUS

Copyright © 1999 by Elizabeth Lord

First published in Great Britain in 1999 by
Judy Piatkus (Publishers) Ltd of
5 Windmill Street, London W1

This edition published 1999

**The moral right of the author
has been asserted**

*A catalogue record for this book is available
from the British Library*

ISBN 0 7499 0481 X

Set in Times by
Phoenix Photosetting, Chatham, Kent
Printed and bound in Great Britain by
Butler and Tanner, Frome and London

For my parents
Alice and Will
with gratitude

My thanks to Mr Greville, consultant orthopaedic surgeon, retired, for his valuable advice on matters of spinal injuries; also to the Heritage Museum, Leigh on Sea, Essex, for providing information on Leigh in the nineteen-twenties and nineteen-thirties; and to those cocklers who provided technical detail in the skill of gathering cockles and knowledge of the Thames Estuary.

Chapter One

Above the wild Saturday afternoon the deep double boom rolled over the Thames estuary to lose itself amid the creeks and mud flats and marshy islands of Leigh and Hadleigh.

In Leigh, Peggy Bowmaker looked up from cooking her men's tea to gaze towards the tiny window of her kitchen.

'That was Southend's lifeboat maroon.' Her tone was sharp but there was no need to further voice the vague concern that came to her. Her four daughters, helping lay the table for their father and brother coming home on the tide, shared the same brief thought, swiftly casting it off.

'They'll be back by now,' Connie, her oldest daughter, murmured.

Peggy hoped so. Daniel had promised only to work the one tide. No cockler, as cockle pickers were locally known, reading the weather signs as Dan could, would be foolish enough to stay out on the estuary for two tides. Dan had lifted an eye at it as he'd left.

'Looks like a bit of a blow coming up,' he'd said. 'Be back tonight.' Never changed his mind once he'd said a thing, knowing too that she'd have his tea ready for him. Always kept his word. Stubborn too. Didn't she know it. That bother with Dick Bryant all those years ago. Nineteen hundred and five, twenty-four years ago. Nineteen twenty-nine now, and the feud still going on . . .

Yes, he'd be tying up by the creek wall at this minute. She felt easier.

Her slow exhalation of momentarily held breath was less audible than felt. She glanced around at her girls, for once all here together: Josie, her youngest and out of work again, Connie the

1

eldest, home from work with a cold, as was Pam. Annie, receptionist at the Cliffs Hotel, would be going in later.

Josie, coming up to eighteen, was first to cheer up. 'Can I go out and see if I can see anything?'

Her mother stopped stirring the casserole she had been getting out of the tiny kitchen range oven as the maroon went off, her full face reddened by the heat. She smiled, but not indulgently. 'It's got too windy out there.'

'Oh, Mum . . .'

Another detonation reverberated in the air, faint here but a mighty boom a few miles away in Southend-on-Sea itself.

'Someone's definitely in trouble.'

'A ship?' Josie was animated by impatience. 'Oh, Mum, can I go?'

The wind had got up, suddenly, around dinner time. Dan had been right, as always, reading the overcast sky. He had chuckled, deep in his throat. 'Anyone working doubles this weather needs his brains tested.'

Doubles – going out on a falling tide to rake the exposed mud banks for the cockles East Londoners loved; as the tide returned, climbing back on board, as it again ebbed, over the side a second time, coming home with a laden boat on the next high tide. Dan favoured the sands of Shoeburyness beyond Southend, where the tiny bivalves were plentiful, but some way out. High wind could be hazardous to a shallow, forty-foot bawley even under engine.

It was nearing the end of March. Visitors wouldn't be coming to the cockle sheds of Leigh to buy the small succulent shellfish until summer – perhaps a few at Easter, but mostly the cockles gathered at this time of year went to Billingsgate fish market in London. Less profit than selling direct to visitors, but still not too bad a living.

'I'll put a coat on, Mum,' Josie was begging. 'I'll only be a minute, I promise.'

Josie's promises were unlike her father's. She could be half an hour, promise forgotten, her dad home demanding where the hell she was. But how could she ignore the girl's pleading tone? Josie, unlike her sisters, was between jobs. She was seldom able to hold a job down, because of her volatile nature, and had been stuck in all day. Perhaps this once. 'All right, but only a minute.'

2

In less than a minute she was racing back from the Strand where people had already gathered to watch what was going on.

'Mum, there's two big ships out there. It looks like one's rammed the other. There's tugs out there too. I can't see very well from this distance but one tug looks in trouble.'

Her eyes flew straight to Connie, who had gasped. But their mother gave a small laugh for all it held a note of anxiety for her eldest daughter. 'There's thousands of tugs working the Thames. It wouldn't be Ben's.'

But Pam had given a disquieting, 'Oh, Connie,' as her sister made for the back door and the back gate beyond the tiny yard, coatless, the edges of her brown cardigan flying.

Annie at the door called after her. 'I'll bring Dad's binoculars.'

The cockle boats had all wisely come in and were tied up to the sea wall beyond which discarded shells several feet deep lay piled up like small mountains, ready to be crushed to help make roads and garden paths. This provided another small source of income. Lorries came for them regularly. And just as well for they filled the air with a heavy stink of rotten fish.

Daniel's smallish haul today had been unloaded into the sheds for boiling. First the men would eat a much-needed evening meal. He, his brothers Reg and Pete, his son Danny and young Tibb Barnard who helped out, had left. Daniel and Danny reached home a quarter of a mile from the sheds, and were on the point of opening the street door when the maroon sounded.

'Trouble?' Daniel, his large hand poised on the half-open door, eyed his son.

Danny, twenty-six, the eldest of his family, his only son now – his youngest had been knocked down on the railway lines five years ago – gazed back and grinned derisively quirking his lips slightly to one side. 'Holidaymaker fell off a jetty? Or some silly rich fool out on his yacht?' It was all possible. His father did not smile.

'Too early for holidaymakers. And anyone going out there willingly has to be a fool.'

'That's what I said.' The quip was mild and his father now grinned, a grin much like his son's, as they pushed into the house.

The door opened into the tiny front room as did all the doors in this short terrace of fishermen's cottages dating back fifty years or more. Facing the old High Street and situated halfway between

3

the rickety clusters of cockle sheds, a couple of pubs and Bell Wharf, they backed on to a cobbled alley overlooking the estuary. They'd all been two-up-two-down when first built, but most had been extended into the back yards to give extra room.

The second maroon sounded as the two men closed the door. Daniel paused. 'Better take a look.'

From the kitchen came sounds of consternation, as his wife heard him come in. She called out fretfully, 'That you, Dan? Did you hear that?'

She came hurrying from the kitchen, her expression all worked up. 'Connie's gone rushing out. Josie says there's two ships in collision and a tugboat that looks in distress. Connie's got it into her mind it could be her Ben's tug.'

'That's damned stupid,' Dan said.

'Yes, but you know how she is about him, what with them to be engaged come June. She says things are going too smoothly for them and something's bound to go wrong – it always does.'

'Where's she now?'

'I told you, out there on the Strand by now. Josie said there's a great crowd gathering there.

'Bugger that Josie,' Dan swore as he followed his wife through to the back, the tall muscular figure of Danny following closely behind. 'Can't ever see her thinkin' on anything but spreading bloody panic wherever place she 'appens to be. Upsettin' Connie like that.'

'Well, they've all gone flying off now,' Peggy said testily, her meal left.

On the square called the Strand and all along the narrow promenade between the shoreline and the main railway line from London's Fenchurch Street and Southend's Central Station local people had gathered, the crowd growing steadily. Adding to it, the Bowmakers gazed out across heaving waves large enough to have been the North Sea itself, the waves breaking right up the sloping sea wall to half drown with each splash those who stood too close. The air had filled with the iodine smell of seaweed.

Dan grabbed his binoculars from Connie's trembling hands. She now wore the coat Annie had brought out for her to wear against the March wind. For a moment he trained them on the two cargo vessels still locked together, then on the several tugs bobbing in the white-topped waves like little bugs around the huge hulls.

'I can't see the names on any of the tugs,' he announced. 'Just them of the cargo ships. One's . . .'

'I don't care about the names of the ships,' Connie shrieked. 'Can't you see more than that? They said one of the tugs is in trouble. Which one?'

'I can see it, gel. But I can't read the name. Not from 'ere.'

'It can't be anything to do with your Ben,' Annie ventured. 'He's probably a long way up river. Probably has no idea. And it would have to be quite a big coincidence, wouldn't it, if it was him and his father on that tug? I'm sure it couldn't be, could it? But you mustn't worry.'

Connie didn't reply. Annie might as well have said, 'But it could.' Whatever Annie said, however well intentioned, she managed to sound doleful, always managed to refer to the more awful of two likelihoods. She and her haughty attitude. Annie worked as a receptionist at the big Cliffs Hotel in Westcliff further along towards Southend and assumed herself a cut above everyone else. With unkind thoughts, Connie ignored her gloomy comments. But it was hard not to react to them.

The lifeboat had appeared from behind the bend in the shore-line. A cheer went up from those around her as it sped its way towards the distant scene, its bows at times almost leaping clear of the waves. The cheer had a note not of relief but of glee. People seemed ever keen to enjoy a spectacle, ignorant of those distant men in danger of drowning, who perhaps had already drowned. They were too removed from the onlookers to possess any significance of suffering and terror – like watching a film at the pictures, where the drama of the silent reel came across only via the accompanying pianist's skill. They were hateful, these people who came merely to gawp. Connie despised them.

The lifeboat would take its passengers back to Southend. An hour or two later she might be informed that Ben had been one of them, dead or injured, for she was becoming more and more convinced of him being there. Through the binoculars she could see men being helped off the tugboat, whose stern was already under water. Some of the lifeboat men seemed to be searching the water around it. Someone overboard. Someone drowning; already drowned. They seemed to be pulling someone or something out of the water. Connie's heart seemed to be up in her throat. The binocular vision picked out a limp form being lifted on to the

5

lifeboat, Ben's form, she was sure of it. With a small strangled cry, she thrust the binoculars back into her dad's hands.

'I've got to get to Southend. They've brought someone out of the water. It looked like Ben.'

'Connie,' her mother said as she rounded on her. 'Don't be so silly, love. You're getting yourself into a state.'

The others had gathered about her, the scene out to sea forgotten.

'You can't go, just like that.'

'It's not Ben. It can't be.'

'You can't go alone, Connie.'

'I have to go, I have to. I have to be sure.' Her heart pumping in her chest was a heavy stifling pain. She knew her face was chalk white, her eyes staring with the visions she was seeing. Her and Ben, so happy. Too good to be true. 'I don't care, I've got to go,' she wept, her voice rising.

'Love, people are looking. If you must, I'll go with you. The lifeboat will take ages to get back.'

'I'll go with her,' Danny said in a commanding way. 'You stay here, Mum, and get on with the tea.' He turned back to Connie, who was standing shaking from head to foot with her visions. His voice was soothing. 'There is nothing to worry about, Connie, but you must go just to be sure, I know. Come on, let's get goin', then.'

Connie returned on his arm, her face still white, her eyes red with weeping. She looked about ready to faint. At her entrance, the family, waiting in virtual silence in the front room for her return, stood up anxiously.

Her mother came forward, arms outstretched. 'Oh, love, no.'

Thus prompted Connie, having held herself together all the way back on the train, burst into a relieved fit of weeping on her mother's shoulder, her words tumbling out in a gush.

'Oh, Mum. It was so awful. It wasn't him. He wasn't there. He wasn't on that tug. But they asked me if I was related or knew him. I didn't know who it was. But he looked so dreadful, all cut and bruised and . . . and dead.'

Her words cut themselves off in a swallowed sob. But it wasn't Ben. Oh, thank God, it wasn't him.

'Then come and sit down, love.' Her mother guided her, still weeping, to an armchair as the whole room seemed to relax.

6

'There's nothing to cry about any more. Your Ben's all right. You'll be seeing him on Saturday. It must have been a terrible experience for you, but now it's all over. Now you must forget all about it.'

'But someone will be grieving,' was all she could say. 'I wish I could take their grief away for them when they're told.'

'Well, you can't, love. No matter how much people care and cuddle, those with grief to endure have to do it alone, I'm afraid.'

The tone of the remark made Connie's heart go out to her as her mother went to make the cup of soothing tea. On the loss of little Tony, only ten years old, on the railway line, had she grieved alone despite all their combined grieving? Yes, she had.

Connie lay back in the armchair, thoroughly worn out by her ordeal, and let herself cry quietly, for her weariness, for the woman who would soon be grieving, and for her mother who had never stopped.

Chapter Two

Who would have believed that a few days ago had seen wild winds and heaving waves? Today the estuary held a strange lurking silence, the water out as far as it could go, leaving mile on mile of brown algae-coated ooze soft as melted chocolate.

The stillness helped calm Josie Bowmaker's angry breast as she let her feet sink ankle-deep in mud. From here she could see Southend's mile-long pier. Two and a half miles away, it looked no more than a grey pencil mark against the pale, cloud-streaked horizon on this fresh April afternoon. The holiday season had not yet begun; few people would be walking the pier, and the small open-sided trains that trundled its length were still having maintenance done to them under the pavilion.

Drawing her cardigan closer about her shoulders against a brief stir of chilly air, she widened her gaze to the distant glint of deep water where cargo ships hardly seeming to move made for or departed from the docks of London. The water's edge itself was completely out of sight, but the tide had probably begun to turn and she'd have to be getting back home soon.

Dad and Danny would be home soon too. Several boats had gone out yesterday, each with four men to work the sands, each team working in a tight circle, throwing back the undersized ones to grow on and replenish their numbers. Cocklers could make quite a decent living, but it was hard work. During the winter when the weather grew cold and the salt wind bit hands and cheeks, they would ease off. But with summer coming, they were now stepping up the hours. In summer they wore shorts and shirts. Today, still in winter gear, it was thigh boots, several polo-necked jerseys. With the season just around the corner, holidaymakers and day trippers would come to the Leigh cockle sheds to buy cockles at threepence a pint in small woven bags to eat with pepper and vinegar. They ate shrimps too, and whelks and winkles, jellied eels, mussels and prawns, but cocklers kept to their own trade.

Most of this sea fare was washed down by pints of beer from dozens of pubs along Southend's bustling sea front, the Kursal, with its switchback and its roundabouts, its fun palaces and its sideshows blaring in the ears of those who converse in loud, sharp Cockney accents, and families taking tea in trays down on to the beach from refreshment booths dotted along the Prom, a shilling deposit charged on the tray. Kids licked ice cream cornets; sucked at sticky scarlet seaside rock with Southend lettered all the way through the white, peppermint centre. Some would buy a few sticks of rock to take home to friends to prove they'd been at the seaside for a day or part of a week (not easy for the bread-winner of a London East End family to give them a full week when he got paid for only three days holiday if he were lucky); kids tore off shreds of fluffy pink candy floss that melted in the mouth and left a grubby rime around their lips. The empty stick on which it had been spun would be used as a flagstaff for a sand castle.

The buzz of Southend-on-Sea was a noise unto itself: tinny music, shrieks from the ghost train, the haunted house, the scenic railway; aromas of hot sausage, fish and chips, vinegar. Shops selling gaudy hats with 'kiss me quick' written on them. Bathing huts and bright swimming costumes, middle-aged women in print dresses, paddling, hems held thigh high to avoid the wavelets, men with trouser legs rolled up to the knee, people who burned their skin bright pink and shiny to peel for the rest of the week in homes, offices and factories. Kids armed with buckets and spades, castles to be built and water to be brought to their moats to disappear as quickly as it was poured in. All rowdy and busy. But here in this back-water fishing community on the far edge of a holiday resort, it was quiet and peaceful.

For a little longer Josie put off that moment when she must turn for home. Even the gulls were silent, feeding far off at the water's edge. The only sounds to be heard were those directly at her feet. They had to be listened for attentively, or one might become aware of them quite suddenly. Tiny sucking, plopping sounds, the oozing of worm casts being thrown up, the brief scurry of a crab, the soft snap of a cockle shell closing at the approach of a foot.

The silence made Josie shiver. She hadn't planned to be out here at all, but she had been so angry. She shivered again. It was getting cold and she hadn't even brought a coat.

It had been Annie's fault, going off at her like that, and Mum taking her side. Anyone with half an eye could see Annie was Mum's favourite. She was so pretty, and she knew it. Tall like Dad, but so waif-like she was the envy of every girl who struggled for that fashionable look. Nineteen twenty-nine dresses made her look even thinner.

It was a dress that had started the row. All she'd done was borrow Annie's second-best one to go out in last night. To hear Annie when she'd discovered it, one would think she'd borrowed the Crown Jewels. It hadn't fitted properly anyway. Thin though she was, Annie was still nearly a size larger than herself. Well, she would be. Annie was twenty-two, and she was only seventeen, well, coming up to eighteen next month. Between them was Pam. Connie was the eldest. Poor Connie.

Josie thought of Connie as she began negotiating her way back to the shore, using the slightly more raised ripples of mud which were harder than the troughs in which mud could come up to her calves. Connie, at twenty-four, though sometimes she behaved like thirty-four, always looked for the dire side of life in a fearful sort of way as though it would pounce on her. Courting Ben Watson, son of a tugboat skipper, she seemed to live in constant dread of anything happening to him in his work. Like last week, when that tugboat sank and she had felt so certain Ben was on board, was drowned. Laughable. Not at the time of course. But everyone had got worked up over nothing. She was always on about the Devil always lying in wait for those who enjoyed life too much and thinking things were too good. As if things could ever be *too* good.

Josie thought again of Annie. When she got back she would snub her. It was what Annie deserved, leading off like she had. She cast her now angry eyes towards the incoming tide. Not easy to pinpoint, but it would steal back in with silent swiftness as if drawn by an invisible magnet, implacably filling hollows and dips, seeping into each, unnoticed, the hollows joining up into pools, lakes, encircling a careless wanderer until the only

10

route of escape was to wade to drier ground. Reaching level parts, the tide became a moving creature quietly lifting the scores of tilted boats upright from their muddy slumbers to set them gently bobbing.

The slippery mud oozed pleasantly between Josie's toes to flow over her instep, causing her to be wary of losing her footing and ending up on hands and knees. Already her shins and calves were coated. No point rinsing it off in a salt-rimed pool if she only had to step again into more mud. As yet there'd be no pools to wash in by the sea wall. She'd clean up when she got indoors and hope Mum wouldn't see her before that.

There was mud on the low-waisted skirt of her pale blue dress, and a streak or two in the waves of her short, light brown hair where she'd touched it with hands that had tried to sweep some of it off her legs. Josie looked down at herself and giggled. No one would guess her to be nearly eighteen, judging by the state of her.

'Look at the state of you. Look at your dress. No coat. Over your sulks now, I suppose. Anyone'd think you was seven, not seventeen.'

'I'll be eighteen in three weeks' time.'

'No one would guess it.'

Peggy Bowmaker glowered at her youngest daughter, who dropped her gaze to look away. Josie knew better than to give verbal defiance. Once angered, Peggy knew she might slap out at Josie; lightly, as a symbolic reminder that she was still worthy of respect, but embarrassing to both of them, since the top of her head reached only as far as the girls's eyes. They had all of them grown beyond her five foot one inch height and were wont to pat the top of her fair hair and call her 'Tiddy Mumma' in playful affection. She put up with it; any sense of being ridiculed even in play would be superseded by pride in her children, their fine health, their good looks, their bearing, their slim but strong build. It wasn't merely that she was blinded by love – they were all of these things. Others had said so.

Peggy, christened Elizabeth in eighteen eighty, over forty-eight years ago, but not called that since that day gave her youngest daughter a small shove of reproof.

'Ought to be ashamed of yourself, messing about out there like some kid. I suppose I'll be expected to wash that dress for you.

11

Well you can wash it yourself. And iron it when it's dry. And put it away.'

'I'll start on it now,' Josie muttered with half-concealed recalcitrance.

'No you won't,' Peggy shot at her. 'I'm getting tea ready. Do it later. And be sure you come down looking like a lady,' she called after her as Josie made for the narrow squeaky stairs to the upper floor with its two bedrooms. 'For once try to act your age.'

It was untrue. Josie did act her age most of the time. But some of the rebellious little girl in her still lingered. Secretly Peggy felt sad it was fading so quickly, her last living child no longer a child. Peggy would never have admitted to anyone how much she clung to the child in Josie. If Tony hadn't been knocked down by a train just a couple of hundred yards away from his home – the irony of it all that the train had been going so slow – she might not still be hanging on to Josie's disappearing childhood.

Five years ago now. Tony had been nearly ten years old, the last of her brood. One small lovely young life got wiped out in seconds. He hadn't known what had hit him. Playing ball with mates, climbing over the level crossing gates to retrieve the ball, excited by his game, full of vitality, and deaf to the warning shouts of people emerging from the station who saw him, the train gathering speed, a driver with his mind still back in the station not concentrating – at least that's how she'd always see it, no one could make her see otherwise – all over in a split second. Perhaps he had seen the train at the last second, known a moment of terror. She hoped not, hoped he hadn't suffered even that fleeting fear. They said he hadn't known a thing about it.

He'd be nearly fifteen now. For a long time she'd felt utterly numbed, couldn't really recollect what she'd done or what had gone on around her those days after it had happened. These days she smiled and sometimes laughed, but it had been years before she could. Even now she often felt she smiled and laughed only on the outside. Before Tony's death she had always lived in fear of losing a child; prayed that no one in her family would die. She herself had died a thousand deaths, as mothers do for fear of losing their children. Even Daniel, her husband whom she still loved dearly, she could have got over in time had he died. But there was nothing worse than losing a child, especially the youngest and, to a mother's mind, the most defenceless.

12

Drawing in a deep sob of breath through her teeth, she straightened her back and turned as her daughter's rebellious footsteps thumped across the ceiling above her, and set about cutting bread for tea.

The front door had opened, Connie and Pam coming in together. The two girls worked not far from each other. Connie worked in the office of a local firm of engineers in Chalkwell, Pam was a legal secretary. Clever. All her girls were clever: no factory work for them. Josie was bright too; if only she wasn't so volatile. She seldom kept a job for long, always looking for something better. She was between jobs now. Annie had said there was chance of an opening at the Cliffs Hotel for Josie. Though now they'd had that row at dinner time, it appeared debatable whether Annie would pursue it.

She'd already been home once today, at dinner time. She didn't usually, but said she'd been stewing all morning over Josie borrowing her dress without permission and couldn't wait any longer to have it out with her. The result had been a row, ending with Josie throwing herself out of the house while Annie had stalked off back to work. Fancy, travelling two stations home on the train at dinner time just to have a row and then two stations back to work, entirely missing her dinner – talk about cutting off her nose to spite her face, but that was Annie. And what of Josie, going out last night dolled up in someone else's dress, trying to make herself look older than she was. Trouble with Josie was, she thought herself a free spirit. Well, perhaps she was. But all this looking for this *something better*, as she called it, meant the only one she hurt was herself.

But she was a good girl. They were all good girls.

She heard their voices talking brightly, then Connie called out to her as they took off their hats and coats. Peggy called back that she was in here, in the kitchen. In that moment the street door opened again and now came Annie's voice, slightly sharp, cultured, the three of them talking now as they came to find her.

'Sorry I'm a bit late, Mum.' Connie sounded breathless as they burst into the kitchen. She was usually home before the others. 'I needed to go and post a letter to Ben and missed my train. Can I help?'

Peggy smiled. Yes, they were all good girls.

'You can make the tea, love,' she said.

'Is the table laid yet, Mum?' asked Pam.

'I was going to do it after I'd done the bread.'

Pam grabbed the tablecloth from the drawer of the old sideboard under the wall shelves beside the kitchen range. Annie, already taking down plates, looked towards the kitchen range and the frying pan noisily sizzling. 'Sausages,' she stated with a snort of contempt.

'We always have sausages on Fridays.'

'They ruin my figure, Mum. I'll only have the one.'

'Hardly anything of you to speak of now.' Peggy smiled. 'How was work today? Meet anyone nice?' She worried about Annie. Nearly two years younger than Connie and no young man in sight yet.

Annie sniffed and said, 'Huh!'

'There must be lots of nice young men going in an out of that hotel of yours. At least one of them ought to be unattached.'

'For heaven's sake, Mum.' Annie stood cuddling the tablecloth to her bosom, what there was of it. Most young girls these days flattened them into the sylph-like fashion with those ridiculous bras, a bit of shapeless material with straps, not worth the two shillings and sixpence they cost. She could have made them herself from pieces of old sheeting for nothing.

'All I ever see is old codgers at that hotel,' Annie was musing.

'You don't go out enough in the evenings to meet anyone,' Peggy told her. 'That's your trouble.'

'Who would I go out with? All the friends I had are getting engaged or married. I'm the only one left.'

'And whose fault's that?' Peggy turned the sausages in the pan, took a peek at the potatoes she was boiling and would mash for the men's meal. She tested them with a knife. Almost done. 'Pam, butter the the bread, will you, love?'

She turned her attention back to Annie. 'You're far too finicky. That nice lad you was going out with last year. He was very hurt, you givin' him up. An' he was so nice, an' all.'

'He was a brick maker. I don't want to live hand to mouth. Anyway, we weren't going steady.'

'About time you were, miss,' Peggy said sternly, sawing a couple of exta slices – the men'd come home ravenous, they always did. She held the loaf against her chest which was far ampler at her age than those of her daughters, perhaps a bit too ample for her small height, but she was past caring about fashion and the slim shape it dictated. 'Trouble is you aim too high,' she muttered. 'What're you looking for, Annie? A lord? An earl or something?'

'That's silly, Mum. I just want someone who can look after me . . .'

'In the style you're accustomed to,' Peggy interrupted with a chuckle. 'That's a laugh for a start. Your dad in his shirtsleeves in a cockle shed servin' summer holidaymakers. And me, helpin' him when it gets too busy. Well, maybe one day Miss High'n'Mighty you might find your earl or whatever you're looking for. Maybe when you're old and grey and the moon turns to cheese.'

She said all this with good humour, faintly surprised when Annie huffed and swept out of the crowded kitchen to lay the table in the other room.

'Now you've upset her,' Connie said. She fumbled in the knife drawer for spoons to accompany the cups and saucers. 'She feels it, you know.'

'Feels what?'

'Not having a steady boyfriend when all her friends have.'

'It's her own fault. She's too picky, that one.'

But Peggy's mind had moved on. This was the first time this evening Connie had come into any conversation, Connie who usually had plenty to say for herself. She had grown very quiet, very thoughtful since that tugboat disaster earlier in the week. When asked if anything was wrong, if she was all right, she'd present a jerky smile and say that she was fine. But obviously she was brooding. It had been traumatic for her, and ever since she had written every day to Ben, hurrying to post it and watching for the postman as though he bore her life's blood with him. Yet she'd be seeing Ben on Sunday. It was hard to know how to combat it, but all Peggy could do was stand by and wait for it to pass.

'I've not got a steady boyfriend yet,' Pam had butted in.

Peggy forced her mind away from Connie and smiled sympathetically. 'You will,' she said. 'Just enjoy yourself while you can. Life's too short.'

Pam didn't reply. She had told a lie and it was important the lie be believed. No one knew about her and George Bryant. Dad would go potty if he found out, because of him and George's dad and that row all those years ago. Something to do with a boat, she wasn't sure. Dad wouldn't talk about it, would not even hear Dick Bryant's name mentioned in the house. Not that it ever was. The families seldom came in contact with each other. The Bryants were shrimpers, trawled the estuary, and saw themselves as proper fishermen, not like the cocklers. Although with the estuary getting more polluted with the growing amount of shipping letting out oil, the finicky shrimps had moved away, were harder to find, and the shrimping industry had been declining for years. Cockles lay buried under sand and mud, and oil didn't affect them. The cocklers did well and always would.

But one day Dad would have to know about her and George, and Pam dared not contemplate the result. It was her constant nightmare.

'You'll find a nice boy eventually,' her mum encouraged, innocent of Pam's thoughts. 'Then we'll give you a nice engagement party just like the one Connie and Ben are having in June. Her and Ben are such a lucky couple.'

Connie turned sharply from replacing the lid on the teapot and swept out of the kitchen with the teapot under its cosy, followed by Pam bearing teacups on a wooden tray. Both girls were very quiet.

The kitchen fell silent. Left alone, Peggy mulled over her daughters as she emptied the water from the boiled potatoes and began mashing them.

Her son she had no qualms about. Danny at twenty-six, had endless girlfriends but no one steady. However, it was different for a boy. It was her daughters she thought of – Annie mostly. For Pam and Josie there was plenty of time for them to meet a nice boy and settle down. Connie would be married next year. But Annie, there seemed no hope for Annie. Always reaching for the moon, with her sights raised so high, she seemed doomed to disappointment. She'd seen it before, spinsters who'd once had such high hopes. Please God, she prayed as she mashed the potatoes furiously, adding a little milk, a little margarine, Annie would find herself a nice young man soon. Twenty-two and not one in sight. Peggy's heart almost bled. To be left on the shelf, and Annie so pretty too.

Footsteps tripped down the creaky stairs. Josie. From the corner of her eye, Peggy saw her youngest girl's oval face peep cautiously around the kitchen door.

16

Josie's voice was small. 'Mum, I'm sorry.'

'Don't be silly,' Peggy said, putting the mashed potatoes aside to give the sausages a last turn in the pan before dishing up. 'And about the dress, love . . .'

'I'll say I'm sorry to Annie,' Josie broke in. 'I won't do it again.'

'I mean your own dress. I'll wash it for you.'

'You don't have to.'

'I know. But I will.'

She received a thankful kiss on the back of her neck exposed by her short hair. In this at least she was in fashion if nowhere else, with her hair shorn off into a back shingle. Two years ago her daughters had finally persuaded her to get rid of the long tresses that had been wound into a chignon which she had worn since she was a young woman before and during the Great War.

'Get away with yer!' But she smiled at the kiss. Doling out a portion of potato on to a plate, laying two piping hot sausages beside it and a dollop of baked beans that had been keeping warm in a saucepan to one side of the kitchen range, she handed the meal to Josie. 'Take your plate and go and eat.'

She was still smiling after Josie grabbed her tea and went off into the other room; the other three had still to come back for theirs. She could hear them talking together, Josie's high twittering voice joining in.

Peggy's smile grew contemplative, broody. Josie was so excitable, so effervescent, so unpredictable, a natural rebel. Whatever would happen to that girl she sometimes dreaded to think. But such fears were dashed away as her other three daughters exploded into the kitchen to collect their tea.

17

Chapter Three

To the gentle throbbing of its engine, the *Steadfast* glided smoothly up the now full Creek. Danny looked about him. It was a perfect April evening, the air still, the water quiet but for the gentle arrowing from the *Steadfast*'s bow wave. Thin flat clouds lay across the fading pale blue in golden streaks that would soon now blush crimson, then purple, after the sun had gone below the empty horizon. The weather held the promise of a fine tomorrow. He glanced at the others in the boat.

Dad was at the helm, while the other three, Dad's brothers Reg and Pete and young Tibb Barnard, sat with backs to the bulwark. The cockles in baskets at their feet sent up a strong fishy tang. Each man felt weary but content, for it had been a good haul, fetching maybe a shilling a basket at Billingsgate or, if they were lucky, one and six, though with often strong competition from the Dutch. Once the holiday trade started in a few weeks, it would be threepence a pint to the public, highly salted water adding to the flavour. Trade remained excellent in summer, but during the approach to it and again at the end of the season, things could be a bit up and down. Salted down for sale in London, though, they'd last up to six weeks, preserved, hard as dried peas, needing to be soaked in fresh water for up to two days before use.

A small pang of hunger ground in Danny's stomach. His dinner would be waiting for him and Dad. Wednesday meant sausage and mash, with baked beans and lots of thick brown Bisto gravy. Apple and custard to follow – Mum never varied her daily meals – and a big mug of hot strong tea, a meal to blow a man out and stop him moving for the rest of the evening. But there'd be no sitting back stretching out on the settee after the meal tonight. As

18

soon as it was over, it would be down the sheds to begin boiling the cockles.

He thought of Lily. It would have been nice to see her tonight, but he'd see her tomorrow, perhaps take her to the pictures in Southend. It was showing *Seventh Heaven* with Charles Farrell and Janet Gaynor. A Harold Lloyd film was the second feature. He might get seats at the back so that while the audience shelled peanuts, mesmerised by the love scenes, and read the words that came up on the briefly darkened screen – *The Jazz Singer* and the second full talkie *Lights of New York* were still reserved for London and other big city cinemas – he would cuddle her, hopeful she might let him steal a kiss. She'd probably balk at any further advances. Maybe later in the dark after getting off the bus home she might allow him a bit more licence but not too much. No girl did. Not a decent girl like Lily.

He rather liked Lily – slim and vivacious, her dark hair bobbed and her eyebrows plucked into that permanently surprised look that girls in the fashion magazines had. She was tall but he still had to bend to kiss her. He had to bend to kiss most girls.

He hoped in a way that Lily would last longer than most of them, who in the end always had a way of becoming possessive. 'We *are* going steady, aren't we, Danny?' 'I've told my mum about you and she's thrilled I'm going out with you.' They tugged his arm to stare longingly at engagement rings in jewellers' windows. That sort of thing. Every time he looked into the eyes of some of them, he could almost hear the wedding bells chiming.

Twenty-six was what people called a marriageable age, but there was still lots of life to live before settling down. None of his mates had as yet, and he didn't want to be the first, be the butt of their jokes. But Lily was different. Every time he saw her or even thought about her, like now, there would be a sort of churning in his stomach that wasn't hunger – well, hunger, yes, but a certain sort which he had to breathe deeply to dispel. Even then it wouldn't quite go away, not for ages, until his mind was distracted by something else.

It was his father who distracted it. Daniel Bowmaker's stare was directed at the shrimp boats already back and anchored out in the Ray unlike the cockle boats which would remain in the Creek. The shrimpers did all their boiling on board. The small crustaceans died fast and a shrimp cooked after having died was no good whereas cockles lived on in their shells, safe and fresh in their own liquid until brought to the shed for boiling.

'Home already.' He said it with a tinge of pleasure in his tone. 'Cold enough today to send shrimp out to deeper water, I suspect.'

Lily put away for a moment, Danny regarded the silent boats and nodded. 'Not easy these days. They say the river's gettin' too dirty for 'em. Lot more cargo boats mucking it up these days.'

His father grinned. 'We're in the best business, lad. One thing about cockles, you know where they are. Shrimps – they can move off somewheres else. Here today, gone tomorrow. Nets get full on seaweed and them useless shore crabs and have to be got rid of before they try again, or get torn on lost anchors and stuff. Shrimpers – huh! I'd soonest use me feet out on the mud any time than mess about castin' bloody nets and cookin' on board.'

Danny could understand his father's devilish glee at the difficulties shrimpers apparently suffered. Further down the road lived the Bryants, shrimpers, the couple old now, their children married and moved away, except for their youngest, George.

'You've never got over it, have you, Dad? All these years. And all over nothing.' It had been nothing much to start with.

'Nothing?' His dad glared at him, oblivious to the others grinning covertly, knowing the old old story. 'Nothing! You call a man what burned me, nearly lost me me livelihood, nothing? No, I'll never get over that, so long as I live. I never want anything to do with 'em and I'll see off any of me family what has anything to do with them, and that's clear to everyone and'll always be so.'

Breathing heavily, he turned his eyes back to guiding the forty-foot wooden bawley towards the hard where he would kill its engine and bring it to rest just off-shore where the beach, strewn high with long-discarded cockle shells, raised its continuous odour of decaying fish into the air.

Danny continued to look at his father. Sad to think of the years that old feud had gone on. Not an open one, merely a silent ignoring, a passing by in the street without glancing at each other. Everyone around knew of it, accepted it, even forgot it, the humour of it long since spent, the gossip long since died. Even the cause of it had now become obscure to many.

Danny had been a toddler, his sisters not yet born. Even to him, from the bits that Dad in his brief recourse to the matter in moments of angry recollection had let slip, it was a sketchy argument over a clod of mud tossed by the then-young married man, Dick Bryant, in a moment of high spirits. The clod had hit Dad on the forehead. Standing there in surprise, mud oozing down his face, his young pride injured with those around him bursting into guffaws of laughter, he had launched himself at Dick Bryant. He'd floored him, almost killed him it was said, others having to drag him off the bleeding face with its smashed nose and broken jaw. To this very day Bryant sported a crooked nose. Seething from his undeserved injuries, Bryant had stolen aboard Dad's boat, so the story went – a different boat to the one he now had – to set fire to it. Those running to the blaze had seen a man hurrying off. Someone had said they'd recognised Bryant. It was obvious to all that he bore Dad a grudge and though Dad had never been able to prove it was him, it wasn't hard to point a finger when afterwards, it was said, Bryant's bruised and battered face wasn't seen for a long time in the pubs Dad frequented.

That had been in nineteen hundred and five. Today, twenty-four years later, the vindictive act was still an open wound in Dad's side.

Those in the boat came alert. The *Steadfast*'s hull gently scuffed the creek mud as they eased the planks over the slowly incoming tide across which they'd make the shore, each with a wicker basket at either end of a stout wooden yoke, both as full and weighty as a sturdy man could carry on to the shell-strewn beach that slithered underfoot, shells crunching and rustling and tinkling together at each step, to the mushers, as the cockle sheds were called, where the small shellfish would be boiled for their meat to fall free.

The boilers lit, it would take time to build up the steam pressure necessary for cooking the batches, so young Tibb was left to watch over it while the rest went home for their supper. After their return and Tibb's departure for his own meal, the round tank and sifting tank would be filled with fresh water. Two steel nets with their weighty three and a half gallons of raw cockles would be placed into each cooking pot, the lids fastened down, the cockles cooked for six minutes. Still in the nets they'd be tipped into a sieve over the cold water tank, be shaken back and forth some sixty or seventy times until the meat fell through the holes leaving empty shells on top to be tossed through the hatch to form a mountain which would be crushed for garden grit and land drains –

21

another source of income. Better than shrimps, Danny grinned, glancing at his dad as he laboured up the beach under his load. Shrimps gave only one income and that was that. His dad had no doubt chortled over that fact in his time.

Once the last of the haul was in the shed, they turned for home. It was growing dusk. Already the tide had turned, was receding. The Thames boasted a hefty rise and fall, and the river to the Pool of London was being constantly dredged to allow the ocean-going liners and cargo ships with deep draughts to reach their docks and wharves.

For some unaccountable reason, Danny's thoughts turned back to Lily. There would be no chance to see her this evening because he would work through the night, boiling and sieving cockles.

Tomorrow they would rest. They'd need it. No good killing themselves and it wasn't yet the holiday season. Tomorrow evening he would see her. She would put her arms about his neck, glad to see him, and maybe she might even be a little more receptive of his caresses. But he was glad Lily wasn't like the others he'd been out with. Maybe she didn't go over the top and let him have his way as some of them did, but then neither did she talk wedding bells. He liked Lily, a lot.

'I suppose you'll be seeing your Ben tomorrow, as usual.' Pam glanced up at Connie with a look of unconcealed disdain.

Tomorrow was Sunday, Connie's fiancé's day off. They would go off to church together, climbing cobbled Church Hill hand in hand, gazing in each other's eyes, daft as brushes, hardly noticing the steep climb that left most people puffing at the top. Connie would wear her best dress, hat and coat, Ben his suit, polished shoes, stiff collar and tie and trilby.

He came every Sunday, or she went to his people. He lived in London, Bethnal Green in the East End, in a flat in what was known as Waterlow Buildings. His family were East End Londoners. Ben spoke with a Cockney accent, and while this family had an accent too, it was certainly better than *Cockney*.

Pam felt jealousy prick her stomach. A common East End Londoner. She had seen some of them, their behaviour when they visited Southend or came here to the sheds. Noisy, brash, full of their own importance, seeing themselves as the salt of the earth and most of them with not two brass farthings to rub together. Yet

22

this whole family were crowing about Connie and Ben's coming engagement. If *she* were to tell them about whom she was going out with, they'd look as though she was telling them she'd just committed a murder, especially Dad. She could almost see his face going purple and his voice booming out that he would rather see her dead at his feet than bring that George Bryant into his house. It wasn't her fault, was it, to fall in love with George, the pair of them asked to pay the penalty for some stupid feud that had started well before either of them had even been born?

Connie didn't seem to notice her disdain. She was living in paradise; saw nothing but her fiancé's face as she carted him off to church whether he liked it or not. She never used to go to church before; probably buttering up Reverend King, the vicar, Pam supposed, paving the way to having the wedding held there in St Clement's. A fine high church if ever there was one. It's stone tower dominated Leigh, had sat high above it on the cliffs for a thousand years, a landmark for miles around. She could have picked a more lowly church, more convenient. Pam could imagine the guests having to toil up that hill to see her wed. She felt a giggle rise up inside her at the vision of everyone in their wedding best arriving at the church door hardly able to get their breath, the church filled with puffing and sighing as they eased into the pews. You wouldn't hear the organ for all their blowing – like a gale blowing through the nave. Though no doubt they would hire wedding cars to take them round by road. Pam felt her pleasant little bubble burst.

Anyway it was more than a year away yet. A lot of money needed to be saved up first, for the cars to avoid the hill, for the cost of the church – with organ and bells, so Connie would keep reminding everyone, though where such money was coming from was all in her dreams.

Ben Watson was the son of a tugboat skipper, the tug not even his dad's, for the man was employed by a large tugboat company. Ben himself worked on a tug. Dirty, smelly work as far as Pam could see.

She looked at Connie over her copy of *Picture Show*. 'So when *are* you getting engaged?' She knew full well when they were, and Connie knew she knew, but Connie appeared quite unruffled, her head bent over a book.

'End of next month. End of May. I'm hoping his family and

ours can have a little get together. The weather should be fine by then, and warm I hope. It'll be a bit of a holiday for them.'

'Not for him and his dad,' Pam said, going back to her magazine. 'Him and his dad see enough of the Thames, I should think, chugging up and down it all week.'

'I don't suppose his mum sees much of it, stuck there in London.'

'Well, I suppose *she'll* be pleased to get out of London. Might as well make the best of a free day out.'

Connie looked up at her, her feathers ruffled at last. 'That's not a nice thing to say about someone. Ben's mum's very hard-working, looking after her family. And she'll be making some sausage rolls and things.'

'No more than she ought, I suppose.'

'What's that supposed to mean?' Connie slammed down her book and Pam realised she had gone a bit too far, been a little too frank.

'It's not supposed to mean anything.'

'It sounded very catty to me.'

Their mother came into the room, a pile of freshly ironed sheets and pillowcases in her arms ready for taking up to change the beds for Sunday.

'What's all this bickering for then?'

When Mum's tone sounded sharp like this, all wrongdoing stopped; memories of a slap across the back of the head as kids still lingered to command respect even though the slaps had ceased years before. Both girls buried their heads back into their reading, but Mum wasn't finished.

'I don't like the way you all go on at each other lately. Pam, you never seem to have a good word for anyone. You and Annie, both sulking, looking down in the mouth. Josie too, sometimes. I don't know what's wrong with you all. Connie never looks miserable.'

'Well, she wouldn't be,' Pam shot back, risking the memory of a slap. 'She's in love. Us other three aren't, are we?'

'Then it's about time you were. At least you and Annie. Josie's still too young, but she'd got her friends to take her mind off boys. It's about time you and Annie started looking for a decent boy each to settle down with.'

So saying, she went off up the stairs, each step creaking at her weight as much as they could for one as small as she, her mind already turning to what she would provide for Connie's engagement party.

George was sitting in the glass-sided seaside shelter halfway between Leigh and Chalkwell when Pam reached him. He was staring out to sea, ignoring the two couples who shared the bench under the ornate green wrought-iron roof and who all but crowded him out with their belongings and their eagerness for a sea view. The bench facing landward, separated from the more desirable one by a glass partition, remained vacant but for a man and a child.

The two couples were in turn ignoring George as they too stared at the gentle waves just below lapping against the sea wall that sloped down to the beach. The strip of sandy beach was submerged but for a small corner by a breakwater where a little family huddled like castle defenders against hostile marauders, the sea their moat, their goods – bags of food, flasks, towels, shoes, windbreak, buckets and spades – gathered about them as if for a siege.

Soon the water would recede, the beach be taken over by dozens coming off the train at Chalkwell from London or off the bus from Southend, seeking less crowded beaches than those of that more popular resort on this warm Whitsun Bank Holiday Sunday morning.

Seeing her, George got to his feet, leaving a vacant space which the man and child behind immediately came round to fill, the now completed group instantly breaking into conversation as though George had been an interloper.

'Want to go for a walk?' George asked her, his voice low and deep and full of adoration as, surreptitiously, their hands joined, entwined, each revelling in the touch of the other's flesh.

'Where?' she sighed.

'Somewhere where it won't be too crowded.'

'Up in the Gardens?'

He pulled a face. 'It's a bit on show up there. Anyone could see us.'

'We could walk into Chalkwell. Along the Esplanade. We're bound to find somewhere quiet. No one we know is going to go that far from here.'

It was settled. Closing together as they left Leigh behind, they walked leisurely, the feel of hand in hand a seduction to savour; occasionally his thumb rubbed her palm and she squeezed his fingers to show her pleasure at its suggestiveness.

Trains carrying the first of the seasonal contingent of day trippers rattled noisily by, making it hard for the couple to hear what each other had to say. But there was little need to talk. The touch of their bodies, their hands, was all the communication they needed.

Soon the rattling railway veered off from its short run along the seafront, leaving the two in a quiet more suited to them. Past Chalkwell Station they began looking about for somewhere to sit. Somewhere alone. Not much hope. Even here the beaches were quickly filling with the overspill from Southend on this first proper sunny holiday of the year.

'What about Chalkwell Park,' George suggested as they searched in vain. 'It's not a long walk and it's bound not to be too crowded.'

'And maybe we can find a spot just to ourselves,' she breathed.

Already she could see herself in George's arms in some grassy hollow hidden by bushes. There they could kiss and fondle to their hearts' content. In her mind she could already feel his hands caressing her breasts beneath the pale blue blouse she wore, chosen today for its convenient buttons down the front, the flat bra loosened to allow his hand to enjoy the released flesh. The thought made her tummy churn with an animal thrill of anticipation as they walked, more purposefully now, up Chalkwell Avenue to the park.

They did find it virtually deserted, visitors preferring the long-awaited seaside. They did find a grassy hollow, and it was well hidden by bushes. The strengthening sunlight filtered through the canopy of park-planted may trees spread above them to weave moving golden patterns across their reclining bodies In this idyllic setting he found her breasts with his hand and his lips, and she sighed in ecstasy, willing him to proceed further. And he did. And she felt him and got him excited, and with the very necessary precautions on his part, they made love with the urgency of the young, over too soon. And no one disturbed them.

They sat side by side, feeling hungry, allaying hunger with cigarettes. They sat now in anticlimax, excitement spent, the world punching its unhappy reality into their heads.

26

'What're we going to do, George?'

'Wish I knew.'

'I want to tell the whole world about us, but I can't. I daren't.'

He remained silent, lost in thought, lost in the hopelessness of it all.

'We could elope,' she suggested, a wild suggestion doomed to failure at the moment of being said. George was already shaking his head miserably. 'No, I see your point, darling,' she added. 'I could never face my family again.'

'No matter what we do,' he said, 'we're up against your dad and mine. My dad might be easier, but he's getting on – too old to change now.'

'And mine's never got over it, that silly business. It's not fair. I wasn't even born then, but I'm the one who has to suffer for what two silly old men got up to.'

'They weren't old then. They were our age.'

'But they're old now. You'd think all that sense that old people are supposed to gather over the years – or so they keep telling us . . . "We know better than you . . ." ' she mimicked what she thought was the tremor of old age. ' "You youngsters don't know nothing." You'd think all that sense they keep telling us they've got would have made them see a bit of it by now.'

'Perhaps they might see some when they know how much in love you and me are. After all it was their fight, not ours.'

'You try telling my dad that.' Pam sucked in a deep lungful of smoke. 'He makes it quite plain that any of us having anything to do with Bryant people are as good as kicked out. I don't know how we're going to get over this one. I'm fed up!' She flicked the half-smoked cigarette away from her.

George laid a placating hand on her arm. 'Don't get upset, darling. It'll all come right in the end.'

'How?' she shot at him, the tender love they'd just made cast aside.

He was equally sharp. 'I don't *know* how.'

'Then what's the point?'

'*I* don't know, do I? How should I know?'

Pam scrambled to her feet. 'If you're going to be like that, George Bryant, I might as well go home. And don't bother to meet me next Sunday.'

He too was on his feet. 'What's that mean? You've had enough of me? We've just been making love, Pam. And that's all it was to you, you telling me you don't want to see me any more?'

She cringed from the pain on his fine looking face. But she wasn't going to be the one to wilt. 'It's up to you, I think.'

'What's up to me?'

'You . . . us . . . well . . . I don't *know*.' Words had begun to fail her. Her voice was shaking with threatening tears. There was even a sob in her throat at the pain she herself was beginning to go through.

'I don't know, do I?' she cried out in despair.

For an answer he grabbed at her, pulled her down on to the ground again, took her shoulders and drew her to him, kissing her mouth hard. For moments they remained like that. Then he said against her lips, 'Pam, I love you,' and his voice was trembling. 'I never want to let you go.'

'I don't want to let you go either,' she replied. 'But what do we do?'

They crouched in each other's arms until she said very slowly: 'If I fell pregnant, then I'd have to get married to its father, wouldn't I? They'd make me. The scandal an' all. And if you was the father, they'd have to bury the hatchet and *let* you marry me.' She felt him nod solemnly, and holding on to each other, each became lost in thought about what she had just said.

Chapter Four

'Are you sure we've got everything?'

Peggy met her oldest daughter's brown eyes. 'Everything I can think of, far as I can see. Now don't worry. Everything's going to be all right.'

Connie moved her hands about in premature frustration on this eve of her engagement party at all that could go wrong. 'I do hope so, Mum.'

Her mother's round face broke into a faint smile. 'Look, we're not entertainin' royalty, love. Ben's people are only East Londoners. They don't come from . . . I don't know . . . Chelsea.' Her knowledge of London was nil. She'd hardly ever been far from Leigh, just a few times to Southend. What did she want with Southend, except its shops of course? But she'd had a field day only last week. When Connie had taken her there to buy a dress for the special day – cream, with brown flowers, a scooped neck and a brown bow, really fashionable. She'd feel a real lady in it, and Southend had been quite a jaunt. Otherwise she didn't know much of the world beyond Leigh and cared even less. But she had heard said somewhere that Chelsea was a posh and wealthy area of London. 'Ben's people can't be so different to us. Well, you should know, Con, you've been to see them often enough.'

It was usually Ben coming here one Sunday, and Connie going there the next. Ben mostly had to work all the week, on tugs, often through the night, Connie said. It depended. And her working too. Sundays were the only time they could meet. She wondered vaguely, as she put the finishing touches to the engagement cake she'd been icing, where Connie and Ben would live when they got married this time next year. She couldn't see Ben coming here. He

29

had his base in London, working with the company his father worked with. It would probably mean him and Connie finding themselves a place near his work in London. Connie would miss the fresh sea air.

She thought on this very intensely as she surveyed the finished cake, mostly to evade thinking of the emptiness Connie's going would leave. But all the thinking in the world couldn't quite dispel the heavy thump that was pounding against her chest wall like a dull hammer, the vision of this once crowded house beginning to empty as one after another left the nest. It had always been full of buzz, full of life, people coming in and out, their friends invited in, house bulging at the seams with people and conversation. The times she had been glad to be on her own for a few hours when they were all out, she regretted enjoying them so much now.

Connie was just the thin end of the wedge. So, the other three girls had no boyfriends yet. But it could come. Right out of the blue, all three meeting that right boy and falling in love, coming home to announce they were getting engaged, would marry in a year or eighteen months. No reason why it couldn't happen all in the space of a couple of years. And Danny, who had one girlfriend after another. He didn't say but she knew. Among them could be that one special girl that he intended to marry. Visions of her and Dan left here alone together loomed. It happened. There would still have been Tony if . . . She stopped herself in time thinking on those lines. But death did come so easily, with no warning; maybe slowly, but inevitably. And if anything happened to Dan, she'd be left . . .

For God's sake pull yourself together! She forced a smile at Connie. 'It'll be the best engagement party anyone round here's ever seen,' she said with conviction. And it would be. She'd make sure of it.

On Friday evening, the sky still light with the sun not yet set, Josie bounded out of her house before she could be stopped again.

Preparations for that silly party tomorrow night, with Sunday for them all to get over it, were sending the whole house into an uproar, with all of them, apart from Dad and Danny, expected to turn to and help. But it wasn't going to stop her going out this evening with her friends and spending some of her wages from the job she'd got last week. Part-time waitressing in the tea rooms at the Cliffs Hotel in Westcliff. Posh.

Annie, who worked there as a receptionist, had put her forward. They had questioned her really closely at the interview, but she had done a bit of waitressing and had lied a bit, exaggerating her skills, putting on the talk which she could when she wanted. Her looks and figure had done the rest.

The money wasn't bad and this evening she was determined to make the most of what she had left after giving Mum her bit. She'd been set on getting out this evening but she nearly hadn't made it.

'Josie, you're not going out, are you?' Mum's tone had contained its usual expectation of instant contrition, instant obedience. She had partially submitted by polishing the best cutlery got from its velvet-lined mahogany case; had polished quickly and skimpily, escaping before Mum could have a go at her for not doing it properly.

'I've done it, Mum! I'll try to get back a bit earlier and do whatever else you want me to do.' And she'd left before anyone could say anything – no need for a coat, just her hat and handbag. She was already in a decent dress and sandals.

She didn't intend getting back any earlier if she could help it. There was always the excuse of a train home being delayed, or a bus too full to take any more. Mum would understand, would forgive.

'Where are we going?' were her first words as they met up, half a dozen girls loitering around the station entrance.

'We thought on going up the Kursal.' They all spoke with a Leigh accent, used 'on' for 'of', in the same way their parents did.

'Bus or train?'

'Whatever comes along first.'

They would sit together on the long bus seats if they could, or if on the train, rush to gain an empty carriage before it filled, sitting next to the girls giggling all the way; would swap anecdotes of what had gone on at their particular place of work; poke fun at whatever odd character worked there, or what the boss had said or done, or if he was having an affair or not; discuss whatever boy had taken their eye, dissecting him and putting him back together again, meticulous as forensic scientists over a corpse.

Josie had no eye on any boy. There had to be something more

31

in life than finding a partner from around here. She dreamed constantly of some rich young man sweeping her off her feet, bearing her off to a romantic life.

She read avidly all the film magazines and, when she could afford them, those giving accounts of society life in New York and Hollywood and in London, probably the furthest she would ever get, despite her dreams of far away places and wealthy handsome sheikhs. Innocently she'd recounted her dreams to friends on one occasion, and had felt hurt and angry when they'd laughed.

'Gee whiz – off to Hollywood? Got your ticket? Who you setting your cap at then, Douglas Fairbanks? John Gilbert? Or is it Charlie Chaplin?'

How could she dare provoke further derision or even outright hostility, losing all her friends by telling them that she thought Southend cheap and nasty and that her sights were cast towards the socialites of London, longing one day to be one of them?

There was one who didn't laugh at her, Winnie Blackman, whom she caught looking as wistful as herself. Confessing her dreams to Winnie, she had been surprised to find a kindred spirit pounding against the barriers of Southend dress shops, local dancehalls and tunnel-visioned work mates.

She and Winnie had grown closer together while staying with the others, and this evening, shrieking with the rest at the sudden curves and dips of the scenic railway in the Kursal, or being whizzed around on some other hair-raising contraption, they continued to keep close together, their eyes searching for that elusive handsome wealthy knight who might sweep them away to the heights of society. How they expected to find him in a place like the Kursal they had no idea. Still it was lovely to look.

'Fancy 'avin' a go on the flyin' chairs with me, darlin'?'

Josie looked into the bright blue eyes of an obviously Cockney lad of about eighteen, his straw boater declaring the ubiquitous words 'Kiss me Quick' tilted rakishly over one eye.

'Does your mother know you're out?' she countered, and he laughed.

'No, she don't, an' wot's more, she don't care. 'Ow abart it then?'

'Push off,' Josie said, and shrugged past him.

He caught her arm, turned her towards him. 'You're some

32

looker, you are. I bet you'd pass fer a film star. You ain't a film star, are yer?'

'No I ain't . . . I'm not,' she blazed at him. 'Now let go.'

He let go with a dramatic flourish, his hands going up in a gesture of surrender. 'Orright, you win. What's yer name?'

'What's it to you?' Her friends were disappearing into the throng.

'I'd just like ter know, that's all. Mine's Arfer.'

'Arthur,' she corrected disdainfully. But he was good-looking, and tall, and slim, and she felt a small twinge of admiration shoot through her. If only he spoke like a prince. After a second she said, 'Mine's Josie . . . Josephine.'

He grinned from ear to ear. 'Not tonight, Josephine!'

'You're right,' she came back at him. 'Now I've got to go.'

Craning her neck to see where the others had gone, she felt dismay to find no sight of them. 'Now look what you've done. You've lost me my friends. They could be anywhere.'

He was suddenly sober. He looked quite handsome without that silly smile. 'I'm sorry. Look, I'll come wiv yer ter find 'em. Keep yer company.'

What else could she do? She didn't care for being left alone in this crowd. He was better than nothing. 'All right. But don't read anything into it.'

'I won't. I swear,' he said, breaking again into that silly grin.

He had taken her arm, tucked it through his in a masterly fashion as she went in the direction she had last seen her friends taking. They had gone quite a way, wending a course through whatever spaces there were between the knots of people; he shouldered his way through, taking her with him, taking over the situation. She had begun to wonder why she had allowed this. Who did he think he was assuming control, practically thinking for her when he didn't even know her, nor she him?

But he had found them. Being a six-footer, he had glimpsed them over the heads of much of the crowd, standing on some steps to the Whip with garishly painted cars being flung around in circles and from side to side to the accompaniment of screams of enjoyable terror from their occupants and some sort of raucous tinny racket that passed for music.

All five girls were craning their necks, ignoring the shrieks and

33

the clatter. Arthur turned to her. 'Five of 'em? Do one 'ave blonde 'air and one really dark? One's in green an' one's in white, an' . . .'

'That's them,' she cut in, glad to have found them and be rid of her self-appointed escort, and as they reached the little group who immediately demanded to know where she'd got to, added, 'Thanks ever so much for finding them for me,' hoping he would now go on his way.

'Ain't no bother,' he said, but he hadn't let go of her arm.

Compelled to explain how she'd come by him, or rather how he'd come by her, though she refrained from going into it too much, for the rest of the evening he had tagged along, commandeering her attention, taking exaggerated care of her on the ferris wheel and the roller coaster, showing her how to hit the moving line of wooden ducks with an air gun, or the tin cans with a fluffy mop, and she didn't have the heart to tell him she wanted only to be with her friends.

She did ask if he had been with friends and he said he had, a club outing, but it didn't matter, he could look after himself and they wouldn't worry. He was chatty but entertaining, and after a while it didn't seem so bad having him along. She listened to practically all his life story, which wasn't that much: he worked in the docks; his dad had been killed in the docks in an accident; his mother did cleaning to keep him and his brother and sister; he hadn't got a girlfriend at the moment, which seemed a bit of a hint. He didn't see her home. She told him it was best if she and her friends went home all together and he'd never get back to London from Leigh – whether he would or not, she didn't pause to concern herself. It wasn't her problem.

He seemed content with her explanation, but she found herself giving him her address when he said he'd like to write to her. She nearly said, 'You can write then?' his speech was so bad, but she didn't. It seemed uncalled for. He'd been so nice. And when she said goodbye at the station, she felt a tug at her heart, found herself hoping he would write as he said he would.

As she lay in bed that night, she thought again of all her dreams of a rich husband and fought to dismiss him from her mind. But it wasn't easy.

That the house was jammed to the doors with guests wasn't due to the numbers but the house itself, which hardly allowed elbow

34

room for the thirty-six individuals who, beside Connie's and Ben's parents and siblings – he had two brothers – included Connie's best friend Sybil, Ben's grandparents in their sprightly late seventies (no doubt pickled by all that London smoke, she smiled), aunts and uncles on her side, their spouses and offspring plus a neighbour with an accordion to provide the music.

Connie elbowed her way to where the drinks were being doled out in the tiny outhouse, crammed with menfolk getting their beer and rum, before taking another glass back with them into the two crowded small rooms, shouldering their way through a kitchen full of women all busy making sandwiches, balancing plates of food already piled high waiting to be served the moment someone spoke of feeling peckish.

Handed a glass of sherry by her Uncle Reg, Connie grinned over her shoulder at Ben close behind.

He had been her shadow the entire evening and she was glad; she would have felt excluded had he spent it with the men and ignored her.

'It's turning out a lovely party, isn't it?'

Ben nodded and took a swig from a pint glass. She hoped he wouldn't get himself drunk, but he seemed very capable of holding his drink.

She felt so proud of him, proud that he hadn't left her all evening; proud as everyone on her side reiterated what a good-looking young man he was and how she'd got herself a good catch there; proud that his family, for all they spoke with clipped Cockney accents, were self-respecting, temperate, decent people. But then she wouldn't have taken up with him in the first place had he and they been rough and coarse. By contrast she felt more ashamed of her uncles, Dad's brothers, already rolling drunk and becoming loud-mouthed. What Ben's people thought, his mother especially who she knew went to church on Sunday mornings, she dreaded to imagine, though none of them had said a word. But Ben's mother was no doubt wondering what sort of family her son was going to marry into.

'Let's go outside for a while?' Connie suggested to Ben, wanting to escape the hubbub and be alone with him, perhaps explain away her errant uncles in the hope that he'd pass the apology on to his parents later.

The look he gave her told her that he too wanted only her and they hurriedly threaded their way through the knot of drinking men into the tiny back yard. But hoping for a moment of privacy, they were disappointed. On this fine June evening with its warmth and lingering afterglow still lighting the sky, her mother's brother Bill, his wife and three of her cousins were already taking advantage of it, all five sitting on a plank supported by beer barrels that served as a bench for the overflow.

'It's really getting stuffy in there,' her Aunt Daphne began in her broad and strident East Essex voice as they appeared. 'And bloody noisy too,' her snub nose and full florid cheeks wrinkling at the muffled unbroken babble of conversation that filtered out to them together with the disjointed singing to the discordant accordion.

Nodding agreement, Connie and Ben made a nonchalant escape out of the back gate and into the cobbled alleyway beyond. No one would miss them for ten minutes or so.

In the gathering shadows of the old brick wall of the wharf with no one about, Ben kissed and fondled her and they made hurried frantic love, standing up, returning to the party refreshed and rejuvenated. No one had missed them and the smile of satisfaction their secret moments had planted on their faces were taken for enjoyment of the attention showered upon them at this party. All Connie now wanted was for the party to end so that they might with luck repeat their tryst before Ben retired to sleep in Danny's room.

The rest of his people had booked a couple of rooms over The Ship pub a short walk away, planned to go home tomorrow after first spending Sunday in Southend. Who in his right mind would go off home without taking advantage of the seaside resort just a stone's throw away?

There was no chance, however, of her and Ben being left alone as the party broke up. At least some of its debris had to be cleared up, a nightcap had to be drunk, and Ben was urged to go settle himself in Danny's room, Danny himself making do with the settee this night. Connie, her bed shared by Josie, the other one by the other two, lay awake for ages listening attentively above the faint snores of her sisters for the faint rustle through the wall of Ben turning over in the narrow bed next door.

She felt entirely happy, gazed at her engagement ring in the moonlight coming through her window, studying the band of five diamonds. They weren't large but together they glistened and gleamed in the silvery light and seemed to embrace her whole finger, transforming the look of her hand. From now on, that hand would be fluttered about for the benefit of all who came near, the light catching it to the full.

'It's absolutely lovely, beautiful,' had come the sigh of admiration from everyone at the party and from her work colleagues the week before. 'You're so lucky.'

The ring had been bought in London the Saturday before, worn all that week, admired, but the engagement was not official until tonight when she had become just a little bored with all the comments it had received.

'I wish it was all over,' she had whispered to Ben. 'I wish we could be alone.'

'Me too,' he'd said, his loving eyes taking her in as the party surged on around them.

Lying here, Connie thought of him now, conjured his wonderful image up behind her closed eyes. Not too tall, but broad and powerful, glowing with health, his broad face strong, his features regular, his brown eyes with a twinkle of humour in them that held her captive whenever she looked into them. For all his physique he was gentle, yet she knew he would never quail from defending her against the world. She in turn would do all she could to make a good home for him. She would bear his children one day and be a wife and mother he'd be proud of. Life was sweet.

She could still feel his hands on her, the uniting of their love, or as near as it could be, for there was still need for precautions – a year remained before they would marry and she couldn't imagine herself pregnant before that, the finger of condemnation pointed at her, walking down the church aisle in white knowing herself undeserving of the purity the gown symbolised. Ben endorsed her sentiment completely and her trust in him was total. He would look after her and never let her down, horrified of the consequence were he to indulge himself selfishly. But she wished they were already married and the fear of that one thoughtless moment well behind them. She was sure he must have the same thoughts, sleeping there in the room next to hers.

'What shall we do this morning?' she asked as he came down to breakfast, one of the first to appear. A strange bed had got him up earlier than intended.

His family had gone off on their own pursuits, and her family were taking their ease after a hard day preparing for the party. She and he had the day to themselves.

Met with his blank regard, Connie answered her own question. 'I wouldn't mind going up to St Clement's for the service this morning. At least to say thank you for the wonderful future we've got in front of us. That's right, isn't it?'

His shoulders lifted a little. He looked tired, had perhaps enjoyed little sleep in a strange room. 'Yes, of course, if you like.'

'Where are you going this morning?' queried her mother, coming in from the kitchen with cutlery and a pot of marmalade before starting on a large Sunday breakfast of egg, bacon, sausages, tomatoes and fried bread. The house bore a forlorn air, as houses do after a party, rather like that of a forsaken hostess. It felt empty, cavernous, silent, in need of some new air.

Connie's reply was stopped by Danny coming bleary-eyed to the table followed by Annie and Pam. Josie refused to get up after such a late night. From the outhouse floated Dad's uneven baritone as he washed and shaved noisily. He finally came to join them as Mum laid the cooked breakfast in front of them all, his grin revealing unnaturally pure white dentures. He'd lost all his own teeth in his thirties to pyorrhoea – the only way to tackle it had been to yank out every tooth. But he didn't wear glasses; his eyesight, used to staring at wide horizons, remained as perfect as the day he was born. Mum had dentures too, an upper set. Her teeth had been lost to childbearing, her own goodness gone into making babies. She did wear glasses, for reading and sewing, first candlelight then gaslight ruining her eyes. She read avidly, two books a week when there was time; labouring up hill to the library in the Broadway.

'Well,' Dad began, starting on his breakfast with gusto. 'Not a bad success, eh, the party? Looks like everyone enjoyed themselves. So how's it feel to be engaged, eh?'

'Nice,' Connie said dutifully. It didn't seem to register with him that they had been engaged since last Saturday, when Ben had put the ring on her finger in Hyde Park in a little ceremony of their own.

'So what'll you two be doing with yourselves today?' Mum cut in.

'We thought on popping up to the church,' Connie said this

time, at the same time gazing towards Ben with a depth of fondness in her eyes.

He looked back at her and smiled. A loving tolerant smile. It was the tolerant part that halted her as she read its unintended message. He was agreeing to go for her sake, not because he wanted to. He'd be bored but he would not show it or mention it and she realised in that moment that she hadn't even thought to consult him, merely assumed he wanted to go. The trouble was that she needed to attend, just this once; it seemed important she should. After this, she vowed silently, she would consult him in everything. He was the man, she must treat him as such or else belittle him, and that was the last thing she would want.

'Just for an hour,' she added hurriedly, apologetically. 'And the view from up there is wonderful.' But they had been up there gazing at the view so many times before.

'Then we could go down to the beach after.' She was thinking for him again. 'It's up to you, dear. What you want to do.'

'Beach'll be fine for me,' he said readily.

That was the trouble. He tended to leave decisions to her, falling in with them without a squawk, because he was so in love. It might make her just a little selfish, if the condition became a habit. She didn't want that. Perhaps it was her fault from the first that he was letting her think for him. Away from her, making decisions came second nature to him in his work. How could he continue his job otherwise, those split-second manoeuvres required to operate a tug in any tight corner or unexpected hazard?

The matter was emphasised for her by her mother as they washed up the breakfast things. Mum was quiet, thoughtful, when asked what was wrong, instead of saying nothing was wrong as Connie had expected, she turned instead to look at her, one soapy hand on the washed cup she had just put on the draining board.

'I'm not keen on all this going to church lark.'

Connie was astounded. It was the silliest statement she'd ever heard her mother make. 'What's wrong with it?'

'Because you never used to. Now all you seem to want to do when Ben's here is go up to that church. It don't seem healthy to me.'

'His mother goes to church regularly and that don't seem to have done her any harm.'

'It's just that it's happened suddenly. None of us are

39

churchgoers. Not that we ain't Christians. We believe, the same as churchgoers, but it's this suddenness that worries me. It ain't natural. Almost as if you're trying to do a deal with God Himself so He might keep you and Ben in the best of health and things. I don't like the smack of it. It looks like you're going there for all the wrong things. And I don't like it.'

'Well, I can't see anything wrong in it,' Connie flared and stalked off leaving her mother with the washing up. That in itself was wrong, but no doubt she'd call Pam or Annie to finish off. That she didn't worried Connie even more as she and Ben left.

It was a steep climb up Church Hill, which was partly cobbled with four or five steps every now and again to help the ascent. Like others going in that direction, she ended at the top quite out of breath. People residing down by the wharf did it daily, labouring uphill to do their weekly shopping if they missed the bus that went the longer, less steep way round, coming down again almost as though walking on the flat. She had seen old ladies in their seventies toiling up here who had done it all their lives. She always took the bus, or else would have arrived in work fit for nothing.

Ben, it seemed, took it in his stride too. He was fit as a fiddle, strong and healthy, from working on the river. She looked at him as they toiled up hand in hand. Was Mum right? Was she going to church in an effort to make a pact with God? 'Please let Ben live to a ripe old age. Please let us *both* live to a ripe old age. But please don't take him before me when the time comes – I don't think I could stand it, being without him.' But what about him? Would he be able to stand being without her when that time came? Even her prayers were selfish. No wonder Mum had spoken as she had. Now she saw the sense of what had sounded nonsensical.

'Do we really want to go to church?' she puffed at Ben's side. Again, selfishness in its way. He looked at her quizzically.

'We're almost there, love. Let's carry on now we're nearly there.'

'I just thought you mightn't really be wanting to go.'

He gave a chuckling laugh. 'So you ask me to come all the way up here and now want me to go all the way back down. I think you're having me on. It ain't April Fool's Day is it?'

Connie laughed too, but they continued, reaching the church as others moved in through the door. But she found herself longing

40

for the service to end, acutely conscious of Ben beside her and the real motive she now saw behind her attendance. Not only that, there was a young curate whom she kept noticing staring at her. Each time she caught his eye, he'd give a flustered smile as though caught doing something wrong and quickly look away. Even with her head bent in prayer she was conscious of his eyes on her and, feeling distinctly uncomfortable, wondered if he might have seen through her reason to be here. It was most unsettling. It was a relief when the service came to an end and she and Ben could escape.

The rest of the day was bliss, just the two of them together, and by the time they'd said goodbye until the next weekend when she would go to see his people, she had quite forgotten the curate and his penetrating glances. But it would be a long time before she went up there again. Mum had been right, there had been an ulterior motive and she suspected that the young curate had known it too.

Chapter Five

Most people who stayed at the Cliffs Hotel had money enough for it. This was where Annie worked as a receptionist. In summer the better class of visitor came to spend a week. Westcliff, called on-Sea for all it sat in the Thames estuary a way from the North Sea, was considered more select than neighbouring Southend with its whelks and candyfloss and public bars, despite its beautiful Palace Hotel at the head of the pier.

To the Cliffs also came the higher-class commercial traveller and company rep staying overnight at his firm's expense and making sure he enjoyed every moment of the comfort and good food. After four years working here, Annie had developed a nice way of speaking, and her slim figure and attractive looks went down well with guests and management alike. She was in fact more than a receptionist, she was supervisor in charge of the whole of reception, one step below the reception manager; and might have had that job but that her employers preferred a reception manager to be male, deeming a woman's temperament not to be up to the day to day running of a large hotel reception desk. It irked, but she had no option, though she certainly made her presence felt, and Colin Wakeman, the present reception manager with only a year's training, was in awe of her, she knew.

He looked to her for guidance and advice should problems arise which he could not deal with. She felt it was she, not he, who ran this place, and it irked to receive far less salary then he for all the hours she put into it.

'Dedicated,' she told them at home. 'That's what I am, dedicated. I'm often staying late when Mr Wakeman has hopped off home. And no thanks for it. Taken for granted. I just hope one of these days I'll find someone with money and get married and never have to work again. Then they'll know what they're missing.'

But she wouldn't add that in truth she loved her job, wouldn't have swapped it for anything else, except perhaps that unlikely marriage she described. Behind her polished oak reception counter she was important, directing arrivals, taking their money, their particulars, solving their queries.

Many a male guest had remarked how civil and helpful and pretty she was, especially pretty. She'd had proposals, but one did not take such spontaneous offers as genuine, ever suspicious of some ulterior motive. Many seemed to think that money would move the proverbial mountain as they flashed their wallets, straightened the lapels of their fine suits. A trilby hat and leather briefcase laid carelessly on the counter were supposed to indicate a disarming gesture of friendly trust to put her at ease enough to trust them in return. She'd seen it all, could cope with that. It was the nervous middle-aged men she didn't trust, who stammered a shy word on how kind she was being and how at a loss they were feeling away from home; who would begin to confide in her how homesick they were away from their wives who of course never understood their position: the hopefuls in sheep's clothing. She preferred the brusque guest with the appreciative eye and no more. Even the young men who looked self-consciously away from her official smile had longings prowling underneath their show of discomfort, their imagining of what it would be like if she were to unbend and tempt them to ask her out standing out a mile. She was a rock against which they beat their hopes.

Yet one moment of aberration was always possible. On one hot August afternoon, she herself experienced a twinge of fancy. She glanced up at the young man waiting among others to check in, her mind, as she handed a man before him his room key, casually noting someone in his late twenties, quite good-looking, with an efficient manner.

'How long will you be staying, sir?' she enquired politely when she was finally able to attend to him.

'Just the one night. I'm meeting an old friend for the evening and going back tomorrow. We were at Oxford together – he's a marine consultant – has his own business.'

Long experience judged him immediately. Beneath that veneer

of self-assuredness lingered a diffident personality, else he wouldn't have begun bothering to tell her why he was here, as though explaining away his single night's booking. Almost as though he thought she might suspect him of some clandestine agreement with a lady perhaps?

Annie hid a smile, hooked a key from one of the pegs behind her and handed it to him. 'Number two-five-seven Mr Willoughby,' she chanted, then smiled openly. 'It has a sea view.'

There had been no need to give him one with a sea view but something about him prompted her to be especially nice to him. Perhaps it was that very diffidence she had detected that drew her to him. He'd signed his first name as Alexander, though why it should matter to her she wasn't certain.

She found her gaze following him across the foyer with its ceiling fans to combat the heat of the August day and its constant movement of holiday and business guests, aware of her preoccupation only when someone on the other side of the counter coughed politely.

'I'm sorry, sir,' she hastened, returning her gaze immediately to a couple with a child. 'How may I help you?'

'We booked a week here, a couple of weeks ago. Name's Morris.'

'Ah yes.' She quickly consulted the booking form he laid before her, her eyes flicking briefly once to the progress of Mr Willoughby up the wide, carpeted staircase before he disappeared for good on to the next floor up.

For the rest of the day she watched for Mr Willoughby, half-annoyed, half-derisive at herself for this ridiculous interest inside her. She saw him go out later that afternoon; he handed his key to the young part-timer who came in afternoons. But she didn't see him come back, her attention most likely having been taken up with something in the office when he did, or perhaps he'd returned after she had finished duty and gone home, he and his old Oxford chum enjoying a late night.

The next day, Sunday, was her day off. He would be leaving that morning for wherever he lived without her seeing him again. It had been just a passing thing, a silly moment of fleeting infatuation, and that his face persisted in hovering in her head made her angry with herself for such foolishness. Her mother accused her of being moody, wanted to know if she was feeling well. To escape,

44

she took a walk, then after Sunday dinner buried her face in a book before retiring upstairs on the pretext of sorting out dresses for the week.

On Monday when she came back on duty he was, of course, gone. Again she chided herself, wondering why her heart should sink as it did. She would soon forget him.

'Oh, Miss Bowmaker.' Colin, coming from the manager's office behind reception, held an envelope with the hotel's brown and gold crest on it. 'One of the guests handed this in yesterday morning when he paid his bill. It's addressed to you.' Colin's eyes held a look that said he trusted she wasn't forming one of those unsavoury alliances with a guest which some lesser hotel receptionists were wont to do.

She almost snatched the envelope from him, not so much because she was eager to open it as in annoyance at the message Colin's uncharitable look conveyed. To further dampen his assumption, she put it into her handbag which she placed in the locker of the office, just to show it held no meaning for her.

'Aren't you going to open it?' enquired an inquisitive Colin.

'It's probably only a thank-you note. Whoever it was has gone now, so there's no urgency, is there?'

'His name was Mr Alexander Willoughby.'

'Oh. Thank you.' Her heart raced, but she controlled herself until lunchtime. In the tiny staff restaurant at the featureless rear part of the hotel that looked out on boxes and wrappings from the kitchen waiting to be taken away by the dustmen, she slit open the flap of the prestigious cream envelope and drew out the equally fine single sheet of paper with its brown and gold embossed letterheading, folded once. On it was written in a bold sloping hand: Alex Willoughby, No.3 Turner's Hill, North Hampstead, London.

In Chalkwell Park on a now dark bench on a snaking little path hidden by shrubbery, George and Pam had just finished making love, and now sat side by side, his arm about her, each deep in thought as they puffed at rather damp cigarettes. They'd made love several times since Dad had told her with no beating about the bush that nothing would ever induce him to embrace George Bryant, son of his bitterest enemy, as a prospective son-in-law.

'You can knock that whole bloody idea of yours on the head,' he had spat at her, his finger pointed threateningly towards her when in July she had tentatively tested the ground.

'We're only friendly, Dad,' she had lied.

'Then you can get *un*-friendly as soon as you like. I don't want to talk on it any more.'

'But Dad . . .'

'I don't want to hear another word on it. Understood?'

She had nodded dismally, had heard him going around the house grumbling under his breath about past injuries, glaring balefully at her if their eyes met. She hadn't dared bring up the subject again, shuddered to think what he would say if he knew the real truth.

'He's never going to forgive,' she had told George and they had sat that day close together, silent, both heavily laden with the hopelessness of it. She had asked what his father would say if he were told.

George had shrugged. 'It's different for me. I'm a man. I could leave home whenever I want. You can't – you're a girl. I don't want to of course. But if we married, we'd leave home wouldn't we? Set up our own home. It's an old, old, silly row – gone on years. You'd've thought they'd have forgotten it by now.'

'Well, they haven't,' she had burst out, tears beginning to pour down her cheeks. 'And we're the ones paying. They're hurting us, not them. I love you, George. I don't think I could exist without you now. It's not fair . . .' She could hardly talk, the words coming brokenly. 'Two silly old men . . .'

She had broken off, her throat closing up, had wept on his shoulder as he cuddled her close. By the sound of his own effort to soothe her, he too had been near to tears.

It was then they'd decided to kick over the traces of that old quarrel. If she became pregnant they'd have to marry, it would be expected of them, no other means to avoid the scandal. Her parents loved her. They'd forgive the young people in love if not the family who had, unknowingly in that dim distant past, caused this desperate measure years later.

Tonight they had made love again, not fearing discovery by anyone passing. August Bank Holiday had been two weeks ago. The weather had grown dull and wet, discouraging Southend visitors. Its coloured lights glistened in the damp evenings to fewer people than it had hoped; Fairyland and Children's

Playground were deserted, the Kursal half empty, dodgem cars stacked against crash barriers, just two or three accommodating a sprinkling of customers, the flying chairs and scenic railway carriages more or less vacant as they continued optimistically to spin and dive for the odd few. The haunted house and ghost train were now truly left to the painted celluloid spirits.

Chalkwell Park, always only the haunt of locals and now deserted, was a haven to them on their chosen bench. But this evening Pam was downcast.

'I was sure I'd have fallen by now.'

'It's bound to take a while, darling. I'm doing my best.'

Pam pouted. Their lovemaking was doing nothing for her tonight – it seemed to her to have become more of a routine than the overwhelming joy it had been. 'If I didn't *want* to get pregnant, you can bet your bottom dollar it'd happen. It always happens to girls who don't want it to. Do you think I'm too old?'

'Twenty?' In the darkness his voice sounded incredulous. 'What d'you mean, too old?'

'Well, you hear of girls of seventeen and eighteen, too young to get married without their parents' consent, falling pregnant after risking it just once. Maybe if I'd been promiscuous when I was younger I might've fallen pregnant more easily now.'

George shot upright. His tone was obviously angry. 'Don't talk like that, Pam. You've not had anyone else, have you, before me?'

She had become angry too, suddenly flaring. 'I've just said I haven't, haven't I?'

'I mean,' he moderated, 'you've not ever thought about it with anyone else before you met me?'

'Of course not. I've not really been out with anyone before you.'

'You must have.'

'Not in *that* way. I'm hurt you could even think that, George.'

He was immediately contrite. 'Oh, God, Pam, I'm sorry. I wouldn't hurt you for the world. I was being thoroughly stupid, but I do love you so much, Pam.'

She melted, sinking quickly back into his arms. 'I love you too, darling. So very much.' And she thought, as he held her to him, that she must get herself pregnant soon so as to be with him forever with nothing anyone could say or do.

* * *

47

'I had another letter from Arthur Monk,' Josie told Winnie Blackman as they made their way on a wet Saturday evening to the pictures in Leigh, the September weather drawing in a little miserably.

'How many does that make since he started writing to you?' asked Winnie. There was a smirk in her tone, a smirk shared by them both.

'Eight.'

'And how many have you sent him?'

'Four.' The question had been whimsically put but Josie now replied with a straighter face, thinking of her involvement with Arthur Monk and did she really want to get involved even only by letter. 'There's nothing much to write about. And his are always full of the same thing. Politics. He seems utterly obsessed with politics.'

'Boring, I should imagine. He talks about other things though?'

'A few things. About himself really.'

The subject falling a little flat, Winnie losing interest, they walked on in silence for a while as Josie thought about Arthur and his letters.

She hadn't seen him once since meeting him in June at the Kursal. This was her fault, for she had evaded every invitation so far to meet him again. So he'd stuck to letters as she'd said, mostly full of politics. He had told her he was one hundred percent Labour, as she imagined everyone from East London to be; that he'd helped canvass on behalf of his prospective candidate during the General Election in June. He was jubilant Labour had got in, overjoyed to see Baldwin's Conservatives lose, saying what a mess (according to him) the man had made of his drawn-out term of office, and that MacDonald, whose Labour Party had earlier seen just ten months in power before being ousted by the Conservatives, should never have lost the election in nineteen twenty-four. Arthur could only have been thirteen then and shouldn't have cared about such things. Instead he wrote as if he'd been an elder statesmen for years, but for his almost childish exuberance at last June's outcome.

Bored stiff by accounts of how from nineteen twenty-two governments seemed to have changed yearly for three years running, when at last he had got off the subject enough to ask to see her again, setting a date for the next Sunday, Josie imagined a day of constant political chat.

48

Fortunately it had rained that day and she hadn't gone. She imagined that would be the last she'd hear from him, but on the Monday a letter had arrived apologising for his not being there – his one pair of shoes had been at the mender's and he had been unable to go out. He expressed his abject apologies and his hopes that she hadn't been too upset at being stood up. If she wasn't upset, could they meet the Sunday after that?

She had written back to say that she wasn't upset, refraining from mentioning that she hadn't even gone to meet him. But she cried off seeing him on that Sunday too, saying she was already booked for a church outing arranged long beforehand. Church was a good excuse for getting out of a date – an invented wedding, christening, an obligation to participate in some fictitious fete or other. Arthur was apparently not at all churchy, so there was no likelihood of his offering to be there with her; and when all that was exhausted there was always Dad to be helped in the boiling of cockles, all hands to the wheel during the height of the summer season she had told him. But now she was running out of excuses.

'It's not that I don't want to see him,' she told Winnie. 'Just that I don't want to get too involved at the moment. And I've only met him once. I don't really know what he's like, do I?'

'You won't know if you don't go and meet him,' Winnie said.

'Well, say if I like him and I was to fall in love with him. Bang goes any hope of meeting someone well off. I still want to see what London is like – see what the well-to-do get up to – maybe even be one of them if I met the right chap. You do too. I don't see why not. We're both attractive enough, you and me. I'm sure we could turn the head of any heir to a fortune.'

'You won't,' Winnie laughed, 'if you go on saying, "you and me". It's you and I. We'd have to remember to put on airs and talk very properly with plums in our mouths.' Already she was putting on an appropriate accent. Josie followed suit.

'We did plan it, Winnie, did we not?'

Again Winnie laughed. 'Did we not,' she mimicked. 'It's all right to say didn't we. All we'd need to get into those sort of circles would be to learn a few of the sayings they use. *If* we ever get that far.'

'But you still want to go, one day?'

'Do I?' Winnie said with fervour, her own life with a layabout father and several brothers and sisters as unattractive to her as anything could be, she'd told Josie many a time. She too dreamed of bright lights and the careless enjoyment London offered.

'Well, I won't be seeing it if I go off with someone like Arthur Monk,' Josie said flatly.

'You can't keep on dangling him on a string though, can you?' Her friend paused, looking thoughtful. 'You know, Jo, I think he could be quite useful.'

'Useful!'

'You could get him to take you around London some time. I could tag along so we could get used to the place with someone who knows about it.'

It was an idea. For several weeks Josie mulled it over, then wrote her letter saying she'd like to see him in London, being that Southend in autumn wasn't all that wonderful. She said she'd have to bring a friend along since she had never travelled up to London before and feared doing it alone.

The plan was set. Arthur Monk fell straight into it, eager to see her at last. But guilt did settle a little uneasily on Josie's shoulders as she agreed a date. They set it for the second Saturday in November, some way ahead, but that being Lord Mayor's Day with a colourful procession through London and crowds of people to watch it, with flags and banners and bands and guards in lovely uniforms on horseback and people waving little Union Jacks, he thought it was a good time for their date and worth waiting for.

'Lord Mayor's Show!' her mother said when Josie asked permission to go. 'I don't know about letting you go all that way up to London on your own.'

'I won't be on my own,' Josie pleaded. 'Winnie Blackman'll be with me. She's twenty. She'll look after me.' Winnie Blackman was only just twenty, her mind no doubt focused on boys by now. Could she look after anyone?

'Two of you on your own then,' Peggy said. 'Two girls. It's as good as you being on your own. Lord knows what you'll be getting up to. And Lord knows what you'll find up there.'

She had never been to London in her life. It struck her as a terribly dangerous step and she was on the verge of forbidding her youngest daughter outright. After all, the girl had only just turned eighteen, easy prey to anyone who might take advantage of her and her innocence. And in all those crowds. All very well saying

Winnie Blackman, her best friend, would be with her. Winnie Blackman at twenty was still under age. A wonder her parents had let her go, but they weren't very respectable people. Her father was a drunk, a layabout, her mother, with loads of kids, had to take in washing to make ends meet. Not a nice family.

On the other hand, it did seem unkind to deny Josie this wonderful day out. Josie promised to leave for home the moment the show was over and not linger in London, and it *was* a straight run back on the train, and it *had* been Josie's birthday last week, and no one had done much about it, no birthday party or anything, just a card from her and her father and a winter scarf for a present. This would be a little extra treat for her. And girls these days were so much more forward and confident than they had been in her day. And Josie's large blue eyes *were* filling with tears at the thought of being denied. Perhaps she would be all right. One couldn't go on and on coddling young people forever. And when they did get to be twenty-one and be adult, they mightn't be equipped to look after themselves if they weren't allowed, just a little beforehand, to sort of have small practice runs.

'Look,' she conceded. 'So long as you start for home as soon as it ends, like you promised, and don't linger about in London.'

'Oh, Mum!' the hovering tears dried miraculously as if they had been sucked away by a syphon. A great kiss was planted on her cheek.

She rubbed it vigorously. 'Don't be so stupid.' But it was nice to be appreciated.

Josie skipped off to tell Winnie the news. She hadn't told Mum about meeting a boy up there. She'd have been even more reluctant to let her go. Anyway, she had no intentions of going serious with Arthur, did she? And he probably had none himself. Hadn't even kissed yet, had they? All this really was, was her passport to London to see what it was like.

Chapter Six

Although Mr Willoughby had left his address, Annie had not taken it up. It wasn't up to her or any respectable girl to make the first move in matters of that sort, and if he thought she would have, he wasn't quite nice himself for all his apparently moneyed upbringing and his obviously well-appointed address. He had probably taken her for a floozy, a gold digger he could have strung along with fine promises and dropped when he had tired of her after getting what he wanted out of her. After a while the thought had made her exceedingly angry and rightly indignant. She wouldn't dream of putting pen to paper on such an arrogant invitation, would rather have died, the way he had taken it for granted that she would indeed. And yet as the months had gone by she felt constantly pricked by a small indefinable thrill whenever his name crept into her mind, which seemed more often than was healthy for her.

So it was in November that the thrill hit her anew when a letter came, via her work, handed to her by Colin Wakeman, his thin fair eyebrows lifted enquiringly at the expensive thickness of the envelope's paper, a move that made her delay until a more private moment to open it. But she had already noted the London postmark and made a guess who it might be from, her nerves jangling with excitement all morning as she went about her reception duties.

Over a snatched lunch of ham sandwich, a cake and coffee, she tore it open before Jean the office typist could come to the table and join her.

* * *

52

Dear Miss Bowmaker,

I am taking the somewhat anxious liberty of writing to you, as I now realise that I had not been entirely proper by leaving my address and no other word for you. I do realise, of course, how unsavoury it must have appeared to you, and I don't blame you for not contacting me. In fact I find it commendable that you didn't under the circumstances so I am hastening to rectify my awful mistake by writing to you now and begging that I may follow it with another letter – that is if you feel you would wish to reply to this one, which I do sincerely hope you are reading at this very minute and haven't thrown away in disgust. At this point may I add my abjectest apologies too?

I shall not at present go into detail as to my reason for leaving you my address, although I hope you will guess why. Our eyes met that day, you know, and I hope I wasn't mistaken in reading what I did in yours. If so, dear Miss Bowmaker, I'm certain I can look forward to your reply, your favourable reply. I shall say no more but look forward to hearing from you. If I hear nothing, I shall understand utterly of course.

Your ardent admirer.

Alexander (Alex) Willoughby.

P.S. Please write.

Annie's joy knew no bounds. She showed the letter to everyone at home, hardly able to sustain herself. Mum bit her lip and said she could be getting into deeper water than she imagined, that everyone had a place in the walk of life and it didn't do to step off the beaten track.

Mum was old-fashioned. People of today were doing things differently, a new decade was approaching, fashions were already changing as clothes became more clingy, women's forms more rounded. Cars had got faster. Silent films had been ousted in less than a year by talkies, and now the only silents left were those starring Charlie Chaplin. Cinema audiences had ceased to be noisy; it was the films that were noisy, hardly anyone understanding what American film stars were saying they spoke so fast and so nasally.

Mum and mothers like her were being left behind the times. The Thirties promised to be an era when women would lift themselves out of their class and marry into a higher one. That it

promised to be a frugal decade with that recent Wall Street Crash
– the papers had talked about thousands in America on the dole
with hints of this country probably following – she was too young
and heady with excitement now to care. A modern woman, with a
salary enough to afford the newest fashion, even if more cheaply
made than those in the large cities, she was good enough for any
young man with a postal address like Hampstead.

She replied that very evening, and two days later received his
letter saying he would be at the Cliffs Hotel on Saturday evening
to take her out somewhere nice, a theatre and a meal if she cared
to. Yes, yes, she cared to, very much.

Josie, who made no secret of her foolish futile desire to one day
join the upper crust and marry someone rich, was jealous. But
Josie at only just eighteen was of no account. Pam too was jealous,
with no boyfriend of her own. Connie, engaged to Ben, held no
envy. But Annie's joy was complete.

The moment Alex Willoughby entered the hotel foyer it seemed to
Annie that he commanded immediate attention. He was the most
handsome man she had ever seen and her heart flipped at the sight
of him. It flipped even more as he came up to her, said hello in a
deep pleasing tone, and added in a quiet, cultured accent that it
was a great pleasure to meet her.

Reciprocating, trying to throw off the vague sensation of being
a pick-up, she purposely made no attempt to adopt any fine accent.
Hers, developed over the years working for this hotel, was good
enough for them; it would have to be good enough for him. Truth
in all things was her motto and she meant to start off this association, if indeed it was one, with honesty and straight dealing. If *she*
felt a little like a pick-up, he was not going to be allowed to
imagine she was. It had been a mistake deciding on this place to
meet, with those she worked with able to witness it. Now all she
wanted was to get out of here as fast as possible.

He seemed to sense her feelings. Preliminaries over, he crooked
his arm for her to take, saying they wouldn't have drinks here but
that his car was outside and they'd motor along to the Palace
Hotel.

'What would you like to do?' he asked as he opened the
passenger door for her and settled her into the seat of a beautiful,
brand new, red American Pierce-Arrow, which is what he said it

was as they pulled smoothly away. She wouldn't have known one car from another. In fact this was the first she had even been in; the experience quite took her breath away so that she sat the whole way to Southend in rapt silence apart from managing to gasp that she'd let him decide what they would do. Her only conscious thought recognised that he was visibly loaded with money, judging by this kind of car, the kind of suit he wore, the way he conducted himself with such casual aplomb. Again came the feeling that she, not he, had engineered this meeting, the sole lure his obvious affluence. She almost visualised being handed a sum of money as they parted company and decided there and then that she would conduct herself with decorum at all times and give him no reason to doubt her integrity.

Over drinks he told her something about himself. As she listened, all her intentions to put her own cards on the table wavered before the facts of her lifestyle that would astonish if not appal him. How he imagined she lived and the sort of family she had, she couldn't begin to think. She was rightly proud of her upbringing, her family, her parents, but listening to him it would be hard to describe her life when finally he asked her about it.

He had visited America, he told her. The imported car, especially designed for his needs on British roads, said that much. His father was a large importer of gems, had agents in Holland and America and India. He spoke a lot about the ins and outs of it, little of which Annie understood. Now that his continuing friendly, almost formal conduct had got her over her initial fears, she heard only his wonderful deep voice and saw only his outstanding handsomeness as she drank in the way his rather large hands moved when he expressed his interests and aims in life.

'I'm a director in the firm at the moment. Not terribly important or overworked. I don't have to do much, obviously. Just learn the business and one day inherit from my father. But I hope that day is still a long way off.

'I've four sisters,' he continued, than gave a small chuckle. 'All older than I and married. My parents must have despaired of an heir – four girls in quick succession, it must have shattered them. Then I came along. I've been spoiled ever since. I am sure my sisters blame me personally. But I see very little of them. One lives in the States and one in South Africa. The other two gad about the world with their husbands. While I was growing up they were all at finishing school in Switzerland. When they came out – debutantes, you know – I was still at public school. They got themselves married off into good families almost immediately – so I see hardly anything of them.'

He looked at her for a moment, his eyes filling with interest. 'And how about you, Annie? Tell me a little about yourself.'

'There's little to tell,' she hedged. But why should she prevaricate? Who was he that she should make excuses for herself? Speak the truth and shame the Devil, and if he didn't like it, then he was welcome to say goodbye before her heart got too lost. She'd be sad, but she'd get over it at this early stage. People have to get over the death of a cherished one – could do nothing else but – and carry on with their lives. So shame on her if she could not get over this sensation that was fast mounting up inside her were he to walk away. If he did, she wouldn't blame him, he of a different class, different tastes to her, but she'd force herself to think less of him and have done with it.

She expected his interest to flag as she talked of her life in Leigh-on-Sea, her father a cockle-picker, no match for a London gemstone importer – but she spoke with pride. She was amazed to see interest glow in his eyes.

'That's so fascinating. My God, you have an interesting life. All that open air and space.'

'You've been to America,' she reminded him severely. 'There's lots of space and open air there.'

'Not where I was. New York. No horizons at all unless you go to the top of the Empire State Building, and then all you see is skyscrapers and the river and hills beyond, all through a mist it seemed to me. No colour. No real fresh air to breathe. All that noise, honking cars, popular tunes blaring swing and jazz, people rushing everywhere, not one of them stopping to give you a second glance. I spent most of my time there sitting in a board-room or someone's office doing deals. Even in London you're restricted. And at home, though the house is in quite decent grounds, and we have the Heath not far away, it's still London in a way. I can just imagine the silence you talked about, out there on the flats with the tide far away and the distant mewing of gulls. You set such a wonderful picture. I think you must be a poet . . . No, I really do,' he broke off to assure her as she gave a scoffing laugh. 'And I envy you your solitude.'

'It can get noisy enough at home,' she said. 'And we have our parties and social get-togethers – we're not exactly living in the back of beyond, you know.' Her tone rang with reproval and he hurried to rectify any misunderstanding.

'I'm sorry if I sounded high-handed, Annie. Look, let's not talk about our lives. Let's talk of something else.'

'What?' She still felt a little ruffled.

'I don't really know.' For a moment he looked so non-plussed that all her indignation melted away and she began to laugh.

He was laughing too, so natural. 'I really don't know. What does one talk about on a first date?'

'First date?'

'There *are* going to be others, aren't there . . . Annie?'

Silently she nodded, unable to trust her voice lest she sound far too eager, but her heart was thumping too fast and too heavily, more so as his hand came across the table and slowly took hers, which had been lying near her sherry glass.

'Annie . . .' he began, to her surprise, hesitantly. 'I . . . I know this does seem a little premature, but I do want to see you again. And again. I've been sitting here utterly overwhelmed by you. It's made me talk too much but I can't . . . my dear Annie, I feel this . . . this electric thing inside me all the time I'm looking at you, listening to you. I'm sure I'm in love with you, but that's silly, isn't it, after just an hour?'

'I don't know,' she answered, recognising those self-same emotions inside herself.

'I felt like that the day I saw you in the hotel. I looked for you again but you weren't there. They said you had gone home. All I could think of was to leave my address. I should have written a letter at least, but I could not think straight. Afterwards, I was ashamed, as though I'd treated you as one might a casual acquaintance. And you were not a casual acquaintance, not from that very first sight of you. Can you understand what I'm saying?'

'Yes, I do.' Her tone seemed to her unusually husky.

'Then may I see you again?'

'Yes,' she said in the same husky tone as though her throat were being obstructed by some web or something.

The rest of her evening had become a haze, with just a sprinkling of recollections approaching anywhere near clarity: of leaving the hotel bar and later entering the rose and gold foyer of the Westcliff Palace Theatre. There had been a film whose title she could not recall followed by some live theatre, drama, its subject matter lost to her as she tried to think back on it. Her only real memory was of a feeling that the future seemed to be slowly unrolling before her, a rosy carpet going on forever. He had brought her home in his wonderful car, riding smoothly, had taken her almost to her door and then, with a murmured request for her permission, had kissed her. The keenest memory she nurtured as she lay in bed next to Josie was the feel of that kiss. It lingered on her lips like the soft touch of a windblown blossom. In her head she could still hear his voice, deep and positive even as it asked a question. 'Shall I see you next week? Saturday – shall we say eight o'clock? I'll wait for you here.'

She had said, full of disappointment, 'I'll be on duty next Saturday.'

'Sunday then. Sunday morning.'

'Yes, Sunday.' Lying on her side, she breathed the words to herself, heard again his wonderful low voice.

'I'll be here at eleven and ask your parents' permission to take you up to London. We can visit Hyde Park, have a boat on the Serpentine, or St James's, or the Embankment. It depends of course on the weather. It could be a little too cold this time of year. If it's too cold or wet perhaps we can visit a few museums. But we have time.' He kissed her again, a tender peck. 'All the time in the world. The rest of our lives, I hope.'

'Yes,' she had whispered again, fervently, and had echoed, 'All the time in the world,' already sure she was in love. The way he had kissed her, at first lingeringly then softly, spoke of no mere brief association but of something lasting, and she believed the kiss implicitly.

In the morning she would tell her parents about him. They would be overjoyed for her. Not just the young man her mother had hoped she'd find one day but a young man of good means. It was almost too good to be true.

'It sounds to me too good to be true,' were her mother's first words, rather stunning Annie. 'You be careful you're not getting too carried away.'

'I'm not being carried away.' Anger prickled up inside Annie. This wasn't fair. 'Don't you want to see me settle down?'

'With a nice young man, yes.' Mum was putting the breakfast on the table, everyone coming to sit at their places in the back room which about gave enough room to squeeze by the backs of each other's chairs. With its small window shielded by the back fence they needed the gas light on to see what they were eating. 'But you can't trust men what tell you about all the money they've got.'

'If he had no money how could he afford such an expensive motor?'

'Could've been borrowed,' Pam put in a tiny bit spitefully.

'Well, it wasn't.' Annie held her hands out of the way for her mother to put the hot breakfast plate in front of her. 'I know it wasn't. He paid an awful lot for our meal and then we went to the theatre. And we had drinks.'

'Mind you're not getting yourself in too deep,' her mother warned, at the same time giving Pam a look. 'Drinking can get you drunk. And with a man you've only just met, don't really know—'

'I've already met him before.'

'If all what he says is true,' her mother continued, 'and not trumped up to impress some gullible young girl, what's he want of an ordinary girl like you? Why ain't he out with some posh girl his own sort?'

'Thanks very much,' Annie struck out. 'Nice thing for a mother to say – that her daughter's not posh.'

'You know what I mean. I mean at your age a nicely brought up girl could be easily led on by a man like that.'

'He's not a *man like that*, Mum. And I am twenty-two and I'm not gullible. I'm old enough to know my own mind and know what the world's about. I work in a big hotel, remember, and meet all sorts of people.'

'And I work in that hotel too,' Josie began, but Annie ignored her.

'I do get to know who's genuine and who's not.'

At the breakfast table, her father moved irritably. 'Twenty-two's no age, my gel. You think you know the world just on working in some hotel? Well, you think again. Sometimes what you thought was a friend can turn on you and you find you don't know him . . . them . . . as well as you thought. Think on it before you go off swanning around London with strange blokes.'

59

'Alex isn't strange!' Annie pleaded, her breakfast going untouched in her disappointment at their lukewarm response to her joy. He's coming next week, personally, to ask permission to take me to London. And he can't be more genuine than that, can he?'

'Anyone can sound and behave genuine when they want,' her father mumbled into his plate. 'Until they get tired on being genuine. That's when it all comes out.'

'Mum . . .' Annie appealed to her.

'Your Dad's only trying to protect you from things you don't know about.'

Annie's hazel eyes flashed in anger. 'How am I ever going to find any young man if you and Dad start vetting him the moment I meet him and telling me I know nothing about the world? It's . . . it's silly.'

She saw her mother eye her father, who shrugged. It seemed to make up Mum's mind. 'Well, experience do make us older. And we don't want to get heavy-handed. But if things don't go right, it's your funeral.'

'Yes,' Annie said succinctly and stuck her fork into her crisp rasher of bacon with such force that it shattered all over her plate and beyond it on to the tablecloth, making her even more annoyed with them but more with herself for allowing them to rattle her. They'd soon change their tune when they saw Alex next week.

Danny threw her a broad grin across the table. 'So what's this fella's other name, then?'

'Willoughby,' Annie supplied waspishly. 'Alexander Willoughby.'

Danny went 'Mmm!' and Josie tittered, repeating it clownishly while Connie enlarged her eyes and pursed her lips towards her mother at the grandiose sound of the name. Pam, however, scowled.

'I don't know how everyone can take it so easily. Picking up with a chap none of us know. And not one of you turning a hair. If it was me come home with someone like that, Dad would find something to pick at about him.'

'If you're talking about that Bryant bugger, you can leave the table!'

Pam shot up from her chair, the back scraping against the fender around the fireplace. 'I go out with who I like.'

'Not that one you don't.' His knife and fork gripped in his fists, a sliver of fried egg white trembling on the prongs of the fork, he glared up at her. 'Any bloke than a sprig off that bloody family. I'd sooner see you dead an' buried than . . .'

'Dan!' Peggy's voice rose full of horror.

Realising what he'd said, he looked down, his jaw set, his gaze concentrated on his plate. But Pam had already given a stifled hiccup of sob and fled the room, leaving her mother to hurry after her.

The rest of them sat unmoving, each gazing down at the food before them. Danny cleared his throat carefully, but his father had gone back to eating, a stolid sort of devouring of food which they all knew he could not be tasting, each imagining it to be as sawdust in his mouth.

Chapter Seven

She had never seen anything like it. Nor had Winnie, the way she squealed and waved the tiny flag on its stick which she had bought from a man with a great handful of them. A penny Union Jack; a coloured waver that was already coming away from its cardboard holder with being frantically waved at the procession; a lolly in a blue and white chequered triangular wrapper bought from a ice-cream vendor pedalling a tricycle with a blue and white ice box on the front; a bag of toffees each had brought from home, plus sandwiches: the girls had their hands full, but they waved their flags and wavers without managing to drop anything. In this crowd, anything dropped would be trodden underfoot and lost.

They were too excited to worry about that too much. This was a day never to be forgotten. Cold and sunny, London smelled of chimney smoke, pronounced in the noses of visitors who seldom if ever came to the capital. The brass bands passed, the music deafening Josie's ears, the big drum as it went by seeming to be pounding inside her chest so that she thought it might stop her heart; the drummer leaned back against the drum's weight on his front as he marched, rhythmically swinging the large-knobbed sticks against the taut skin . . . boom-boom-boom-boom. Horses, not a bit disturbed by the noise, moved past, harnesses jingling. Beautiful shiny-coated horses, the riders' breastplates and helmets and swords glinting in cold November sunshine. Then came the gold coach bearing the new Lord Mayor of London towards Mansion House.

'I've never seen anything like it,' Josie yelled her thoughts to Winnie as it all went by, but every word was lost in the renewed fervour of cheering that rose from the crowds around her.

62

She and Winnie had got here early, had been waiting for hours. Even so, others had got here even earlier and it had been a hard job finding a place at the barriers that lined the route. They'd never have found one but for Arthur; being tall and skinny, he had been able to shoulder his way through the growing throng to find a place at the front for them, giving back as good as he got from those he edged aside.

The girls, both ecstatic, had a full view of the passing spectacle, but he took it all in his stride. He'd seen it all before. He had, he told them, attended this annual parade from a child, with his parents when his dad was alive, and his brother and sister; they would take sandwiches and beer and flasks of lukewarm tea that tasted lovely after the parade was over and the crowds dispersed to London's parks if it was sunny, and home if it was cold and wet. He came less often now he had grown up. 'Well, yer see one, yer've seen 'em all. It don't change, only the bloke in the coach.'

Today he looked on his charges – two of the most prettiest (well, one at least) girls he had ever escorted anywhere – with nonchalant pride in *his* London glowing on his narrow face.

'It must be really wonderful living in London all the time,' Josie gasped as the cheering died away.

'S'all right,' Arthur said with that same nonchalant pride as, with the crowds miraculously thinning, they made their way from the now uncoveted vantage place at the barriers. Some were already being taken down for stacking in batches by grinning, tall-helmeted police while cloth-capped street cleaners began sweeping up horse manure as well as the litter of twenty thousand Londoners' day out.

'Where d'yer want ter go?' Arthur asked the two girls. He still looked proud, a girl on each arm.

Josie glanced round him at Winnie on his other side. 'We don't mind, do we, Win?'

'I don't know London,' she supplied. 'We'll go wherever you say.'

'Fancy one of the parks? It's a bit cold but it's dry, and they are nice, our parks.'

'I'd rather see what West End London's like,' Josie put in quickly.

She had been waiting for a chance like this. She felt she could never have ventured there alone – tales gleaned from this person

63

and that of Soho, the hidden dives and the opium dens of Chinatown and all the other seamier back streets lurking just behind the bright lights of Mayfair and Piccadilly Circus making her eyes boggle.

With her arm linked in Arthur's she would feel safe. But she wished now that she hadn't brought Winnie along – not that she particularly wanted him to herself, but Win would want to go one place and she another. Two's company, three's a crowd.

On this occasion, however, Winnie was in full agreement. 'Oh yes, I'd love to see all those theatres and things.'

Arthur was looking concerned. 'Can't afford ter take yer into any. I ain't got the money fer free of us, not even if we line up fer the gods. Could prob'ly take yer ter the pictures.' But he didn't look too keen on spending on two girls. Josie he might, but not Winnie as well – Josie was his date.

'All I want to see,' Josie said excitedly, 'is just what it looks like up there. I want to see all the moving bright lights around Piccadilly Circus, all those electric advertisements.'

'Aint you never seen em?'

'No. And all the people in their lovely limousines and their furs, and men with top hats and canes and their evening dress. I want to smell what it's like – all that expensive perfume and powder, and peep into one of those nightclub places, just to see what it would feel like if we went in, which I know we can't – we're not dressed for it. And watch people getting out of taxis . . .'

''Old on, 'old on!' Arthur was laughing. 'I fink I get the picture. It's up West fer us then.' Again his pride in his city knew no bounds. He'd show these girls from the sticks the night of their life. He would even go to three cheap seats in a moderately priced cinema to finish up with – a cowboy film maybe, his favourite type of film, full of blazing guns and tough lean men, men like Tom Mix.

Darkness, but for the blazing lights, having closed in hours ago, the time sped by until it was nearly ten o'clock. An electric sign proclaiming it drew a horrified breath from Josie.

'Oh, God, look at the time, Win.'

Winnie too looked astounded, and just as worried as Josie. Her father could belt her one when she appeared. Though Josie knew her dad would do no such thing, his displeasure would be just as painful, and Mum's too.

64

'We've got to go,' she told Arthur. 'It's going to take at least an hour and a half on the train if we go now. Half past eleven before we get home. Our dads will kill us.'

Arthur, who lived just twenty minutes from this city's heart, grinned at them, but then realising the distance they had to go, sobered quickly.

'We'd best start off then.' He would have loved going to the pictures to see Tom Mix, but Josie had been so absorbed and overwhelmed by all she had seen of London's just-awakening night life, she didn't want to sit in any dark picture palace. And Tom Mix films were still silent ones.

Her whole being cried to stay here, to be, if only in imagination, part of this scene, imagining herself getting out of one of those taxis, entering a nightclub on the arm of an evening-dressed escort, having her fur wrap taken from her by a cloakroom girl, producing from her gold lamé clutch bag a long ivory cigarette holder into which she would insert a fragrant pink-coloured Turkish cigarette. She yearned for that life even more and as they made their way down Piccadilly Tube Station, she promised herself that she would come back, but not to gape, to be one of those society women who tonight had moved past her without even seeing her.

The Wall Street Crash last Autumn hadn't touched Annie's family business. Theirs was insignificant except to them, isolated, specialised, the trauma that had hit prominent business organisations and sent them tumbling, had passed the Bowmakers by like a puff of summer breeze, although it had shaken Alex's father's business a little. Fortunately his firm relied not only on America for its sources but on countries as far flung as Argentina and India – diamonds from South Africa, opals from Australia, rubies from Burma, emeralds from Columbia and India, topaz from Brazil, turquoise from Tibet.

Nevertheless, Alex said he was struggling, the States being one of their major customers. But the world was wide and the business would survive, he told Annie. She was fascinated. But she was fascinated by all Alex told her, and he by all she told him. They were in love. Her delighted family knew all about it. His family didn't know.

65

'I thought you would have told them about us by now,' she harried.

'I will,' he said, staring out over the estuary as they huddled within an otherwise deserted storm shelter against a stiff, snow-laden January wind. The water looked an angry mud-grey, its bottom churned by the white laced waves far too enormous for a mere estuary. The promenade pavement looked as though it were on the move, minute frozen pellets of snow, driven by the wind, racing across its surface in thin white clouds. But such was love that lovers would be alone together no matter what the weather, feeling nothing, or at least enduring it so long as they had each other.

Annie studied Alex's face. 'When? When will you tell them?'

Alex bit his lip, kept his eyes on the scene beyond the glass shelter, refusing to look at her. 'Annie, my darling. Please don't take this the wrong way, but you and I, we come from different walks of life. *I* don't care. I love you, Annie. And I should hope that it is no one else's business but our own. But families are particularly protective of their children. They presume to make up their minds for them, for the sake of themselves. But it's important to them despite what we feel and want. I want you, Annie, with all my heart. I want us to be together forever. But my family think that one day I'll marry into a family they deem fit for me. They've been badgering me about it since I was twenty-one. But I never met anyone I fancied. And I didn't intend to marry anyone just to please them.'

Annie listened in silence. She had taken her eyes off him and she too was staring out to sea, her heart slowly plummeting. This was his way of telling her that although he loved her desperately, she'd never be acceptable to his kind of people and that their relationship might have to cease.

'Then I met you, Annie,' he continued. 'And I knew you were the one I'd been waiting for, and nothing, no one, would ever make me stop seeing you.'

Seeing her, that was it. One day he would marry someone of his own kind. And he was expecting to go on seeing *her*, for her to become his paid mistress. Good God!

She shifted on the bench, but his arm around her tightened. 'I know we probably have a rough time ahead of us, darling. Not from your parents but from mine. They'll create merry hell about

66

this, I know they will. But they won't shift us, my darling.' He lay his head against hers while still staring ahead. 'I intend to marry you, no matter what they say.'

'Marry?' Annie found her voice, moved back to turn her face to him, wondering if she'd heard correctly. She wasn't sure what to say, how to react. She had assumed, had hoped, these past months but they'd not talked purposefully of marriage. 'Did you say marry?'

She saw his expression full of anxiety, alarm. 'You do want to marry me, Annie? You've not just been playing along, have you?'

She too had begun to feel alarm. What if he had taken her surprised tone for what might seem a rejection and at any moment jump up and walk away? 'I love you, Alex,' was all she could blurt out.

'And I love you . . .' The fear began to melt from his eyes, replaced by revelation. 'Oh, my darling, I see what's wrong. What a way to propose. I'd meant to make it an occasion, go down on bended knee and ask for your hand in marriage.'

It sounded so comical but he meant it seriously, taking her hand in his. 'Annie, my precious darling, I'm asking formally now. Annie, will you marry me?'

No more fear. Her mind again serene, Annie relaxed against him. A wonderful glow began to surround her. The snow was getting heavier but she didn't care. It was beautiful, romantic, sitting in this cold shelter safe from the biting wind outside. She felt secure, knew he would guard her from harm and the pitiless tongues of those who would have them separated.

'Yes, Alex, I'll marry you. With all my heart,' she said.

'George! I'm pregnant!' It was far from the way an unmarried girl would usually say this to her boyfriend, nor usual for the boyfriend to stare back in pure joy.

'Are you sure?'

Pam nodded eagerly. 'I waited to be sure. This is the third month I've missed . . . you know what I mean. I didn't want to say too much, in case it was a false alarm. But this morning I woke up queasy in my tummy. I *know*, George. I know. Isn't it just wonderful? They can't stop us now.'

He was thoughtful. Standing with her in the icy cold park, the only place they could ever be sure of being undiscovered by any

67

who might know them, he grew businesslike, the first flush of joy overshadowed by doubt.

'We'll have to go about this carefully. I know it's what we'd planned, but I don't think we should say anything to anyone just yet.'

Pam looked astounded. 'They *can't* stop us marrying now.'

'There are things like abortion.'

'That's illegal. Mum wouldn't even consider such a thing. She loves me too much. She wouldn't risk harming me. And she wouldn't expect me.'

'It's your dad I'm worryin' on. Him hating mine like he does, and mine not far short of that himself. What if yours threw you out?'

There was a moment of dismay that Dad could do such a thing, but she laughed it off. 'He'd never do that. But if he did, surely I'd be free to marry without having to ask his consent. It would solve all our problems.'

George didn't laugh. He gave her a long stare. 'I don't think it would. Not for you. The people you love – d'you know what it'd mean to you?'

Pam shrugged. A flake of snow touched her face. It was coming down quite heavily and she'd not noticed when it had started. The weak sunshine through which they had walked had gone, snow clouds gathering as though from nowhere, a brief fall of large soft flakes that promised not to last before the sun struggled out again. The crisp fresh smell of the snow was in her nostrils as, her head bent, her arm through his, they wandered without any real idea or care which direction they took.

Not knowing whether to feel despondent or cheered, they walked in silence. Finally Pam's despondency or whatever it was began giving way to new hope as a thought that hadn't made itself apparent until now came to her. She stopped staring at the movement of her feet and lifted her head.

'George, hasn't it ever occurred to you that us *having* to marry could bring our two families together?' Enthusiasm for the idea began to mount, visions of her part in this reconciliation invading her mind.

'With us married, my dad and yours would have to make it up. I bet neither of them has ever wanted to be the one to make the first move – pride and all that.' She began to giggle. 'There's never been anything to get them together until now. Imagine, all

68

those years. Before I was born. So long ago it's almost become a myth.' She broke out into a joyous laugh. 'George, a myth. Oh Lord, how daft can people get? And we can be the ones to bring them together. My family and yours.'

His arm tightened about her in a gesture of reassurance. She heard him laugh, and if it sounded a fraction cynical she didn't notice. All she had to do was weather her parents' wrath for a while then all would be well.

In the pale glow of the central gas lamp, her mother held her arms up, and from her small height wrapped them about her daughter's neck in pure joy at the news she had just been given this February evening.

'Oh, Annie, Annie, dear, I am so pleased for you both!'

Dad was shaking Alex by the hand. 'Best bit o' news in a long while. I know you're goin'ter look after her, Mr Willoughby. My Annie's a lucky gel.'

'I consider myself the lucky one,' Alex said, looking across at her.

'Well, whatever, still good news, Mr Willoughby. I wish the pair of you all the joy what you both deserve.'

Annie looked across at them and smiled in amusement. Dad had so far never addressed him as anything but Mr Willoughby. To him Alex's life was so far removed from the one Dad led. Also it was such a short while since she and Alex first met – just five months ago. Some parents might protest that it was too soon for engagements, that young people should wait to be certain of their own minds. But Alex was wealthy. Such doubts did not come up in the excitement of such fortunate circumstances. Almost like a form of greed, Annie deliberated indulgently. She didn't feel greedy or avaricious. She was just deeply and helplessly in love.

The rest of the family sat about in the small front room, all except Danny who, as usual, was out seeing his Lily for whom these past four or five months he had forsaken all other girlfriends.

On the sofa with its flowered loose covers, Josie leaned over towards Connie and whispered behind her hand. 'You and Ben mightn't have to save so hard for your wedding now. He might help you. You never know.'

'Don't be stupid,' Connie whispered back fiercely and looked quickly at Ben lounging beside her. He was very much part of the family now with their wedding just four months away.

Arrangements were already in hand, the date booked with St Clement's church, the banns to be called as appropriate, the church hall booked too, for far too many guests were invited to cram into this house or his parents' cramped third floor letting in Waterlow Buildings. All his family lived in and around Bethnal Green, some in Corfield Street, some in Wilmott Street, some in Three Colts Lane, and some on the other side of the arches in Tapp Street, a close-knit family, and a lot of them. They would come to Leigh in a body, making it a weekend holiday as they did for the engagement party last June. That was the last party they'd had, the usual one at Christmas foregone with everyone saving like mad to help with the cost of the wedding. She just hoped Ben hadn't caught what Josie had just said, that was all.

'I wouldn't dream of asking him for any hand-out,' she hissed.

Josie shrugged, listening to congratulations flying around the room, and before jumping up to add hers, hissed back: 'Well, I must say, it does look as though he's going to be part of the family, doesn't it?'

These days she spoke very correctly, echoing the way the wealthy in London spoke, happy to risk ridicule from friends and family. She had been to London several times, with Arthur, who had taken her up the West End, proud to show it to her. Dressed in her very best, many a polished young man's eyes had turned towards her, and she would flutter hers at him in apparent surprise at the unspoken compliment given her. All without Arthur noticing a thing.

Nothing came of it, of course. No matter how fashionably she dressed, they saw at a glance she wasn't of their class, especially when Arthur opened his mouth. Not that either of them could afford to ever step into those expensive nightclubs. But they could linger outside while the wealthy went in. Arthur would boast how used he was to seeing it all, and she would merely gape and wish; dream what it must be like inside, how it would feel to be on the arm of some handsome, filthy-rich escort. But it was only dreaming. There was occasionally the odd one or two in a group who was without a partner, who appreciatively glanced her way, but only briefly. All she could do was dream, ending up at the pictures or in some ordinary dance hall with Arthur.

Worse, it had grown less easy to run up a dress such as the wealthy used to wear. The sleeveless, knee-length, drop-waisted dress that had been in vogue for nearly four years until it felt that it had come to stay, had gone. Suddenly, drastically, this very month hemlines had fallen to calf length, a dress once more following the body's contour after years of shapeless little shifts with fringes and beads and sequins to round them off. Suddenly the line was slinky, bosoms that had once been flattened had come back in fashion, backs plunged to reveal naked flesh. Even hairstyles were changing to longer marcel-waved coiffures. It was not easy to afford such hair styles, nor such dresses, even made at home. Unable to copy the fashionable set at all, Josie's dreams had become after all just the dreams of an ordinary girl hopelessly yearning for the unreachable.

'To think,' Mum was saying, holding firmly now to Annie's hand with both hers, 'a few months back there was me despairing of you ever finding yourself a nice young man, much less a nice young man like Alex. Annie, I'm so pleased for you. And so proud. It was a real surprise. What's his parents say?'

'We . . . haven't told them yet.' Annie remained straight-faced before her mother's joy. Her mother leaned away from her.

'Well, I'm sure they're going to be pleased as us when you tell them. They'll be thrilled he's found himself a nice respectable girl like you. When are you going to tell them?'

Dad was calling Alex Mr Willoughby again. Annie turned on him, taking Alex's arm possessively. 'Dad, please call him Alex.'

Dad cleared his throat, awkwardly fingering the collar and tie he had hastily donned when she and Alex had come in unannounced this evening from their day in London buying the gorgeous solitaire diamond ring – a huge great thing – to tell everyone their news. 'Er . . . Alex.'

The ring flashed and glinted in the cold light of the gas lamp above it as if it were under electric light. Those like Alex's people already enjoyed electric light.

Pam, seated on a hard chair, a little removed from the rest, couldn't take her eyes off it. Silly great ostentatious thing – Annie showing off with her posh boyfriend.

What sort of engagement would she have? None at all, she felt. She still hadn't summoned up courage enough to tell them about

71

her condition. Four months – she'd start to show soon. Then what?

Already she was having to evade awkward questions from Mum on not seeing any soiled towelling from her monthlies by saying she had been washing them out herself as her monthlies had not been very heavy and she had actually missed one occasion the month before last, then come on just a little this month for only three days.

Her mother had looked rather concerned. 'Shouldn't be that light that they don't need a boil now and again. You sure you're not ill? Shouldn't you go an' see the doctor? Could be something wrong with you. Anyway, where are you drying 'em?'

'I only need to use a couple or so. They just need a quick rinse. They usually dry overnight.' It was a poor excuse, something her mother would eventually see through.

'Well, I think you ought to go and see the doctor, Pam. It ain't right.'

So far, that was all that had happened. But soon Mum must or would know.

Chapter Eight

Saturday, the first day of March. Today Alex had promised to take her to introduce her to his family. Now he was saying it wasn't possible as they'd be away at their country home in Berkshire.

'Well, can't we go there? Surely it's not that far in your car.' He had a new car, a Daimler ADR8, he told her; had got it for a song straight from the Austro-Daimler factory in Germany, because the stock market crash last year had affected the luxury car market badly. It was to be used for business as well, he'd said, so it wasn't really his, but he used it as though it were.

Two weeks ago life had felt wonderful. He had his car, she had a lovely engagement ring that cost as much, the times did not seem to be affecting him or his family too severely. While unemployment was growing worse all across the world, their family business appeared to be holding up without much trouble. Diamonds, or any gem for that matter, must be keeping their worth around the world so long as one avoided investing too heavily on the stock market. Alex said that his father had always been prudent, thus escaping last year's disaster that had struck down so many.

'Can't we motor out to Berkshire to see them?' Annie pleaded, the thrill of the luxury she was marrying into taking second place to her need to see her future in-laws. It struck her as odd that here she was engaged to Alex yet so far hadn't met any of his family. 'I'll have to meet them some time.'

'You will.' He put an arm around her as they strolled along Southend's Prom in the pale March sunshine. 'It's just awkward at the moment.'

A bolt of anger she wasn't expecting flashed its way through Annie in a wave of heat. She pulled away from his arm.

'*How* awkward is it, Alex? *Why* awkward?' He was smiling at her, a sort of confused smile – confused and uncertain. Annie read its message instantly. 'It's me, isn't it? You want me but you're ashamed of me.'

'Of course I'm not.' There was still the silly grin marring his usually handsome face, his wonderful face. She wanted in a moment of impulse to wrench his ring from her finger, the huge wonderful ring she had been so proud to wear, and throw it in his face.

'You are!' she railed instead. 'If I'm not good enough for your fine family, then how do you expect us ever to get married if you can't even bring yourself to introduce me, this poor girl of working-class parents, to the sort of people you belong to? Why did you ever choose me?' She was beginning to cry, her voice wavering, bereft of strength, taking on a tone of disbelief, of pleading. 'You knew my people were nowhere like yours. Yet you made yourself known to me, knowing how it would end up. Selfish. Cruel and selfish. You thought only of yourself. You said to yourself, my God, she's a good-looker, I'd like to get to know her. Who cares about the consequences?'

'That wasn't how it was.' Now he too was angry. 'All right, I was very attracted to you, Annie. But I fell in love with you too. From the very start. I loved you, Annie. It's not my fault they expect me to find myself a girl of their sort. You'll be marrying me . . . me, darling, not my family.'

It was an old cliché, spoken at some time or another by all those in love as truth. But there were families involved and she stood in the middle, caught between it all. She would be the sacrificial lamb for his own needs. And he, of course he was in love with her, but if they parted, if she threw back his ring, he'd go back to his fine family, in time get over her, find himself a wife *of their sort*. And what would she be left with? Having known, though only for a short while, the luxury he had shown her, how could she go back to her own sort and find herself a man who must work for a living, take his wages each week and eke them out until the next pay day? She couldn't. It was impossible. Annie felt herself dissolve.

'Alex. Do you mean that? You mean you wouldn't care what your family said? That you'd marry me no matter what they say?'

Her body was leaning heavily against his. He guided her to a seat by the promenade that was vacant, sat her down and sat down beside her, his arm about her holding her to him.

'Now listen to me.' His voice was low and soothing, and held a note of command, melting her completely. This was why she loved him so; why she couldn't imagine ever being without him, why she was so afraid of losing him. 'I know it sounds old hat, the bit about marrying me not my family. But I mean it, with all my heart, darling. I *will* introduce you to them. What worries me is how you, not they, will take it – how you'll take the way they might probably look at you. They might not. I don't know. But I'm scared.'

She looked up, her eyes faintly flushed from crying. 'Scared?'

'Not for me . . . well, yes, for me. In case you decide we can't make a go of it. But for you too. I don't want you hurt. Yet again they might be nice as pie about it all. I just don't know. That's why I've been holding fire.'

'Well don't,' she told him. 'It'll make no difference whether you tell them now or later. But we can't go on like this.'

'Listen, I'll speak to them, tell them about you and how strong our love is. I'll tell them this very week. And no matter the outcome, we'll never be parted.' He bent and kissed her and all his love was in that kiss.

It was all that had mattered, Annie kept telling herself, but three weeks had gone by and not a word from him, not a letter, not a telegram to say why he hadn't got in touch. At first she merely thought something, some workload in his father's company, had come up to keep him away, and had felt just a tiny bit annoyed that he hadn't found time to let her know.

Mum had asked where he was and she had fobbed her off by saying she had known about it and he couldn't always be here at every turn, but he would come here next week or she go there to his people in London.

'You've met his parents, then?' Mum queried. 'You never said. Are they nice people?' Annie almost flinched.

'Oh, yes . . . Nice. Not a bit stuck up.' Lying, with its habit of needing to be embroidered upon, took hold in even more fabrication. 'His dad is . . . really nice, though his mother's a little reserved. But . . . but she kissed me. They really welcomed me.'

'Oh, that is nice.' Annie cringed from her mother's trusting voice. 'We might be meeting them soon, then, eh?'

'I suppose so.' Her reply tersely cutting the cross-examination short before she was compelled to elaborate even further, Annie had made herself scarce. But she had neatly scuppered herself. Impossible now to confide her woe in her mother even if she had wanted to sink her pride. She sought Connie out instead.

'I'm so miserable.' Pride might prevent her confessing her white lie to Mum and gaining her sympathy, but Connie, always full of sympathy and understanding, was someone one could turn to at any time, and safely. Nothing said to Connie passed her lips. She'd listen with that intense look of concentration, thinking about what was told her, and could always be relied upon to come up with some comforting words even if she had no solution to the problem.

'I don't know what to do. It's the third week I've not seen him. Until now we've seen each other every weekend since we first met. He always says he can hardly last the week without seeing me. There must be something wrong.'

Connie reached out and touched her arm as they stood in the back yard in the dark. She had called them out to see the stars, the dark sky so clear they stood out like sequins. A dreamer was Connie, when she wasn't looking on the dark side of things in connection with herself. With others she was all hope and reassurance.

The family – that was Mum, Dad and Josie – Pam was out with friends and Danny out with girls or a girl – hurried back in out of the cold after indulging Connie in her star-gazing, so she and Annie stood alone. A chance arose for Annie to tell someone about her misery.

'I thought he might write. I was going to write to him or telephone him from the box, but it looked silly then, running after him the second he didn't turn up. I really thought I'd hear from him. Then when he didn't come this weekend and sent no word, I wouldn't let him see I missed him. But again this week. How can I write now, begging him? It's all over. I know it is. The waiting's been sheer hell, Connie. Whoever said no news is good news? If it had been good news, I'd have had a message from him by now, or he'd have come himself. He promised to convince his parents that nothing they said would part us.

76

Obviously he hasn't convinced them, has finally been persuaded that I'm not for him.'

All the while she poured out her heart Connie's hand was still on her arm, the touch light yet reassuring. 'I think you might be jumping the gun a bit. It might be nothing like you're imagining. Something's just delayed him, that's all.'

'Yes.' Annie heard the rasp of her own voice. 'Cold feet.'

Sure of it, while Connie and Ben went off to church and the rest of the family did what they most liked doing, lounging around the house, Annie took herself to Southend to be on her own and escape the inevitable awkward question from Mum on why she and Alex hadn't seen each other this weekend. Despite a drizzle that had followed the clear night sky that Connie had dragged everyone out of doors to see, Annie spent the whole morning here summoning up her resources enough to come to a conclusion that it was indeed all over. She resolved that under no circumstances would she be the one to get in touch. She had never begged in her life and wouldn't do so now even though her heart was breaking. Her hands in the pockets of her raincoat, she finally turned and made her way back to the station and home. Lovely while it had lasted, she and Alex, but since he was a rich man's son, made for disaster. She would put it all behind her. She wouldn't write, wouldn't beg, wouldn't lower herself, her pride good as any the wealthy could summon up. Now she must tell her parents that it was all off. And that was the worst part of all.

Lounging on the settee, Danny thought of last night. Lily lying under him, giggling, saying he knew how to make love all right and how marvellously strong he was, masterful. He had lapped it up. Well, any man would. Lily was the prettiest girl in the world, so slim, so pliable, and so ready for him.

'Go on like this, love,' he'd puffed, 'and I'll have to marry you.'

'Ooh, yes, darling,' she had found enough room between gasps of ecstasy to reply. 'I want you to marry me.'

It had been wonderful making love under the stars, on damp grass, and he had almost proposed. Only afterwards when he'd rolled off her, spent, was he glad he hadn't. Not yet anyway. She'd be ideal for him. They were ideal for each other, but he still needed a little more freedom, just in case. In case of what? In case

77

another girl came along? He loved Lily. He couldn't get her out of his mind. But marriage ... such a big step. Planning, a white wedding, church, reception, honeymoon ... well, honeymoon was all right ... people to invite, having to grin like a bloody cheshire cat at them. God. Yet it was worth it to have Lily. What if someone else claimed her while he was dithering around? He sat up quickly. Tonight he'd start the ball rolling when he saw her. Mention it, seriously. Lily would jump at it.

A knock at the door and his mother's voice as she opened it made him sit up hastily, check that his fly was buttoned, his shirt, collarless though it was, at least done up to the neck, that his dark curly hair wasn't sticking up from contact with the settee. Too late to find his shoes upstairs.

'Do come in, dear,' his mother was saying, her voice adopting an odd sort of accent intended to sound nice. 'Lovely to see you, dear. Annie is out. She shouldn't be too long. She went off to Southend. Heaven knows why. She never said noth ... anything about you coming today.'

Everyone else discreetly withdrew; she and Alex sat in the tiny back room after Annie had confessed her lies to her mother, in tears of relief telling her everything. Now, sitting with Alex at the dining table, she wondered at her premature happiness.

'I could not ... I dared not contact you to let you know what's been happening,' Alex was saying. 'My parents and I have been having row upon row. My mother in tears, my father in a rage.'

Annie looked at him, her eyes sad with understanding, sad too with what she still saw as the inevitable as he told her of the hell he had gone through these past two weeks. His parents had no intention of meeting her no matter how he had argued and pleaded his case.

It had come to her as she listened that it was all hopeless, that she must be brave and let go of him, but she couldn't. She had just sat silently listening as he went on, his story sounding worse with every word.

'My father is threatening to send me abroad.'

Now she spoke. A father threatening to send his son, a grown man, abroad, sounded ludicrous. 'How can he, Alex? You're twenty-nine. He can't do that.'

His expression was grim. 'He can, my love. That's to say the company can. I'd be transferred to one of our overseas agencies for a spell. To sort out business on behalf of our company. I've done it before. The States, South America, South Africa. I enjoyed every minute of it, begged to go. Broadens the mind, makes a man of one. But now . . . He says he will arrange for me to go to India for an indefinite period and in time I will forget you.'

'You don't have to go.' Indignation at such outrage against a grown man, son or not, gripped Annie. For the first time Alex smiled.

'I do if I want to stay with the company. My father's ultimatum. It's tantamount to my being disinherited if I refuse under these circumstances, though he'd never cut me out of his will exactly, I know that. What it will mean is that he would ask me to resign from the company if I refuse and I'd be left to fend for myself.'

Annie felt her muscles relax. 'You could get a position anywhere. You know management and buying. We'd get along.'

'What would I have to offer you then? We'd have nothing.'

'We'd have each other.'

'And when we have no money? I have always been in the family business. I know no other work.'

'You could do what you're doing now, but with some other company.'

He shook his head, his fingers drumming nervously on the table top. 'Annie, I couldn't. It's not as easy as that. Whoever I go to will ask who I previously worked for. What do I say? That I'd been asked to resign from my own family business? My father would admit to that, if asked.'

'I think your father's a vindictive man.'

Immediately she wished the outburst hadn't been said as Alex's face changed, growing stubborn. She had blotted her own copybook. He would not now fight for her against his own father, whom she saw he loved, no matter what. It was all at an end.

'Alex,' she pleaded, pride thrown to the wind. 'Darling, I love you. I know you love me. There must be something we can do. Please, darling, please say there is. Say you still love me.' Her voice had risen so that those in the house must hear. She didn't care.

He had reached out his hands and was holding hers, his grip fierce. 'I will have to do as he says. There's no work here, businesses everywhere are going to the wall and unemployment is rising. I will be going to India. I can't forsake the family business, Annie.' For a moment he said no more and she remained silent, enmeshed in the hopelessness of her situation. Then he spoke again.

'But they still can't stop us getting married.'

'What?' Confusion smothered her senses.

'We could get married secretly.' His voice had fallen to a whisper that no one in the house could have heard. 'In a registry office, not even your parents knowing of it. Would you do that?' When she didn't answer, unable to for the shock of it all, he went on swiftly. 'We could do it quickly, go to India together and live there. No one will know for a long while.'

Now it was her turn to worry, relieved and overjoyed though she was by Alex's proclamation of love against all odds. 'I couldn't deceive Mum and Dad like that.'

'I'm ready to deceive mine – for you.' She wanted to say, it wasn't the same, but he was going on. 'I thought you loved me enough to throw everything overboard. It's what you were asking me to do.'

Yes, he was right, but still she hedged. 'My parents' view is different to yours. They want to see me married to you. They want to see me happy.'

'But would they be prepared to see you going off to the other side of the world where they'll not see you for years? What if they insisted you stay here?' Annie said nothing, and his tone grew confidently coaxing. 'You can write to them, tell them why you did it. I in turn would write to my parents revealing that we are married, only a little later.'

She had to say it. 'Your father could still dismiss you from the family business and we'd have gone through all that for nothing.'

'That's a risk I'll be prepared to take. By then I don't think he will.'

'Why not?'

'What will he gain? We'll be married. He can hardly undo that, and I don't think he'd be so stupid as to try. You see, my darling, it's a threat, to stop me marrying you. He'd never carry it out once we're married.'

'But he could transfer you to India.'

Alex chuckled, got up and enfolded her in his arms. 'And we'd go together, just as we're planning to do now. You see, we're going in circles, darling. Are you willing?'

Yes, she was willing. But she still told her mother, on Monday evening while Dad and Danny were in his cockle shed, the day's haul being steamed and made ready for Billingsgate market.

Dad would have gone off the rails had Annie told him direct of her intrigue. Mum could break it to him later, gently, in her usual careful way. There would be argument, but not so stinging as if it came straight out of the blue from Annie's own mouth.

All the same, Mum looked as though she had been bitten, her hand flying to her lips, her small rounded face filled with fear. 'Annie, dear. You can't go off on the other side of the world where we'll never see you again. You can't.'

'You would see me, Mum.' Annie tried to keep the empathetic tears hidden by lowering her face. 'I shall come home on a visit whenever I can.'

'No you won't. The tone, so firm, so full of wisdom, made Annie look up. Mum might just as well have said: out of sight, out of mind.

'It won't be like that, Mum. I'll make every effort to come home on visits. At least a couple of times a year.'

'And where will the money come from for that?'

'Alex isn't poor, Mum.'

'Paying for a passage home just to visit people eats into a good deal of money. And it'll take a good couple of weeks I should think for you to sail home, and the same going back as well as the time visiting us. Do you think your husband will stand for that every six months or so?'

Annie pushed that argument aside, too painful and too accurate.

'We won't be away for ever and ever, Mum,' she changed tack. 'It'll only be for a year or two. You're not losing me for ever.'

'I thought Alex said he was being sent there for an indefinite period.'

'That could be as long or short as it needs to be, Mum.'

'My guess is, when his dad learns what you and him have done, he won't call him back. Not in a month of Sundays. Do you think, Annie, them in their standing'd want their lives turned upside down and be the butt of all their high and mighty friends with their son introducing a wife what to them looks beneath them? Them sort of people only marry within their own spheres. They need to keep things like this out of the limelight, and somewhere like India or China or some other far-off place is just what the doctor ordered, even though it'll hurt them just as much as it hurts us, hearing all this. They love their son too.'

She hadn't thought of all that. Suddenly the rosy future didn't seem so rosy. The rest of her life, away from home, never seeing her family again. Quickly, Annie shrugged off the momentary depression. She was prepared to make a life for herself. She loved Alex with all her heart; would follow him wherever he went, to the ends of the earth if need be. Together they would be, must be happy. Stay here just to stay clinging to her family and she'd never see Alex again. That prospect was unbearable. Anyway, despite what Mum said, if it was to be so long away, then she would make efforts to come home at least once a year even if it did take weeks and weeks. Her future lay with Alex, and it *was* exciting. She felt her heart lighten, the future turning ruby again.

'I know what you're saying,' she said. Poor Mum. How she'd miss her. And she in turn would miss Mum, dreadfully; Dad and Danny too, but mostly Mum; and Connie and Pam and Josie, the arguments they had, the turmoil of this house, borrowing each other's things and fighting over them. But the companionship as well, confidences shared, advice offered, comfort in numbers. Away from it all she would only have Alex to comfort and advise her. Would it be the same? But then, Connie was getting married in a few months' time. She would leave home, set up her own, have her own life. True she would be nearby, in London maybe. But London could be a thousand miles away when she wanted Mum's advice quickly. So what was the difference? Annie felt cheered. Saw Pam and Josie one day married. And what if she stayed here, too frightened to follow Alex, who would she find to compare to him and would she forever remember the day she got cold feet and backed out? Maybe she would end up settled with some man who would never take Alex's place, or, because she could find no one to compare, be the last of Mum's daughters to remain at home, an old maid, destined to look after an elderly couple, be their nurse and when they finally died, be alone? All this thought choked the tears in her breast. She took a deep breath.

'I know where I'm going, Mum. I know what I'm doing.'

'I just hope so,' her mother said, turning away. Then suddenly she turned back, took Annie and clasped her to her with such strength that Annie felt she was being suffocated, drawn down to her mother's height by the embrace. 'I shall miss you, darling.' The words were muffled by Annie's shoulder, and by tears. 'I can't stop you, love. I wouldn't. But I'll miss you so much . . . I wish you all the happiness in the world, love.'

As suddenly as she had clasped Annie to her, she let go, giving a little laugh that sounded nearer to weeping. 'Your Dad's going to be a sod to handle, when I tell him what's goin' on. But we'll sort him out, you an' me.'

Two weeks later they were married, a brief registry office thing with no one in Annie's family present except for Uncle Bill, Mum's brother, and Aunt Daphne as witnesses. Annie had begged her family be there but Mum was right as usual.

'I don't think it'd be proper for us to be there, love. Not because we don't want to be. I'm goin' to be really upset not seen' you married, love, but it'd be underhanded if we was there and not the groom's people, and them with no idea of what's goin' on. I hope you won't feel too hurt about it, love, but you must see it's for the best. We don't want to be seen as accessories to any conspiracy,' she had added firmly, adopting a little of Alex's manner of addressing a thing, adding her own simpler version: 'or anything like that.'

It was hard not to weep, the wedding she had once dreamed of as far removed from it as any could be, but she had Alex to herself for a week before he left. He'd be going on ahead alone, his parents at London Docks to bid him *bon voyage* in the belief that he'd be staying in Jalapur eighty miles out of Delhi, working at the agency for his father's company, dealing and sending back reports until he finally got over this infatuation he'd confessed to. He had told them fiercely that it could be years before he did get over it, scotching any hope his father had of forgiving and recalling him too soon.

'We'll make a life for ourselves out there,' he told Annie as they came away from the registry office, man and wife. 'You'll be following me on the next package out. By the time you reach Jalapur I shall have selected a nice residence for us and done all the arrangements about servants.'

'Servants?'

'You didn't expect to do *housework*, did you? It would be too hot for a start. No memsahib does housework. That's for the servants. All you'll do is go to the club, socialise with the other wives, play cards and croquet and tennis . . .'

'I don't know how to play croquet.'

Instead of exciting her, a small fear had gathered inside her breast all the way to the Strand Hotel in London where they were to stay for a few nights before Alex left for London Docks. She intended to go back home for the two or three days until her own passage was due.

The full prospect of what lay ahead of her hit her suddenly as they unpacked their clothes in the room he had booked for them both, its splendour paling beside the new thoughts and fears. Who were these wives who played croquet and tennis? What were they like? Would they take to her, accept her? They no doubt spoke beautifully and correctly, these rich wives of colonials whom Alex had casually referred to as the Raj. Would her broad East Essex accent, that lingered no matter how well she'd learned to speak as a high-class hotel receptionist, be detected and sneered at?

'I don't know how to play croquet, or golf, and I'm no good at tennis.' Her life hadn't included such luxuries apart from one game years ago when she had hit the ball clear over the outside net. She had never bothered to play again.

Alex remained undismayed. 'You'd pick things up easily enough, my darling. But there are scores of other things for you to do. There's polo we can watch, and we can go to the races. Swim, play bowls, go motoring or horse riding – I'll teach you to ride.' His enthusiasm grew. 'I'll teach you to play golf as well, and tennis. We'll go to dinner parties, and lunch at the European club. where there are Europeans residing abroad, there's always a club – a haven for wives with little else to do. You'll go shopping and play bridge . . . all right,' he broke off to laugh. 'You can't play bridge, but you'll learn. We'll become part of the Raj in no time at all, you'll see.'

He was sitting up in bed, the huge canopied bed that dominated this bridal suite. He was in pale green pyjamas, the top half unbuttoned. She stood before him in a pale blue satin nightdress and wrap, part of her small trousseau, having shyly undressed in the huge bathroom, even there too worried by what lay in store for her in India to see its pink tiled opulence.

'But for now . . .' he held out his hands to her, inviting her to come to him and she, overcome by a wave of demureness, shed her wrap and, not daring to look at him, slipped in beside him beneath the smooth bed covers. Soon, all fear of the future forgotten as his hands, cool from his bath, moved over her body beneath the satin nightdress, she gave herself up to him with all the delight she had ever dreamed of.

Chapter Nine

Pam sat with all the family listening to Mum reading Annie's first letter. Annie had been gone a few weeks now; her letter arrived yesterday saying how lovely India was. Northern India, its heat cooled by soft breezes from the Himalayas all those hundreds of miles away. India with its sights and its smells, a blend of spicy cooking, dust, exotic scent and cattle dung, she said, not as unpleasant as it sounded; streets crammed with humanity, everyone busy doing something, selling, buying, bartering, mending things, fashioning things – all accompanied by a great deal of noise; buildings of pinkish-brown sandstone; the windows unglazed to let the air blow through; roads brown and dusty, trees to give shade, and the sky deepest blue. Elephants, camels pulling carts, hundreds of people on foot, on bicycles, in two-wheeled tongas and ancient charabancs, never a still or silent moment, even at night.

'India lives totally outdoors,' proclaimed the letter with a note of awe before going on to describe the residence she and Alex had, a spacious yellow and white-painted bungalow surrounded by a white painted wooden veranda, lawns, fruit trees and toddy palms, a pond shaded by a very large peepul tree and an Oriental plane tree, vivid purple bougainvillaea growing over all the boundary walls, flower borders with irises, narcissi and crown imperials. 'They have a lot of English flowers here,' she added. 'I expect they have been brought over by the British. We have a gardener to keep it nice – a mali. See, I'm learning a few words.' Annie seemed to gush with the pleasure of all this new experience.

Then after all that, the letter took on an odd and vaguely subdued note: 'I haven't made any friends yet. Most people here already have their own groups of friends. It'll probably take time to get in with them.'

'Sounds a bit cliquish,' Connie observed.

'Sounds like it ain't what she was expectin' it to be,' their father put in gruffly. 'Socially, I mean. Scenery sounds all right, but it's people not scenery what makes up a life.' He hadn't got over her leaving despite Peggy's caution.

The letter had also said that Alex was away a lot, involved with the agency and travelling between Jalapur and Delhi. It said the servants were helpful, polite, smiled readily, but were so quiet and unobtrusive it was almost as if they weren't there at all, silently coming and going to her bidding. As yet she wasn't finding it easy to issue orders to people although whatever she asked was done immediately without question. 'I'm still not used to having servants. I feel a bit unsure of myself, but terribly pampered.'

'Don't know about feelin' pampered,' Dad said as the letter was at last folded and put reverently back into its envelope. 'Sounds more like a bit homesick to me. And lonely. What's he doin' leaving her alone out there?'

Listening between the lines, it did seem the whole thing wasn't quite what Annie had expected, scenery apart.

Pam thought about Annie. Thought about them all. Annie had now gone. Connie and Ben, planning for their June wedding, would soon be off too. Danny had brought home a girl called Lily Calder to meet his parents, which in itself proclaimed her something more than just a friend. Mum, taking to her, said she was demure and sweet. He would probably decide to get married and leave home, since at twenty-six he had nothing to wait for. Josie had made it known she was seeing a London boy, Arthur Monk, on a regular basis, which was taken as equivalent to going steady. He was working in the docks, a good job with prospects. Mum, with an approving look on her face, said that although Josie was still a bit young at eighteen to go steady, a couple of years or so would soon see her going off and getting married.

Pam, apparently with no boyfriend, felt herself looked on by them all with something like pity. All but Mum, whose eyes she noticed the next evening as she came in from seeing George, shedding her outdoor coat, turning towards her midriff and growing just a fraction concerned, not for the first time this week.

Pam felt aware that even her winter jumpers and cardigans could no longer disguise that she was beginning to show.

'You puttin' on weight, Pam?'

'No, Mum.' Pam avoided her mother's scrutiny. 'Not as I know of.'

'You seem to be. Around the waist, mostly.'

Now was the time to confess voluntarily before she was forced into it. But words wouldn't come. Not the right words. Bad enough admitting to being pregnant, but by George Bryant? 'I'm eating a bit too heartily lately.'

It cut no ice. Mum came close to her, looked down at her and then took her arm quietly. 'Come in the kitchen a minute, love.'

She drew her away from the others who were busy listening to the wireless, the evening news with the football result soon to follow. During those Dad would demand complete silence while he and Danny checked the scores against their individual crosses in the crimson-edged squares of their individual pools coupons. 'I want a quiet word with you.'

Reluctantly Pam let herself be guided from the room. In the kitchen, away from everyone's hearing, her mother turned on her, her expression no longer one of anxiety. Now it was a look of determination, of certainty and of anger. But her voice remained low.

'Now tell me the truth, young lady. You've not been indulgin' in food, but you've been indulgin' in something, ain't you?'

Pam drew in a deep breath. 'I've been intending to tell you for a long time now, Mum.'

'So I am right.' Her mother was nodding. 'When's it due?'

'Some time in August. But it's not what you think, Mum.'

'What am I supposed to think then? That it was one instance, the first time you ever did it, you was taken by surprise, didn't understand what you was doin' – you a woman old enough to know what it's all about? And if it was a one and only time, did you think it didn't matter? I'm ashamed.'

'Mum, don't be ashamed. Do listen. There's something I've got to tell you about this. Me and . . . and the young man I'm going with . . .'

Her mother interrupted immediately. 'You're goin' with a young man and you've not said a word?'

'There's a reason.'

'What reason?' Her mother's expression was still angry, obdurate, and it took all Pam's courage to begin her explanation, an explanation she was sure would shock her mother to the core as much as it would Dad.

'Because the young man is someone you might not approve of,' she began. 'In fact I . . . we know you and Dad won't approve and you'd forbid us ever to see each other again. But we love each other, and we want to get married, no matter what went on in the past, and we thought if I was pregnant, we'd be made to get married and no one could do anything about it. I know this is going to hurt you, Mum, but I waited until it was too late for anyone to do anything about it before I told you. But now I've got to tell you. It's George Bryant. His dad is Dick Bryant.'

'Oh, God! Pam . . .' Her mother grabbed her arms, her plump fingers like talons through the sleeves of Pam's cardigan. 'You can't.'

Pam forced herself to remain calm. 'We knew this is how you'd both be. And George hasn't told his family either, not yet. He says they'd be just as upset as . . .'

'You silly little fool!' her mother's voice hissed at her. 'D'you know what you've done?'

'It's the only way we could see for us, Mum. We want to get married and I didn't want us to elope and get married secretly and hurt you both. I wouldn't have wanted to be that underhanded. We both thought if I was pregnant, we'd have to get married, and that old quarrel would have to be laid to rest.'

Her mother let go of her, a limp sort of release as though her hands had lost all their strength. 'You couldn't have been more underhanded if you had got married in secret.'

'Why?' Defiance took hold of Pam as she thought suddenly of her sister off in India, the marriage known to them but not his family. 'Annie and Alex have kept their marriage a secret from his parents, and you even went along with it. Then what's so underhanded about what me and George has done? At least we're being honest. We've not married in secret.'

'Because . . .' Tears were forming in her mother's eyes. 'Because you don't know how deep that trouble between your father and that Dick Bryant went, the way he wounded your father, and me, and our whole family.'

'But I wasn't there.'

89

'But it's reflected on you ever since, on you all, though none of you know it. But for what he did to your father, we might have been wealthy by now and you'd all have had a fine education and . . .'

'How do you know?' Pam's voice rose, growing exasperated. 'All sorts of other events could have cropped up to stop you and Dad being wealthy, not just Dick Bryant. And I don't want any fine education. All I want is to marry George. I love him, and your old quarrels have got nothing to do with me.'

The door opened and her father came in, his face creased with faint irritation. 'What's the bother with you two? I'm trying to do my pools and I can hear your two voices right through the wall. Can't hear a thing on the wireless properly.'

His wife took her daughter by one arm and turned her to face him. 'This girl's got something to tell you. I can't tell you. I can't bring myself to. Pam, tell your father what you told me. See what he's got to say about it. Then try and tell me you think you've done the right thing. Go on.'

Unable to defy her mother, Pam found herself mumbling over the same ground, a penitent before her father's blank look, no challenge or entreaty in her tone now.

Her story finished, she stood watching that first look of mild irritation becoming ludicrously fixed on his face as though carved there. By now it should have been suffused with fury, yet she knew that below the paralysed features rage did indeed lie, a well of magma beneath a dormant volcano. And when it finally burst out, Pam sensed an end to all she'd once known.

But nothing came as without a word he turned and went back to the room he had just vacated to voice his petty complaint. Her mother moved off after him, and after a moment of hesitation, Pam felt compelled to follow.

In the living room with the news reader's voice still coming over the wireless, unheeded now, all eyes trained on the silent three in vague premonition, Pam found her father standing gazing into the low fire, his back to her. Her mother had sat down in his chair where she was picking at a loose thread on her pinafore, intent on the task as though it was her sole interest at this moment. Pam felt her legs quaking.

'Only one thing I've got to say to you,' her father began without even bothering to turn round, as though the sight of her would have been offensive to him. 'Get rid of it.'

Pam found her voice. 'It's too late. I can't.'

'No, she can't,' her mother put in but they might as well have remained dumb for all the notice he took.

'And you don't see him any more – else you're out of this house.'

Listening from the chair where she had been sitting, Connie felt her heart leap with shock. Just after Christmas Pam had confided in her, as they all did at different times, letting slip her affection for George Bryant. Connie had done her best to dissuade her, pointing out the hornets' nest she'd be opening. Pam had sworn her to secrecy, thus putting her in an awful awkward position, but now it seemed Pam was pregnant. She wished now that she had confided in Mum at least, giving her some forewarning, but a vow was a vow and she had hoped Pam might see sense or that her fondness might only be short-lived and George Bryant be given up. Apparently not.

Running to Pam's defence was instinctive. Leaping up from her chair, Connie hurried over to her sister, her arm going protectively around Pam's shoulders. 'What d'you mean, Dad, she'll be out of this house?'

'What I say,' he said, turning now to glare around the room at them all: Danny still with his pen poised over his pools coupon, now forgotten; Josie, her library book, a gripping romance, open on the table where she'd been reading, her elbows still where they had been propped either side of it but her eyes on her father now instead of the book; Peggy, her eyes lowered as she continued to fiddle with the loose thread, running it between finger and thumb. 'She's been bloody messin' about with that Dick Bryant's son and the little sod's got her in the family way and she thinks we'll be willin' an' happy to see 'em wed. Well, that's what she bloody thinks.'

'But you can't turn her out,' Connie cried, the only one to challenge Dad's authority. It seemed solely between her and her father.

'She must've known what she was doin' of, the way things stand twix' us and them Bryants. It's been spoken on enough all these years.'

'Has it?' Connie flared. She had always been a match for her dad and now made full use of it. It had occurred to her in the past that she was his favourite of all his daughters. Surely he would listen to her. 'That family has never been allowed to be mentioned in this house as far as I know, Dad.'

'It don't alter things.'

'It does when you're so crabbed up by what happened all those years ago that you can tell your own daughter to destroy what's alive inside her and then order her out of the house. If that happens, Dad, I'll never speak to you again. And you won't need to come to see me married either.'

'I see. That's how it stands,' he roared. 'Right then, there'll be an empty place – two empty places, mine and your mother's, at your wedding.'

'Dan!' her mother's strangled voice came through the argument. 'You can't do that. You can't refuse to be at your own daughter's wedding.'

'I can, an' I will.' His hands were flailing in temper. 'We didn't go to Annie's. That was a fine state o' things, I must say. Now we're barred from our other daughter's weddin'. This time she's the one what's barring us. Well, I go along with that, if that's how she feels.'

Connie stood facing him squarely. 'You'd hold a grudge against me, Dad, just because I'm sticking up for Pam? It seems to me your whole life has been a grudge against something.'

It was an unfair statement. She knew it and her father certainly did. Livid with fury, a roar broke from his lips, and snatching up the first thing that came to hand, the tightly folded newspaper beside him, he flung it blindly across the room. Still folded, it was a missile, hitting the as-yet unlit gas mantle, smashing the thin glass shade, sending slivers of glass tinkling on to the cloth-covered table.

Josie shrieked and ran sobbing from the room. Her mother cried out something which no one actually heard. Danny called out, 'Watch it, Dad!' But no one heard him either as Danny immediately began to gather up the larger pieces of shattered glass to hand them to his mother who accepted them dumbly in the palm of her cupped hands, her eyes trained on her husband. He, ignoring the devastation, was roaring like a bull, perhaps because of the havoc he'd wrought: 'I said I bloody won't be at your weddin', and I won't if you stick up for that connivin', schemin' little cow!'

Connie stood her ground, her own voice raised. 'I don't believe you. I don't believe you could turn Pam out either.'

92

Pam was becoming hysterical. Her voice screamed above them all. 'I don't know what everyone's so upset about. I'm leaving anyway, that's what I'm doing. I'm leaving right now, so stop arguing about me. I don't care what everyone does. I wouldn't stay here . . .'

Connie turned on her. 'No, Pam. Dad's not going to throw you out.'

'I bloody am!' he bellowed. Pam ignored him.

'He's not throwing me out. I'm leaving on my own accord. I don't want to stay here another minute. I'm going to George's.'

'An' see how they'll take you in,' her father railed at her. 'They won't. That bastard Bryant won't take you in any more than I'll have you and his silly bugger son here, or the bastard you two've spawned. You couldn't even be careful . . .'

Pam's laugh was high, wild. 'Careful? What d'you mean careful? We planned it, didn't you know?'

'Pam! No!' Connie cried out, but Pam wasn't listening.

'We love each other and we mean to get married. We knew what you'd say, so we planned I'd get pregnant so I'd have to marry him. So there. And there's nothing you can do, Dad, to make that any different. I thought it might make peace between everyone when I told you how I was. But it looks like even that wouldn't stop this silly feud between you and his dad. Something we're all expected to take part in, even to giving up our own lives and happiness, even though it's got nothing to do with me or Connie or Josie or Annie. Over before we were born.'

'It'll never be over,' he began, but Peggy, her hands still cupped around the broken glass, moved to his side, suddenly with him against what her daughter was saying.

'You call it a stupid feud, Pam?' she said evenly, softly, but there was a stern note of obduracy in her tone. 'Is that what you call it? Let me tell you, Pam, because it's never really been discussed before. We took it there'd never be any need. So you've never really known how it was and . . .'

'Stop tryin' to reason with her,' Dan cut in viciously, but she stopped him by raising one of her hands, a piece of glass escaping from the lower one to tinkle on to the lino at her feet. But neither she nor any of them went to pick it up.

'Let me tell it as it was,' she said and looked intently into her third daughter's angry blue eyes. 'Yes, love, it is a feud. And like all feuds it started over nothing much at all. An argument in the Peter Boat. Started as a bit of fun over a pint and ended in a row. Your dad hit out and knocked Dick Bryant clean off his feet. You know how quick-tempered your dad can get. Nothing's goin' to change him. That's how he is. Well, it started a fight and your dad wiped the floor with Dick Bryant. Two nights later the boat, the one your dad had saved and scrimped so hard to get . . . his dad, your granddad what you never knew, was a gambler and gambled away his money and then sold his bawley to pay a bookie. Bawleys them days was sailing boats only.'

The room had fallen quiet, Dad sitting down heavily in his chair as though exhausted by his fit of temper, or perhaps subdued by it. Though Connie, glancing away from her mother to look at him, didn't think so.

'But I'm gettin' away from the subject,' her mother was saying, taking a deep breath and glancing briefly at her husband to catch any reaction from him. 'As I was sayin', your dad when we first got married, and that on not a brass farthing between us, scrimped and scraped to get a boat of his own. Poor little thing it was, in bad condition, but he worked on it, every day, and me with a young baby and tryin' to live on stale loaves from what the bakers had left over, and a bit of jam. That's all we had. And a bit of fish some of our neighbours'd be able to spare. None of us was that well off them days. Well, your dad worked hard on other men's boats, doin' what his dad had done before him, cockling. Then he bought his boat, and so proud of it we was. Then two nights after the row in the pub when your dad floored Dick Bryant, our boat went up in flames. It was deliberate because we could smell the oil used to set it alight. And some-one told us they'd seen Dick Bryant coming away with a can of oil in his hands just as the first flames got up.'

Connie saw a glimmer of light. 'Did Dick Bryant ever admit to doing it?'

'No, but he was guilty. He went around grinnin' all over his face and sayin' your dad had got all he deserved.'

'But that's not proof.'

She was stopped by her mother's look, a look that froze her marrow, so fierce it was, so full of angry support for her husband. 'You don't know nothing about it, love. We didn't need what you call proof. We saw it in his manner and his boasting, boasting so

94

much that he might just as well have admitted it was him. And if it wasn't, a man's livelihood, what he'd struggled to build up, seeing a good future goin' up in flames, meant nothin' to Dick Bryant. If it wasn't him, and we all know it was, the very way he acted and spoke was enough for us never to forgive or forget and to hate that family to the day we die.'

Silence lay about the room, its occupants standing or sitting stiff and tense, feeling the weight of this old, drawn-out feud descend upon all their shoulders.

'So you see,' Peggy went on. 'Nothing, no marryin' into that family is goin' to alter what we went through and the loathing we feel for them.'

'But Mum ...' Pam began, falling silent immediately, her mother's gaze moving from one to the other, full of sadness.

'No one knows how your father had to work to get us where we are today. We're fine now, but it's no thanks to the Bryants. I can't go into how hard your father fought to get to owning his present boat, but he did it, and you should all be proud of him for where you are now.'

Her eyes had turned on Pam in particular. 'And you think you can heal twenty-four years of sweat and toil and heartbreak by gettin' pregnant by that George Bryant? You think sayin' you and him intend to marry is goin' to make a speck of difference? No, my girl. I'm afraid it won't. I'm not turning you out, Pam. But I do think it's best you and the father of your child go and set up your own home somewhere, as all married couples do.' She spoke with simple dignity. 'We'll give you a few pound, enough to find somewhere to rent. Then it's up to you.'

'It's what I intended to do,' Pam said, her voice conveying relief.

'I know. But just one other thing, Pam. We don't want you or that father of your child ... ' To Connie it sounded disquietingly odd hearing her refer to George Bryant as the father of Pam's child rather than by his name, as if to utter it would have burned Mum's mouth. '... to come visiting.'

'What d'you mean?' Pam's overt relief was now overt alarm.

'I mean, we don't want you to come here. Not you or the man.'

'But the baby! When it's born. It'll be your grandchild.'

'It'll be impossible for us, me an' your dad, to see it as that. I'm sorry, Pam. That's how it is. You won't really need me to help in its birth. There are plenty of people what'll help you. There always are. But we'd rather we didn't see you again.'

Connie heard the gasp from Pam but otherwise she said nothing, seemed incapable of saying anything.

In all this Dad had remained silent. And as Mum turned away from her daughter, he took her hand in his rough, hard, weather-beaten one and the two older people became a unit before the eyes of their stunned, silent children, the two of them united in their mutual enmity for a family whose name they still found hard to utter after all these years.

Watching them, Connie felt her own insides dry up as though she too were being cast out. It was a hateful feeling. Yet there was no doubt Pam had done what she had done with the best of intentions as well as for love, and that love can never be put down no matter the intensity of adversity. She knew that although her parents would never mention Pam or see her as long as they lived, in her Pam would have a friend and confidant no matter what they said. The worst of it was, Mum and Dad must never know of her association with her misguided sister, but Pam was her sister and she loved her.

She felt a tear trickle down her face. Josie, who had come back into the room, was crying silently, her head bent, only the crown of her fair hair visible. Danny stood by the table, a few shards of glass which his mother had not taken from him still gripped in his fist and Connie saw a thin line of crimson staining the crease of his hand just below his small finger as Pam without a word turned and went out of the room.

Chapter Ten

'What's the matter, Jo? Yer 'ardly larfed once at that Laurel an' Ardy. An' that King o' Jazz film . . . Yer didn't even wan' an ice cream when I ast yer.'

Josie turned a miserable face to Arthur as, blinking at the lingering glow of an April evening after the darkened cinema, having sat almost twice through the continuous film performance, they emerged from the Excelsior Kinema into a Bethnal Green Road still full of late Saturday shoppers, the air filled with the stale odour of cooked meats from butcher shops selling dripping, pigs' feet, saveloys and faggots.

'I'm sorry, Arthur. It just didn't seem that funny.'

He tucked her arm through his. 'Well, I nearly split me sides at that cartoon. But you . . .'

'I wasn't in the mood, I suppose. We've had such an awful upset at home all week.'

She needed to tell someone. Dangerous confiding in local friends. Too near home, it didn't do to let them know all about your family's business. She said as much to Arthur, who grinned, preened himself on being the one chosen as a confidant and said blithely, 'All some people live for is ter know the ins and outs of every cat's arse. But there ain't nuffink yer can't tell me what'd make me blush – or chortle. My lot's bin all fru it in their time.'

He was a comfort, was Arthur. Salt of the earth, as they say. Pity he wasn't the rich, well-brought-up man she still felt in her bones she was looking for, discard the idea as she might. There were times she really felt she loved him. Then he'd do something or say something, kick up his heels in a pub or come out with a swear word in public, and she'd think again of the wealthy young man of her dreams who knew how to conduct himself in society and speak beautifully without having to resort to some embarrassing epithet. She still wished for all the things those women in the heart of the West End wore: beautiful fox furs about their shoulders, slinky, backless dresses that fluttered around the calves of their silk stocking'd legs, lovely matching satin high-heeled shoes, hats whose broad brims flapped over one eye giving them a look of mystery as they hung on the arm of elegant young men in evening dress.

Arthur didn't own any evening dress, wouldn't have been seen dead in one, would say he wasn't no bleedin' pansy toff. She could almost hear him saying it. And yet even in his cheap pinstripe suit and his trilby he was so handsome. In expensive evening clothes (and with a nicer way of talking) he'd be a knock-out. She'd be so proud. But he would have laughed like a drain at the notion that he should try to better himself, and she wouldn't dream of stooping to mention such a thing because it would have been insulting to him.

'So wot's the trouble at 'ome?' he asked as they made for the bus to take her to Fenchurch Street to catch her train home. He would leave her there; she always insisted she was safe enough on a train, not only because he'd have to go all that way back home, but to let him accompany her would be a declaration of something she wasn't yet prepared to declare, that he was her steady and that she was putting behind her all her dreams of something better than Arthur could give. It wasn't something she was happy to acknowledge for it made her out in her own eyes to be a gold digger, playing a decent man along just for her own aims, probably to ditch him were that dream ever realised. She hated herself, but there it stayed in the back of her brain like a little black imp.

But she would tell him about the trouble at home, even though the mere effort made her voice tremble dangerously and her nose tingle with the tears she fought to hold back.

'My sister Pam's got herself into trouble,' she began, startled when he chuckled.

'Oh, that's all.'

'No, Arthur,' she corrected hastily, angrily, wishing she hadn't embarked on this. But she wasn't going to have him sneer at something he didn't as yet understand. 'That's not all. She did it deliberately.'

Arthur's dark eyes were turned to her with interest, and she went on to explain all that had happened. She saw his expression grow awed and sympathetic as his arm tightened against hers.

'Cor, that's a bleedin' 'orrible shame fer your mum an' dad,' he said when she finally finished, the bus pulling up outside Fenchurch Street. 'What the bloody 'ell's your sister goin' ter do?'

'I don't know.' She was no longer thinking of Pam, but the thought of going home to a house full of downcast faces made her heart sink. As they got off the bus, she turned to him, suddenly smitten by a small bolt of rebellion.

'I don't want to go home yet, Arthur. I've had enough of it, all the squabbling and nastiness. Mum's long face and Dad you can hardly say a word to without him getting all uppity. My brother Dan's out every night and isn't bringing his young lady home any more. My sister Connie sits all quiet on her own upstairs writing letters to her fiancé. Pam's gone, taking all her clothes with her, and we've not heard a thing from her since to say if she's all right or not. Connie keeps in touch – knows where Pam is but hasn't said where. Not that Mum and Dad ask. But she says Pam's all right and her boyfriend has got her a room which he's paying for. She says they're getting married by some special licence in a registry office next week. But it's so miserable at home with all that hanging over our heads. I just don't want to go home yet. It's only just gone seven. Another couple of hours won't make any odds.'

Arthur looked worried. 'How yer goin' ter let yer parents know?'

'I don't care. I'll just be late that's all. Let them stew.'

'Yer making an 'eap of trouble fer yerself,' he said. 'It ain't right, wot wiv them already worried.' Then he laughed. 'Don't want ter see anuvver one of yer slung out of the 'ouse.'

Josie didn't laugh. 'Look, it's still early. Let's go to the West End for a couple of hours, wander around Piccadilly Circus and watch the crowds.'

He looked at her. 'Well, if yer fink that's orright. I can get yer straight back ter Fenchurch Street an' yer can catch the ten-fifteen. It'll be dark by then but your 'ome's only a couple of minutes from the station.'

'Then let's do it!' She grasped his arm with renewed joy.

* * *

Piccadilly Circus in the fading evening light held a magic brilliance, though not yet in full flood with the April sky still streaked translucent green and vivid crimson. Once that faded and the sky grew pitch black, Piccadilly's lively electric signs would blaze out in their full exhilarating glory.

'This is lovely,' Josie gasped as she always did when they came here. The air smelled of taxi fumes and eating places and of those warm wafts of perfumed dust from foyer carpets as theatre doors opened and closed. The brightly lit theatres confused her eyes. 'I'd really love to see a show.'

Arthur looked dubious. 'It's three hours and you'd never get home at anything near a respectable time.'

Above her the shimmering electric sign announced 'Private Lives' with Noel Coward and Gertrude Lawrence. 'Oh, Arthur!' Josie grabbed his arm, bringing his attention to it. 'I'd just love to see that.'

Arthur pulled a face. Slapstick comedy was more his taste than clever plays. 'If we went, it'd 'ave ter be up in the gods. I ain't got enough money fer anyfink posher. An' anyway, it's too late finishin'. An' look at the queue. The doorman's 'and'd come down long before it's our turn ter go in.'

Seeing her crestfallen look, he squeezed her arm. ' 'Ow abart next week? We could do a matinée next Saturday an' 'ave a bite t'eat after.'

Josie knew his bites to eat – a portion of fish and chips wrapped in newspaper and a cup of tea in a café to wash it down. But that faded into paleness against a chance to see a good witty play. 'Could we?'

'Means linin' up and takin' a chance. But if we get there early.'

'Oh, yes, please,' she burst out, loving him with all her worth.

It did occur to her to suggest meeting tomorrow, Sunday, maybe in Southend, but if he spent too much money coming to see her in dreary old Southend, dreary compared to London, he mightn't have enough to take her to a proper London theatre next Saturday. On what she earned as a part-time waitress at the Cliffs Hotel, it wasn't easy forking out the fare to London if she suggested meeting him there.

Not only that, if it rained tomorrow, and Dad had said it looked very much like it would, Arthur would have to spend more hard-earned money on some indoor activity which always cost.

Best really to bide her time until next Saturday. Then, wearing the dress she intended to make for the occasion, spending out on a couple of yards of crepe-de-chine – green she thought, to show off her fair hair – she'd look as stunning as any of the rich people in the dress circle or the theatre boxes.

That week she cut it out, carefully, on the dining table, using a *Vogue* pattern she'd found in the material shop in Leigh. The very latest fashion, the dress called for far more material than would have been needed only a year ago, when the rage had still been for those silly shapeless Charleston frocks. This was figure-hugging, and her figure was just made to be hugged by a slinky dress; the back cut as low as she dared, an evening dress with narrow straps and two tiny sequinned clasps which she also intended to buy – yet another expense. She was glad she hadn't tried to afford more train fare on the Sunday.

On Mum's old treadle sewing machine she ran the garment up and hung it in the wardrobe she shared with her sisters. Or sister now. Both had plenty of room with only the two of them sharing the one room.

It was odd lying alone in a bed once shared by another. The bed felt vast, less cosy, and all those sounds that had once gone unnoticed, the soft breathing of the other girls, the odd mumble and rustle as Pam or Annie in the other bed turned restlessly, now remembered and missed. She lay in her lonely bed, Connie in hers, listening to all the sounds outside: a train rattling by not far away, the light wind that had got up in the night, the distant slap of rigging against the mainmasts of moored sailing boats. A lonely, deserted sound.

The whole house, once full of the bustle of a large noisy family, now had the same deserted air with Annie and Pam gone. The only advantage it had brought was that she and Connie had become closer than ever before when the other two girls had been here. As she lay in her bed, Connie in hers, there was more opportunity to talk, exchange confidences, their voices murmering into darkness, stygian in this bedroom. No street light burned in the back alley and the sea was black as pitch.

Tonight, unable to sleep for the thoughts tomorrow's trip to a London West End theatre were generating in her head, Josie's mind was mostly on Arthur. Where were the pair of them going? Did she really love him or was she still using him for her

101

own ends? One thing she did know: when such questions arose, guilt followed, and self-derision; who did she think she was that some wealthy, handsome young man-about-town would look her way with any more than that one brief appreciative glance? Yes, she was still aware she could draw such looks, but one glance didn't make a love affair; didn't promise inclusion into that social whirl she so coveted. It remained just a lovely dream. The trouble was, the dream was getting in the way of reality, her feelings for Arthur that were beginning to persist above all else, try as she might to stifle them. They'd have grown even stronger by now if it wasn't for the way he spoke and his amusing (to everyone) but embarrassing (to her) moments of exhibitionist clowning whenever they were in company. He'd do something crazy, she knew he would, as they entered the foyer of the theatre for tomorrow's matinée, do a silly little jig waving the tickets in her face in triumph at having got them, or something equally stupid to make her cringe before the well-dressed people going up the wide, thickly carpeted staircase to their Grand Circle and Royal Boxes. It did occur to her that few such people would attend a matinée, but some might, and what a fool she'd feel with Arthur making an idiot of himself.

Kept awake by all the guilty thoughts, Josie wondered if Connie had yet fallen asleep. After all, it was said that sharing a problem was halving it. Josie stirred restlessly. 'Connie? You asleep?'

Connie's mind snapped back from wrapping itself around Ben and the wedding in five weeks' time. Tomorrow morning, five weeks from now, she'd be getting up, hopefully to a sun-filled morning and the house full of bustle and excitement. It seemed hardly possible. Months and months of waiting, preparation, planning, and now it was almost here. Looking back, the time had gone so quickly and was still rushing by, flying towards the day. Four Saturdays to go; with so much still to do, would it all get done in time for her to walk down that aisle in her beautiful dress of clinging white satin, her lovely short veil and her huge bouquet of pink roses and white mock orange?

At Josie's whispered query, Connie stirred and made an appropriate grunt to signify she was still awake. She didn't want her thoughts interrupted but it seemed unkind to pretend to be

102

asleep, judging by the diffident tone Josie had used. Something was worrying her.

Connie turned fully to face the other bed, only dimly seen even though her eyes had by now become accustomed to the darkness. She could see nothing of Josie until the girl propped herself up on her elbow, and then only to become an indistinct shadow.

'What is it, Jo?'

'Just that I'm worried. I've been worried for months.'

The worst came to Connie's mind, a thought she tried to brush away. Yet she still felt it must be probed. 'Jo, you're not . . .'

'Oh, Con, no! If that's what you're thinking.' The tone had come sharply but now moderated again. 'Connie, it's about that Arthur Monk I've been going out with in London.'

'What about him?' She wanted to get back to thinking about her wedding. There was so much still to be done. She would see Ben tomorrow, travel up to London and stay overnight at his parents on the sofa in the living room. Ben and his three brothers shared one of the two bedrooms of the tiny flat in Bethnal Green.

She and Ben would spend the day looking around for cheap furniture to fill the flat they had put down their first rent on two weeks ago, a two-bedroomed one in Wilmot Street, just off Bethnal Green Road, very near to the shops, and one street away from his parents and in the same Waterlow Buildings, but a top flat on the fifth floor. Lots of stone stairs to climb, especially when a family came along. By then they might have to move to a lower, more accommodating flat when one came up, so a pram wouldn't have to be pulled up so many stairs. But for the moment this had some lovely views across London on a clear day, if smoke from countless chimneys didn't obscure it all. She would gaze out of the bedroom window across London's roof tops whenever they went to inspect their new haven, see the distant tower of Big Ben and the huge dome of St Paul's dominating everything. From the front could be seen Victoria Park, with its trees making it look like a little bit of the countryside. No sight of the river though, that side of the letting, as flats were called, adjoining the wall of the one next door.

Connie wondered vaguely if she would miss the wide horizons Leigh presented, and the refreshing breath of its salt-laden air. Would she ever get used to living in London and the smell of chimney smoke in her nostrils? She guessed she would. In time everyone gets used to an enforced new environment, and being in love went a long way towards helping.

On Sunday Ben promised to take her on a tug early in the morning. This was not normally allowed but he'd wangled it; they would go just a short way along the river and back. She was looking forward to sharing a little of what he did day after day, to smelling the warm whiff of oil and sooty reek of smoke. She would stand there with Ben, who would have one arm on the steering wheel and one around her, the breeze in her face. Then they would come back here and pop up to the church to see the vicar about calling the banns. Then after that, weather permitting, they'd go on to Southend, on to the beach.

Putting all aside she concentrated on Josie's worries. Josie asked if she thought her selfish to be questioning her feelings towards Arthur Monk and her yearning for just a little of that life she was describing.

'If you want my honest opinion,' she told Josie, a little cautiously so as not to upset her, 'I think you're just reaching for the unreachable. If you did come anywhere near it, you'd be a fish out of water.' She cringed at both clichés, was in danger of adding more and had to steel herself in the darkness to find words that sounded halfway philosophical and wise. It was a battle she was swiftly losing. 'You see, Jo, it's like asking oil and water to mix. What I mean to say is I know we don't exactly live in poverty, we're not poor by some people's standards, but we are, or would seem to be to those sort of people you admire. We both have different standards, and I'm sorry to say it Josie, but their standards . . . or more their morals aren't like ours. They stay up till all hours, they live a free and easy life, get up to all sorts of things that would horrify people like us. I mean, look at film stars. There's always scandals about divorces and remarrying and things. And some of the dresses those sort wear, well, nothing's left to the imagination, is it? You wouldn't fit in. Ever. You'd be made to feel a laughing stock. What society people are is born in them. They'd spot you coming. Honestly, Josie, I'd say forget all that. Concentrate on your nice young man. By what you've told me he sounds as if he'd make you a really good husband one day, But you're too young yet of course to think of getting married. You must be certain of your own mind and that the man you have is the one you really love. Why don't you bring him home to meet Mum

104

and Dad? Perhaps that way you get your mind made up to what you really want, or what's the best and sensible way for you. I don't think you ought to go getting all excited about what's only wishful thinking after all.'

She was coming to realise that she must sound like a Dutch aunt giving out all this good advice, so she shut up abruptly, merely to finish on, 'Well, think about it, Josie,' and hurriedly turned over with a whispered 'Goodnight, and hope I've not hurt your feelings.'

In the darkness she heard Josie murmur, 'No,' and then 'Goodnight.'

It was easy for Connie to say. She was settled, with her wedding all planned, with no ambition but to be married and bring up a family, no doubt rejoicing that she could give up working as girls usually did when they got married. Being a housewife and in time a mother was work enough.

All Connie had said, she had said with a sincere heart. There was no more sincere heart than Connie's. But she was wrong in this instance. It wasn't so easy to forget a dream you've had for so long it has become a part of you. But there was something else too, something that wouldn't affect Connie but would her. Annie and Pam had gone, Danny spent most of his free time with his girl, and was seldom at home. Five weeks from now when Connie would be married and living in London, there would only be herself, rattling around in this room that once held the four of them. It felt alarming. She was quickly beginning to hate this house, this fast-emptying house she had once loved so much. She could hardly wait for tomorrow and to be out of it for a few hours, lording it up London in her new dress. She wished she need never have to return, apart from missing Mum and Dad, and Danny of course when he was there.

As it was with Josie, so it was with Danny, and even their father. It was as if the house had lost its soul. Danny made all sorts of excuses not to take Lily home; he spent much of his time at her house with her parents. She was an only child and made much of by them. It made him feel wanted seeing the way they behaved about her, and him too: 'She's a very good girl,' they'd say as though putting her up for the marriage market. Yes, she was a good girl, and very lovely, delicate and lovely, so that he was sometimes scared to hug her too strongly in case he broke something. Yes, it would be nice to marry her, but he wanted to bide his time for a while yet. Meanwhile he was having to make all sorts of excuses why he wasn't taking her to his home any more, evading questions like, 'Are you going off me, darling? I sort of feel you are.' He swore he wasn't and said the only reason for not taking her home was all the preparations for the coming wedding. It seemed to suffice for the time being. Later, things at home might revert to normal, but it felt it was going to be a long time before that happened.

No one felt the atmosphere more than Daniel himself. Peggy went around all silent. She sided with him on the business of – no question of putting a name to it, but it didn't stop the hurt Peggy must be feeling caused by her own daughter.

It was a relief to be out of the house sometimes. Out on the boat with his brothers about him, and his son and an extra lad to stay in the bawley while the four of them raked the mud for its harvest, Daniel could forget his life and all that had happened in such a swift time. Yes, he could stare at the horizon and forget all about home troubles. It was calming, seeing the low hills of Kent and the deep break where the River Medway pierced them, the North Foreland of Thanet, a headland reappearing as a misty promontory between water and sky, then the bare line of the North Sea meeting a cloud-streaked sky; on this side of the estuary the blunt protuberance of Foulness before land was lost from sight running up towards the seaside towns of Essex and Suffolk. He could stare at it all and pretend to himself that after a double out here on the mud flats, the wicker baskets full to the brim with cockles, as heavy as a man could carry, the holiday trade already stepping up, that he'd return to a home that was busy and happy. It was only as he came into the Ray to chug quietly up Leigh Creek that the reality of home life would hit him again and he'd be sullen and silent, incapable of saying a sociable word to anyone.

For now he felt good, the sting of a stiff clean breeze on his face, its salt taste on his lips full of the tang of seaweed and the cockles they had already gathered. The tide had turned, was rolling back in; this would be their last haul before turning for home if done quickly. Just enough time remained to fill the final two baskets before the water reached them and got too deep for them to rake. They mustn't be greedy, and with the mud covered, the trail, the seed of the cockle, would be washed away. It must be left here to grow into young.

The four skilled men worked as a team, each raking at the mud towards a central point, then starting again a little further to the left until a whole circular area was raked. The smaller shellfish got thrown back to grow on, conserving the stocks.

'Right!' Daniel bellowed, as three of them went down the narrow-runged ladder. As he was about to step on to it after them, Daniel glanced up. 'Bloody hell!'

'What is it, Dad?' To his ears came the faint puff-puff of a small engine.

Ignoring his son, Daniel scrambled back, grabbed for the binoculars hanging against the bulwark and trained them on a boat passing a short way beyond in deeper water with its brown sails unfurled. Even before he clapped the binoculars to his eyes he had already identified it. Intuitively he knew whose it was. Shrimpers, their craft anchored out in the Ray, each with sails furled looking identical to other folk, could row out unerringly to their own boat in the darkness of early morning without hesitation. Many in a close-knit fishing community could identify the boats of others. Daniel identified this one immediately.

'Tauntin' us!' he roared. 'Damned swine's tauntin' us. That stinkin', Godforsaken shrimp-catcher's got the bloody audacity ter come out within range of us out 'ere.'

'Who is it?' Danny asked, but he already knew by yet another string of rich epithets.

'You know who I'm talking on. Takin' the bloody piss out of us. I bet he's set his bloody snivellin' son up in a place with that . . . with *her*.'

Unable to utter his daughter's name, even now, Daniel threw down the binoculars and clambered blindly over the side of the tilted vessel, with a vague notion to race dementedly through the incoming water, swimming the rest of the way to the shrimper to do physical battle. Even as the men on the mud watched, rather than let himself down by the free swinging ladder, a slow way to alight, he leaped the full six feet from the boat, landed on an unexpectedly firm area of sand amid the mud and went over in an awkward heap, letting out a cry of rage and pain.

'Aah! Me ankle! I've done it in. Sod that damned Bryant.'

107

Sitting in the mud, splattered all over, clutching his left ankle, he was rocking in pain.

Danny and the others were at his side immediately, helping him up, and back on board. It was a long job. By the time Daniel Bowmaker was over the side with a good deal more swearing and cursing than might be necessary, more out of fury than pain, sitting on the deck nursing his throbbing ankle, the rakes and the two still-unfilled baskets hauled up too, the shrimping boat had gone and the incoming tide washing an inch or so deep around the *Steadfast's* hull.

'That bugger can't leave me in peace,' swore Daniel, and glared at the horizon, now empty of shrimping boats though busy with other shipping. The shrimpers had departed for cleaner waters; a long haul now for many years with the oil-polluted Thames driving the shrimps further round the coast. That point seemed to have escaped Daniel, blaming this injury solely on his bitter enemy whose boat he had just seen.

'But for him, the sod, I wouldn't've ricked my bloody ankle,' he raged as they waited for the *Steadfast* to come afloat. 'All these years and he's still driving me to drink cold tea! And two on my baskets empty still because on him. An' my own daughter sides in with 'em. I'll see her dead afore I ever see her set foot in my house again, treacherous little bitch.'

Danny let his father rail on. The man was in pain; saw himself abused and insulted by the mere sight of his adversary's boat passing so close by, awakening old scores. It eased him to strike out at anything and anyone, Pam leaving as she had without a backward glance, or one word of apology or regret. Danny couldn't say who was to blame, Pam or Dad. His father nursed an old hate that for him would never heal, and Pam hadn't been born at the time of the trouble. All Danny knew was that his father would make life hell for everyone at home with his hurt ankle and his hurt pride, would be impossible to live with for the next week or so.

As his dad said after they had got him home and bound his now-swollen ankle which Dr Freeman said was a torn ligament, bad as any break to heal, after they had got Dad to bed where he wouldn't stomp about and make it worse as he was sure to do, he just hoped he'd be fit for Connie and Ben's wedding in four Saturdays' time.

Chapter Eleven

After Connie left, Pam stood gazing about the living room-cum-kitchen, one of two rooms she and George had found themselves at the top of a house in New Road. Lovely Georgian houses they were, but that was where the similarity to good living ended. The top two rooms of this house were no more than attic rooms, furnished and let out to those who could afford nothing else. Still, they were home for now. Perhaps, Pam hoped, they might be able to afford something better one day.

These two rooms had only come to them out of the good graces of his parents, because she and George possessed hardly a bean between them. Mr Bryant, whom she had seen only from a distance for much of her life, when she had come face to face with him proved to be a mild sort of man, grey, thin, and of medium height like his son, with a moustache that had grown bristly and strong with the years: the only strong-looking thing about him, she'd mused. How he and her father had ever got into a fight beggared the imagination, he looked too frail. But then, perhaps all those years ago he hadn't been so. While not too approving of what the pair of them had done, he had at least stood by his son to some extent, more than her father had done by her, enough to pay for the small, plain, registry office wedding with no frills, no reception, and with just him and his wife there. No one of her own had been present except Connie and Ben who'd attended without telling anyone else.

One hand caressing her growing stomach, Pam thought about her sister's visit, paid before she went up to London to see Ben, having been allowed that Saturday morning off from work for the occasion. Connie had come once a week since Pam had left home, saying it was no one's business but hers what she did and always asking was there anything she needed. And she always brought a little something with her, a loaf of bread, a tin of corned beef or fruit, half a pound of butter – something well beyond Pam's reach – best butter from Wainwright's Dairies with its distinctive daisy imprint from the butter bats that shaped it into a brick. Pam accepted her sister's gifts with humble grace and her visits with tearful longing for things to have turned out so much better than they had.

Over a cup of tea, Connie had talked of the coming wedding – her and Ben's coming wedding. Not intending to provoke envy and regret, Connie could not help but talk of the dress she had chosen, the two-tiered cake Mum was making, the car they had booked to take them up to the church, her amusement at everyone else having to negotiate the steep climb up to it on foot. 'I just hope it doesn't decide to rain,' she said and had then turned serious. 'Pam. I've decided, whether anyone likes it or not, you're invited to the wedding service. You *and* George.'

Pan had vigorously shaken her head, aghast at visions of the look on the faces of her parents seeing her and George sitting there in the church as they came in, or turning to see the pair of them enter. She couldn't begin to imagine what they'd do, but she did know that the atmosphere would be such that she would run straight out again.

'No, Connie. Nice of you to invite us, but it'd spoil your whole day.'

'Don't be silly. I know it would be difficult asking you both to the reception afterwards, with everyone so on top of everyone else . . .'

'No,' she'd cut in. 'But I'm glad you asked me. It makes me feel a bit better, as though I've got an ally.'

Connie had put down her finished tea and took both Pam's hands in hers. 'You'll always have allies in me and Ben. And when we're married we'll come down here as often as possible to see you and George. Dad was wrong in what he did. But you know him, he won't change. But soon you and George will have your own family and move on. We all move on. But look, it's my wedding, Pam. I can ask who I like to it. Neither of you have done anything wrong except to love each other and you getting pregnant in the hope that it'd mend something.'

Still she'd shaken her head, obdurate. 'That's not how it works. You'll spoil your own wedding day having me there, and you won't forget it for the rest of your days. But I will be thinking of you. And thanks, Connie.'

Connie had finally left with a parting shot. 'We'll come straight across from the wedding as soon as we can, to see you, and I'll still be wearing my wedding dress so you can see me in it. And I'll send you a piece of cake too.'

She had nodded her thanks as she saw Connie out, thinking to herself that the cake would choke her if she took one morsel of it, made by Mum's hand. Mum's hand had turned her out as much as had her father's. She'd stood by and watched her leave, without so much as a farewell smile on her face. No, the cake would choke her.

Leaving during the morning to go up to London, Josie had no idea of the small drama that had unfolded in the late afternoon with Dad injuring himself and ending up ordered to bed to rest a torn ligament. So the anxiety that dogged her not to be too late getting home that evening and incurring his wrath was to some extent needless. When Arthur spoke about having a meal afterwards she could see it going on until it would be a rush for her train, a train that on Saturday nights seemed to take ages with people going home after a night out alighting in droves at every station along the route.

'We'll make it sharp,' he promised about the meal as the doorman for the balcony and the gallery, the gods, the cheapest seats, let them in with crowds still lining up behind them. Some had no hope of getting in, the Noël Coward play was so popular.

The foyer as they entered was bright and exciting, full of people and noise. Josie stood waiting to one side while Arthur joined the long queue for the tickets. She felt at ease, good in her silky green dress, a piece of the material of which she had sewn double to make a stole for her shoulders.

A group of young people, obviously with money, had alighted from a couple of taxis and were crowding in, in couples but with two men apparently unattached for they came in together. The men, top-hatted, each in evening dress, each carrying a slim, silver-topped cane, looked out of place without a girl on their arm. And one was quite drunk, Josie was sure. She was aware of staring

111

when one of them, the one who wasn't drunk, caught her eye and winked broadly at her.

Josie was on the point of lowering her eyes quickly, caught staring, but somehow she didn't. Wide-eyed, she stared back. The young man smiled. Josie smiled too, shyly. Before she could take a breath he was at her side, his slim cane held in both white-gloved hands.

'I say, not on your own, are you?'

'No . . .' she managed, coughed awkwardly, started again. 'I'm . . . I'm waiting for my friend.'

'Girl or chap?'

'Chap.'

'Ah. Well now, not engaged to him, or anything like that?'

'No, not really. But we have been going out together for a while.'

'Pity, that.'

From the small group came a woman's impatient call. 'Nigel, dear, we'll miss the beginning. Don't want to cause a disruption finding our seats as the curtain rises.'

He looked round, waved at her, then looked back at Josie. 'Well then, might see something of you in the interval.'

He wouldn't of course. Those of the orchestra stalls or the dress circle congregated in a different, more fancy bar from those up in the gods. Arthur joined her and together they climbed the thousand and one stairs to the very roof of the theatre, then negotiated the steep and dizzy descent down the steps to their seats.

The orchestra ceased tuning up, got itself together. The curtain rose. The magic began. The players looked such a long way off from where she sat; mere dots, faces not easily recognisable, but the voices carried clean across to the furthest listener – Noel Coward's studied vowels captivating all, Gertrude Lawrence's clear diction perfect, Laurence Olivier's measured, almost whispered drawl, even so reached her quite magically. Josie sat riveted to her seat, hardly noticed Arthur's fidgeting. He was bored but suffered his boredom manfully.

Enthralled, during the marvellous scene with Gertrude Lawrence and Laurence Olivier, she in full-length mink coat over a flame-coloured silk pyjama suit falling off the sofa on to the stage while fighting with him, Josie felt hot with envy. Even on stage, mock-fighting with Olivier, G.L. was the epitome of all

112

Josie imagined the world of wealthy socialites to be. That scene almost ruined the rest of the play for her; she felt hardly able to watch it for wishing she was Gertrude Lawrence or someone like her. What did she do or where did she go after leaving by the stage door and getting elegantly into her chauffeured motor car? It had to be a chauffeured car. Did she go on to a wild party with other actors, a dinner party maybe? And when she finally returned home to some luxury apartment, did she lounge on an equally luxurious sofa full of soft cushions in silken pyjamas similar to the flame-coloured ones?

All through the play, Josie could visualise her amid the costly comfort of drapes and elegant furnishings, wafting perfume while a maid poured a glass of sparkling champagne for her to sip; the maid going to turn down the bed, folding back silk sheets, plumping up billowing pillows, dozens of them, Gertrude waving a pale nonchalant hand at her, saying 'That'll be all, Rawlings.' Or maybe there was a man with her . . . Josie shivered deliciously and thought oh, how she wanted so much to be like G.L. and savour all that wonderful opulence, take it for granted as she too sipped champagne . . .

The audience had broken out into rapturous applause. Josie clapped too, energetically. She remembered it all, yet she hadn't concentrated as she might. In the interval Arthur had got her an ice cream, lining up for ages for it. She had licked it all through the first part of the second half, hardly tasting the stuff. Now it was all over. Arthur picked up his jacket, left her to put on her own stole, and together they made their way out of their seats up the steep seating steps and down the endless stone stairs amid crowds of others and back into the glittering foyer.

A voice hailed her. 'I say, there!' Turning, she saw the young man called Nigel pushing his way through the exiting throng towards her.

'I say. Didn't catch a glimpse of you in the bar. I didn't expect to see you again.'

'No, we didn't . . .'

'And I don't even know your name.'

'Josie.'

'Charmed.' He was looking now at Arthur, and Arthur was looking at him, and their expressions were as unlike as chalk and cheese, Nigel's full of enquiry, Arthur's bordering on baleful.

113

Nigel leapt to the rescue instantly. 'Are you the one Josie, as she says is her name, is going steady with?'

'Steady?' Arthur repeated, somewhat stupidly.

'I take it you are. Well now, look here, my name's Nigel Hobbs.'

'Arfer Monk,' Arthur said.

Nigel blinked no eyelid at the mispronunciation. 'Look here, we're going on to a party. Still light out there you know, but Virginia's parties get going early. Lots of fun. They go on till all hours. She's having it in her flat in Park Lane. Owns it, you know, so can do what she likes really. So we're going on there. No point stopping for a bite to eat, she's got masses of food usually. Bit of a Bohemian, but rather nice. Come along.'

'Well, we . . .'

Nigel's crowd were leaving, some already getting into taxis. Nigel was moving inexorably further away, backwards, needing to follow them. Josie made a decision as she saw a golden chance slipping away because of Arthur's hesitancy, and leapt in, interrupting him.

'We'd love to come.'

'Then right.' Nigel had taken her by the arm, had wrapped it about his own, was pushing through the crowd taking her with him, as Arthur followed on behind, scared of losing them both.

The next instant she and Arthur, Nigel and his now somewhat more sober friend, were in a taxi, speeding away into the still sunny evening against which the electric signs of Piccadilly glowed pale and unreal.

Josie found herself glancing with more frequency at the golden clock over an ornate mantelpiece, its hands creeping nearer ten o'clock. She didn't want to leave. The centre of attention for most of the time she'd been here, at first she had wondered why she had come. The luxury flat was bereft of anyone who looked like a guest other then those she and Arthur were with. Piles of food were being brought in by outside caterers while the fabled Virginia, whoever she was, a bandeau around her black wavy tresses and her dress hardly able to keep on her thin breasts as she hurried energetically from room to room ordering about the caterers and the waiters whom she had obviously hired for this occasion, whatever it was, ignored Josie completely. Though she had ignored Nigel and his friends too, apart from a casual wave of a hand to indicate they please themselves what they did until more people arrived.

As they did, Nigel introduced Josie, forgetting poor Arthur who took himself off to a chair between a window and a corner and managed to stay there for the rest of the evening, sipping sparingly of a mere glass or two of wine.

With the rich young people gathering around her at Nigel's instigation, Josie found herself being asked about her home in Leigh, which she had let slip, what she did for a living, how big was her home and 'how many people fitted into it?' their tone one of utter disbelief.

'Fascinating!' someone said, and looking at her dress, asked, 'And where did you buy such a singular creation, dear?'

Her heart swelling with pride that her dress should receive attention as though it were a Chanel creation, she told them honestly she'd made it.

'My, you must be so clever!' gushed one girl whose dress was most obviously Chanel and whose delicately bleached hair had cost her a fortune to have done.

Another of the cluster around Josie had also remarked on the dress, saying, 'I must get you to run up a dress for me. I could put heaps of work your way. You could make a fortune!'

Josie preened, putting on an accent she hoped passed for cultured. 'I like to think I have something of a gift for it.'

'You most certainly have, darling.'

From time to time she overheard other comments, the voice carrying, and if she hadn't felt she knew otherwise, meant for her to hear: 'Makes her own dresses, can you believe?' 'Is that a fact?' 'I couldn't put two stitches together – just get mine from Paris and have done with it.' 'She *is* unique, though, don't you think? I wonder where he found her?'

One comment: 'Nigel's a one for picking up odd sorts,' fortunately she didn't hear.

To her, Nigel was attentive the whole evening, guiding her from one cluster of people to another, introducing her as 'my little Josie', his slim, cool fingers entwined in hers. She felt Queen of the May, celebrity of the year. It was a most wonderful feeling, her first-ever venture into the world she had always only dreamed about, and everyone was so kind, so attentive and so amused by everything she said.

But now it was fast approaching ten o'clock. Even Cinderella hadn't needed to leave until the stroke of midnight. But Cinderella hadn't had a train to catch all the way back to Leigh and a father to go off at her for being out so late and him worried sick where she might have got to. She wouldn't lose her lovely dress as midnight struck, but she might as well have done, going back to that dismal world, that tiny dull house after all this grand glittering opulence. Gertrude Lawrence was after all only a dream. But at least Josie knew she must be thankful to have sampled a tiny fraction of that dream. Trouble was, she wanted more.

The hands of the clock on the ornate mantelshelf had moved on ten more minutes. Arthur still sat in his corner. He was looking at her. As she looked back at him, he jerked his chin at the time. Josie nodded. She would have to go. She felt suddenly guilty ignoring him the whole evening, but she had been having such a lovely time, the centre of attention as she joined in conversations and nibbled at food she had never tasted before in all her life and making everyone laugh uproariously as she pulled a face at this or that delicacy. Caviar had nearly brought the house down, and aspic too, people hurrying to get her some other titbit from the laden buffet table to see her reaction. She had played on it, revelled in it. But now it was over. Arthur was getting up, coming over.

'It's time yer went, Josie. You're goin' ter miss yer train.'

Nigel swung round from chatting to someone, his fine-boned, darkly handsome face creased with startled disappointment. 'You're not going, already?'

Josie forced a smile. 'I have to. I've a long way to go to get home.'

'But I can take you in the old Rover. All the way home. It'll take us only a quarter of the time a train would take.'

The temptation was overpowering. To ride home in a car, a Rover, even if it was old. For a moment she hesitated. She turned to Arthur, then back to Nigel. 'Could you drop Arthur home on the way?'

'No bother at all.' He smiled towards Arthur, but Arthur had a scowl on his narrow face.

'No fanks. I can git a bus.'

116

Josie felt embarrassment for him flood all over her. He couldn't even bother to correct his speech, just for that short sentence. It occurred to her for the first time that he didn't even notice how he spoke. Humility ignited a flame of anger within her.

'Well, I've decided to stay. You can go if you want, Arthur. Nigel will take me home.'

'I certainly will.'

She watched as Arthur turned without a word and shouldered his way through the clusters of guests with their drinks in their hands towards the door. Instantly guilt consumed her. She couldn't let him go like that. He'd treated her to a theatre, sat bored all through 'Private Lives', not his cup of tea at all, yet hadn't uttered a word of complaint, and here was she selfishly pushing him aside.

'Just a minute,' she said to Nigel. She pushed past everyone, hearing an amused comment: 'Where's she going?' but, no longer interested in being the centre of attraction, she ran out of the door after Arthur. She was just in time to see the private lift door closing, enough to catch a glimpse of his face, its expression. It was tight, sort of anguished. Then the two edges of the lift door met and she heard the light whine of it descending.

For an instant she wanted to run down the stairs and catch him at the bottom, but with two flights of stairs, he'd be already gone. But she needed to at least try. Standing there uncertain, she heard a voice calling from the door of the flat. 'Oh, there you are! Everyone's wondering where you went to, darling.'

The decision made for her, Josie turned and, still full of remorse, followed the speaker back into the hot, overcrowded, over-perfumed apartment.

The next hour did its best, but Arthur refused to be forgotten if purely in a conflict of arguments within herself. After all they weren't engaged or anything. She could please herself. Had they been engaged it would be a different matter. He had paid for their theatre tickets but she had offered to pay her share and he'd refused to take it, so she didn't owe him anything. But none of it made any difference, all she could see was him walking home, alone, head down, hands thrust into his pockets and there was a heaviness in her breast even as she laughed and chatted.

Arthur began to be replaced by another anxiety, small prickles of panic started to arise as the clock showed five to eleven. She'd been out all day. Time enough to have been home by now. She told Nigel so, carefully. What if he wouldn't now take her home?

'What?' Nigel burst out. 'It's an unearthly hour to leave any party.'

'Well, when does it finish?'

'God knows. Could go on all night. Virginia does tend to throw some long parties, could go on forever. Sunday tomorrow, you see. Usually stay the whole night, fall down in some corner, and tomorrow pop off to someone's country place to round everything off, tennis party or something. If it don't rain. Then we lounge about. Billiards, cards, or generally mess around. It just rounds off the weekend, sort of.'

He was so nonchalant, easy with himself. Did money make people like that? No care in the world, not even for anyone else. Had he forgotten that, unlike the sort of people at this party, she must be home at a certain time? Surely not all rich people had such easy views about time and having fun. There had to be some more staid rich people about. What sort of crowd had she got herself in with? A trip up to the bathroom, fabulously furnished with black tiles and pink suite, confirmed the sort of crowd. As she opened the door, two bodies lay entwined full length on the floor before her, the girl with her breasts exposed, her legs in the air, the man with his trousers and pants around his ankles, his naked buttocks heaving up and down. 'Oops!' the girl cried and let out a giggle as Josie hastily closed the door, feeling hot all over.

Downstairs, she pleaded with Nigel. His reply was, 'An hour or two late shouldn't matter.'

'I must go. Please.' Perhaps if she left on her own there might still be a train. But it would take an hour or more to get home.

'Listen, old thing, I said I'd take you home in the old Rover. We'll get you home in time if you're really worried what your old man will say.'

'Can we go now? Please.'

She watched him give a sigh, glance at his gold watch, then look around the chattering, laughing gathering, and give a second sigh. 'I'm getting bored with all this, anyway. By the time I get back from taking you home, it might have livened up. But you'll be missing a treat tomorrow, I can say. Well, come on then. Get your wrap, darling, and we'll be off.'

The *old* Rover turned out to be spanking new and shiny, just his joke. Open-topped, it took her breath away speeding a little too fast through the city and the suburbs and even more so through darkened towns, villages and country lanes. In no time at all they were leaving the Southend Road and were in Marine Parade where he glided to a stop at her command.

'I can walk from here.' She felt suddenly ashamed of the tiny narrow High Street of Leigh and its all-pervasive reek of decaying fish coming from the banks of empty cockle shells by the sheds, its line of tiny terraced houses.

Whether he divined her thoughts or not, she wasn't certain, but he said, 'Are you sure?'

'Yes, this is fine.'

He leaned over. 'Then this is fine with me.'

His arms came around her, his face closed on hers and he kissed her mouth, a long slow kiss, his mouth a little open. For a moment she wasn't sure what it was in her mouth, warm and wet and slippery. Then she realised with a shock that it was his tongue, forcing through her lips, exploring hers. At the same time as the shock hit her, she felt his hand on her breast, already pushing away the material of her dress and bra, making contact with her bare flesh.

She let out a squeak, stifled by his mouth on hers, put her hands on his shoulders to try to force him away. She was relieved to feel his grip lessen, his lips leave hers. But it was merely to say, 'Come, isn't this what you asked me to take you back for?'

'No.'

His reply was a low chuckle. 'No? I like it.'

'No!' she yelled again. Her hand came up and across, the slap on his cheek resounding in the quiet night.

For a moment, he sat back looking at her, his hand on his stung cheek. 'What the hell was that for?'

Josie was sobbing. 'Because I'm not that sort of girl, even if you thought I was.' Her hand flew to what she hoped was the outside handle of the open car. By some good luck she found the unfamiliar object, pushed it down and the door flew open. She followed, almost falling. Free, she slammed the door to. Bold now, recovered, she bellowed at him.

'I might come from people less well off, but I think our principles can knock yours into a cocked hat. Who did you think you were?'

It now dawned on her that all those wonderful comments about

119

her dress, her way of life, the offer to have her run up a dress just like it for someone, all that had been fun at her expense. To them she was an oddity, a curio, the lower classes seen at closer quarters, as people go to a zoo to see something they might never encounter in the wild.

He was looking at her. In the reflected light from his headlamps she could see his expression. It was one of wonder not derision, respect not contempt.

'Look, I like you a hell of a lot, Josie.'

'You've a rotten way of showing it, making me feel like a prostitute.'

'But I do like you. I'd love to see you again, Josie. I'm sorry for trying to do what I did. I just got it wrong, that's all. Look, how about tomorrow?'

'No thank you,' she said haughtily, and turning on her heel marched off with all the dignity she could muster, adjusting her dress straps as she went. She half feared he would follow, but he didn't. As she turned into Billet Road, with only a few more yards to go, she heard his car start up, a deep soft throb, the sound of the motor finally fading into the distance.

Only then did tears come into her eyes, the black water of the estuary through a gap in the houses misting up before her gaze. She'd been such a fool, on the verge of being offered a wonderful life with him. Her dream would have been fully realised and she could have been taken away forever from this dull little fishing village whose only excitement was holiday visitors in the summer.

But had she really been a fool? What if she'd let him do what he wanted? Would that have been any guarantee of a lovely future with him? She would have been made to feel cheap, and he would have gone off into the night satisfied. No, she hadn't been a fool.

She did, however, feel chastened, much wiser, and next morning cringed in remembrance of how near she had come to disaster on ground she knew nothing of. And she thought of Arthur too. She would write to him. But when it came down to it, she couldn't bring herself to. What words were there to say to him? Best not to write just now. Perhaps later.

One surprise was that there had been no scolding when Mum let her in to the house. Mum had stayed up waiting for her, and hadn't looked too pleased, but some of the stuffing had been knocked out of her since Pam had gone, and her scolding had lost much of its sting.

'Your Dad's in bed, lucky for you,' was all she said. Turning up the gas light in the living room where she had been sitting waiting, she told Josie to turn it off before going up to bed.

'I suppose you'll need to make yourself a cup of tea. The kettle's simmering on the kitchen range in case you do. Take it off before you go up or it'll simmer dry. Your Dad had a bit of an accident today on the boat, sprained his ankle. He'd not in a good mood and it's lucky for you he went to bed early because of the pain. See you in the morning.'

It was all said tersely, with no enquiry about how she had enjoyed herself and Josie, taking the kettle off the range and turning out the gas before following her mother up, was glad about that.

Chapter Twelve

After leaving Pam, Connie went straight on to the station, catching the ten forty train to Fenchurch Street to get a bus going on to Bethnal Green.

Sitting there in the rattling carriage, empty but for an elderly couple on the opposite seat, Connie gazed over their heads and studied the four pictures set in a long, dark wooden frame beneath the sagging net baggage rack and the bold capitals: London Tilbury and Southend Railway. They were of seaside resorts. One announced itself to be a view of Eastbourne.

Connie felt a tingle of anticipation thrill through her. She and Ben would be spending their honeymoon there, returning home to their new flat the following Saturday. Ben had saved hard for their honeymoon. With so much else to pay for, she was proud of his achievement. It would be so romantic.

She only realised she was smiling broadly to herself when her eye caught that of the elderly couple; they returned her smile somewhat self-consciously, no doubt wondering what she was grinning at. Hastily she allowed her smile to fall away without looking too rude, lowered her eyes and thereafter remained straight-faced, gazing out of the window to avoid looking in their direction again until the two of them nodded off a little. Then she felt safe to look where she pleased and smile when the fancy took her. When two more people got on to bury their faces in their newspaper she felt equally at liberty to muse absently on the tinted pictures and their romantic scenery – one the Highlands of Scotland, one of Margate and the other Scarborough – while she dwelt on all the shopping she and Ben would do this afternoon, especially for bedroom furniture, an expense but important, a big item. She felt the thrill of excitement pierce her stomach, a most delicious feeling.

It was a wonderful afternoon, as she knew it would be. Buying all the things their money would stretch to, sighing after all it couldn't. There were curtains still to be ordered but they could wait for a week or two. They still had to think seriously about what they would sit on and eat off, what they would sleep on. She and Ben held hands as they looked at a double bed, a bedside cabinet and matching chest of drawers in oak and weathered oak.

'I think oak?' Ben said, his voice a question. Connie nodded.

'I think so too. But can we afford it?' At six pounds seventeen shillings and sixpence it was slightly the dearer of the two woods. With the chest of four drawers costing five pounds two and six, they were looking at twelve pounds.

Soberly they considered the hire purchase payments of two shillings and sixpence a week for the next couple of years. They'd also be looking at another couple or so shillings a week on the two rep-covered spring-seated fireside chairs and a drop leaf table and four upright chairs they'd seen, the combined cost another eleven pounds sixteen shillings. The whole lot added up to twenty-three pounds. It was a vast amount.

Totting up, standing in the shop while the shop attendant hovered nearby hoping for his commission from a sale of some sort, Connie and Ben gazed at each other.

'Let's see,' Ben whispered. 'There's rent for the flat, seven shillings and sixpence a week. There's insurance in case we need to pay a doctor's or hospital bill – another shilling a week. There's gas and electricity. That'd be another, say, six bob. So let's call it twenty-one shillings to be safe. Take that away from what I earn. Can be overtime of course, but we can't count that – it's never regular. It leaves us about one pound and nineteen shillings for grub.' He drew in a doubtful breath and she did too. 'Then there's them incidentals what come up what you don't expect. It don't leave much for saving. And if we have a family . . . Could we manage?'

'We'd have to, darling,' she whispered back. She had always been a bit of a saver – the reason why they were buying new and not secondhand furniture now, having a nice wedding and even a honeymoon. The two of them pooled their wages every week into a kitty and spent carefully.

She took another quick look at the bed, the cabinet and the chest of drawers. They looked beautiful with the bright electric lights making them gleam. But more, they were solid, serviceable, none of that art deco stuff they'd looked at in other shops. They needed things to be sturdy, and they were for a lifetime. And a bed and a chest of drawers were necessary things. She came to a decision, conscious of the shop attendant shuffling his feet impatiently behind her. 'If we leave the bedside cabinet, that'd save a bit.' Even so they were cutting close to the bone but what could they do?

Ben looked at her face and she knew he read accurately what lay there, her soul pleading for a good start in their new home: no secondhand stuff used by others, please. He melted to it.

'We'll get the cabinet another time. We don't need it yet. No need to go mad all at once. Haven't even got a table lamp to put on it.'

They both chuckled, decision made. The shop assistant's face beamed as he took their order; he did not note or want to note the apprehension on their faces that they could scarcely afford all they'd bought.

Ignoring any fripperies taking their fancy they hurried back to inspect their flat for the sixth time since putting down the first month's rent, Ben having had to get in enough overtime to make it up after that to kill a horse. But it was worth it as hand in hand they walked around the three empty rooms, the tiny kitchen, the little toilet and balcony, seeing them all as they would be furnished a few weeks from now.

'It really is heaven,' Connie sighed as she looked out over towards a misty Big Ben, then began planning for the umpteenth time where their new furniture would go once they moved in. A lot of the space would stay bare for a while but it would fill as their lives together grew. Ben's parents had said they'd be giving them a wireless set for a wedding present, which would provide a little diversion on winter evenings as they sat conserving their savings for a family when it came.

After a Sunday breakfast the next morning of egg and bacon, tomatoes and fried bread, Ben and Connie made their way to Wapping where the tug was moored.

'Are you sure this is all right? Connie queried as he helped her on board. Ben grinned, his grin impish, broadening his already broadly handsome face even more.

124

'Had a bit of a word with the foreman. Said he'd turn a blind eye. Not supposed to but lots of blokes give fiancées trips up or down the river, so long as they don't go too far.' At this he gave a significant chuckle, and knowing what he was alluding to, Connie laughed too, blushing a little. She and Ben had had their moments, enough to make her blush now, but there had never been any opportunity to go to bed together, not even in the new flat, which as yet had no bed in it. But next week it would be delivered, and then . . . She grasped Ben's hand tightly as he helped her down into the boat.

It was just as she had imagined, the muddy smell of the river, the oily smell of the tugboat, the light scent of Ben's brilliantine as he put his head close to hers, one arm about her shoulders, the other on the wheel, his hand on her feeling cool through her pink print summer dress. Now and again he let her take the wheel and she laughed with delight, feeling the power of the tugboat beneath her grip.

'You don't have to strangle her,' he laughed. 'Gently now. She'll respond well enough.' He seemed so proud, even though the boat wasn't his but belonged to the firm for which he and his father worked.

Around midday they took the train back to Leigh for dinner with her parents. Her father, with his ankle strapped up in bandages, behaved like a bear with a sore head, moaning and groaning about his incapacity.

'How did it happen?' she asked.

'Just a bloody accident,' he grunted, irascible and inconsolable, but very obviously unwilling to go into detail.

He sounded almost embarrassed and Connie thought best to leave it alone. Especially as her mother gave her a look that signified things had happened that were best left unsaid, which merely pricked her curiosity the more. Still, she said nothing. Whatever had caused Dad's accident it obviously went deeper than it might have. Dad's pride seemed thoroughly jarred.

After a lovely roast beef Sunday dinner such as only Mum could cook, Ben and she stood in the back yard in the sunshine for a while. Secluded by its wooden fence all round, it let the sun beat down into it, trapping it. Ben loosened his tie and undid his collar.

'Fancy popping along to Southend?' he suggested, his broad face a little ruddy. 'We could spend the afternoon on the beach.'

Connie was in agreement. Even her summer dress felt too warm. 'Let's take our swimming costumes. I really do need to cool off. We can take a few sandwiches and a flask of tea. Mum'll make that up for us.' It was imperative they spent as little money as possible after yesterday's outlay and she knew Ben's wages this week must already be dwindling alarmingly.

The train was hot but not crowded, the usual cram of holiday-makers having eased much earlier that morning. This evening coming back would be crowded.

Gratefully, they alighted at Southend Central Station and made the long hot walk down the High Street, down Pier Hill and along Marine Parade past the pier where the beaches were crowded with people.

Near the Kursal, where there were more people than on the beach, Connie stopped and puffed. 'This is far enough. Don't forget we've got to walk all the way back.'

She might have grown hot from walking, but while they had been doing so, the wind seemed to have changed from the morning and a chilly breeze had sprung up. Where the sky that morning had been a clear blue, it now harboured a sweep of high thin cloud that dulled the sunshine a little, with darker puffs of smaller clouds appearing below that.

'We'd best get our swim in quickly,' she suggested as they went down some stone steps to the beach. Some of those already there, feeling the slight chill, were leaving, gathering up their belongings, although the sun was still bestowing its warmth upon the narrow strip of sand, the tide well up.

'At least there's a place to sit,' Connie added gratefully as they settled themselves against a breakwater sheltered from the slightly chilly breeze, taking advantage of the relative solitude of the beach, though there were quite a few people walking the prome-nade while the raucous music from the Kursal proclaimed a good trade on all its pleasure rides.

'There'll be a lot more people here next week,' she went on as they sorted out their costumes. 'Whitsun Bank Holiday next week. They're most likely saving their pennies for then.'

'Like we are,' Ben laughed, already beginning to get himself into his costume under a large towel he'd wrapped around himself for modesty's sake. Connie stood up and helped hold it around him in case it did fall and cause them embarrassment before the few people left on the beach. Ben did the same for her, at one time putting his hand between the fold to touch her naked bosom, making Connie cry out and tell him to pack it in.

She emerged respectable, but shuddered a little. 'Ooh-ee . . . ! It's cold!'

Nevertheless, with Ben's hand in hers, she let him lead her down to the water's edge a few yards away. The beach here shelved steeply before it met the submerged mud that would then continue for half a mile or more, soon to be exposed with the tide showing obvious signs now of being on the turn. She ventured a foot or two up to her knees, but the tender flesh of her thighs could take no more.

'I'm sorry, Ben, I'm going back. The water's freezing!'

'Coward,' he laughed at her, let go her hand and to show that cold did not trouble him, took a header into the deeper water. Thick-set, strong and muscular, he came up to look back at her. 'See you in a tick, darling,' he said, and struck out with a strong overarm stroke, moving away at a rapid pace.

'Don't go too far,' she called after him. His voice came faintly back as his face turned momentarily clear of the water. 'I won't.'

Connie waved but he didn't see it. Turning, she made her way back up the few yards of sand, sat down and began briskly towelling her wet, chilled legs. That done she wrapped the towel about her shoulders, untouched by water though they were, and poured herself a cup of steaming tea from the flask to swill down the warming liquid in one comforting gulp.

Removing the towel she slipped her cardigan over her swimming costume. Cursing it's inconvenience on the warm walk here, she was glad of it now. Her knees up under her chin, her arms wrapped around them, she stared out to sea.

There were four or five hardy souls out there (she didn't bother to count), all apparently good swimmers. Ben too was a good swimmer – he was probably one of them. Connie settled down and waited. She felt suddenly lonely and a little shiver passed over her although she wasn't that cold any more. She wanted Ben's arm around her, to feel its warmth on her shoulders. As soon as he came out they would go into some tea room for a real cup of tea and a cake and damn the expense.

She waited. A clock above a holiday souvenir shop across the promenade, when she stood up to look, said quarter to three. The

127

next time she stood up to look it showed nearly three. Two swimmers, young men, were coming out, rubbing their arms briskly as they pounded up the beach to a group of people entrenched behind a barrier of clothes and deck chairs against the wall of the promenade above. The sun, struggling through the ever-thickening high cloud, gave some warmth still, reflected back from the concrete. Connie wished she had sat on that side now, taking advantage of the wall's warmth.

Another swimmer was coming out, making for the same group. It left just two in the water, their heads bobbing up and down between the small waves now being stirred up by a stiffening breeze. Connie watched, tried to identify Ben. If he didn't come out soon, she would go to the water's edge and call him. She got up, wandered down to the edge, negotiating a smelly line of dried seaweed, then a wet and glistening line of it that smelled much fresher with little creatures still moving about on the fronds. The sand here was wet and steeped down to a narrow strip of now-exposed mud. The tide was going out, swiftly as it always did, drawing back over the mud flats as if eager to be away from the chattering holidaymakers to languish out there in its own silence. Soon it would be too shallow for swimming. She stood watching the two remaining people coming towards her. Giving up the battle they stood up sharply, surprising her that the water came only up to their chests, rising out of the water like rabbits being popped out of a magician's hat. They were wading in now. Connie recognised neither of them.

Frowning, she cast her gaze across the deserted, choppy surface. Idiotically she turned round quickly, looked at the place where she'd been sitting, her and Ben's own small entrenchment of clothing and bags, half expecting him to be sitting there among it all, surprising her in a joke.

Her gaze moved itself along the prom above. He might have swum around the loading pier of the gasworks further along to come up there, might even now be walking along the prom to get back down on to this beach. There were plenty of strollers up there, none of them Ben, all of them dressed for strolling.

Sudden anxiety clutched at her breast. One of the swimmers passed her without looking at her. She let him go. The last one she reached out to, in a sort of unreasonable panic.

'Excuse me.' He paused, warily. She went on hurriedly, her

voice breathless. 'I'm sorry, but is there anyone else left out there?'

Almost stupidly, he looked back at the small waves. The sun, having steadily grown more brassy, had given up the struggle with the thickening haze of cloud. The heavier lower clumps had slowly united without her even noticing. The sea had turned quite quickly from its original summer blue, taking on an ominous steel-grey hue.

The man looked back at her. 'No one out there now.' He went to go on but the look on her face stopped him. 'Are you all right? What's the matter?'

'My fiancé . . . He . . .' It was hard to acknowledge what was gathering in her breast, hard to form words to explain how she was beginning to feel, the disbelief, the panic, the impossible. 'He was out swimming. He is a strong swimmer. But he's not there now.'

The man stared at her without speaking, then turned sharply and looked back at the water as if the sharpness of his action would produce a swimmer ploughing his way back to the beach.

'Are yer sure?' he asked stupidly like a man not knowing what next to do.

'He was out there.' And then panic really took hold, bursting through her breast in a torrent of terror, her voice rising. 'He has to be out there. Where is he? He has to be out there.'

The man had come to his senses, was holding her cardigan'd arms with his hands. His hands were large and wet. She could feel the wetness soaking through to her flesh. They were cold too. So very cold.

'It's all right,' he was saying. 'Probably gone up the beach a way.'

But the way he spoke held no comfort, his voice a little too high, a little too fast. She pulled away from him, ran into the receding water, uncovered mud squeezing between her toes. Her voice came shrill against the stiffening wind. 'Ben! Ben, for God's sake, where are you? Come out. Stop being silly!'

The man had hold of her again. The group by the promenade wall had got up and there were people coming towards her.

'What's 'appened?'

' 'Er bloke – 'e went in swimmin' . . . 'ow long ago?'

'Twenty . . . twenty-five minutes ago. I don't . . . I don't know.' She was stammering with fear.

'She can't find 'im,' the man supplied to the listeners now crowding round, their faces striken by suspicion of what could have happened.

'He must be *somewhere* . . .' Connie's voice trailed off, had become a useless thing, her throat seizing up, there were tears coursing down her cold cheeks. She felt herself turning to each of the people around her, trying to gain some hope, some defence against what her heart was telling her had happened, the final word itself refusing recognition.

All her senses told her to stay at the water's edge, as if her presence in some way would compel him to reappear, but she felt herself being led up the beach by friendly, concerned hands, with no willpower of her own.

'Looks bad,' someone said. 'Someone best go and get a policeman.'

She was being sat down in one of the deck chairs she had seen the group sitting in. But she didn't want to sit down. She wanted to go back to the water's edge, wade in, search for Ben until she found him.

' 'Ow'd it 'appen?' someone was saying.

'Could've got cramp. I got it a bit meself. That's why I come out. But the water was goin' out and by then it weren't deep.'

'Cramp?' echoed someone.

'If it gets yer when yer way out, it's a killer. People can drown.'

Connie found her voice. It issued from her in a cry that didn't seem to be her voice at all. 'My Ben's a strong swimmer. He's got medals. He's got . . . He can't be . . . He can't . . .' Still the word refused to be uttered.

She was being patted on the shoulder, cuddled to a strange woman's breast. 'There, there, luv. It's probably orright. Look, 'ere's the policeman. 'E'll deal wiv it.'

How the hours went, Connie had no idea. The beach was suddenly filled with men: policemen, men poling about under the Gas Corporation loading pier further along, ambulance men, an ambulance drawn up on the prom above her. She was taken up there to sit inside the vehicle in the warm. A cup of sugary tea was brought her, a tablet given to her to take, a woman from the nearby first-aid hat beside her on the bunk patting her hand, looking after her. She could hear the roar of the lifeboat's motor as it searched

130

the area where Ben was supposed to have been last seen, though no one had taken any note at the time. And all the time she had the feeling he would turn up, his handsome brow creased, his eyebrows raised, and ask what all the fuss was about.

Later, having been asked if she had any family nearby who could come to her, hearing her own toneless reply supplying her address to whoever had asked for it, she sat in a hospital room with a feeling that she was floating. Her mother, her own face creased with grief and anxiety, came to sit with her.

It was ten o'clock at night when a doctor came into the room and stood looking down at the little family group, the bereaved girl, her mother, and her brother, so he gathered. It was the brother who stood up and came over to face him as he said the words in a low, respectful voice.

'A body has been found. I'm afraid the police need Miss Bowmaker to identify it if she will. I think someone should be with her.'

'I'll be with her,' the brother whispered, half turning to look back at his sister. 'We'll both be with her.'

Chapter Thirteen

One hand holding open the wardrobe door that always persisted in swinging shut again if not held, Josie surveyed the two dresses hanging within, both swathed in tissue paper.

That in itself was sad. There should have been four dresses. It had always been expected there would be four when the first of them married: a bridal gown and three bridesmaids' dresses. Always. But Annie was living in India, her connection with the family now only by letter. Pam, disgraced, did not even communicate. Any letter she tried to send was thrown into the fire unopened – Dad's orders. Dad remained bitter beyond belief.

Josie gazed at the two sad, lonely dresses, and her eyes filled with tears as they had done continuously since yesterday. Only one bridesmaid dress left and now there wouldn't even be a wedding.

The knuckles of her hand holding open the wardrobe door whitened. Her pretty face crumpled and she let herself weep – for Connie and a little for herself. Yesterday she'd been so happy, thinking of Saturday when a really wealthy young man had brought her all the way home from London. He had hoped to get something out of it of course. But she had been strong and refused him and he had said . . . what was it? He liked her a hell of a lot. All yesterday she'd reenacted that scene, full of a wonderful sense of elation, of being in control, of walking away from temptation with his words ringing in her ears: 'I'd love to see you again. How about tomorrow?' and her own haughty 'No thank you.' She kept on repeating it all day. 'No thank you.' Wonderful.

They had tried to make a fool of her, those rich young socialites, she realised that now, but she'd risen above it, had even put her hopeful escort in his place. Of course she had cried, but he hadn't seen that. Dignified, that's what she had been. He had been defeated by it. The power of it had stayed with her all through Sunday.

She had still suffered some regret about Arthur, leaving him in the lurch like that. But he was still just a casual boyfriend. She would drop him a note of apology for her behaviour and see how he'd take it. She'd do that some time in the week, she had told herself, trying to ignore the whisper at the back of her mind that it seemed important she did.

Yes, she'd been so happy yesterday. Then had come the awful news. Perhaps the most awful news ever. A policeman knocking on their door. Mum and Dad stricken dumb, Mum putting on her hat, her hands trembling, Dad looking helpless, still unable to put his injured ankle to the floor much less stand on it even with a crutch. Danny had gone in his place, but when Josie had asked to go, Mum had said to stay here and be with Dad. Left with him, she had made tea for them both, her thoughts, like his, following Mum and Danny to the hospital as she automatically laid the table, cut bread, put out the cheese and jam and the cake Mum always made for Sunday tea, nothing of which either of them ate, sitting mostly in silence, waiting. She had paced the house, gazed again and again from its upstairs windows, had shed tears until her throat ached, had tried to kill time by reading magazines – the same sentences over and over, unable to concentrate. From a happy, happy morning, Sunday had become wretched.

A police car had kindly brought them back later that night. Josie remembered the dull feeling of uselessness as they came in, holding Connie between them, followed by a policeman who had asked if there was anything else he could do as they sat Connie in an armchair. Dr Freeman had come to give Connie some pills to make her sleep. Mum had refused the ones he'd offered her, saying she needed to keep her wits about her should Connie wake up and need her.

'She won't,' Dr Freeman had said, his middle-aged heavily jowled face wise. He had been their family doctor as long as Josie could remember. 'She'll sleep through the night.'

'Maybe so,' Mum had said stubbornly. 'But tomorrow she'll need me and I can't be all muzzy when she does.'

Connie had slept, drugged. This morning she had awoken

133

looking ghastly, glazed eyes staring at nothing, her face pale and expressionless as though all her feelings and sensations and emotions had been drained out of her like blood drained from a vein.

The worst part was, she still hadn't cried. Josie, biting back tears, had said without thinking: 'I was going to be Connie's bridesmaid,' and her sister's blank stare had momentarily switched towards her – the most awful look. Hating herself, Josie had fled to the kitchen, Mum hurrying after her to cuddle her and say Connie knew she'd not meant it as it had sounded, and everyone said silly things in the midst of sorrow. But unable to bear even Mum's comfort, she had fled up to her bedroom where she now stood unable to go back and face Connie after what she had said.

Gnawing at her lips, Peggy stood alone in the kitchen. Josie never thought before she spoke. She knew what Josie had meant, but it could never be explained in words. There were no words to explain grief. Even scholars with all their learning were never quite able to describe what it was that clutched the heart with such claws as to drain all feeling from the body, leaving only empty yearning, that too indescribable. It took another bereaved to know how it felt: her heart, still carrying that other grief of five years back, had never completely healed.

The day they had come to her with the news of Tony's accident, the slow dawning of reality while still clutching a belief that it had not happened, the shapeless, primeval sense of loss that all animals feel – it still assailed her whenever she thought about it. She only hoped Connie's grief would not last as long as hers had. But now she must push it all aside, go back to Connie and give what comfort she could, even if it only meant sitting nearby watching the pale expressionless face of her eldest daughter.

Connie felt stiff and withdrawn. It didn't seem like her sitting in this chair, but someone else. As if she watched herself from afar. Time had long since lost all meaning. All day people had been coming in – she vaguely recognised them as relatives, neighbours, friends – leaning over her, making awkward attempts to cuddle her and managing only to make a travesty of it. If only they would just keep away, stay on the other side of the room and say nothing. She didn't want to be cuddled and cried over. Why couldn't she cry? People were supposed to cry. Everyone else was crying but she couldn't feel anything. She should be feeling something, but there was a void inside her around which floated this outer frame which people came to clasp to them in an inane fruitless effort to comfort.

'Want a cup of tea, dear?' Her mother's voice came wafting towards her. She had thought she shook her head. What could tea do for her? But the cup appeared before her and she took it automatically because it was there. She sipped it automatically because it was there, tasted nothing, but its heat made her wince.

'Blow on it, dear.'

She blew on it.

'That's a good girl. Drink it down. It'll do you good.'

Sipping, she drank most of it, and the cup was taken away.

For a few moments at some time during the day the room emptied of people. In that pause, Connie stood up to look at her reflection in the mirror over the fireplace. The person it mirrored stared back, unrecognisable, yet familiar. Was it her? It felt it shouldn't be her at all, that someone else should be gazing back at her.

Disembodied thoughts had begun to wander in and out of her mind: Ben's parents who would never now be her in-laws – someone would have told them by now. Consumed by their own shock and grief, they would be in London with their own family comforting them, too bereft to come here.

She'd have to go and see them – sometime. Her mind shrank from the thought. Ben's body would be taken there, to their flat, to lie in one of the bedrooms until the funeral. They, not she or hers, would make all the arrangements, register the death with the Registrar of Births, Deaths and Marriages, see the undertakers, choose the coffin, the funeral cars, the hymns to be sung, the food for those attending the funeral. She would be told, perhaps consulted, would be expected to view the body. Who'd come and fetch her? Was she supposed to go under her own steam? And the flat they had rented, would that have to be let go? She could go and live in it all by herself . . .

Thoughts which had begun to run on wildly broke off suddenly and she fell back into the chair, her mind shutting down mercifully to shield her from reality as people again filled the room. It still seemed hard to think of Ben as no longer here. She kept half expecting him to appear and hold her hand

135

protectively. And when one of her aunts came offering a neatly cut crustless sandwich on a plate to say that she should try to eat something, she took the unwanted plate with a blank nod of appreciation, and she really did think Ben would be there to take it away for her.

A night and a day had passed, another night with the aid of sleeping pills. Someone said it was Wednesday. Connie had eaten, sitting at the table with the others putting food into her mouth to order, masticating it by force of will. She'd dressed to order, washed, combed her hair, cleaned her teeth to order, incapable as yet of thinking for herself.

Today Danny was taking her to London to Ben's people. Danny had asked her if she was up to it and she had nodded, feeling strong enough so long as he was with her. Even now very little of it had sunk in, everything, all that needed to be done, seeming to close in on her, crowding out the unreality of Ben no longer being here.

On the train up to London – she now wore black, having been taken out that morning by Mum to a local shop to buy it – she and Danny sat saying little other than a few words.

'Are you all right?' he had asked, and she had nodded.

'Glad it's not raining,' he'd said on another occasion and again she had nodded, then surprised herself by asking, quite out of the blue: 'How's Lily?'

He had looked startled but gathered himself. 'She's fine.'

'You don't bring her home to see Mum and Dad any more.'

'No. Well, the business of Pam, the house so upset. I didn't want to subject her to all that. Maybe later.'

'Yes. I'm glad you're seeing a girl.'

They lapsed into silence, Connie's head suddenly emptying of all thoughts, as it had on the day of Ben's accident.

Peggy stood ironing one of her husband's shirts left over from last week. It could have waited but it was something to do. She should have started on this week's washing but that was something too much to do. 'I wrote to Annie yesterday,' she said absently. 'She'll be upset not being here.'

Seated by the kitchen range, Daniel winced as he moved his painful, bandaged foot to a more comfortable position on a

136

wooden stool with a cushion under it. 'She'll want to come home for the funeral I expect.'

Peggy stopped ironing to look at him. 'Why should she want to do that? I know this is all terrible and poor Connie. But Ben means nothing to Annie. Not really. Not enough for her to come all this way home for. It's just that I thought she should know.'

Dan grunted and Peggy resumed her ironing, spitting delicately on the smooth surface to see if it was still hot enough for the moisture to hiss. It still was, and her elbow moved back and forth with it across the grey twill working shirt tail before the heat went and the iron had to be put back before the low fire in the grate to heat up again.

She wasn't thinking when she said, 'We ought to tell Pam too.'

Dan stiffened, sucked in a painful breath and swore as his injured ankle twinged in response. 'Who the bloody hell's that? No one I know of that name.'

With a clatter that betokened irritation, Peggy banged the iron down on its stand. 'For heaven's sake, Dan. Not at a time like this.'

Of course she understood how he felt. Knew how deep his hurt went. Sympathised with him. Wouldn't have gone against him to save her life. But all hurt put aside, Connie was Pam's sister. She should at least know what had happened.

Until this had all come about she hadn't even been able to bring herself to find out where Pam was living. Connie had tried to tell her, some weeks ago, but she, God forgive her, had closed her ears, said she didn't want to know, and when Connie, giving up, had written it on a scrap of paper and pressed it into her hand, she had lifted the round iron lid of the kitchen range where she had been cooking the evening meal and had dropped the piece of paper in among the coals, turning away so that she wouldn't have to see it flame up and shrivel into blackness.

It was Josie who went. The morning after the news of Ben's death, when all those who'd crowded in to announce their dismay had left, she had plucked up enough courage to come down to face Connie again. Connie had smiled faintly at her and, encouraged, she had come and crouched in front of Connie, had taken her hand and looked up into her face, trying to hook on to something that might be practical instead of inane or foolish.

'Someone needs to let Pam know,' she had said, and Connie

137

had come partially to life, making her feel she was at last doing some good.

'You know her address, Connie?' she had prompted.

'It's in my bag,' Connie had murmured, and finding the bag, Josie had stood aside while Connie fished in it, seeming for the moment to be herself again, though it had all gone once more into reverse once the job had been done and the energy fled.

Armed with the piece of paper, Josie found herself welcomed with open arms into Pam's poky little top flat.

She had never been here before. The climb up the bare stairs to the very top of the house, past two floors utilised as private flats by the look of them, had been depressing enough. Connie's glowing description of the flat she and Ben had rented, built for that purpose with its own knocker and letter-box, had made it seem a real home, but this sharing of what had once been a complete house had a dejected air about it, as if one trespassed by merely entering the building. All was silent as she ascended, adding to the sensation, as if people lurked rather than lived behind those doors.

Reaching the top floor, no more than an attic space, Josie had looked at the scuffed door with 89D inscribed on it. There was no knocker on this door. No letter-box. Tapping on the wood itself with her knuckles, she had heard movement on the other side. A voice asked, 'Who is it?' Pam's voice.

'It's Josie.'

The door handle had rattled loosely and there was Pam, her hazel eyes, so like Dad's, lit up with the joy of seeing her, almost ecstatic with joy.

'Josie! Oh, how lovely, *you* coming to see *me*. Oh, come in, Josie!'

'You didn't think I wouldn't come and see you?' Josie queried as she stepped into the tiny living-cum-dining room so poorly furnished with bits of this and that, and all so obviously second-hand, that it made her feel sick with pity for Pam's state.

'It's only Mum and Dad who feel the way they do about you,' she went on, taking Pam's offer to sit in one of the fireside chairs that had seen better days. 'The rest of us, Connie and Danny – Annie's not here of course – haven't any axe to grind. It's not our affair.'

'And it wasn't mine,' Pam added, standing over her with her

138

square features, again so much like her father's, creasing up a little. 'But it feels as if it is. All I did was fall in love with George Bryant. But you'd think I'd gone off and murdered the King of England the way I've been treated. I never thought Dad would throw me out. I feel . . . Honestly, I feel . . .'

Tears were forming in her eyes at the plight she had been forced into. Josie felt she was on the point of collapsing on to her knees before her to be cuddled as she fell into a fit of weeping. There would be weeping but not for herself when Josie divulged her sad news.

'Look,' she cut in before Pam could dissolve into self-pity. 'You make us a nice cup of tea.' (The tiny, odd-shaped oil stove with a little door on one side could hardly have heated more than a kettle or saucepan or a frying pan, and then only one utensil at a time, and again Josie felt that wave of pity flow over her thinking of the lovely meals Pam used to enjoy from their mother's shining black kitchen range in whose oven she still baked fresh bread as she'd done all her life.) 'Then I'll tell you why I'm here – apart from coming to see you because I wanted to.'

Innocent of what news lay ahead of her, Pam dried her eyes quickly and grabbing the kettle off the stove, said a little more brightly, 'Shan't be a tick,' and took herself out of the room. Josie heard her descending the stairs to the floor below, distinctly heard the sound of a tap being turned on and water running into the empty kettle, then the footsteps lumbering back up the bare stairs. Pam's body was heavier now with her child waiting to be born in August.

Back in the room, Pam placed the kettle on the oil stove and fiddled about getting the thing to light. That done, she turned to Josie with a smile bleak with apology. 'It takes a while.'

Her head bent over the small cloth-covered table, she arranged two cups and saucers, got spoons from a cardboard box on the floor where the cutlery was apparently kept. Milk she got from a bottle standing on a shelf together with a half packet of sugar and a packet of Lyons tea.

Josie looked around. 'Where do you wash up?'

'Oh, in the sink on the next floor.' Pam's tone was falsely cheerful. 'The landlady had a butler sink and tap installed there when she turned all this into flats. We all use it.'

'I didn't see any sink when I came up.'

139

'It's in the corner behind the stairs. It's a bit dark there.'

'Where do you wash?'

'There's a bathroom. Quite a big one really. We take turns. Our turn is on Wednesdays. But we can use the sink there for a morning or evening wash when the bathroom's free. We pay for the heating. There's a boiler on the ground floor. The water's usually warm enough, though at the moment, being summer, Mrs Carper sometimes doesn't light it very often. In winter so I'm told, we get hot water through the pipes to keep the place warm, so it's not too bad.'

'Good God,' Josie sighed, watching the kettle for some sign of steam coming from it. 'You don't reckon on still being here by wintertime? You'll have the baby to worry about by then. There's no room.'

Pam smiled her wan smile. 'We'll have to see. I mean, George don't earn much, the shrimping industry's going down the pan all the time, and I'm not working. Can't. We do our best.'

'Don't George's parents help you at all?'

A small flutter of anger passed across Pam's face. 'Do ours help at all? They couldn't care if we both died.'

Then the anger passed. 'How can his parents help? They're nearly as poor as we are. There's virtually no shrimping industry now. It began dying when shipping started mucking up the river and shrimps went off elsewhere. And it's getting worse. George and his dad have to go miles out to sea now to catch anything worthwhile, sometimes nearly to Harwich, and they're out in all weathers. At least cocklers know where their cockles are. Shrimpers have to go chasing all over the place for their catch. And Dad thinks *he* was hard done by when his boat caught fire. George's dad never talks about it. At least Dad has done well. George's hasn't.'

As though exhausted by her tirade, Pam sat down on the other, even more worn, fireside chair next to Josie's.

The kettle had only just begun steaming and Josie felt it could be hours before they ever got their cup of tea. She must start to relay the news about poor Connie. It would be unseemly to embark upon light chit-chat, if Pam in her present frame of mind permitted such a thing, and then to go on to report dire news that should have been told at the very outset.

'Pam,' Josie began. 'I've something to tell you. It's about Connie.'

Pam tilted her head slightly, her smile warmer. 'The wedding?'

Perhaps she was hoping to be invited, all finally forgiven. Connie had said that she had indeed invited her but that Pam had declined, for obvious reasons. Any hope Pam might have must be quickly quashed.

'No, not the wedding. Well, yes, it has something to do with it, but . . .' This was going to be far harder than she in her impulsiveness had thought. 'You see, Pam, the wedding . . . it won't be . . . it's off.'

'*Off*?'

The whistle on the kettle had begun to hum, very low. Soon its note would rise to a scream demanding to be taken off the stove. Desperation clutched at Josie's chest. She leaned forward.

'Pam, something dreadful's happened.'

Was that glee in Pam's face, glee at something gone wrong in the Bowmaker family, compensating her in part for what had been done to her, even if it came from Connie's corner, Connie who was still nice to her? 'They haven't split up, have they? They haven't had a blazing row, have they?'

'Pam . . . Ben's dead.'

She hadn't meant it to come out like that. How did people convey the terrible news of death? She'd never done it before; never experienced death before except for her young brother. She had been only thirteen then and awful as it had been, she had only the luxury of crying to contend with, the sad knowledge that Tony was no longer there hitting her only when she came in from school or from playing with friends. At all other times, she forgot that he was no longer there.

Now she must convey the worst news of any to another, and it wasn't easy. So it had been blurted out. Pam's face had frozen in the midst of her smile, a fixed grimace. The kettle's whistle had risen considerably.

'What d'you mean, dead?'

'I mean . . . what I say. Ben was drowned. Sunday.'

The whistle was shrieking. Pam took the kettle off and put it on a stand on the table for the while. She seemed now to be moving like an automaton, holding the empty teapot close to her. 'Drowned? How? What happened?'

'I don't know. Just that the police came for Mum. Danny went with her. Dad has an injured foot, from jumping off the boat on

Saturday. He couldn't go. They left me behind to give eye to him. They came back but all they said was Ben had been drowned, an accident off the gasworks jetty – someone said it was cramp.'

Pam's voice sounded far away. 'But Connie said he was such a strong swimmer. She wished she could swim like him. Said she should have learned. Just self-taught. Perhaps he'll turn up all right after all.'

'Pam – don't be silly. He's dead.'

'I'm not being silly . . .' She stopped abruptly and they both looked at each other.

'They found the body some hours later,' Josie said, her voice low. 'Connie had to go and identify him.'

She saw Pam lean over the table. Head bent, she was weeping, sudden great gulps of weeping. Leaping up, Josie, more distraught at the way she had blurted it all out than for any other reason, went and took Pam in her arms.

'I'm sorry I had to be the bearer of such news. I didn't think you'd take it this bad. After all, Ben wasn't family, not yet anyway.'

Pam's voice came fast and fierce and angry, gulping its way through her tears. 'I'm not crying for Ben. I'm crying for Connie, she didn't deserve to have that. Apart from you, she's the best of the bunch, she didn't deserve to have that happen to her. She's been good to me, better than any of them, and this had to happen to her. I wish . . . I wish it had been him, Dad, to go through that. Then he'd know how it feels. I wish . . .'

Josie leaned back in horror. 'You mean you'd want him to lose Mum? Pam, you can't wish a thing like that.' She too was in tears, that Pam could say this, almost as if Pam had cast a curse upon them all. 'You can't wish a thing like that.'

Pam's words could hardly be heard through her crying. 'Of course I didn't. Of course not. But I wish it could have been anyone rather than Connie. Oh, Josie, I miss Mum and Dad so much.'

There was nothing Josie could say, wishing, as they stood in the centre of the poor little flat with only lino to stand on and second-hand chairs to sit on and a rickety table to eat off and an oil stove to cook by and washing done by rota, that Pam could be forgiven, called home, and they could all be happy again, and Ben could still be alive. And she wished that Annie was here.

142

Chapter Fourteen

Annie sat in one of the deep bamboo armchairs on the covered veranda, the letter from her parents unopened. She thought of Connie, the wedding. Probably the letter would be full of it and she had not been there. She felt left out, wondered if they had missed her, if Connie in her happiness had stopped once to miss her. Perhaps she had, but only fleetingly on that her special day.

It felt odd imagining Connie married. She had sent her a unique wedding present, a pair of pure silk bed coverlets and four cushion covers and an ivory statue of a group of Indian dancers. Something different from the usual run of wedding presents. Connie would have been delighted, she was sure. She thought of Connie and Ben settled in their Bethnal Green flat. Then she thought of herself, here.

She didn't want to open her letter yet. Hearing about the wedding and all that had gone on as well as the day-to-day trivia which always provoked feelings of homesickness that were growing worse as the months went by would only destroy her for the rest of the day.

It had been wonderful here at first, still winter, the air despite the sun's fierce heat freshened by cooling breezes from the Himalayas hundreds of miles away. Her arrival here had filled her with wonder and excitement as she'd wandered about the villa, which seemed almost too spacious for just her and Alex, and of course the obligatory half-dozen servants, or boys as he called them. Running from room to room she had been struck speechless but for cries of wonder at each new discovery.

Alex had watched her progress as she'd run out to the wide veranda and on into the well-kept garden, his face creased by a grin. 'Well, what do you think of the place?' he'd asked needlessly, already knowing her answer.

She had ran back and embraced him. 'We're going to be so happy here, Alex darling.'

Those first couple of months had indeed been happy. Homesickness had no place in her happiness, and what did it matter if she hadn't immediately taken to the Raj, as the English out here were called by the Indians? She had Alex. He was all she needed. She spent each day eagerly waiting for him to come home of an evening, her time completely taken up by the large house she lived in. Each evening was spent together in rapturous bliss. He had said he should write to his parents telling them of this marriage, but her joy in the place had been such that she had feared it being ruined and he had indulged her and not written and their life had gone on happily. It was with the arrival of that intense heat of summer, when even the punkah, that efficient long strip of stiff material moved back and forth by a sleepy punkah-wallah, failed to do more than stir the humid air around a little, that homesickness began to make itself felt.

Sitting on the veranda, its slim colonnades twined with vines limp with rain from the thunderstorm that had raged all morning, Annie stared with glazed focus at the sodden garden, its dank odours rising up to fill her nostrils. Pale daylight lightning flickered from cloud to cloud and thunder rolled continuously around the sky – a foretaste of what the monsoon in a month or two's time would be like. Clothes stuck to her. Perspiration didn't just dampen her temples, it actually trickled, and she often wondered how on earth the other Britons-Anglo-Indians as they termed themselves – could appear so cool all the time. Used to it, she supposed. But how long did it take for a body to get used to this climate? And when this storm abated as it would towards afternoon, the sun would batter the soaked earth with its heat filling the air with rising mist to make the whole place as sticky again as if the storm had never been. And they said this could continue for months once the monsoon did arrive. Annie felt she couldn't bear the thought. Already she was hating the place, but it was so hard to make Alex see.

He was in his element here, had made friends so quickly. When she complained, he'd laugh and say she was just taking a little longer to get used to it, that was all. He just didn't understand.

He'd spend the hottest part of the day with colleagues lunching in the shade near to his office, to come home in the evening wondering why she was so down.

Knowing the letter from home would only make her feel worse, she put it aside until Alex came home when she would probably feel a little more well disposed towards life here. She contented herself instead by reading a book until lunchtime when the gong thrummed softly announcing tiffin, lunch, and she came to eat in the dim and quiet room. The storm was finally going away. Morarji, her house boy, padded back and forth; she desultorily watched his movements as he served the meal, cleared away after her, brought a pot of tea out to her on the veranda. Now the sky was clearing but none, as she could notice, of the clammy feel to the air. After lunch she bathed, had a little lie down, trying to make the most of the movement of air from the punkah, finally got up, washed again, changed her frock and tidied her hair, to be served more tea. Dinner would be held back until Alex came home. He came home full of high spirits as she knew he would. She lifted her face for him to kiss.

'So, what've you been doing with yourself today?' he asked brightly, but added, seeing her more low-spirited than ever as he helped himself to a whisky and soda, 'Surely you've not been hanging around here all day? No wonder you're bored. Why don't you go down to the club during the day? That's where everyone is, there being precious little else to do in this heat. You'd enjoy yourself, chatting, playing a bit of bridge, sharing a bit of gossip.'

'I didn't feel up to it,' she told him, getting a drink for herself. Now he was here it tasted much better than when she drank alone. 'And I don't really get on with them.'

'Don't be silly, Annie, of course you do.'

How could he understand? He came from a wealthy, socially confident background, and from the very start felt at ease with people such as these, while she still sensed that they looked at her with distaste, her speech, as nice as it was, not theirs, which featured a certain accent she had never acquired. Hers echoed in her ears as soon as she opened her mouth. She'd rather stay away. Trouble was she was getting a reputation of seeming a little odd and the more she kept to herself the odder she was appearing to become. Yet she felt so ill at ease with all of them. It was becoming a vicious circle.

With a sudden thump she put down her glass on a side table, her anger bursting out against them all with their haughty sidelong glances and their awkward . . . no, censorious silences.

'What is it about the people out here? They behave as if they think they are gods or something.'

'Perhaps they are in a way,' he said, unruffled, sitting himself down in one of the deep bamboo armchairs on the veranda. 'Out here they are.'

'Out here, yes,' she replied stiffly, still on her feet, leaning her pelvis against the low fretwork railing in an agitated series of thumps and gazing out at the rain beating down on the lawn below her. 'At home they wouldn't behave like that. At home they'd probably be fawning around someone higher up on the social scale than them.'

'They,' he murmured behind her.

She turned, frowning, her train of thought broken. 'Pardon?'

'They, not them.' He was contemplating his glass, and she continued to frown at the fair crown of his head as his correction dawned on her.

'Is that all you're concerned about, Alex, the way I speak?'

He looked up, his fair handsome face loving and helpful. 'You keep telling me, darling, you feel you don't fit in, that you wished you could speak better than you do. To me you speak perfectly. But you won't be convinced. I was only trying to help you along. If you're going to get on with these people . . .' it sounded to her as though he were gently admonishing her '. . . you've got to mix with them, speak the way they do. It would help. All I'm trying to do is . . .'

'And you . . .' Anger made her splutter. 'You act like the biggest god of all.'

His turn to frown. 'What god?'

'One of the ones these English think they are – out here. Honestly, Alex, you've changed. I don't know if it's since our marriage or this place, but you always seem to be on your high hat all the time, as if you feel you mustn't put a foot wrong before the Indian population. Like you were a god.'

'I've not changed, Annie. You have. You used to be so lively, happy. Now you're just morose and silent and sulking all the time.'

'It's because you're away from me so much. You seem only

146

interested in your work, your silly exporting of gems, meeting clients, eating away from home.'

'It takes up a lot of my time, darling.' He was sitting stiffly in his chair now. 'It's part of my job. I don't want to be away from you any more than you do from me. If you started socialising a little more you wouldn't feel it so much. You're beginning to behave like a hermit. Soon people will start gossiping, wondering what I'm doing with you.'

'There seems too much gossiping goes on. None of them have nothing better to do than talk about someone else. I suppose I do as good as anyone. Trouble is, they won't show it, but they're all as bored as me with this place, this country.'

He was getting a little irritated, his voice a little snappy. 'Then you're in good company, aren't you? So learn to mix with it better, can't you?'

'Company,' she shot back. 'I feel as if I'm in a glass case, everybody noticing everything we do, everything I do whenever I set foot at the club. They go out of their way to make me feel I'm an outsider, an intruder, not their sort. Whatever I say, do, wherever I go, I feel it's being scrutinised, chewed over, judged. Sometimes I feel as if I'm expected to behave as servilely as the Indians themselves.'

'You mean the servants? Not the Indians. They're not servile. They are proud of what they are. I think they even laugh at us.'

He was trying to be humorous but she didn't want to see it that way. All she heard was sarcasm, him having a dig at her.

'Yes.' Her voice was sharp. 'The servants, if you like.'

His light smile faded. 'Then it's time you snapped out of this feeling. And please do not mistake the Indian's pride in doing what he does to the best of his ability as servility or inferiority. He's not your English worker who often begrudges whatever he does for his employer. I'd ask you to remember Annie, the Indian is totally different from us. I'd ask you to respect that.'

Annie realised they were having a row. Voices unraised, very civilised, but a row nevertheless. The first. And all because of India.

'I don't care!' Now her voice did raise itself. 'I hate it here. I hate the people, the Anglo-Indians. And the Indians. I hate the way they do all they're told without complaint. I feel ashamed ordering them about, seeing them complying. I say please but it

147

still feels I'm just giving orders and they're doing anything I tell them even if it's against their better judgment.'

Alex put his drink on the side table as though he had lost his enjoyment of it. His voice also sharpened though remaining controlled. 'They're our servants. We pay them for what they're employed to do. What else?'

'We! Them!' She moved, jerkily, a short way along the veranda and back. 'We, us, all cast in the same mould, behaving as if we see ourselves better than them . . . they. I'm beginning to hate myself for it. Hate it all.'

He watched her pacing. 'So you keep saying, Annie,' he said, his voice low and even.

'But it's . . . it's all wrong, us treating them as inferiors.'

'I don't think I do that. Annie, enough of this. It's getting silly. You've been fed up all day and you're taking it out on me. I'm afraid you will have to adjust to this place and the people who, like us, have to live here or continue being miserable. We're going to be here for a long time, I'm afraid. I've written to my father about us.'

'What?' Annie stopped pacing, her pique forgotten.

'He would have had to know sometime. Now he has two choices – either recall me, and he won't do that. Mother wouldn't allow him to ask for my resignation and risk her friends talking and making her feel a fool. Or keep me out here for as long as he can, out of harm's way. I think that will be the route he will take. So be prepared, Annie, for a long stay out here.'

He probably saw the look on her face before she was even aware of it herself at the thought of years here instead of the one or two she had expected. He got up and came towards her, his arms held out to her, and she could do no other than come willingly, wanting only for this argument to be over.

'Annie, I love you, my darling,' he murmured into her hair. 'I'm sorry you're unhappy, but it won't last and together we'll make it work. We will, I promise. Seeing you sad makes me feel sad too.'

He bent his face to hers and she let herself be kissed, feeling the smooth warmth of his lips on hers, comforting, desirable. He leaned back to look at her. 'Now, let's see you smile, my love.'

Complying, she smiled, saw the satisfaction on his face. Alex was content again and assumed she was too. Well, she was, now that he was here to kiss her. When they kissed, embraced, made love, she felt she could conquer this place, could conquer the whole world. Only when he was away did she fear this new life, India and the people who ruled it, who had ruled it for two centuries until they had come to believe it theirs and any gauche newcomer a threat to their supremacy unless she fell into their ways unreservedly. Their territory. It belonged to them, not to the Indians, and people fresh from England were expected to be integrated into that narrow insular niche they had carved for themselves in a foreign land.

Alex had already achieved that. He enjoyed his work, felt free and unfettered by the England he'd left behind. For her was still the trauma of facing that old brigade barricaded behind the boundaries of its English Club, enjoying life with that peculiar social snobbery typical to the English abroad which Annie was fast coming to recognise and shy away from. She saw herself, the newly arrived, as the lowest on the social rung, expected not to say too much, to be respectful, subservient, not as the Indian was expected to be, but with an awareness that she must bide her time in order to be accepted fully into their circles.

The men were nice enough; it was their formidable wives she feared, with their studied silences, as she saw it, should she speak out of turn or say too much at once. She hated their patronising, their questions, veiled a little, as to her upbringing. At home she'd been at the top of the tree in her job, respected as head receptionist of a high-class hotel. Here she was considered nothing. Her only defence was to think of the lives of these people as a charade, slightly unreal, as though beneath their laughter and camaraderie, their pomposity and their social rules they too longed for home, the soft lines of the English country-side, the orderly cities. Perhaps Alex was right, there was nothing for them but unite against India and Indians with their so-different approach to life lest it rub off on them, and against the brash newcomer who might upset their order of things that seemed not to have moved on from the turn of the century. Even their homes reflected a life at the turn of the century. Victorian mirrors and drapes, colonial furniture, elegant but outmoded, bolstered the impression of a past regime.

But Alex was right. If the two of them were going to be here for years she'd have to become one of them or remain isolated and

149

miserable, ostracised as odd. But oh, to enter the Jalapur English Club, was, as she'd told Alex, like being an exhibit in a glass case.

As they both dressed for dinner, even though there were only the two of them, (the done thing she had come to learn; standards must never be lowered before the eyes of the Indians, certainly not the servants) she put her woes firmly out of her mind. This was the hour she looked forward to, and it must not be upset by her going on about her miserable day.

Coming indoors, shutters closed against biting insects (though the higher region of Jalapur was so far free of the malarial mosquito) allowing in only night breezes, they ate a light meal of salad, chicken in a mild anglicised sauce, vegetables and fruit. Annie's palate had still not adjusted to hot curries. The brief Indian twilight had gone, leaving the night outside black. This evening's short burst of rain with its distant lightning and faint rolls of thunder had ceased and night insects were singing in full flow as she and Alex sat on the Edwardian sofa after dinner. He had put a record on the gramophone and now the air filled with quiet dance music 'With a song in my heart . . . I behold your adorable face . . . with a song in my heart . . .'

It was still warm. The sofa's cushions seemed to heat her legs under the soft clinging silk of the pale blue dress she wore. With Alex close beside her reading the Indian edition of *The Times*, Annie fanned her face with a small delicate fan and thought about India and her journey to this place.

Nothing of India inspired her. Of course, the temples were beautiful, the people quick to smile, the pink buildings of the city lovely, the scenery breathtaking. Beyond both sparse and full-leafed trees through which green parakeets skimmed, the distant hills were blue and misty under a cloudless sky – though not today. But one could take in just so much of temples and smiling people and scenery. The land, still dry as dust an hour after a downpour had passed, would become waterlogged and miserable with the arrival of the monsoon and the clammy heat made life unbearable.

She'd had such high hopes coming here. Had been so excited, for all the tearful goodbyes to the family at Tilbury Docks. But the pang of emptiness mingling with the anticipation of all that lay ahead of her had soon been swept away by her longing to see Alex as she had waved to them from the upper deck, leaning over the handrail the better to glimpse her family among all the others crying their farewells.

The P & O liner had been huge. *The Viceroy of India*, built just the previous year, had dominated Tilbury Docks, a glistening black-painted leviathan, her two funnels issuing the faintest trace of lazy smoke swiftly swept away on the stiff March breeze.

From the deck where she'd stood she'd been able to look down upon the street lamps of Tilbury. (Later in that awful storm in the Indian Ocean that had laid her low, waves had towered above that same deck.) And when the liner had manoeuvred out of the dock it seemed its length might never turn round in such small space. Heaved round by tugs, the engines had shaken the whole ship and herself almost to bits, roaring and shuddering enough to frighten the life out of her though the seasoned passengers had taken not a bit of notice as they went off to their cabins to sort themselves out or to the dining rooms for their dinner. The juddering and roaring dying away, the ship at last eased out of the narrow docks. She too, calming, had gone first to her cabin to sort herself out, thrilled by the splendour of a first-class cabin for which Alex had paid, then down to dinner, suddenly hungry.

In the equally opulent first-class dining room – there had been a different one for second-class passengers – surrounded by the low babble of conversation coming at her from all sides like gentle sighs, the light clinking of cutlery against fine crockery, everything bright and lively, she had felt utterly pampered. She'd found herself sharing a table with a middle-aged American woman, a Miss Rita Tessland from New England, and her paid companion, a quiet little mouse of a person named Nancy Green. They had been such nice people, with Rita Tessland proving to be quite a talkative woman, who instantly befriended Annie. They had become her companions all through the voyage.

Gliding majestically out into the Thames, a few street lamps starting to glow from the Gravesend side in the gathering dusk of late March, the land slipped by, the river widening. The banks had soon merged with the darkening countryside of Essex and Kent, finally disappearing until they seemed to sail on in a black void but for tiny far-off pools of light denoting small towns. One pool of light she was sure she recognised.

'That's where I live,' she told a couple standing by the rail where she had gone after dinner, speaking in the present tense but suddenly realising that that part of her life would never come again. But she wasn't dismayed.

'I'm going to India. Delhi,' she chattered on. 'A town not far from there called Jalapur. They say the buildings are all pink. I imagine it's quite wonderful to see. My husband's there waiting for me. He's in the precious gems trade. He went out there for his father. He has an agency there.'

The couple listened, smiled, but said nothing apart from a remark from the man that she would like Northern India, and after a while drifted away.

The Bay of Biscay had been choppy and she had experienced her first bout of seasickness. Miss Tessland's high but cultured New England voice ordered her not to stay in her cabin but to go up on deck, take deep breaths of sea air and keep her eyes on the horizon. It had worked. By the time the liner called at Gibraltar to take on more passengers, called at Marseilles to take on mail, then Malta and on through the spectacular Suez Canal that took Annie's breath away, she had begun to feel very much a sailor born. But later during that storm in the Indian Ocean nothing had worked and she had lain prostrate on her bed, her head reeling, her stomach churning, heaving up what little food remained inside her.

It had been a relief to finally reach Bombay, saying farewell to Miss Tessland, who was going on to Calcutta. Her first impression of India had been one of shock and bewilderment that to this day hadn't diminished. And if her family had seemed far out of reach during her voyage, they had felt even more so as she'd made for the train to take her on to her final destination.

Wrinkling her nose against the strange smell that had immediately surrounded her, a mixture of spicy food, bodily odours, unsubtle wafts of perfume, engine oil and stale steam from the trains, all hanging on the heat of midday, she'd followed the porter taking her luggage to her compartment. Victoria terminus, an amazing edifice at once cavernous and suffocating, a jumbled mix of Victorian gothic and Indian sculpture, had echoed with a constant deafening babble of voices. It teemed with humanity. Smart businessmen had virtually rubbed shoulders with humble native travellers in colourful sari or white dhoti squatting beside their linen bundles, unaffected by the modern world about them.

The train had been another shock, one she would never forget, the journey in it long, tedious, hot and so uncomfortable that it far outweighed her awe at the unaccustomed scenery of arid plains with sparsely-leafed trees, low blue mountains, towns and villages that amazed her with their squalid huts and grubby inhabitants, their dusty streets where skinny cattle wandered freely. Camels, asses, even men pulled laden carts, and the children looked in need of a good wash; all were seen fleetingly as the train rattled by. Stopping at stations en route to Delhi where Alex had arranged to meet her, she'd been dismayed at the apparent thousands of people scrambling on. The train was unable to accommodate them all inside, so they clambered on its roof and clung to its sides. She had offered up a prayer of gratitude for a first-class English compartment and cultured English fellow travellers.

As with her voyage across the Indian Ocean, so she had been heartily glad to have the journey over. On her arrival, when Alex caught her to him in an overwhelming show of loving welcome, she'd once again fostered high hopes of her future here, but her life here had proved no more inspiring than the sea voyage or the train journey. And here he and she were together, at least some of the time.

Beside her, Alex put down his *Times of India* with a sudden rustle that made her nerve endings jump briefly.

'Aren't you going to open your letter from home?' he reminded her, getting up to change the record on the gramophone. 'I noticed it sitting on the sideboard when I came in, unopened.'

She had forgotten all about it. Laughing at the oversight, surprised at herself for having overlooked it all this while, she got up almost guiltily and retrieved it from the sideboard. It was perhaps the first time ever she hadn't opened a letter from home straight away. She should at least have had some curiosity as to how Connie's wedding had gone.

It was as she slit the flap that she noticed for the first time that it was quite a thin envelope. Slightly intrigued, she drew out a single sheet. Usually there was a whole wad, full of the goings on in Leigh, sometimes with an added note from Josie. Nothing came from Pam any longer. Mum had written telling her about Pam, a short, sad and bitter letter.

Annie had written back saying how upset she'd felt. It had been an awkward letter to write, because she hadn't wanted to take

153

sides, knowing how her parents felt and also how Pam must feel. Distance had made the on-going feud nonsensical and the casting out of Pam petty. But she hadn't dared say so.

She looked at this other single sheet, a premonition of bad news already assailing her. Seconds after reading it she was lying with her face against Alex's shoulder, weeping for Connie while he scanned the terrible news, his arm tightening in the sad knowledge that his wife could not be in England to comfort her sister.

But they both knew the true reason for this unconstrained weeping was not for her sister's loss – after all, Ben hadn't yet become one of the family on the day of his tragic death – but for her own, a culmination of her disillusionment with life here, a sense of isolation and a deep longing to be home. He could have sent her home; could have afforded it, but as he held her close, Alex had a frightening feeling that were he to let her go away from here she might never return, her obvious unhappiness with this place overriding even her love for him, and that he could not have borne.

Chapter Fifteen

Danny lounged on the well-worn settee after tea, his eyes narrowed against the shaft of late August sunlight coming in through the window from the west. The tide was well out, the day's haul done, the boiler lit with half an hour yet to go before a build-up of steam could allow the cooking to begin. He had time to relax.

Young Tibb Barnard would come and tell them when all was ready. Then Dad would get up out of his armchair to stomp heavily and awkwardly along to the cockle sheds – his ankle had never been the same since he'd injured it in May, the dreadful day Connie had lost her Ben. These days he suffered from a nagging ache in it and a need to rest it where once he'd have been active about the shed. These days he'd growl to Danny: 'Well while we're waitin', might as well pop on 'ome, see how your mum is,' indicating Danny go with him, that way avoiding the embarrass-ment of appearing to have difficulty leaving on his own. Nothing was said but his brothers Reg and Pete would often say they might as well pop off too for half an hour, which made him feel a bit better about it.

They'd all be back there on time, poor young Tibb puffing from having to run one way up the road and then the other to say the pressure was good and the tanks full with fresh water.

But once in the shed Dad pulled his weight well enough, lifting the steel nets full of raw cockles into the cooking pot, fastening down the lids for the shellfish to cook at a pressure of fifteen pounds for six minutes. Six minutes to rest his foot, his expression betraying the pain that sometimes plagued him. Then the cockles, still in their nets, must be lifted out and Dad was the first there,

155

allowing his brothers no time to do it for him. He'd have none of
their humiliating sympathy. He'd tip them into the de-sheller, the
sieve hanging over the large sieving tank full of cold water, lifting
their weight with a grunt of pain. There he'd stand watching the
sieve shake back and forth, quick to spot any unopened shells as
the cockle meat fell through the mesh. The empty shells left on top
of the machine he'd take his turn with his brothers to toss through
the open hatch on to an already formed mountain of them waiting
to be taken away by lorries for crushing.

If small-shelled cockles fell through the finer sieve he at least
left Tibb Barnard to fish them out of the sifting tank. It was Tibb
who put them into a smaller tank to stir round and round until the
meat flowed free as their shells sank to the bottom.

It was a long day after the gathering, three or four washes, and
the rubbish had to be removed from the tanks to allow the process
to begin all over again with a fresh batch. At the end of it Dad
would look grey with pain but he would never give up, growling
irascibly should any of them suggest he take a rest.

At the moment he was resting, his foot up on a stool. To
Danny's eyes it looked a little swollen under the thick socks, but
it was more than he dared to mention it. Dad would grit his teeth
and suffer.

Instead, Danny glanced across to where Connie was sitting
staring out of the back window at the setting sun. She did a lot of
staring of late. She'd become oddly reclusive at home, gone that
light happy way she once had. She hardly ever went out after work
except to travel down to Bethnal Green in London to Ben's
parents, spending Saturday evenings with them just as though she
were their daughter-in-law and family. (Whether they welcomed
her or not, for maybe she awakened a hurt they'd rather forget,
Danny was uncertain.) Sunday mornings she'd invariably go to
church. She had begun attending the week after Ben's funeral,
never inviting anyone to go along with her. Unnatural, Danny
thought as he regarded the back of her head and shoulders framed
in the shaft of evening sunlight through the window, elbows on
the windowsill, chin supported by her cupped hands, her head
very still, her mind . . . God alone knew where her mind was.

Danny stopped thinking about Connie and thought about
himself instead – him and Lily. Lately he could hardly stop
thinking about Lily. Even now, turning his thoughts to her, he felt

156

his insides twinge with excitement. Lily had begun to be very generous with her body, that they would one day become one was now a foregone conclusion. Though he had never proposed as such, it was understood, and in dark corners they were as good as man and wife already.

He thought now what it might be like actually making love on a bed, properly, instead of in isolated places, standing up, or in a deserted park just before it closed, hurriedly, agitatedly, lying on his coat behind a clump of shrubbery, half their attention distracted by fear of being caught in the act by someone coming by. The risk of discovery, contrary to belief, did nothing to heighten the experience of making love. Not only that, the use of a French letter and the haste with which they were compelled to culminate their deed did little to stimulate a climax and they often came away vaguely disappointed, Lily in sulks and not far from weeping, leaning miserably on his arm as he saw her home. They would talk of the day when they could go to bed together in their own home and they would make up fantasy stories of how they would make love until he would feel himself harden afresh, but unable to take her as he wanted, he would himself be made miserable and frustrated.

They'd been going out together for a while now and he wondered if he should soon propose properly or just drift into it as they had been doing. The ring that would officially announce their engagement was an important item, but what ring? He couldn't afford much. What was Lily expecting? She often dragged him back in the midst of strolling along the road to gaze into a jeweller's. Her eyes would go immediately to the ring trays and she would point out those that had caught her eye, to his dismay mostly the expensive ones on the ten, fifteen, twenty-pound trays. His eyes would go guiltily to the three-to five-pound rings.

He wondered now, should he buy a ring and surprise her, or would she prefer they seek a suitable one together? The latter, he imagined. Lily was very particular. Tall, lithe, long-necked, graceful, beautiful of course, she took care with her appearance. Her nails were well manicured and never without pretty pink varnish, her lips tastefully rouged, eyebrows plucked. She wore delicate perfume, had her hair marcel-waved, suffering her locks to be tightly wound in hot metal curlers and strung up by wires to the electric gadgets on the hairdresser's ceiling for hours while the perm took. She chose her clothes with care and looked like a million dollars in them. He was proud to have her on his arm, delighted to see other men's heads turn as they passed, and women's too, their eyes brilliant with envy at her looks, her graceful movements.

Yes, Lily liked beautiful things, expensive things. Couldn't afford them, of course, but she made damned sure that what she did have came pretty well near to looking expensive. Resourceful to a point of fanaticism, she'd study all the latest fashions in magazines, then go out and buy the material and make them up. Lately she had taken up dreaming what sort of house she would like when she got married – the perfect house, nothing too ostentatious of course, but a nice little house she could furnish and titivate to her own taste. Well, he would do his best for her, but saving for a house like that started with not buying too expensive an engagement ring. Maybe tomorrow or Sunday he'd pop the question, formally. Then they might talk of money, sensibly.

Josie sat at the table reading her newest cowboy book she'd bought for her usual shilling every pay day. Mum said she was too old for such stuff and by now ought to have extended her reading to a bit of better literature. But cowboy books were full of handsome heroes doing marvellous adventurous things in the romantic Wild West, righting wrongs, seeing off the baddies, riding off into the sunset with the girl of their choice. They were strong, good, courageous characters and Josie loved to steep herself in their deeds.

Having helped Mum clear the table after Dad and Danny's dinner and helped wash up, her time was now her own. Coming to the end of a short exciting chapter, she glanced across at Connie. Instantly her eagerness to start the next chapter to see if Ward Gainer would struggle free of his bonds before the Indians returned to bury him up to his neck in sand for ants to devour, evaporated.

'It's time she snapped out of this brooding of hers,' Mum kept saying, not unkindly, only wanting her daughter to be happy again. 'It's not as if Ben had been her husband, even though she did love him so.'

Josie couldn't agree to that last bit. Ben had been as near to being Connie's husband as anyone could be. But she did agree to the first bit. Connie ought to snap out of it, for her own good. But it wasn't her business. Connie would come round in time. Shrugging off contemplation of Connie, Josie bent her head to her book again. But the tale had palled with the interruption. Her mind turned on to herself and the acknowledgement that she was feeling more than a little fed up.

Friday and nowhere to go. None of her friends were going out tonight, at least not with her. It had been like this for several weeks, because all of them had settled down with boyfriends now. Gone were the days of going out in a group looking for likely boys, and she was the only one left without a steady boyfriend. Of course there were plenty willing to take her out. She could have had her pick still. But somehow it wasn't the same any more.

It had been a couple of months since she'd last set eyes on Arthur Monk. She kept telling herself she'd got over him, but none of the boys she'd met since had pleased her, not one of them looked as handsome as Arthur. For all she tried to convince herself she *had* got over him, she thought of him all the time and kicked herself for having lost him the way she had. Numerous times she had nearly gone to humble herself and write to him but each time had quailed at the thought of his reply – if he replied at all. While she wasn't writing to him there was at least the lingering hope that when she did he'd ask her to go out with him again, but to get a negative, perhaps nasty reply would have dashed all those hopes once and for all.

A thumping on the back door brought her thoughts to an end. Danny sprang up from the settee, Dad hoisted himself out of his chair to retrieve his muddied boots from the outhouse. Josie could hear him grunting as he thrust his stockinged feet into them.

'See you later,' Danny called from the rear door, which closed with a bang. The two men made their way back down to their cockle shed from whose open door steam would be issuing along with the steam from many of the others, a gathering of cocklers already calculating the profit from their day out on the mud flats. At this moment the fishy smell of steaming cockles from those sheds already operating was wafting on the air past the small row of houses. The men would work into the night, coming home Sunday morning.

By Sunday afternoon a different crowd would gather, the August trade, holidaymakers and day trippers savouring the delicious feast from little crude pottery bowls with pepper and vinegar or bearing away a bagful for their Sunday tea back home. August trade was always a good one for cockle people, and made up for the slightly leaner winter months when the only customers were from Billingsgate Market in London. But the tiny shellfish were always in demand. Cockling families never really had poverty staring them in the face, not like the shrimping families whose existence these days was far more precarious.

The reflection made Josie think momentarily of Pam and wonder for a moment how she was. But her book became suddenly more important, lying there still open at the next chapter. She couldn't go bothering herself with other people's problems. She even steeled herself determinedly against her own, and buried her head again into her book.

Ward glanced around him, saw the jagged edges of rock lying scattered around the foot of the nearby butte ... if he could wriggle to them, sever the bonds on his wrists – he might tear flesh from his arms in doing so but it was a better fate than that awaiting him. Would he do it in time before those savages returned? Ward began to ease his prone body towards the butte ...

Josie shivered deliciously, savouring her hero's courage in the face of pain and danger; all else forgotten.

Alone on this lovely Sunday morning, Connie trudged up the steep hill amid a scattering of other early worshippers going towards St Clement's church. Alone among the as-yet sparse congregation she entered, eyes down lest she glance inadvertently to distant Southend with its long jutting pier beyond which Ben had lost his life. The water looked as still and benign on this day as on that one, the resort as busy and joyful as ever in August, life there going on oblivious to that one beloved life it had taken from her. Had she swam that day he might still be alive ...

Grateful for the dimness of the church interior, Connie found a pew and knelt on a ready hassock, its hand-embroidered cover faded from long use. It felt dusty, grubby, unwashed. The church smelled dusty too, overlain by the taint of ancient wood, old bibles and stale incense. People still entering immediately lowered their voices to a whisper so that the air sighed with what they had left to say to each other.

Connie remained silent. She had no need to speak, no one to speak to. Lowering her head upon her clasped hands, closing her eyes in dark absorption, she sought to pray. But for what? Pray for Ben that he was in heaven? Where else would he be – good, honest, generous Ben? Pray for his parents that they would be succoured in their grief? But grief was natural and they shouldn't be deprived of it by a well-meaning girl seeking to ask God to forbid them that human luxury. Pray for her own family? They hardly needed her prayers, except perhaps Pam. She prayed for Pam, that her child be born whole and well, for her to be delivered of it safely, for her and George to be a little better off, for Mum and Dad's hearts to be softened by the birth enough to take her back into the bosom of their family.

And herself? What did she want other than to have Ben back with her again? That was impossible. Pray to follow him and be with him instead – that too was futile. A small voice inside her whispered: You aren't ready to die, and she hated the voice because it was the truth and the truth wasn't what she wanted to hear.

To avoid it, she opened her eyes and looked up quickly, sensing someone's gaze on her. But she was shocked to note that someone's gaze was indeed riveted on her – that of the young curate she'd first seen when she and Ben had come to rehearse the wedding ceremony. He had been present during her every attendance since, but he mostly took no notice of her. He looked hastily away as she lifted her head and continued putting out the rest of the hymn books. She wondered now, had he not so much ignored her on earlier occasions as avoided her? It provoked a small shiver to be so much in someone's eye when all she wanted was to be left in peace to think her own thoughts, indulge in her own loneliness.

Bad enough Mum having a go at her every Sunday.

'You're doin' too much on this religion business,' she said in a voice of disapproval as Connie left this morning. 'You never used to go to church so often. It ain't natural for a girl your age, goin' to church every second of the day. It ain't good for you, Connie.' She might as well have been saying, find yourself another chap.

Connie sat back in her seat as the organist began softly to play and more people filed in to the pews, the air filling with their

161

whispering and the rustling of hymn and prayer books. The smell of dust mingled with the faint perfume of rose water and lavender, of Sunday best brought out of moth-balls for this one day of each week. The curate had finished doling out his hymn books and was putting up the hymn numbers for this Sunday.

Connie watched him reaching up to the wooden slots, his arms raised to slot in the numbers. He looked tall and lithe, the black cassock he wore making him seem thinner than he was. He had a nice face, open, smooth, gentle. Connie looked away as he turned, settled her gaze on the chancel as the organ music swelled and she stood with the others to receive the priest and choir now moving with measured and swaying dignified grace down the aisle towards the altar, the great cross held before them. She watched it pass, and so began this morning's service and she thought no more about the curate.

'George!'

He sat up in bed, suddenly, coming awake with a start. 'What?'

She knew he was constantly on edge and alert these final days of her pregnancy, but his abrupt rise from deep sleep made her start for all the moment was urgent.

'What is it? Has it started?'

'No, love. But the alarm didn't go off. You're late for work.'

It hadn't needed an alarm to awaken her, the kick the baby had given her had been responsible. Such a kick it had made her instantly wonder if this was her time. But it hadn't been. Just that one kick low down in her stomach and then a lot of lazy flexing of tiny limbs, unseen but imagined.

Smiling at the thought of the life inside her that two weeks from now would be lying in her arms, she had glanced at the clock and been shattered that it was quarter to seven. George should have been up and washed by now.

He no longer helped his dad on the boat except for Sundays. There was little enough money in it lately for his parents to live on, let alone him and her. When a little job had come up, a bit of building work, he'd jumped at it first and thought about it afterwards. His father had been somewhat taken aback, hurt even, but had understood that with a baby on the way, money was needed. The shrimping business had suffered after a cold winter and spring. The shrimps sought deeper, warmer water, even burying

162

themselves in the sea floor out of reach of nets. The Wall Street Crash of last year had begun to make itself felt in Britain; unemployment was growing.

George had been lucky to land this job. But being late could cost him that job as easy as winking with dozens waiting in the queue to jump into it. Nineteen thirty hadn't so far been a good year for the working man. If George lost this job what would they do, the baby coming and all?

Panic had consumed her. Her first impulse had been to leap out of bed, calling to him as she hurried to put the kettle on for a cup of tea and start on his breakfast. But she was too large in the stomach for that, too cumbersome, too near her time to take chances.

George had sunk back. 'Oh, God, that all? I thought you'd started.'

'No such luck.' She laughed briefly, then sobered, glancing again at the alarm clock that hadn't gone off. 'Come on, love, hurry up. You mustn't be late.'

He was out of bed in an instant, urgency taking the place of relief that she was still not ready. She was having the baby at home. Hospital treatment had to be paid for. A midwife and one visit from the doctor if needed was far cheaper. He had the money for it saved in a biscuit tin, along with the rent, neither to be touched at any cost.

Pam struggled slowly to a sitting position, eased her legs out of bed. They were swollen, as they had been all this last month. They worried her a bit but the baby seemed lively enough, so she cast aside the concern for her own self. So long as George's baby came whole into the world, it was all she wanted. She often thought that if anything bad should happen with the birth, all the sacrifice she had made in marrying the man she loved, hoping to mend the rift between two families, would have been for nothing. Then she'd push the thought aside angrily. George was all she really wanted and they could always have another baby. But this one seemed more important than anything else.

Now she came to life. Getting to her feet she waddled in her nightdress to the stove and lit the burner under the kettle.

'No time for that,' George called, coming back into the flat after running down to the bathroom, feeling his chin after a scrape round with the razor. In his haste he had left a patch of bristle but there was no time to remedy it as he struggled into his work clothes. 'I'll grab a mug at break time.'

'There's your sandwiches,' Pam said. Her stomach had begun to ache a little, a hardly detectable throb. 'It's a good job I always do them overnight, that's all I say.'

A quick kiss on her cheek and George was gone. She heard him race down the bare wooden stairs, already ten minutes late for the bus he should be catching on the corner. The journey took half an hour to Southend where they were building new council houses to take the overflow of people looking to get out of East London for more open spaces, the current whim of city people. If George missed that bus he'd have to wait another ten to fifteen minutes for the next one. He would definitely be late. Pam prayed as his footsteps faded away, then turned to put out a cup for herself. She'd have a slice of bread and jam for breakfast, save George's egg for tomorrow morning.

All morning as she tidied their home, made herself a sandwich of bread and cheese for lunch, then lay on the bed for an hour, the ache in her stomach persisted, not much but becoming more noticeable, seeming to creep around to her back at times. By afternoon it had become a real nagging ache that became more pronounced when she made to get up off the bed. It would go. She'd probably strained herself this morning getting up just a little too fast for all her care.

She was still lying on the bed when footsteps were heard coming up the last of the stairs, a trudging sound. She wondered who it could be this time of the afternoon. Not Josie. Josie was at work. So was Connie. For a second she thought of Mum and her heart gave a little leap of hope. But instead of a tap on her door, it opened and George stood there.

Pam sat up in surprise, wincing at the sharp pain in her belly. 'What you doing home? You've an hour yet before you come home.' It was a nonsensical statement but he didn't smile. His face was expressionless.

'Lost me job,' he said, his voice that of a man worn out from a long day's hard graft. 'Six minutes late. Someone jumped in two minutes before I got there. Foreman said he couldn't wait in case I didn't turn up at all.'

'Oh, George.' Pam felt the tears well up from the pit of her

stomach as though about to consume her completely, so strong
was the disaster she saw before them.

'I've been wandering around Southend and Westcliff all day
looking for something, but there ain't nothing. Nothing at all.'

Pam stared at him. 'Oh, love, what're we going to do?'

'I don't know. I just don't know.' She watched him sink down
on a chair like a man suddenly bereft of muscle, and felt the same
herself.

Chapter Sixteen

The pains persisted through the weekend; if getting no better at least getting no worse and as Monday came round she put it down to the way she had clambered out of bed on Friday, a bit less carefully than she should have done in her panic to get George off to work. All a waste of time, he'd lost his job anyway. Six minutes late. It didn't seem fair. Clusters of unemployed hung about building sites and everywhere else like hungry vultures, showing no scruples about jumping into a man's job the second he tripped up. The dole queues grew every day. Yet some people could still afford day trips to resorts like Southend. And here she was, cooped up in this tiny two-roomed flat with a husband out of work.

George under her feet when he wasn't hunting for work made the place even more cramped, practically claustrophobic. She longed for somewhere to go to get away from it, but even if there had been someone she could have gone to see, the weight of her stomach and the nagging pain in it would not have let her go far.

George's parents came on Monday as they often did, and, as they often did, looked around themselves at the cramped rooms with constant glances of guilt that they were unable to do more for their son and his wife. It would have been better to have said nothing, but his mum couldn't keep her thoughts to herself. A small, thin, prematurely wrinkled woman, with a head of exceptionally light grey hair that spoke of once-blonde locks, she seemed to relish the worst side of most things – what some people would term a Job's comforter. Pam had the measure of her by now, a woman who lorded it over her husband, he a follower who did all she told him, who took her advice, had probably taken her

166

advice in not attempting to heal the rift between himself and Dad long ago. In fact, Pam saw Milly Bryant as the sort of person who would actually get satisfaction out of being an enemy. Pam was sure of it as she continued to regard their humble habitat.

'No place to bring up a baby, this. Only got a week to go now, ain't you? You should've got somewhere better to live than this. Lord knows me an' George's father did our level best for you, what we could do under our circumstances. But . . .' the rest of the sentence going unsaid, accompanied by a long intake of breath, a shake of the head and a slow significant shrug.

'We're OK here,' Pam lied, smiling. 'It's not too bad. Don't have to do so much cleaning in a small place, and the way I am at the moment I can do without that.'

She had tried to make light of it, a joke, but Mrs Bryant wasn't done yet. She sat stirring the cup of tea Pam had handed to her. 'Nice if you'd had a bit of help from other sources, I say. But . . .' Again the rest allowed to go unsaid, the sigh, the shake of the head, the shrug of the shoulders. Milly Bryant was adept at leaving sentences hanging meaningfully. Pam knew what she was getting at: her own parents' lack of assistance, though this woman for all her apparent conviction hadn't courage enough to finish what she was implying. Just digs and references, leaving nothing for one to say in defence. Pam hated it.

'We're doing all right,' she said again, but the woman's dig had her thinking about her family which at most times was only too easy to do.

There had been an effort at contact from her mother – a letter from her some time in early July. Still blistering under the way she had been treated by her own parents when she'd needed them most, unable to forgive them, a feeling she thought at times would never subside, she had torn up her mother's letter unopened in a fit of rage that she dared to write after all that had happened, regretting her action only when the dustmen came and emptied the communal bin in which she had thrown it. Mum hadn't written again and her own chances of healing the rift had receded even further.

But bitter as she was against her own people, that bitterness turning itself inward so that she hated herself more for having such feelings, it wasn't for some outsider to criticise her own flesh and blood.

'How's the work?' Dick Bryant was asking his son.

Pam saw George redden, knew he hadn't told his father about losing his job. George had spent Sunday with his dad on the boat, for once bringing in a relatively good haul. He had come home excited at his share of the profit which would come as a small godsend during the week when the catch was sold.

'Work?' she heard him echo as she listened to his mother going on about what baby clothes did she have ready for the birth.

'The building lark,' Dick Bryant reminded him. 'I'm sorry, son, you havin' to do jobs like that. You're a fisherman, like me. But trade just ain't there. Some on us shrimpers is havin' to go out of business altogether. But your mum intends us to hang on as long as we can. Things'll get better in a year or two if we hang on.'

'Yes,' George said as his dad glanced across to his tight-faced wife for confirmation. He was a small man, once agile but now become bowlegged, which made him even smaller. Pam wondered how her father could have socked him on the jaw all those years ago and kept his self-respect. Even today Dad, a well built man, stood at least five inches taller than Dick Bryant. According to legend, Dick Bryant had made some nasty remark, but that was no reason for a big man like Dad to belt into a man several inches shorter and quite a bit lighter than himself. No wonder the man had gone creeping off in the dark to get his revenge. Though burning down someone's livelihood had been unjustified, she had to admit, no matter what the cause. Yet she found herself liking George's father. He seemed a man who wouldn't say boo to a goose, not now, not then.

'As soon as things get better,' he was saying, 'you and me, we'll take out the boat together, an' you can get shot of the job you're doin', son. Ain't no job for a born fisherman.'

George's blue eyes had brightened suddenly. 'What if I pack the job in and come on board with you permanently again? We could make a go of it.'

His father shook his head sadly. 'Not a chance, son. I couldn't pay you.'

'But we did well enough yesterday.'

'Drop in the ocean. A fluke. It's like that sometimes as you well know. A spell of fine weather and up come the shrimp into shallow water, just askin' to be taken. A week later, back comes the cold an' out they go again. An' there's the competition, everyone trying to get at 'em. An' what with all the oil in the estuary nowadays, shrimp like clean water. It's a lost cause, son. You're probably better off doin' what you're a-doin'. Me, I'm too old to give up and go into something else. I'll stay in it till I'm in me box I expect.'

'Dick!' Milly Bryant turned on him, then turned back as Pam gasped at a sudden sharp pain in her womb. 'My guess, Pam, is you'll be havin' that child in the next couple of days, if not tomorrow. George, you'd do well gettin' hold of that midwife, alertin' her to what's to happen in a day or two.'

'This business'll see me in me box afore long,' Dick mumbled to himself and had his wife turn on him again.

'Dick!'

Josie's Sunday had been a miserable one. Fed up to the back teeth with nowhere to go, no friends to go out with, she felt left on the shelf.

'It's a lovely day,' Mum had said. 'You should be out, a lovely day like this.'

Mum didn't understand, when Josie had told her that all her friends had begun courting, and had voiced what seemed to her the simple solution.

'Then go out and find some more friends. Look up some of them you used to know at school. Some of them could be at a loose end. Better than moping around here all day. Ain't healthy.'

She said that a lot these days. 'Ain't healthy.' About Connie and her new preoccupation with church. 'Too much religion. It ain't healthy. That girl's moping and she ought to be snapping out of it. I know we're all sorry for her. Terrible thing to happen to her, my heart goes out to her every day to see her, but she's still young. She'll find someone to take poor Ben's place one day. Can't go on living in the past, her with all her life ahead of her. Moping about going to church won't help her. But what can you say. It ain't healthy.'

'Go for a walk,' she said as she put the meat into the oven for their Sunday's dinner. 'Get a bit of air into your lungs. Staying indoors on a lovely day like this, you'll make yourself ill.'

She hadn't wanted to go out only to see other girls her age arm in arm with their boyfriends or fiancés. In desperation she'd sat down that afternoon and had written a short letter to Arthur, had posted it this morning and now waited in a fever of anticipation for his reply.

With the tide well out, and plenty of cockles to pick, Danny, out on the smooth sand with Dad and his uncles, thought of his Sunday with deep satisfaction.

He had come to a decision. He wouldn't go buying Lily a ring and presenting it to her out of the blue, like they did in films. On Saturday he had taken her to the pictures, the resplendent Rivoli in Southend. They had sat in the cheaper seats – he had to be a bit careful with an engagement ring to buy, for all he'd been secretly saving for ages. In the film they'd seen, Greta Garbo had been presented with such a ring by a prospective suitor to her obvious delight, but it was all make believe. He couldn't see Lily being so overwhelmed except to say it wasn't quite what she'd have chosen especially as she'd be wearing it for the rest of her life and it didn't quite suit her fingers etc. He knew Lily well, and understood. So after they came out from the cinema he'd said, almost matter of factly: 'Lily, do you think it's about time we got engaged?' And when she had said, 'Ooh, Danny, please,' he had added, again casually, 'Then what about us going to choose a ring next Saturday if I'm not working?'

What had followed, in the darkness of her porch, had not been at all casual as they cemented their engagement prematurely.

Thinking about it as he worked the sand with the others, he could hardly wait for next Saturday to come. Already reckoning the tides ahead to next Saturday, it appeared they'd have plenty of time to go and buy the ring, display it first to her parents then his, both of whom were already anticipating a union.

'Oh, Danny! Darling! Look – that one there!'

The forefinger of Lily's right hand stabbed decisively at the window pane of the jeweller's shop. They'd spent all morning and part of the afternoon wandering up and down Southend High Street – Danny had balked at going into London as she would have wished with the prices they charged up there – and he reckoned they must have gazed into every shop there was.

Nothing seemed to satisfy her, and now he was hot from all this fruitless searching although Lily still seemed as fresh as a daisy and as equally excited and enthusiastic as she'd been when starting out.

'I'm looking for a special one, darling. It has to be a special one.'

By special, Danny could only see every last penny in his pocket disappearing. He had £12, the result of months of careful saving. He had hoped, in fact banked on a ring costing definitely no more than £7. A lovely five diamond cluster they'd seen had cost that. On an ordinary man's weekly wage of around thirty shillings, £7 was a ridiculous fortune to fork out. Something around £5 would buy a fine enough ring. But Lily was worth more than that.

The one she now pointed out flashed and glinted in the August sunshine. Danny peered doubtfully at the band of five diamonds; the centre one looking alarmingly huge. He was surprised to see only £7 on the price tag. Even so . . .

'It's a bit expensive,' he ventured. It was the wrong thing to have said.

'Oh!' The single word spelled pique.

'But if that's what you want,' he hastened.

Pique vanished like a spark falling on water. 'You mean I can have that?' Beaten, he nodded to her cry of, 'Oh, darling! Danny, I do love you!'

Fifteen minutes later they walked from the shop, her eyes glistening with tears of joy. On a bench at the end of the pier which for a moment had become their's as another couple got up and walked off, he ceremoniously slipped the ring on to the third finger of her left hand, and with sea breezes ruffling her hair and the hem of her skirt, kissed away her joyful tears.

Josie was over the moon. A reply to her letter must have been on its way almost at once after the postman slipped it through Arthur's letterbox. He had been thinking about her lately – coincidence he should get a letter from her – maybe they could meet in London – perhaps next Saturday – around twelve o'clock by the Salmon and Ball Pub on the corner of Cambridge Heath Road and Bethnal Green Road, just under the railway bridge there – perhaps go up town for the afternoon – could she let him know with a quick telegram if she agreed or not – would be nice to see her again.

That it was worded rather formally didn't seem to matter as

Josie hugged it to her. Only later as she hurried in a fever of joy to send off her answer did she think about the coolness of his reply, wondered if he'd had a string of girlfriends in her absence and had merely contemplated adding her to his list so he could fall back on it when needed. After all, he was so very good-looking, the best-looking boy she'd ever met. It was only his rough Cockney ways and speech that spoiled it. But then, girls in the East End he must have been going out with in the interval would have fallen over themselves to have him as a boyfriend. They, who spoke exactly as he did, would see nothing detrimental in it, only that he was a good catch.

Josie felt jealousy roll over her in a hot wave as she entered the post office; jealousy she firmly shrugged off, as, with heart braced, she worded her telegram carefully so as not to appear too eager.

'TIME AND PLACE SUITS ME FINE STOP JOSIE'

Brief, but all she could afford, and perhaps it was just as well not to appear too chummy as yet. She'd know one way or the other on Saturday how things stood between them. If it was the other then she'd have to dismiss him from her mind and get on with her life. This she told herself with stern determination. Trouble was, her heart was beating so fast after she'd sent the telegram – partly in misgiving that she had made a fool of herself, partly in a welter of doubt that she had cheapened herself in his eyes, partly from a overwhelming desire to see him again – and beat hard enough all that day to make her feel almost sick at the thought of Saturday, that determination didn't have a chance to come into it.

Her men out in the estuary, Josie and Connie at work, Peggy was left with time to think. She hated these times where others would have revelled in being alone for an hour or so out of the reach of a busy demanding family. But having time to think was a bane to Peggy. Visions of those no longer here plagued her. Annie, answering her letters, wrote regularly every fortnight, pages filled with the wonders of India yet, reading between the lines, that girl didn't seem quite as happy as she made out. It was more than homesickness, some unhappiness, she felt it, and that she was too far away to be reached caused Peggy untold heartache.

Then there was Pam. Living virtually around the corner she might as well have been as many thousands of miles away as

172

Annie. But it did not stop her thinking about Pam, which she did constantly, despite herself, thoughts of Pam invading her mind as involuntarily as breathing or the beating of her heart. It was in a fit of remorse one day in July that she had sat down and written to her.

She hadn't told Dan what she'd done – he'd have hit the roof. But men were able to hate far more easily than women. They did not have that maternal instinct natural to every woman to defend the fruit of her womb, even though she might deny it. Cast out her child in anger, ignore it all the days of her life, a mother would jump into a freezing river to save its life if the occasion called, and then paradoxically continue to ignore it so long as the hurt it had done lived.

Knowing Pam's time was only just a month away, Peggy had felt an instinctive pull in July to put aside all wrongs and make contact of some sort. The ache which had been slowly growing of its own accord practically from the moment Pam had walked out of the house, had suddenly become too much for her, and in a fit of impulse she had sat down and written the letter, seeing her daughter back with her again, all forgiven and forgotten.

Pam hadn't replied. The hope of a truce had been destroyed, and with it all Peggy's hopes of ever contacting her daughter again. But today, here in the house on her own, she thought of Pam, and several times felt on the verge of putting on her hat and going to see how she was. She condemned herself for letting the girl go as she had, for not even attempting to go and see her even though she knew if anything dire should happen news would travel to her with the speed of light. But each time the prospect of what she'd say when she got there, how she'd be received, the danger of opening the wounds even more, stopped her.

Peggy longed for her family to come back home and take the thoughts away in a round of busy family life, and by the time they did, it was too late to carry out all the intentions she'd had during the day.

On Thursday morning the twinges which had been niggling all week came on in earnest. Getting out of bed, Pam doubled up as a great wrench convulsed her middle.

Instinct alone would have told her this was the start of the baby's arrival had it not been for her mother-in-law predicting it with certainty to be imminent. 'I notice your stomach's dropped a lot. I bet you'll have it this week or I'm a Dutchman's uncle.'

So she knew this was the start. 'George! Get up, love! The baby's started.'

George, who had been sleeping the exhausted sleep of the despondent, awoke reluctantly. 'What d'yu'say?'

'The baby. I think it's ready to come.'

Fully awakened and instantly in a panic, he was out of bed. 'What do I do?'

'You've got to go and fetch the midwife.' It was all she could think for him to do. She too was on her feet, the wrenching pain already receding, leaving her to wonder if it had only been her imagination. Perhaps she only needed to go to the toilet. But the thought of getting herself down all those stairs to the lavatory on the floor below was daunting. Perhaps it was too soon to call out the midwife, who could charge for the wasted call.

'Hang on for a while,' Pam said, getting herself to one of the fireside chairs, still hanging on to her bulging stomach even though the pain had gone completely. 'It could have been a false alarm.'

The relief on George's face was evident as was the peeved expression that immediately followed it that he had been dragged from a deep sleep for nothing, but, bless him, he kept his opinion to himself. 'Shall I go back to bed again then? It's only seven o'clock. After all, I've nowhere to go, have I?'

She was about to say that he hadn't when another, somewhat lesser wrench began to build up, not enough to make her cry out but enough to send warning signals again to her brain. 'Oh, George, love, I don't know. I really don't. It's come back again. Perhaps you should go for the midwife, just in case.'

Visions of a child bursting from between her legs and damage – she wasn't sure what – being caused to both it and her made her decide. In her ignorance she saw only the threat of something dire if just she and George were here should it happen.

'No, get the midwife, George.' She would feel safer. 'Hurry!'

By the time he'd scrambled into his clothes and run out of the house unwashed, unshaved, the pains had gone. She felt a fraud. The midwife would arrive, see nothing amiss, and put the cost of the inconvenience on her bill, small as it was. But there was nothing Pam could do. She got up, made a cup of tea, and

174

was about to drink it when ghastly agony searing through her middle made her cry out and fall back in the chair, the tea spilling on to the lino.

Entirely alone, she was in a state of terror. She should have sent George to get his mother before going to the midwife so there could at least have been someone here with her.

A knock on her door brought a surge of grateful relief. 'Oh, come in – door's open.' But it wasn't the midwife. It was the woman who owned the house, her landlady, Mrs Carper.

Mrs Carper was a widow in her forties. Her husband had been killed towards the end of the last war as she was fond of telling everyone; sent to the front one month before its end and killed after only two weeks there. A tragedy, but twelve years had softened it. She was a sharp, lively woman, who took great pride in her looks, perhaps in the hope of one day finding herself another husband.

'I saw your George running out of the front door,' she said, coming forward to where Pam was sitting hunched in the creaky fireside chair, her arms still curled about her stomach. Gently she took the empty tea cup from her and put it on the table. 'I guessed what it was. I wondered if there was anything I could do for you. Keep you company perhaps?'

In gratitude, Pam looked up at the tall slim woman clad in a bright expensive-looking dress even at this time in the morning, her hair immaculate and her face made up as though she had spend hours on it. She even wore light orange nail varnish, the nails beautifully manicured, all the things Pam hadn't indulged in since her marriage. Even in the midst of a fresh stab of pain that now caught her, she felt envious of the woman's position in life, all but hated her for it where she herself had to exist in the squalid top flat of this house.

Who was she to come up here with her offer of help? Who did she think she was coming up here . . .

'Ohh . . .' A long drawn out groan of pain escaped Pam's lips, cut off all other thoughts. The woman's carefully made up face took on a worried look.

'Shouldn't you be in bed, my dear?'

'I would . . . if I could get there,' Pam sobbed erratically. 'I don't think I . . . I can m-o-v-e . . .' The last word sounded torn out of her in a mixture of pain and fear.

175

'Can I help you?'

'I just . . . want to stay . . . where I am.'

The pain was receding. Her breath coming easier, Pam wondered at herself for making such a fuss a moment before. She straightened in her chair, aware of the tea spilled on the lino. 'Can you make me another cup of tea? I'm so thirsty. This came on as I was getting out of bed. I wish my mother was here.'

'Shall I go for her?'

'No! No,' Pam added less harshly. 'She can't come.'

'Why not, dear?'

'She just can't.'

'What about your husband's mother? You should have someone here with you, not just me. Where does your husband's mother live?' Unthinking Pam told her the address and found herself devastated to hear her say as though she had found her niche in life: 'Oh, it's not far away. I'll go there myself and get her. We'll be back in two ticks.' And she was gone, the cup of tea Pam longed for unmade. She was alone again in the flat, terror beginning to fill her that if the pain started again she would have no one to help her.

In fact, Mrs Bryant was the first to arrive. Mrs Carper, tactfully, perhaps gladly, withdrew to leave them to it.

'Right,' Milly Bryant announced. 'Let's get you into bed. Midwives take their time, but she shouldn't be too long now. When did George go for her? I'm going to get you a cup of tea, with lots of sugar in it, help you keep up your strength. There now.'

Pam settled between the sheets. The kettle began to sing as she watched her mother-in-law gather a sheet from the cupboard in the corner, pull out a piece of water-proof American cloth used for lining.

By nightfall Pam was still trying to deliver her baby. A concerned midwife had detected it to be a breach birth if she couldn't turn it. All night she tried without success and by Friday morning Pam was in shock and growing weak with pain and the effort of it all. The doctor was sent for.

He looked concerned, rolled up his sleeves, washed his hands and arms in soap and water and, setting out his instruments, bent to his task. Downstairs in the parlour by kind courtesy of Mrs

Carper, George was beside himself, pacing to and fro, downing cups of tea she had made for him, trying to shield his ears against the cries of his wife above. His mother, banned from the scene, sat nearby, at a loose end. His father stood now at the open door to the garden taking in the morning sunshine and looking as if he wondered what he was doing here. His wife came to join him.

'Pam's exhausted. It don't look good. The doctor's working hard on her, but he's not very happy.' She was whispering, out of her son's hearing. 'Someone should go and let her people know. It's not right how they've treated their own daughter, but her mother should be told. Say if something happens to her?'

Dick Bryant gnawed his lip, worried that Milly was going to hurry off to bear the dire tidings, leaving him alone with his son should he find himself suddenly bereaved. He needed Milly by him. 'Who's to go?'

'We can't ask that Mrs Carper to do our errands for us. And I can't leave George at a time like this. I think it's best if you go.'

'Me?' Visions of meeting his old enemy flashed into his mind. But Dan Bowmaker would be out with his boat, though Dick as a fisherman was already reckoning the tides, which would be coming in by now. If he was quick, he'd get to the house before Dan Bowmaker, deliver his message to the mother and get off as quick as he could. Compared with being here alone with George, this choice might be the better of the two. 'OK, I'll go now.'

His wife nodded briefly and went back into the house where George still paced listening to Pam's weakening cries.

It was unfortunate. Knocking on the Bowmakers' door he received no reply. In a dither, unsure what to do, he knocked on the door of a neighbour. No reply there either. On a Friday women had all gone out shopping for their weekend food, what else. In desperation he turned to go back up the hill via Billet Lane, though why he should take that route he didn't know except that he was loath to go back and say he had failed to deliver his message.

Dick felt desperate. He had to tell someone in Pam's family. Perhaps he should have waited for her mother to come back from her shopping. But that could take a couple of hours, and God knows what would happen while he was waiting. Pam could die without one of her family being there. Milly would kill him.

Dick felt his heart beating sickeningly against his chest wall.

177

The only other course was to go and wait at the cockle sheds for Pam's father to come in with his boat. Feeling physically sick, he retraced his steps and turned down the path that ran past the cockle sheds. There he made his way down to the water's edge, empty cockle shells crunching under his boots, the familiar stink of rotting cockle flesh filling his nostrils.

He stood there a second, his heart fluttering. The tide was flowing into Leigh Creek at walking speed, trickling into gullies, around raised patches of mud. Soon it would engulf them. A fleet of cockle boats was coming in too. They'd come to rest off shore and the men would put out long boards from the boats to dry land, then with a basket full of shellfish slung from a sturdy wooden yoke would negotiate those springy boards to the beach, no mean feat with the baskets weighing between them something over a hundredweight. Men like these had muscles. Dick thought of Dan Bowmaker's muscles and felt his own quiver. But someone in Pam's family must be told of her plight.

He watched the *Steadfast* moor up in the fast filling creek. No one on board seemed to have noticed him here. Almost grateful he stood his ground, though his knees shook. What he really wanted was to leave, but he didn't.

He was trying to make himself look small as Dan manoeuvred the yoke across his broad shoulders, the two wicker baskets at each end swinging heavily. Stepping on to the planks he swung his way along, head bent, watching his step, each hand supporting a well-filled basket as he came on.

Dick felt a prick of envy that the pickings were always so good. No lean months for these people as there were for shrimpers, and shrimpers worked a lot harder, forever chasing the elusive shrimps, here today and Harwich tomorrow. And all people like Dan Bowmaker had to do was go out at low tide and bloody well scrape up a bit of mud for their livelihood. It wasn't fair.

He watched Bowmaker reach the centre of the springy planks, his son about to clamber overboard with his load. He saw Bowmaker look up briefly, heard the hiss of his intake of breath as Dick went forward to convey his urgent news. The man, taken off guard by the sight of him, let his foot go forward unguided. It caught the edge of the plank. Bryant saw him stagger under the weight of the baskets, topple forwards, then sideways.

The movements were almost clownish. Bryant heard one or two

men nearby chuckle a little. He too felt nervous mirth rise up in his throat, sweeping away his previous trepidation. The man did look comical, his old enemy tottering about like a comedian on a stage, baskets swinging wildly on their yoke as Bowmaker tried to regain his balance to no avail.

He seemed to fall slowly, helpless under the weight of the baskets, until as though at last coming to a decision on which way to land, his foot slid over the opposite side of the plank sending him backwards across it, his legs in the mud on one side, his head plowing into it on the other.

Bryant heard the chuckling die as the fallen man was seen not to be moving, the baskets lying on their sides half emptied of their contents, the thick heavy wooden yoke across his chest, his eyes staring, turbid fingers of tide beginning to cover the mud to seep gently around his head.

Chapter Seventeen

'Dad!' Danny, standing at the gunnels of the boat, let his own load fall from his shoulders on to the deck. 'You all right?'

It was a silly question. No movement came from the man below him, the pale blue eyes staring apparently sightlessly up at the sky. In seconds he was over the side, dropping down into the mud beneath its thin covering of water with a splash, to plough through it towards his father.

It hadn't been a big fall, twelve inches or so, normally no more than an annoyance to a man measuring his length in soft mud. Dan would have reared up, roaring, ready to vent his fury on the man who'd sent him off balance with his sudden appearance. But with a heavy yoke on him burdened down by its unsteadily swinging baskets, each a dead weight, it had the power to snap a man's neck as easily as if he'd fallen thirty feet.

Danny's shout had added to the concern of those offloading the other two bawleys, their laughter already falling silent. Dropping their loads, they hurried forward, coming to see what was up as Danny knelt in the slowly deepening water beside his father.

Helping him push the yoke aside, several of them eased Dan off the planks so that he could lie flat. Danny lifted his father's head on to his knees, clear of the incoming tide.

On the shore, Dick Bryant was looking on helplessly. 'Is he all right, son? Anything I can do?'

Danny looked up, his eyes darkly brittle. 'You've done enough, you. Go on, sod off! Or I'll come an' belt you meself.'

'I only came to say your sister's having her baby. It don't look good.'

'I said, sod off!' Danny bent his head again to his father. 'Come on, Dad, wake up.'

The blue eyes focused, swivelled to the face of his son. The weather-battered lips twitched into a grin. The voice came low. 'Looks like I made a bloody fool of meself.'

'Are you hurt?' Danny asked, full of relief, and saw the brows knit.

'Legs feel a bit funny.'

There were men all around them now. Whether Dick Bryant was with them or had made himself scarce, Danny wasn't much caring so long as his dad was all right.

'What d'you mean, funny?'

'Just funny. Can't proper feel 'em. Jarred meself. But I'm OK. Just help me up out of this damned water.'

As requested, Danny put his hand under his father's shoulders, began to lift him to a sitting position where he'd be able to stand on his own, but the body felt heavy, limp, there seemed to be no muscle power there. He saw his father wince with pain and immediately stopped trying to move him.

'Come on, Dad, help me get you up, or we'll both drown sitting here.' He said it in jest but already a light was dawning in his brain, one that had begun to put the fear of God into him. It echoed in his voice. 'Dad, move yourself, for God's sake.'

'I can't, son.' There was fear in those words too.

Someone crouched down beside Danny, the water around his ankles, and whispered in his ear.

'We best get 'im on shore, lad. An' one on us oughter go an' call an ambulance. Yer dad's bad hurt, I'd say. I'd say he could of broke his back.'

It was only echoing what had already gone through Danny's mind. He let his father lie back down again as several men moved forward, between them tenderly, gently, lifting the helpless body, a heavy man needing six of them to do the job with care, one of them supporting a suspected injured back as best he could. Laid carefully down on a flat piece amid the rattling, tinkling mountains of shells, they tried to make him comfortable. He, his teeth clenched against the pain that moving him had caused for all their care, his face a grey colour, kept his eyes screwed tight shut, perhaps not to reveal the knowledge they held as well as pain.

'You'll be all right, Dad,' Danny kept saying, thinking of Mum,

181

no doubt at this moment out shopping, blithely oblivious of the drama going on a few hundred yards from her home. Connie and Josie would come in at lunchtime, all unsuspecting of the prospect that possibly lay ahead with Dad in hospital, paralysed. And . . . Danny put aside the family feud that had encompassed his own sister Pam, who had thought she'd been doing something constructive in marrying George Bryant . . . Pam should at least be told.

He suddenly, vaguely, remembered Dick Bryant's words as he told him to sod off. What was it? Pam in labour? Didn't look good?

It had to be something bad to make Dick Bryant come here seeking Dad. Why hadn't they been alerted to the closeness of the birth sooner than this? But, of course, Pam has been slung out, hadn't she? Stupid attitude to take. He, Connie and Josie still went occasionally to see her to show that they had no axe to grind. The last time he'd seen her had been three weeks ago. She had seemed all right then if a bit like an elephant around the middle, waddling about the little flat she and her husband rented. He'd spoken of it to Mum but she'd gone quiet, had changed the subject. But she should have known when Pam was due. Even if she chose to ignore it, word should have been got to her prior to this. He found himself blaming Pam's in-laws, the Bryants. Easy to blame someone else. And George her husband too – a letter at least would have been decent of him if he hadn't the gumption to come round in person.

Danny returned his attention to Dad. He'd opened his eyes again, but his legs lay as they had been when he had been placed down on the ground. And when Danny reassured him, 'You're gonna be all right, Dad,' he merely turned his head towards him with a wan smile and closed his eyes again in a sort of waiting, as they all waited, milling around unsure what to do. Once he spoke, as though to himself.

'Bloody Bryant – wants to see me in me grave, do he? And then he'll dance on it? Ain't agoin'ter give 'im no chance o' that. I'll see 'im there first.'

Otherwise he said little else, not even when Danny said, 'He came to say Pam's having her baby and that she ain't doing too good havin' it, Dad.'

Pam knew little of the birth, waking up in hospital, confused and woozy from anaesthetic. After the dim light of the room in which she had begun labour white light dazzled her, bleary though she felt as she opened her eyes to three hazy faces gazing down at her.

One was that of a nurse, distinguished by her cap and white clothing. Pam's eyes, focusing within seconds, picked out first her mother-in-law, then her husband. She came fully awake, realising with a start where she was.

'George.' She tried to rise but her stomach hurt so across the middle, like something pulling at the skin, stretching it with a pricking sensation that wasn't pleasant. She lay back weakly. 'Oh, George. How'd I get here?'

She realised that his hand was holding hers. 'The doctor had to send for an ambulance. You couldn't get the baby out.'

'Oh, no!' She realised the worst now. She'd lost the baby. They'd had to take her to hospital because she had been so weak, near to dying herself. It had felt like it, no strength left in her even to scream from the pain of trying to deliver it. She recalled vaguely hearing the doctor saying, 'She hasn't a chance of delivering it . . . growing too weak . . .'

She had known little after that, except for a feeling of floating, hands bearing her along, downwards, of swinging about, of lying on something hard and being swayed from side to side, strange faces looking at her, bright lights, then nothing.

She felt wretched, empty, destroyed. 'Oh, darling, I'm sorry. I lost it.'

'The baby?' He was smiling down at her. 'Turn your head a bit. This way. Take a look.'

Doing as she was told, she saw the crib by the bed, so close she could have reached out and touched it had she the strength and the stitches not pulled. She realised now that the pulling meant stitches. From her angle, though she was propped up by pillows, she couldn't see properly into the crib but she saw the mound within it, a cosy little mound that moved from time to time.

'It's a girl, Pam. We've got a baby daughter.' George's voice was in danger of breaking. She thought he was near to tears. 'She's doing all right, Pam, and so are you. Mother and daughter doing fine.'

'It was a breach,' Mrs Bryant's voice cut in sharply, but her son took no notice of the interruption.

'The doctor couldn't turn her so he sent for the ambulance. They did a . . . Caesari . . . thing section, they called it – opened up your tummy and got the baby out that way. Isn't it wonderful what they can do? They said you'd never've brought her into the world on your own. But she's perfect. They say she weighs eight pounds twelve ounces. They said it's very big for a girl. I think she's a-goin'ter be tall, like you. Well made, like your dad.'

He had been gabbling, now he paused. 'I'm sorry we couldn't get any of your family here.'

Pam had been regarding the bundle in the crib all this time. Now she lay back on the pillows, staring at the walls, her eyes filling with tears. 'I didn't expect them to come. They don't want anything to do with me, not even interested in their own grandchild, their very first grandchild. I'll never forgive them. I don't care if I never see them again.'

George said something to the nurse who said something back and he turned to Pam, quickly interrupting her. 'The nurse says you can hold your baby if you want. So long as you're careful. The stitches, y'know.'

Wordlessly, wrapped in her own misery about her uncaring family, Pam nodded, had the bundle laid gently in her arms by the hovering nurse who folded back the hospital shawl from the tiny screwed up red face with such tenderness it might have been her own child.

'There you are, dear. Isn't she beautiful?'

Pam tilted her head, drawing in her chin to look down at her new daughter. Red-faced she might be; grimacing she might be, the little mouth already seeking nourishment, the eyes alternately opening to slits and screwing tight shut again, the head being turned this way and that, but the nurse was right, she was beautiful. Pam saw Connie in the tiny, working face. If she grew up like Connie she would be beautiful indeed. She looked a bit like Annie too. But then they were sisters, her new baby's aunts.

Perhaps it was anaesthetic that made her so, but she thought of Connie and of Annie – Connie, the man she'd so loved taken from her and Annie thousands of miles away, maybe never to come home again – and she let herself dissolve into weeping, her head bent over her child who would never be visited by her parents, its grandparents, as if the child too must be blamed for her mother's actions, just as they had all been expected to take up their father's feud with a man who had wronged him long before they were

184

born. At that moment she hated her parents as she had never hated anyone before.

'They wouldn't come even when I was in danger,' she sobbed against the baby's head, its warmth penetrating the flesh of her wet cheek. 'Not even my own mother.'

George was gripping her hand as it lay over the baby. 'They couldn't,' he whispered. 'Something happened that stopped them. There was an accident.'

Mrs Bryant's voice cut through his whisper like a sharp knife through butter. 'Your father had an accident. All because he can't abide my husband. The man's eaten up with enmity against us. He'll never see it wasn't planned. He don't want to see. In my opinion he deserves all he . . .'

'Mum!' George said, the terse command shutting her up.

He turned back to Pam, who suddenly felt bewildered and alarmed. His hand tightened its grip on hers as she cried out, 'What's happened? What's wrong? What d'you mean, accident?'

'You dad had a bit of fall. I don't think it's bad but they did take him to hospital – this hospital.'

While Pam cuddled her baby ever closer to her, concern for her father growing steadily, he told her all that his father had told him of the incident; how he'd gone to fetch her mother but had not found her in, so seeing the cockle bawleys coming in on the tide had gone to the sheds to meet her father; how he, furious at seeing Bryant there, had slipped, the laden baskets of shellfish making him fall awkwardly.

'Dad said he didn't know what to do,' George went on. 'He just backed off while they carried your dad to the shore and an ambulance came to take him to the hospital. Your family is here, but round your dad's bed.'

'What's he done to himself?' Pam's question was hardly a whisper.

'While you were asleep I went over to find out. I didn't go into the ward, didn't want to start another row. But I explained the situation to the ward sister and she said you're not to worry, your dad's not in any danger. Except that is . . . well, he's injured his back. They didn't tell me how bad it was, but at the moment he can't move his legs.' Trying to lessen the blow for her, he hurried on. 'It's probably just temporary until they sort him out. But as I wasn't immediate family, so they said, even though I explained

185

about you, they wouldn't tell me any more. But you're not to worry, darling.' Pam was crying. 'He'll be all right.'

'I want my mum,' she sobbed, getting steadily more distraught.

George gave his mother a despairing glance and she hurried off in search of a nurse to help calm the girl.

'Where is her mother?' the nurse asked in surprise and frowned when told the situation. 'It doesn't matter what ill feelings there are,' she said briskly. 'This girl had just had a Caesarean section. She is worn out by a prolonged labour. She needs her mother. It doesn't matter what the circumstances.' She turned towards George. 'You say her father's injuries are not life-threatening, so for your wife's sake, go and find her mother. She need only stay a few minutes to comfort her. Tell her she is needed here. It is her duty to be here with her daughter.'

Ten minutes later Pam and her mother were holding each other in an embrace that could only speak of long lonely months of separation and the secret pain that had gone with it, each woman weeping quietly upon the other's shoulder as the past for the moment was put aside.

'Will you tell Dad?' Pam asked quietly as they moved apart, the other two people by the bed momentarily forgotten. 'About you coming here to see me?' She had already been informed that her father knew nothing of her mother's presence here. Mum had slipped away while the doctors were attending to her father, after hearing that his immediate condition wasn't as much a concern as his long-term condition might prove to be. She'd come to Pam's bedside already upset by Dad's accident and what might lie ahead of him, of them all. It had only taken her daughter's pale, wan face to send her weeping into her arms.

Now, having dabbed at her eyes with a handkerchief, she put it away in her handbag with an excessive amount of concentration on what she was doing, using that action as a shield against her reply.

'I don't think so, dear. Not yet.'

'He'll never forgive me, will he?'

'It's not that, dear. He's too ill at the moment to be bothered with other things. We've enough on our plate.'

There was silence between them, each alone with her own thoughts while George and his mother, relegated to a place far outside this reformed bond, stood back as spectators only. George gave his mother a warning look at the slightest sign of her making to interfere.

Pam watched her mother turn her attention to the baby, who had been put back in her crib. Peggy kept her eyes concentrated on the flexing bundle. 'What're you going to call her?'

There had been so many names passed back and forth between Pam and George during the pregnancy, a dozen boys' names and as many girls', she and George laughing over some of them while over others they had nodded, almost agreed, coming to a decision until dropping them for something that seemed even better. But now, Pam looked with tear-moistened eyes at her mother and said simply: 'Elizabeth. We'll call her Peggy.'

She saw her mother's eyes begin to glisten, her own too prickling afresh. She saw George's face split into a grin of agreement while behind him Mrs Bryant sniffed her plain disapproval of this sudden unequivocal reunion between a mother and daughter for so long estranged by the feud between the two families.

Josie had written another, sad, letter to Arthur Monk. Sad in two ways, because of the thought that Dad might never walk again, and because Arthur, expecting to see her yesterday, would have felt stood up. There had been no way to tell him on a Sunday and until her letter arrived today explaining what had happened, he would still be feeling angry and let down. She just hoped he'd understand.

She wasn't being unfeeling about Dad's accident. She was as worried as any of them. She loved Dad. Could not visualise him stuck in a wheelchair at the mercy of other people's dictates, unable to work any more, only half the man he had been. It made her cry every time she thought of how the doctor had taken Mum into a side office to speak to her at length.

She, Danny and Connie had stood outside, close together as though needing protection from some exterior force beyond their control. Through the window they had watched the man's lips moving, his head held at an earnest sort of angle towards Mum. Time and time again she had nodded. She'd had a handkerchief to her lips but she didn't seem to have been crying.

When Mum came out she had walked slowly from the ward and down the green and cream painted corridor. They all followed, not knowing how to ask what the surgeon had said, sensing it too dire

187

for her to tell them until she could keep her voice steady. A few yards along she'd stopped, allowing them to gather around her. Then she had spoken in a quiet controlled voice.

'It seems your dad won't be able to work, ever again. In fact . . .' she had paused and taken an easier tack. 'The doctor's told me they can't do anything for his back. I don't understand all he said. Bit over my head, I suppose. But we've got some hard times ahead of us with your dad. He said something about an upper lumbar spine what's been injured – something about a complete something-or-the-other of the spinal cord that they can't do anything about. They're watching him in case he develops some sort of bladder infection which'd be serious, so he's not out of the woods yet. But I'm afraid your dad's legs'll be paralysed for always. I'm going to have be with him everywhere, lift him about, get him in and out of a wheelchair and into bed, though he might be able to do that much for himself in time, and dress himself and that. It all depends on his strength of will, the doctor said. And your dad's got a lot of that.'

They had all listened in silence. Once or twice Danny had said he would always be there to help her with him, and Connie had nodded that she too would be there, and Josie herself had joined in the general encouragement, at the time firm about her own role in all this.

But after two weeks, doubts had set in. The bladder infection, though held at bay, was still the hospital's prime concern. They said it would take about six to eight weeks for him to have some sort of control over it. Meantime, he lay humiliated by the tube that ran from him into a bottle, a strong man brought low and belittled. The hospital had promised that in eight weeks he would be given a wheelchair; they spoke about his being sent home after that, that Mum should arrange for him to sleep on a sawdust bed which would give him support – they would explain to her later what this comprised, and of course he would have to sleep downstairs, no hope of him ever going upstairs again. They asked her if she could cope. Mum had lifted her chin and said yes she could, thank you very much. They had told her that in about three months things would be quite reasonable with him and he might even manage getting himself from the chair into his bed and out again, and one day even try to get around on crutches, again depending upon his willpower.

Meantime, morose and sullen, speaking little, he was aware without being told what his future would be. Josie wondered about all their futures. How would they live with him not working? They couldn't ask his brothers to keep them even though the *Steadfast* was jointly owned by the three of them. Obviously they would help, being family, but it would be like charity. Danny of course would become the breadwinner now, no question about it. He had already spoken of it, though out of Dad's hearing, had taken it as expected of him.

She posted her letter to Arthur and for the rest of the week waited for his answer. It didn't come until Thursday. Three wretched days during which she slowly came to realise that she was in love with Arthur – really in love. Going to work while she waited, the waiting made worse by not knowing if he would even reply, was misery, the most miserable three days of her life.

Each evening after work she visited Dad along with Mum. Sometimes Connie and Danny came, and sometimes Danny with Lily. Afterwards, she and Mum and Connie would pop along for a brief look in at Pam who was due to leave in a day or two. Her stitches had come out, and she was walking about the ward nursing her baby. Dad knew nothing of these calls. 'Best not to upset him,' Mum said.

He was obviously worrying deep inside about the future though he said little to anyone except Mum, and whatever he said to her she didn't divulge. It made visiting hours uncomfortable, as he remained silent while they tried to find something to talk about. There were long silences when Josie wished she could see Arthur, that things had been different.

She felt heartless thinking more of herself than Dad when the doctor in charge of his case spoke words they couldn't comprehend about the future: words that were supposed to cheer but rang only dire.

How could she think of spending time seeing Arthur while Dad was in this plight? Yet waiting for the letter that never seemed to come, she was falling more and more in love with Arthur.

On Thursday the letter she waited for arrived. Ripping it open Josie read the short note:

Dear Jo. Ever so sorry to here about your dad's acident. Shame we didnt meet on Sunday. I wated a long time but you never turned up and I went home. I wos upset but I understand why you didnt come. Hope your dads alrite. please rite and tell me. I still want to see you and hope we can meet soon. I miss you. I wuld like to see you everso much, can we make a date Sunday after next same place same time. Looking forwood to seeing you again. Sorry, I aint much of a writer. love. Arthur.

At least he'd spelled his name correctly. Josie clutched the letter to her bosom in an ecstasy of delight and forgave him, even loved him for his hopeless spelling. It made him dear to her. She could hardly wait to put pen to paper, send her reply flying off to him as quick as the post office could get it there. And she could hardly wait to see him again. This time even hell freezing over wasn't going to stop her.

Danny sat by his dad's bedside. 'I don't think you can come home yet, not until they say you can. You've got to be up and used to a wheelchair before they'll let you out. Mum can't lug you about. She's only a small person and you are a bit hefty, for all the accident.'

His father, flat on his back, glowered at him. 'I don't want this lot messin' about with me any more. Food here's bleedin' awful. What I want is a bit of your mum's cookin' inside me. Never been in hospital in all me life an' I don't intend being farted about with in 'ere for much longer.'

'But they're still keeping an eye out for bladder infection. And you've not got your functions under control yet. They've got all the ways and means to look after that. You can't ask Mum to do it. They wouldn't allow her to.'

His father's expression didn't alter; became even more belligerent at talk of his personal waterworks. Not only that, his present lack of bowel control left him unhappy. 'It's bleedin' humiliatin', young bits of stuff in uniform pullin' me about, lookin' at all me privates, puttin' a nappy on me like some soddin' baby in case I shit meself.'

'They're trained for that, Dad. You don't mean nothing to them. You're a case they have to see to.' Danny fiddled with the edge of the bed cover, that stiff board-like hospital material that seemed designed more to tie a patient down in a vice-like grip than keep him warm. 'They said you could be out in six weeks if all goes well.'

190

'*They* said.' Dan gave a harsh humourless explosion of a laugh. 'I could discharge meself anytime I please.'

'Dad, you've got to be patient.'

'Got to? Me, got to?' He dragged his hand away when his son tried to take hold of it and savagely tapped his own breast with a hard tight fist, his weather-beaten lips curling downward. 'I'm still me own master. Remember that. *I* say whether I've got to do *anything* or not.'

'It'd be unfair on Mum,' Danny pleaded. 'And I don't think you can really insist on leaving in your condition.'

'I don't want to be farted about with any longer,' came the reply.

So that was it. Danny came away to tell his mother that Dad had made up his mind to come home.

'Always was stubborn,' she said as she pulled their Friday dinner out of the oven. It still felt strange not to be cooking for him. 'Though what I'm going to do I don't know. How's he going to ever leave the house again when they bring him home? I'm going to have to push him about, him a heavy man. I won't be able to take him out, uphill to the shops or anything. It'll be like a prison for him, and me.'

'I could push him outdoors,' Danny offered. 'And anyway, they won't let him come home yet, no matter what he says.'

But she wasn't really listening as she contemplated a future that held only labour and care and an utter change to her life. 'We'll have to turn the downstairs back room into a bedroom for him. I can see meself doing everything for him.'

'He'll be able to do some things for himself, wash, shave . . .'

'And go to the toilet, and dress himself, and get in and out of bed?'

'The hospital will show him how to do all that before he comes home.'

'He's a proud man, your father. Him having to have other people do things for him, it'll cripple him . . .' She broke off, realising the cruel truth behind that thoughtless aphorism. She hurried on. 'I don't know what we're going to do, how we'll survive for money, him not able to work.'

'I'm here, Mum,' Danny said with a sense of effrontery that she had not once considered him, twenty-eight years old, capable of supporting this family. 'What d'you think I'd be doing? Sitting here on me backside?'

191

She turned to him. 'You've your own life to lead, Danny. We couldn't expect you to support us all.'

'Why not?'

'Because . . . well, apart from the bit you give me for house-keeping, what money you get from the business is yours. You're not like a married man, all your money going out. You're a free agent.'

'If I got married I wouldn't be.'

'That'd be different, going into it with your eyes open. But I'd never ask you to keep us.'

Danny got up from the table where he'd been sitting, knowing the tide would soon be on the turn and he and his uncles ready to take the *Steadfast* out to the cockling grounds. Things had to go on, with or without Dad. 'Then let's say I'm volunteering to take Dad's place. He'd expect that.'

And he'd tell Lily what he'd decided. They'd get married as soon as possible and live here. Mum would need an extra pair of hands with Josie and Connie at work.

Chapter Eighteen

It was good to get away from it all. Mum stayed in the hospital all afternoon, coming home to make a tea that was no longer up to her usual standard, since she gave herself hardly any time to make it, and went back again to the hospital to spend nearly half the evening there with Dad. She came home on a late bus worn out, to go straight to bed after a cup of cocoa and a cheese sandwich.

Josie longed for the old days back again. It had been three weeks since Dad's accident. Connie had gone with Mum on several occasions after work. Josie herself had gone only three times, a trundling journey by bus, a long sit by Dad's bedside, bored stiff with the same old conversation, which consisted of him grumbling, Mum reassuring, as he talked about the rotten hospital food, the way the nurses were treating him, and she tried to fill in the gaps with home trivia. Josie was glad it was Saturday.

No Saturday morning work loomed this week. She now did alternate Saturdays as assistant receptionist at the Cliffs Hotel. She was going up to see Arthur, meeting as they had done twice already, at the Salmon and Ball Pub, under the railway arch on the corner of Bethnal Green Road and Cambridge Heath Road. The weather remained pretty warm for mid-September so they might take a walk in the park if Arthur was strapped for cash. Half of his money went to keep his mum, his younger brother helping too. His sister was still at school. Sitting on the train, Josie mused that the same sort of fate was befalling her own brother, keeping the family, with Connie helping, and her too, a bit.

Yes, it was good to get away from it all. With a heart that

seemed to renew itself with each mile the train travelled towards London, she turned her thoughts away from family problems towards Arthur.

Three times she'd seen him. That day in April when she'd been stupid enough to leave him standing to go off with some fancy bloke had been put well behind her. She wouldn't do that again in a hurry. Arthur was worth fifty of them sort of people, she had learned now.

He was there waiting for her as she got off the bus from Fenchurch Street, the train having got her into London just before twelve. He looked so tall and handsome in his well-brushed brown Sunday suit, his brown trilby at its usual rakish angle as he stood looking out for her, his neck stretched to see better over the teeming Saturday shoppers.

She hurried up to him and saw his bright blue eyes all a-sparkle. She too smiled broadly, seeing some exciting news in those eyes. He held her in welcome, kissed her cheek, an appropriately restrained greeting in this crowded area.

'What?' she asked, his eyes still shining down at her.

'I've booked seats fer us. Fer tonight. Ter see *Show Boat*.'

'Tonight? Oh, Arthur, my mum'll be worried stiff, me getting home so late. She's had enough trouble about Dad.' She had, of course, written to him about Dad, about their changed circumstances, pouring all out to him so that her mind would be eased of the weight of not being able to tell friends who might purr at the thought of a slightly better-off family than theirs coming to grief. Arthur, who knew all about changes in circumstances, cuddled her to him now.

'Whatever 'appens, it ain't no good goin' ter meet it 'alf way. It'll right itself in time an' yer'll all learn ter go along wiv it. An' yer'll be s'prised wot friends yer've got when yer look ararnd. I'm one yer know.'

Yes, he was. She thanked the Lord she had found him again.

'Could yer send 'er a quick telegram,' he suggested. 'She'd get it in an hour or so . . .'

'Oh no!' Josie was startled. 'She'd think it was about Dad.'

'Telephone then?' They were starting to cross the wide busy junction towards the park, taking that direction automatically, each looking this way and that and in all directions for oncoming traffic, his guiding arm around her waist as protection. Later in the park his arm would be around her waist for a totally different reason as they sat on a secluded bench and he kissed her long and firmly on the lips.

'I don't know anyone with a telephone.'

'Not even a shop wot might run a message to yer mum?'

'Only one of the corner shops. They know her well. I know their name but I don't know their telephone number. Never had to bother before.'

'We could ask the operator.'

'Yes, we could.' She began to feel excited. This was adventure, this staying out late and telephoning someone. Arthur was so clever. 'Of course we could.' But something else dawned on her quite out of the blue, what he had first said. She looked at him as they reached the other side of the crossroads. 'You booked seats?'

It was usually a case of joining a queue for the gods, often in a dark side street away from all the bright lights of the theatre frontage. Everyone in the thick patient line hoped they'd get in, hoped the uppermost gallery, the gods, wouldn't fill up before their turn came to be let in by an indifferent male usher.

'You *booked* seats,' she said again. 'For *Show Boat*.'

He was grinning from ear to ear, his eyes sparkling. ''Ad a bit-a-luck,' he said, his 't' becoming the usual back-of-the-tongue click that served in its place. 'On the gee-gees. Me an' anuvver geezer went ter Sandown races last Saturday on a coach outin'. I went barmy an' did an accumulator – that's puttin' wot yer win, if yer win, on an 'orse in the next race, an if yer win on that, it all goes on the next race, and so on. I won each time. Free times. An' one of 'em a rank outsider. I put five bob on ter start, and ended up wiv twenty quid. I give me mum 'alf. She weren't 'alf pleased. I put a few quid away, for when somefink crops up – yer never know wot. An' wiv the rest, you and me's gonna 'ave a smashin' time ternight. I've booked seats in the dress circle. I'll buy yer a box of choc'lates ter go in wiv, and after that we'll 'ave a slap-up dinner at Lyons Corner 'Ouse. Right?'

Josie felt thrilled. The dress circle. She'd never been in a dress circle. At the same time she felt worried. And guilty. 'You shouldn't be spending all that money on just one evening, Arthur.'

His arm tightened about her waist as they reach a quiet seat in the faintly chilly but sunny park. 'I ain't spendin' it all on *jus' one evenin'*. I'm spendin' it on *you*.' With that, his arm still firmly

195

around her waist he sat them both down as one person and kissed her with a long lingering kiss, ignoring any who happened to walk past. 'You're my gel,' he whispered against her lips.

It was a gorgeous show. Sitting in the fourth row of the dress circle was an experience in itself. Each seat had a tiny pair of binoculars in a slot in front of it, so that the players could be observed right up close. Josie could hardly get enough of it all. The songs were quite marvellous. 'Old Man River', 'Only Make Believe', 'Why Do I Love You?' filled her with joy as she munched on her chocolates from the midnight-blue box, Arthur having paid the girl in the sweet kiosk for them as if he'd been doing such things all his life. Together in the dress circle they shared them as she sat with her eyes virtually glued to the stage when not riveted to it by the binoculars. The only thing that marred it all was that she hadn't come dressed for such an evening. A lovely surprise, yes, but if only she had known and had dolled up to the nines for it. But she was utterly pleased just the same.

The first of the two intervals was equally wonderful, standing amid a throng of well-dressed people, none of whom seemed to notice her lack of evening wear, though Arthur had bought her a small corsage of two pink roses to go with her plain moss-green dress, which passed as near appropriate for theatre-going. All in all she felt presentable enough.

Waiting for Arthur to come out of the gentlemen's toilet, she held her glass of sherry he'd bought her, enthusiastically lavish with what was left of his winnings for all she had protested that he should look after what little was left. Someone standing behind her touched her on the elbow, lightly but deliberately. Startled, she turned to find herself gazing into a pair of deep brown eyes and a narrow tanned face beneath immaculate smooth hair.

'I say, don't I know you?'

The smile was suave but questioning. Recognising him instantly, Josie felt a thrill of fear ripple through her, but she managed to present a blank mask. 'No, I don't think so.'

'Yes I do.' The frown on his forehead cleared. The dark, gathered eyebrows drew apart. 'Aren't you the girl I took home to that place on the east coast, Leigh-on-Sea, wasn't it? Good Lord, last May, wasn't it? Or was it April?'

'I'm sorry.' Her nerves had begun to jangle. She just wanted him to go away. Arthur would be back at any moment. He mustn't see her with this person. He would recognise him straight away. It would ruin everything with her and Arthur, and this time she wanted nothing to do with these sort of people and their debauched way of life any more. 'You've made a mistake.'

'No I haven't. It's Josie something-or-other. You remember, you refused to let me kiss you. And after me taking you all that way home. You just leapt out of the car and disappeared into the night like some elusive little sea-witch.'

He was speaking very fast, excitedly. 'I almost felt you had sunk into the sea never to return to land again. I was most disappointed, you know. Not for not having any thanks for taking you home all that way, but because I was really taken by you. I've thought of you ever since and wondered where you went to. I began to think you must be magic, a sea-siren allowed to come up on to land for a single short spell . . . I can't believe my luck seeing you. Look here, can I get you a drink? I really cannot believe . . .'

'Look, I'm sorry, I really am. You've made an awful mistake . . .'

She broke free of the hold he had on her elbow, light though it was, as though he'd had a tremendous grip on it. Then she was edging away through the throng as swiftly as it would allow, a backward glance through a gap revealing him with his hand still in the position of clutching her elbow, his smoothly handsome features caught into a half-amused, half-questioning expression. She was heartily glad when the brief gap closed between her and him and she saw Arthur emerge just as the bell sounding the end of the interval reverberated loudly.

The musical had been spoiled for her. She watched it in a growing ferment of anxiety as the time for the second interval drew nearer, no longer bothering to peep at the players through the binoculars, the rest of the chocolates in the lovely box uneaten except by Arthur who devoured them, oblivious to her torment.

'Let's not go back to the bar,' she pleaded as the curtain came down on the second act. 'Let's just sit here. All that jostling to get us a drink. I'd sooner have an ice-cream from the girl there.'

As the lights came up to reveal the trim young woman with her

197

tray full of ice-cream tubs, Arthur followed her pointing finger and pulled a face at the long queue already forming there.

'I don't relish standin' in that queue,' Arthur muttered. 'Oh, fer God's sake, let's live it up a bit, Josie. We won't do this very offen I can tell yer. Let's make the most of it an' 'ave anuvver one at the bar. I can get yer anuvver sherry. I can just abart afford it and 'ave enough left fer a bite-ter-eat at Lyons Corner 'Ouse. Come on.'

He was up, pushing past those few left in their seats, so she felt forced to go with him.

In the bar, Josie looked around with veiled eyes, praying her tormentor would not find her, or even bother to seek her out, his curiosity slaked. But there he was again, coming towards her. And there was nowhere to go.

'I say, there you are. We seem destined to meet again and again. Providence. Though I expect you're with someone.'

'Yes, I am,' she replied tersely, her gaze on the brown-suited figure of Arthur struggling to get near the elegant gilt-wreathed bar. 'And I don't want to upset him like last time.'

'So you do recognise me.'

'I never said that.'

Arthur was coming back. He'd got served quicker than expected, a man who knew how to get to the front of a crowd at any bar. Fortunately he hadn't yet seen her.

'Look, please go,' she pleaded. 'I mustn't be seen with you.'

Nigel Hobbs – she remembered the name only too well – gave a small chuckle. 'Ah, the chap you were with last time. Serious then, heh? Well, I shouldn't really cause you embarrassment, should I?' He was speaking quickly. 'But really I couldn't get you out of my mind last time. Having seen you again, it'll be an even harder job. I'll look for you in the foyer when the show's over. I've friends in it, you know. Came to see them really. But I need to see you. You won't let me down, will you? I'll be waiting in the foyer. Be there, Josie. For the moment then, *au revoir . . .*'

It sounded like a command. Josie bit her lip as he slipped away into the throng as Arthur came up grinning and handing her the sherry.

When the show finished, they got their hats and coats from the busy cloakroom desk and put them on. They heard someone say it was raining.

'We'll 'ave ter sprint fer a bus,' Arthur remarked. 'Just

'ope there ain't a queue, but I bet there is. Never thought of a brolly.'

He conducted her down the carpeted staircase. Surrounded by others making their way out, the going was slow. The conversation on the musical just seen, low and appreciative, moved around them like the waves of a serene ocean. He too was asking how she enjoyed it and she replied automatically that she really had, and all the time her gaze roved over the top of the people in front to see if Nigel Hobbs hovered below.

If he was there, she'd ignore him, sweep by him, but he'd only call her name. If he moved into her path she'd have to stop. Either way she'd have to introduce him. It was a pickle. It was all so plain now – robbed of a bit of fun and made a fool of that evening in April, having bumped into her again he was after revenge, to belittle her, wreck her happiness with Arthur.

Josie wished she'd never consented to see this show, wished she'd never let herself get mixed up in the first place with that dissolute crowd of socialites of which he had been one, wished she'd never been naive enough to have allowed him to see her home.

There he was, standing at the foot of the staircase, checking each face. Josie tried to make herself small, hoping he'd miss her in the crowds pouring down the stairs and out through the doors. He didn't, not at all.

'Hi, there you are!'

He was in front of them, blocking their way, grinning at her. Arthur pulled up, the people immediately behind coming to a temporary stop and then flowing on around them like liquid mud around an obstruction.

'Scuse me,' Arthur said mildly. Stepping down the last step, he was as tall as the man blocking his way. But the other stood his ground, still smiling at Josie.

'I said I'd meet you here, my dear Josie.'

'Wot's that?' Arthur's hold on Josie tightened protectively. 'Oo d'yer think yer talkin' to, mate?'

'The young lady here,' came the easy reply.

'Sorry, mate, yer made a mistake. She don't know you. Let us fru.'

'No mistake, old chap.' People were still flowing around the hold-up. 'I take it you don't remember me, but the young lady

199

does. Last April. Came back to a party with me. You went home. I did the proper thing and took the young lady home myself. And I must say she was very . . . grateful.'

Arthur was glaring. 'Wot yer mean, *grateful*?'

'What I say, old chap.'

'Don't *old chap* me.' Arthur's voice had risen. People were looking, held up by those who, seeing the rain outside the theatre, had paused, themselves causing a hold-up. Attendants dotted around were bracing themselves for trouble.

Josie was gazing with pleading eyes from one man to the other, now realising what Nigel Hobbs was intimating, aware that Arthur knew too.

'It's not true, Arthur,' she cried. He didn't even glance at her; his glare fixed on his adversary commanding the man's own stare. To Josie it seemed he had ignored her, believing the other man's words and challenging him. 'Arthur, it's not true,' she cried again.

'I know.' His glare hadn't faltered. 'And you . . .' he said to Hobbs. 'Yer a liar, mate. An' I fink we've got noffink ter say ter each uvver. Come on, Jo, let's go.'

Gripping her arm firmly, he sidestepped Hobbs in the now fast-emptying foyer and led Josie away. Hobbs was left staring after them, the theatre attendants relaxing as the troublesome couple stepped out into the rainy night.

They didn't speak at all on the short bus ride to Fenchurch Street Station. The meal at Lyons' wouldn't have seemed right after the incident at the theatre. Arthur's expression looked set and Josie felt at a loss how to redeem herself if that were necessary. Had he believed her for all he'd said 'I know' or was that just to shut her up at the time? All the way to the station, a weight seemed to have settled beneath Josie's ribs. She predicted that Arthur would take her to the ticket barrier and there say he wouldn't be seeing her any more. She could hear him saying it. It made her feel as if at any moment she would be sick.

At the platform barrier, Josie got out her return ticket ready to go through. She lifted her face to Arthur's.

'I'm sorry about tonight.'

'So am I.' The tone sounded sharp, hard. Josie bit her lip, hovered.

What she felt she ought to do was turn away, go through the

200

barrier without saying another word. But she couldn't. She stood there looking up at him. Arthur was looking along the platform where a few people were leisurely getting into carriages; the train was not due to leave for another ten minutes. At the far end the engine was breathing gently like a slumbering giant, steam issuing quietly from beneath it. She could hear the echoing slam of doors, the hollow trundle of a half-empty trolley bearing letters and parcels ready to be sorted in the mail compartment once the train moved off.

'Will yer be orright goin' the rest of the way on yer own?'

'Yes, I think so,' she said, her tone formal.

'Don't want me ter see yer all the way 'ome?' Like Nigel Hobbs had, she silently finished the sentence for him. Obviously he had believed him for all he'd called him a liar, and was now accusing her.

'There's no need.' The ten minutes were ticking away. She wanted to be away too, away from all this, yet it seemed all she really wanted was to stay here with Arthur, thrash out this difference that had arisen between them. 'Arthur . . .' He looked at her, his head slightly on one side. 'Arthur, you didn't believe what that . . . what he said?'

'No.'

It wasn't good enough, just – no. 'I didn't let him touch me. He tried. I was worried about going home alone that time of night and he seemed so nice, and you had left.'

'I fort yer'd decided to stay the night. Yer was 'aving such a good time. I fort, this ain't fer me. She knows wot she wants.'

'I didn't know what to do, when you left. I was angry. Arthur. I let you go because I was angry. I thought I could look after myself. But I was wrong. I felt confused and a bit scared all alone there, and when he said he'd take me home, I thought it would keep me safe. He took me all the way home to Leigh in his car and then when we got there, he tried to . . . he . . .'

'I don't need ter 'ear any more, Jo. I said I know yer didn't do anyfink yer shouldn't of done. When 'e tried ter tell me a bloody pack o' lies.'

'Then why've you been so quiet on the bus all the way here?' she taxed, suddenly annoyed that he couldn't have told her this earlier instead of tormenting her that way. So much that she forgot to feel relieved.

'Because you was,' he said simply.

The train had started panting, getting up steam. People were beginning to stride more urgently through the barrier and along the platform. Doors closed more sharply, abruptly. A guard was walking up and down the carriages, checking the doors, a whistle poised in one hand, a small green flag in the other. Josie glanced anxiously at the train. She mustn't let it go without her. She'd be so late home. Torn between leaving and seeking reconciliation, she put both hands on Arthur's arm. 'And you're not cross with me?'

'I'm cross with everyfink,' he said bluntly. 'That sod spoilt our ev'nin' an' I wanted it ter be special for yer.'

The ticket collector had moved towards them, He touched her shoulder. 'Train'll be goin' in 'arf a minute, miss, if yer wants ter git on.'

'Thank you,' she rapped out. 'Arthur . . .'

'Best get on,' he said. 'See yer next week, same place, time . . .'

He deposited a quick peck on her cheek as the ticket collector all but hauled her through the barrier. She ran off along the platform to the nearest third-class carriage as the train began laboriously, slowly, to move at the shrill command of the whistle.

As she yanked open a door of a moving carriage, leaping on to the running board, she glanced back. Arthur was waving. She heard his voice float distantly towards her, only just audible above the stentorian puffing of the engine ahead, smoke from its funnel now billowing up energetically to the bevelled glass roof of the station.

'Take yer ter see me mum nex' week.'

In the carriage, deserted but for herself, Josie gave herself up to tears of joy. See his mum. As good as a proposal. Usually, a boy did not take a girl home to see his mum but for one purpose, to declare his intentions. Surely Arthur was no different.

Chapter Nineteen

Pam stood gazing at little Elizabeth in her cot. She'd had every intention of calling her Peggy after Mum, who'd been so wonderful after the rift. But George had shortened the name to Beth, our little Beth, and it had stuck.

They had bought the cot secondhand from someone Mum knew. Repainted white, the covers cut and sewn from the better parts of old sheets, thinning blankets and worn coverlets given to them by her and George's mothers, it looked as good as any bought expensively from a shop.

So far Beth was proving a good baby, thank God. She slept all night and most of the day and stayed quite content except when hungry. Then Pam would sit in the old fireside chair with a cup of tea, the baby at her breast. She would stare into space while the baby suckled, thinking of things: of Mum coming round after what had at one time struck Pam as unresolvable, unending, although Dad, still in hospital convalescing, knew nothing of Mum's decision to make up; of George, in work at last, in a boat chandler's as an odd job man, with luck a long term thing where he might learn a bit. It wasn't good pay but it fed them if little else. Compared to what she'd been through Pam was beginning to think they'd struck lucky at last. Perhaps one day they'd move, live better, one day be rich . . .

Such dreams of what she'd do if she ever got rich would drift through her mind as little Beth drank her fill, and after dozing off Pam would come to herself again, the cup of tea stone cold and Beth fast asleep, the nipple having slid out of the tiny mouth to drip milk on to the little face, the rosebud lips a tiny O as if still attached to the breast. The other side would be full still, unused,

203

that too oozing nourishment on to the shawl in which Beth lay wrapped. The breast would later have to be expressed to relieve the hardness, because she was making far more milk than one baby needed. At the turn of the century, Pam mused, still not yet fully awake, she would have made a jolly good wet nurse, earning good money for it.

Today people frowned at the idea of someone else's breast being stuck in the mouth of their darling baby. Baby milk was bought from stores instead, and God knows where that came from. In hospital the nurses had come round with basins calling out, 'Dairy time! Anyone needing to express?' She always had enough left to fill her basin for babies whose mothers could not feed.

Beth started to stir, whimpered. Pam lifted her out and set to work changing the nappy, washing the tender little bottom with warm water already poured from the kettle into a tin bowl, by which time the round blue eyes had screwed themselves up again in a fit of crying to be fed. Beth was a chubby baby who enjoyed her nourishment, but easily satisfied, and absolutely adorable.

'All right, little one,' Pam crooned, clutching the now-clean Beth to her as she sat herself in the chair and pulled aside her cardigan and yanked up the old jumper underneath. October had grown cold and the heating here was never sufficient, so even Beth had to be clothed in three little knitted jumpers and a cardigan to keep warm. Pam presented a heavy breast to the urgently nuzzling mouth.

George wouldn't be home yet. After feeding Beth she'd put her down and start getting his tea. He had sandwiches at midday, so his tea was more a dinner – today sausages, mashed potatoes, baked beans, and the remains of yesterday's jam roly-poly pudding warmed up, with a bit of custard over to make it moist again. She'd eaten hers at midday. Settling down, she wasn't prepared for a knock on the door.

'Who is it?' she called, getting ready to take Beth off the breast and cover herself. She remembered the door was not locked after she had gone down to fetch water from the landing tap. 'Just a minute.'

But the door was opening. Taken off guard with Beth still feeding greedily, Pam swung round to see her in-laws standing there.

'Coo-ee! All right to come in?' But they were already in,

204

advancing on her. It would have been an obvious show of over-modesty to have dragged Beth away from her feeding and she'd only have created at being deprived and have to be presented to her grandmother in a fit of rage. And after all Mrs Bryant had suckled kids of her own. But to Pam's horror it was Mr Bryant who came forward first.

'God, Pam, she's really growing, ain't she? Likes her food, don't she?' With that he bent forward, ignoring Pam's bared breast, and planted a kiss on his grandchild's forehead, his bristly moustache actually brushing Pam's flesh before he stood back once more.

Pam's felt her cheeks grow hot. It had been a simple gesture of love for the baby, but Pam couldn't help feeling it was something more. In fact the words flew through her head: 'You dirty old man.' But for all her insides cringed she found herself smiling sociably up at him, knowing it would have been imprudent to make a fuss. It was his wife who made the fuss, her voice shrill and censuring.

'What in the good Lord's name, Dick, do you think you're doing? Let the baby feed in peace. You'll get time to hold her before we go.' Not criticising him for his impropriety but merely for his interference. Pam felt near to hating them both. Yet they had done as much as they could for her and George, more than her own had done, until now.

Mrs Bryant went to the little stove and lifted the kettle to gauge the amount of water it held. 'I'll make a cup of tea, dear. I've brought some milk. What time's George home? I'm glad he's got a decent job. You might both get back on your feet now. For heaven's sake, Dick, stop hovering around the baby and sit down. What time did you say George'll be home?'

Pam could still feel the heat in her cheeks, glad as George's father did as he was told, rather like a small dog coming to heel. 'In about fifteen or twenty minutes,' she said. 'I'm doing sausage and mash for him.'

'I'll do that for you, dear. That's what we're round here for, to help.'

They did this often, popping in unannounced, his mother going down the shops to save her having to go out, offering to look after Beth while she and George went out, which they only did to go for a walk to get out of the poky flat for a while. His income came

205

nowhere near meeting the expense of a proper evening out, except maybe for one drink in one of the nearby pubs. Pam was alternately grateful and irritated, feeling she was quite well enough to do for her and George; yet it was good of them to put themselves out. She didn't go round to their home much. In the first place there was a tiny sense of disloyalty to her own family, in spite of the way she had been served. Also she never felt at home at the Bryants. He would ask after her dad as if the accident had been solely his fault, which in a way it probably had been.

'All right if I smoke me pipe?' Bryant asked. His wife swung at him.

'Not with the baby in the room. Go out on to the landing.'

He got up and went out and Pam felt her entire being relax. By the time he came back, Beth would have been fed and she would be in a state of decency, as far as he was concerned. But the sense of having been somewhat outraged hung on for the rest of the evening long after George had come home.

'I wish they wouldn't come barging in without telling us they're coming.' She and George sat one each side of the fire. Beth was asleep. She mostly slept right through to morning now, to Pam's relief.

'How d'you mean?' George murmured. He had his nose in a boat chandler's catalogue picked up at work, which would help him to know everything they stocked so he would not have to keep asking the proprietor if something was in stock and if so where it was kept. He meant to hang on to this job. He could see prospects in it.

'I mean like today.' Pam, her head bent over some darning, did not look up. 'They just walked in. And there was me feeding the baby. I felt really embarrassed.'

'No reason why you should be. Mum fed all her kids herself.'

Pam forbore to mention the episode of his dad. 'It's just I never know when they're coming. They just walk in.'

'Wasn't the door locked?'

'No. I'd just been down to get some water to wash Beth. I wasn't expecting them. It'd be nice if they'd *tell me* when they're coming!'

He looked up sharply at the tone of her voice. 'So what d'you

206

suggest – they telephone us? Send a telegram? One of 'em come round to say they're coming round?' It sounded sarcastic.

'There's a telephone downstairs.'

'Which Mrs Whatsername owns and won't let anyone use except for emergencies. You call Mum and Dad coming round an emergency?'

'Don't be sarcastic, George!' Her voice had risen. 'I'm only saying . . .'

'That you don't want them round here,' he misinterpreted, putting down the catalogue. 'They've done a lot for us, Pam, since we got married. More'n your lot's ever done. You ain't forgotten how they threw you out?'

'Don't say that!' she railed at him. 'Since Beth was born, my mum's been here once a week regular. And she brings things. For us, for the baby.'

'So she should, after all them months ignoring you like you was dirt.'

'Don't talk about them like that, George,' Pam cried, throwing down his sock, her face beginning to crease up. 'You know how deep that trouble went between our families, and it was your dad's fault as much as mine. But because of me and the baby, it looks like it all might clear up one day. And it was my idea in the first place, remember, to have a baby and try to bring everyone together. And all you can do is put my family down. And me. It's unfair!'

'Then don't talk about mine as if they was interfering. They've done all they could for us, and Dad not far from poverty street himself.'

'It's your dad I'm talking about,' she burst out before she could stop herself.

George leaned forward. 'What's wrong with my dad?'

'The way he acts.' Embarrassment, uncertainty how to finish what she had started, calmed her, moderated her tone. George was looking at her, his blue eyes challenging.

'What you talking about?'

'When I'm feeding Beth. He's done it a couple of times. I don't like it.'

'Like what?'

All this hedging had to be put aside. Pam took a deep breath, lowered her eyes. 'I mean . . . today, when I was feeding Beth,

207

your mum and dad came in, and your dad came straight over and kissed Beth on the top of her head – while I was feeding her. I mean, I had all my nipple on show and he came straight over and did that. I felt his moustache touch my skin, he was that close. And he did the same thing last week as well, him and your mum walking in when I was feeding and him kissing the baby like that. It's not nice, not decent, and I don't like it. I feel so . . . I felt . . .'

She couldn't go on, her face growing hot and her mouth dry at the recollection of a man other than her husband so close to her naked breast. It was all too horrible. She felt she would never get over the horrid sensation of her father-in-law taking liberties, which was how she saw it, no matter what anyone, even George, said.

He said it now, just as she would have predicted if she'd been a clairvoyant. 'Don't be silly, Pam. Dad is family. You're part of our family.'

'Not that much part of it,' she snapped back, her sense of outrage rising afresh to conquer embarrassment. 'My dad would never dream of doing something like that. He's got more decency. It *was* indecent, darling. I *felt* it was indecent. And my feelings must count for *something*.'

George's face had grown angry. 'You're just being silly.'

'No I'm not.' She was angry too, now. Furious. 'You're telling me you condone that sort of thing – a man . . . I don't care if he is my father-in-law, he's still a man – a man almost laying his face against my bare breast on the pretext of kissing my baby, and me *feeding* her at the time? And you think I'm just being silly? *I* felt as if he was taking advantage of me. I felt just as if I was being molested.' That was what she'd been trying to say. But George was looking at her aghast, not at what his father was alleged to have done but that she, his wife, was accusing him of something he wouldn't accept.

'That's a bloody awful thing to say,' he said quietly, coming to his feet. 'I can't believe you, saying things like that about Dad. He didn't mean nothing by it and he'd be shocked to think you've got yourself in a state over something entirely innocent. I don't want to talk about this any more. I'm going to bed.'

'And I'm locking the door *every* time after I so much as set foot on that landing from now on,' she yelled after him, beside herself that he had not even raised his voice while she had resorted to yelling, but he took no notice, undressed himself in silence and got into bed.

But her raised voice had disturbed Beth and for the first time in weeks she sat awake pacifying her while, whether he slept or not, George lay with his back to her and not once asking if she was all right with Beth or wanted help of any sort.

There was only one person she felt she could confide in – Mum.

Peggy came to see her daughter on Wednesday afternoon, as she always did. There was no visiting at the hospital on Wednesday afternoons, when the doctors did their rounds, so it was a good day to see Pam. She found her with eyes puffy and cheeks mottled as she opened the door to her light tap.

'Good Lord, Pam!' Peggy got quickly out of her coat and came back to take her by the arms and look into her face. 'What's the matter? You look as if you've been crying for days.'

'I have.' Pam was on the verge of fresh tears. 'We've had a row.'

'You and George?'

'He's not spoken to me for two days. It wasn't so much a row, not shouting. Well, I shouted. He didn't even raise his voice. Just went to bed and hasn't said a thing to me since. Apart from asking if I'd done his sandwiches, things like that. Apart from that he's just ignoring me.'

Peggy sat her daughter down. 'I'll put the kettle on, make us some tea. I brought a packet of tea and some milk.' She fished in the shopping bag she'd brought. 'And a bit of bacon.'

It was on her mind to say that she had never considered George to be a sulky man, but that would have been putting in her oar, and Pam was upset enough. It was one thing for man and wife to row, but woe betide anyone else who put him down. It was best to keep quiet about what she thought of George and his conduct.

'Do you want to tell me about it?' she asked as the kettle began to heat up on the slow little oil stove.

Pam shook her head, but minutes later was pouring out her heart to her mother. Peggy listened in silence until Pam fell quiet except to sniffle and swallow and clear her throat of choked-up tears. She was appalled by what Pam had said. And to think George couldn't see what was in that dirty mind of Dick Bryant's. Didn't Mrs Bryant see what her husband was about? She felt like

209

going to the Bryants and confronting them about it, but that wouldn't have done Pam any good.

The kettle began to steam and she went and set out two cups.

'Men,' she said, busying herself putting tea into the pot and milk into the cups. 'They never see beyond their noses. Maybe George wasn't upset at you, but at his dad. Sort of felt guilty for him. He was probably angry with himself because he knew who he should blame but couldn't say so because it was his dad. Maybe that's why he's being quiet, why he didn't shout back at you. Because he can't admit that his dad did wrong. After all, he is his dad. He must love him.'

'And I'm his wife. He should love me more. He should have taken my side as his wife. He was the only one I could tell and he acted like that.'

Pouring the tea, Peggy came over and handed one to Pam. 'I'm glad you told me. As I said, men don't understand. Pam, you've always got me. I'm sorry about that business earlier this year and I should have understood, being your mum. I'm ashamed of myself.'

In a rush of impulse Pam put her cup down on the floor and went to her mother who only just had time to put her own cup down before Pam flung herself into her arms, sobbing.

'Oh, Mum, don't ever be ashamed of yourself. That's all in the past and we're friends again. I'm glad we're friends. You're the only friend I've got.' The words poured out through the weeping while Peggy held her, rocking her gently.

'You've got your family. You've got Connie and Josie and Danny, and you've got me.'

'But I haven't got Dad.'

'He'll come round in time.'

Pam was firm. 'He won't never forgive me. He'll never get over that business of him and George's dad. Though now I can see why. But I'm married to his son, and I love George. But I've lost my own dad through all this. I hate the Bryants. Oh, Mum, I feel so unhappy and confused.'

Peggy sat cuddling her daughter to her, unhappy for having no words of comfort to give her save that it would work itself out given time. There came to mind that most useless of all maxims that time healed all wounds. Of course time would solve this row between Pam and her husband. As for the rest, she didn't know.

210

Time heals all wounds? She didn't believe that for a second as she sat with her arms about the kneeling girl, trying to be a comfort to her. Trying to be a comfort was the hardest of all achievements. How much of a comfort was she really to Pam, except that she was holding her close?

Her mind went back, as it did so often, even after all these years, to the loss of her youngest son. Time would never heal that wound. She had needed comfort then, but had not received any, not really. Friends and relatives had come to sympathise, felt deeply for her at the time, but all the while they had silently thanked God it wasn't their loss. They had wrapped their arms around her, said how dreadful it was for her and asked what could they do for her, had even cried for her. They had talked among themselves about how awful it was and how badly they felt, but at the end of the day they had gone away and carried on with their own lives and she'd been left with her loss that no one could assuage, not even Dan.

Comfort was more to do with firmness. At that thought Peggy put her daughter from her, held her at arm's length. 'Now, no more of this. You've got to pull yourself together, love. It's not the end of the world and there are far worse things can happen. So don't say any more about it to George. And don't let him come home and see you crying. Brighten yourself up. Put on a bit of make-up, cook him a really nice dinner, give him a kiss on the cheek, and make sure his dad doesn't have any more opportunities to get near you while you're feeding Beth. It could be George was feeling a bit embarrassed, even ashamed, and the only way he had of fighting it was to act the way he did. If the truth's known he probably feels as bad about it as you, but he won't say so. That'd be putting himself down, and men can't abide being put down, not by anything.'

No, men couldn't, came the thought, her mind racing to Dan. But his downfall was a different kettle of fish which she must face for the rest of their lives together.

She smiled at her daughter and received a tremulous little smile in return. 'That's better, love. Now, remember what I said, and I promise that come tomorrow you'll both have got over your tiff.'

If only it was as easy as that for people like her. Tomorrow she'd go and visit Dan, in a convalescent home now, listen to his griping and his unending rage against Dick Bryant on whom he even blamed this accident as though he relished it having happened just to lay the responsibility for that too at the man's door. It had become his only joy in life now, blaming Dick Bryant. It was no longer a feud, it was an obsession.

Chapter Twenty

On the matter of wedding arrangements, Lily was completely blinkered, her sights set on what she wanted the day she would walk down the aisle of St Clement's and nothing else.

'We could have it in May, darling.'

For all he wanted her for his wife so much it was an ache inside him, May had to be out of the question, at least the sort of wedding she had in mind – one that would ape a society wedding if she had her way – hordes of people, family and friends, three bridesmaids – 'I can't leave my nieces out, I promised they'd be bridesmaids when I got married' – in pink, together with her oldest sister's four-year-old son as pageboy in blue, the reception held in one of the big reception rooms at the Cliffs Hotel.

'You work there,' she'd taxed Josie. 'Maybe you could get them to give us it a bit cheaper.' Which had put Josie on the spot and embarrassed him into telling her she couldn't go around manipulating people like that. Josie was just a part-time assistant receptionist and nothing to do with the hotel management. The result had been a stand-up row with Lily finally falling into a pouting sulk.

But it hadn't put a stopper on her idea of a May wedding as well as a honeymoon afterwards.

'Bournemouth would be nice,' she mused as they ventured along a deserted spray-drenched Southend prom, the only fools in sight on a Sunday morning like this, their heads bent sideways before a buffeting late November wind.

The tide had come right up; grey wind-driven waves bashed themselves against the sea wall with a hollow booming and threw up white plumes of broken water, the wall's curved rim deflecting them back to sea to collide with other incoming breakers in mighty bursts of foam, so that every now and again flecks of the wild spray landed on the couple's faces to make Danny screw up his face and Lily squeal.

Hard to imagine warm summer Sundays with the water gentle, the triangles of shelly beaches between the low breakwaters alive with holiday makers, what little soft sand there was before the mud began, a haven for children with buckets and spades. Now with the slap and pound of waves against the sea wall, the sea was a raging creature with the ability to drag out and drown anyone fool enough to venture the other side of the iron railing and stand on the few steps down to what beach the waves might expose. He thought momentarily of Connie's Ben; claimed by a sea which that day had been merely choppy, but the cold had no doubt caused cramp enough to cripple even the strongest swimmer. Poor Connie – it had come out of the blue for her, one minute so happy, the next . . .

'We ought to be getting back home. It's too cold here.'

Lily tutted. 'It was you who said we should go out for a while.'

He'd suggested a stroll along the prom to get her out of her house for a while where her horde of siblings as well as parents butted in on every word she spoke on the subject of the wedding, putting in their tuppence-worth, eyes lighting up at the thought of this splendid do she described.

He had been glad to get her out of the house but he hadn't reckoned on the strength of the wind and now they were both cold and slightly damp. Soon Lily too was eager to get back home in the warm for all they had needed to be alone to discuss the wedding. Well, Lily wanted to discuss it. He would rather have let the subject drop, at least for the present. He had enough on his mind without that too.

'So what would you think? About Bournemouth then?' she pushed.

Danny stayed silent. How could he make her see the impossibility of the sort of wedding she wanted, and so near? May, of course, was all of seven months away and could still be achieved, if on a more modest scale, but much of his money was already going to keep his mother. Dad would never work again and Mum refused to take a penny off Dad's brothers, drawing herself up to her small height and saying almost haughtily, 'We're not doing too bad. We're managing.' With winter coming on, the holiday trade long gone, money was tight anyway.

He still hadn't told Lily about the arrangements for when Dad came home. Dad kept saying he'd be back in time for Christmas even though that depended on what the hospital said. Danny himself dreaded the homecoming, his dad reduced to being helped about, a man who'd always told others what to do being himself told.

In hospital he was a bad patient, and Danny felt sure that when he finally came home he would plague Mum's life out of her from dawn till dusk and probably half the night. Danny worried for Mum. He had to be there, for her sake. No one else would be – Connie, still strange and withdrawn, was forever up at St Clement's these days; Josie, all for her fun and that Arthur she was going out with, spent her time dreaming and jotting the signature Josephine Monk on bits of paper which stated plainly what was in her mind. Neither girl would be able to support Mum, stand up to Dad and his dominating nature which would become more pronounced with him in a wheelchair. And he was a heavy man, too heavy for Mum to pull around. The hospital had told them he'd never walk again. His weight on Mum's shoulders, his cussedness and newly acquired irascibility would wear her down. She needed another man in the house.

His heart like a ton weight inside him, Danny knew that under these circumstances there'd be no question of him and Lily thinking of a house; he had to try to pay the rent and keep Mum, and when he wasn't working, be round there helping her with Dad. It wouldn't be fair on Lily, and in time – he could see it happening – she'd start to complain and their marriage would falter and have to be shored up with promises to divide himself into even smaller pieces to please her. Divide himself and what money he brought in. It would be easier and far cheaper to live at home after they were married. Connie and Josie would sleep in one room, Mum in his small room at the back because Dad would have to be downstairs in the back room, so he and Lily could have the big front bedroom. They'd cope, he was sure of it. But he couldn't tell that to Lily yet, still dreaming of her own home and her fine wedding.

'We might make it around July,' he said cautiously. 'Give me longer to save up.' He saw her smile, nodding agreement, satisfied

215

with that, and, temporarily relieved, he put the rest of his bad news aside for the moment.

Connie knelt for a final private prayer before leaving for home, the coarse fibres of the hassock prickling her knees through the thick stockings she wore against the cold fog through which she had felt her way uphill to Sunday morning service.

She tried to pray for Ben's soul. Instead her thoughts seemed more filled by the fog outside, hoping that it might have abated a little with the coming of December rather than getting thicker – more like November really. Perhaps by now it would have cleared a little, enabling her to go back downhill with more confidence than she'd come up. Perhaps later the sun would break through, watery and pale, enough to cheer her up. Foggy days made her spirits, never far from plummeting even in bright sunshine and balmy days, plummet even further. She longed for spring. But spring would be ever nearer the anniversary of Ben's drowning and she felt she needed to hold back next spring, as if by some physical force, which was foolish, but with her eyes tightly closed it seemed she might even be capable of doing so. Like a dream . . .

Bending her head deeper into her hands, she pushed away thoughts of the weather and supernatural deeds, and tried to conjure up Ben's face behind her closed eyes. It would not come. What came was a blurred image of a photo they'd taken somewhere, her face still far clearer than his. Why couldn't she see him when she loved him so? But he would not come.

There were times when she wished she could be a spiritualist and bring him to her with ease. There had been times when she had almost gone to a meeting of that sort to see if he would come to her, but her religious beliefs, grown so powerful these past months, prevented any dabbling in the occult, as spiritualism seemed to her. There *was* a hereafter. There *was* heaven and hell. Heaven, if not up among the clouds, a notion this enlightened age of science seemed to be dispelling, was *somewhere*. That she did believe, because a pure soul like Ben's could not just lie rotting in the ground of the East London Cemetery. It had to be rejoicing somewhere beautiful as it deserved to. And hell? Hell was here, on earth, a testing ground. It couldn't be anywhere below because this planet was as solid as any of those in the solar system . . .

Connie lifted her head in alarm. What was she thinking of?

216

When she should be praying for Ben, her head was full of stupid thoughts of planets. She opened her eyes to find the church almost emptied and a black-clad figure standing not far away looking at her.

With a feeling of guilt at having delayed the closing of the church doors, she got to her feet, gave him a smile of apology and gathered up her bag and her hat.

'I'm sorry,' she mumbled self-consciously.

He came towards her. 'Are you so unhappy?'

Connie stared at him, a tall slim figure compelling her to lift her head to look up at him, tall as she was. She'd seen him more or less every time she came here but had never bothered to find out his name or consider him closely.

'Unhappy?' She was offended. 'Why should you think I'm unhappy?'

'You look unhappy.' His voice was deep, the timbre of it echoing in the now-empty church. 'I hope I don't intrude, but if there is anything I can do, if you need anyone to talk to . . .'

How often had he been watching her to so define her private feelings? Connie felt slightly invaded. Something inside her automatically stepped back from the intrusion into her soul. Yet an impulse to unburden a weight inside her made itself felt, and a strange surge of gratitude. It was the need to recoil that triumphed and her voice felt harsh in her throat. She didn't want anyone sorry for her.

'Thank you. I'm fine. But nice of you to take the trouble.' Probably part of his duties as a curate but all she wanted was to get out of here. 'I must go . . .'

He moved in front of her, virtually barring her way.

'Please. Would you stay and talk to me awhile?'

'Why?' Now she was irritated. Confused too, by the nearness of him, by the maleness of that proximity for all the cassock he wore. His nearness disturbed her. 'There's nothing I need to say about myself.'

'There's something I'd like to say,' he broke in. 'About myself. I hope you don't mind, but I need to talk to you. I see you every Sunday morning. You never miss.'

It *was* about her, but he was ploughing on, his hand lightly beneath her elbow now, gently persuading her back down the aisle to one of the front pews.

217

'I know of the loss of your fiancé, of the wedding having to be cancelled. I thought I'd never set eyes on you after that, but I was glad to see you. I have come to look out for you every Sunday since.'

Connie found herself sitting down without having realised that she had. He sat beside her.

'One thing I do know.' His voice was low, no longer echoing around the church, so it must be a whisper, she thought abstractedly. 'I'd be upset ... can I say devastated, if you stopped coming now? That's why I have never approached you before now, in case I drove you away. I look forward with eagerness to every Sunday, sure you will be here. I am so overjoyed when I see you arrive and for the rest of the week I seem merely to be waiting for the next Sunday when you will attend again. But I am terrified that you will one day cease to attend, your grief healed enough for you not to. And that day to me is unthinkable. So ... please forgive me for saying all this to you, but I had to take this chance.'

In all this he had not looked at her, sitting very still with his head bent, his eyes regarding his hands which were clasped unmoving in the lap of his robe. He still did not look at her. 'You think me too presumptuous.'

She wasn't sure what he meant by that. 'Presumptuous?' she echoed.

'Declaring ... no, I mean speaking to you in this manner.'

What manner? But some sixth sense was already telling her in what manner he had spoken to her. Her heart leapt then grew angry. He couldn't be trying to usurp Ben's place in her heart.

She almost shot off the seat. 'I'm sorry. But if it's in your mind to say what I think you're trying to say, then please, I'd rather not hear.'

He was on his feet too, both hands on her arms in a desperate grip. 'No, don't run off. I don't mean to offend you, but there is no circumspect way to say this. I know your Christian name and I need to say it. Constance. I have watched you throughout the summer and autumn and all that time I have become conscious of a growing affection for you.'

'I ... oh ...' All her reserve could not combat this statement pouring out in a torrent. She knew she should have drawn away and said haughtily, 'I beg your pardon, please allow me to leave.'

218

But all she could do was stutter, 'I . . . oh . . .' as his hands gripped her arms, his voice continuing.

'I know you don't have the same feelings for me. You couldn't have. You still long for the one you lost so tragically. I understand that. But I can't bear to see you continue so unhappy. I want to ease your pain and I know I can't – not unless you allow me to. And you won't do that, I know. So I had to tell you how *I* feel, and now I've said it and you can forget about it. All I say to you, Constance, is that if you ever need someone to help ease your pain, I will be here.'

How she got out of the church, blinking in the light of a pale sun that had at last broken through the layer of fog, she wasn't sure. Her hat was still in her hand, her handbag on her arm. She felt he had kissed her, but she knew he hadn't. What was his name? She felt she'd been told it sometime in the past but she couldn't remember. At the church gate she turned round, expecting to see him there, but he wasn't.

Dan Bowmaker was home. As he had been a bad patient in hospital, so he was at home; his spirit had gone out of him and all that was left was a complaining, irritable, irascible man, seeing nothing ahead of him but a life of being cared for, told what to do. He was filled with recriminations against one who years ago had begun all this by setting fire to his boat, his livelihood, and all over a small punch on the nose, and who had finished it by goading him into the accident that had robbed him of his legs, his very masculinity; finished him.

'Your husband must begin to learn to accept his disability, for his own sake,' the doctor had told Peggy as if such a thing need only be learned by rote. 'He has his bladder under some sort of control now. His bowel movements too. But I am afraid, Mrs Bowmaker, you will have your work cut out in helping him to regain his old self.' He made it sound the easiest thing in the world to do, like boiling an egg. Then he was discharged, to return at ever-lengthening intervals to be 'seen' and dismissed until the next appointment was due. The rest she must shoulder as best she could.

A wheelchair had been provided, a heavy, rattling old thing a ninety-eight-year-old wouldn't have felt any self-respect in, but they had said it would have to do unless she could afford something grander and more suited to her husband's requirements.

219

But she couldn't afford anything grander, not with just Danny to bring in money (the girls' small offerings she could dismiss) and with him hoping eventually to get married to Lily. Dan refused to be seen outside the house in it, though she suspected that if she could afford the Rolls-Royce of wheelchairs he would have refused just as vehemently.

Christmas was a dismal affair. 'I don't want no one spendin' it here,' he told her. 'Sittin' there gloatin' on me.'

'They won't gloat. Every single one of the family is sorry on what's happened. They're all sympathetic. They all want to help.'

'I don't want none o' their sympathy. An' I don't want no one here.'

She explained to them how it was, hoped they understood. But for all their nodding and chewing of lips, she was sure they condemned her for not inviting them for Christmas, it being her turn this year to have them to her house. To her it looked as if she were trying to wriggle out of her responsibility and she felt bad on that score alone. It wasn't even as though it was easy to sneak off and pop down the road to see one of them.

'Where you goin'?' he asked when she attempted to on Thursday, Christmas Eve, around three o'clock. Connie had come home early from work.

'Just popping up to see my sister Anne.' Anne and Bill lived just up the hill off the Broadway, a five-minute walk. 'I'll only be gone an hour.'

'Without me?'

'But you won't go out. And I couldn't push you uphill.'

'What'm I supposed to do stuck here on me own?'

'Connie's here.' Connie would go to church later, to its Christmas Eve service. She bore a worried look lately, said she might not go, though in the end she would. Peggy hoped she was getting over Ben and all that religion she had acquired. Unhealthy, too much religion. Too much of anything could become unhealthy.

'Connie!' came the snorting response.

'I'll only be a tick.' Peggy could hear the pleading in her voice, and felt the humiliation of it deep inside her. She had never been one to plead with anyone – stated a fact and to blazes with what people thought.

'Just to have a few words just to say Merry Christmas to

220

Anne and Bill and give them a card. I can't ignore them completely.'

'Merry bloody Christmas! Some merry bloody Christmas this is goin' to be – me stuck here and you gallivantin' off.'

She should have said, 'What're you going to do about it then?' But she didn't. She loved him. For all his irritability, his irrational attitude that after only a few weeks was driving her up the wall, she loved him; the strong and handsome young man she had once known still in her mind's eye.

So she said instead, a little huffily, 'All right – I won't go out then.'

But when he was asleep the following afternoon, helped out of the chair by Danny and into his bed in the downstairs back room where street noises would not disturb him after the quiet Christmas dinner of which he ate hardly anything, she crept out and hurried off to her brother Harry and his family who lived just off the London Road. It meant a bit of a walk but she had to see them. Pam and George and the baby were at his parents', so she had no need to see them.

With her she had a little bag of presents, nothing much, just a little something for Harry and Daphne and their two children who were now in their early teens and awkward to buy for: a boy's annual for Jimmy which she guessed he might already have grown out of at fourteen, and a pretty box of two embroidered hankies for young Joan, bought, as she always had done, ages ago in readiness for Christmas, well before Dan's accident.

She would also express regrets for not having them at her home for Christmas Day. Her sister Anne, and Bill and their children, would be there with Harry's family, so her apologies would encompass them as well. As she made her way there, thinking of them all together, she already felt excluded, isolated, lonely. They welcomed her heartily enough, brought her into the overheated living room, but the sight of everyone together without her and her family accentuated the feeling and she was glad to come away after an hour, making her excuses after exchanging presents that she couldn't leave Dan for too long.

Huddled against the damp breeze she almost wished she hadn't gone. Over a cup of tea, a glass of sherry and a piece of Anne's Christmas cake, they'd asked after Dan, had tutted when she told

221

them how he was, had made much of waving aside her apologies for not having them to her house, saying they understood.

Now she hurried back through the quiet streets, eager to see how Dan was, wondering what temper he would be in if he had woken up to find her not there. The house would have an empty feel to it after the over-bright, over-hot, busy Christmas cheer of Harry's.

If Dan was still asleep when she got in, all well and good. He'd never need know she'd even gone out. If he felt hungry she'd reheat some of the Christmas chicken and pork for him while she, Connie and Josie ate their tea of cold pork and sweet pickle sandwiches, pickled onions, mince pies and cake. Then Danny would go out to Lily's parents, spend the rest of the evening with them. Only right he should, now they were engaged.

There had been trouble between him and Lily, she thought as she hurried along the cold deserted streets. Everyone was staying indoors digesting their Christmas dinners around a blazing fire, maybe listening to the wireless, maybe snoring in armchairs and settees. Danny, feeling he was needed to help cope with Dad, had told Lily last week that he'd be staying at home for dinner. He had wanted her to be there, but not only had his father got upset about having 'some bloody stranger' round the table gawping at him, but Lily had declined anyway. They had sat at opposite ends of the settee, hardly speaking a word to each other. Lily's face had looked downcast, her eyes sulky, Danny's troubled, his lips compressed. They had left early and at the door Peggy heard her say, 'I'll see myself home,' and him ask, 'What's the matter with you?'

'I just don't want to spend the whole of Christmas Day looking at you pulling your Dad around.' There had been a sharpness in her voice. 'Some Christmas that'll be for me. At least at home we'll be having a good laugh and a bit of fun, all the family round for dinner.'

'I'll come round in the evening,' he'd said, but she hadn't sounded at all mollified.

'*Late* evening I expect.'

'As early as I can make it.'

'They'll be asking where you are and I'll have to make some excuse.'

222

'Just say I was needed here to help Mum with Dad.' His voice had sounded hard.

'I can just see what's going to happen when we're married – you stuck round here looking after your dad. What about me?'

Feeling like an eavesdropper, Peggy had moved quickly back to washing up as noisily as she could so she wouldn't have to overhear any more in the house where every voice carried.

The last thing she wanted was to see strife between these two. She had enough on her plate already. Dan, Connie haunting her church still moping over Ben whose memory by now she should be starting to lay to rest. Josie was no bother, a typical young girl with her ups and downs, but there was Pam. It was getting harder to creep off and see her as she'd been doing once or twice a week while Dan was in hospital, but now he timed her when she went shopping, looking only for her to get back. She'd begun to feel like a trapped animal. Rushing round the shops making herself out of breath, she tried to fit in perhaps twenty minutes to look in on Pam, telling her how things were and seeing her nod and shrug. Peggy thought of Annie too as she bashed the cooking pans in the sud-filled sink. Pam at least had George's family to go to this Christmas, and might even be enjoying herself. But what of Annie? What sort of Christmas was she having thousands of miles away in an alien land? Peggy's heart wept for the girl.

Chapter Twenty-One

'Alex, I want to go home on a visit.'

She knew the best time to go would be in the hot season, but she was pining for her family ever more acutely. Nearly a year had gone by since she left, and so much had happened at home since. Connie's trouble, Pam's, Dad's, Danny courting, Josie growing up and travelling to London to see what Mum said appeared to have become a steady boyfriend.

Annie thought of London, of Southend, of Leigh, and instantly an ache for it all made her heart feel heavy within her. It would be snowing there now. Maybe heavily inland, but spasmodically on the coast, melting quickly in the salty air.

Here it was dry as a bone, the plain with its dotting of scrubby trees dun-coloured, its low distant hills made blue by the hazy air. The sun came up without splendour, always a disappointment after the almost thunderous crimson of dawn, with nothing of the quiet vibrancy of an English winter morning, and set in the briefest blaze of glory, night descending even as one took a breath.

The weather at the moment was like nectar during the day, warm, mild as any English summer. But this was January and the night temperature dropped to near freezing, for all the daytime warmth, the moment that brief twilight faded. Annie derived at last some comfort sitting by a good fire, the wooden shutters of the overstuffed living room of their Jalapur residence closed to the night air, she and Alex reclining in deep cushioned armchairs, the wicker ones they used in the hot season put away. But she did so want to go home, just for a few weeks.

'I wish I could have gone sometime in July, or in August,' she said, her book idle on her lap, the soft crackling of the wood fire the only other sound in the room apart from her voice and the rustle of Alex's *Times of India*. She could have escaped the heat of summer and the clammy misery of the monsoon had she gone then.

'It was too near coming out here,' came his soft voice, his face hidden by the newspaper. 'Couldn't afford to send you, darling. Cost enough to get us out here and set ourselves up.'

'But your father paid for your passage.'

He did not look up. 'Not yours. I had to pay that.'

Annie fell silent. She hated being reminded what he had paid for her to come out here, almost as if he blamed her for the problems this marriage had raised regarding his parents, yet she knew that was bunkum.

But would it have cost so much to go? She wouldn't have asked again. Instead he'd insisted she go stay in Simla, the hill station to which most of the wives from here went to escape the heat of the Northern Plains and the debilitating monsoon.

Between July and September the Club – that haven of gentility set amid the seething mass of the Indian population, the villas, bungalows and administrative buildings reached by wide roads that allowed very few of the Indian community to enter unless authorised – was virtually deserted but for those menfolk who needed to remain, and a sprinkling of diehard older woman who couldn't or wouldn't leave, declaring that they had weathered a quarter of a lifetime of Indian summers and saw no reason for being packed off to some hill town with all the resultant upheaval to their ordered lives.

But Annie, in her first year of marriage and so in love with Alex, had not wanted to leave him until the heat finally made her ill and she had seen the wisdom of going up to a hill station out of it all.

Simla had been beautiful and miserable. She had missed Alex dreadfully, because he too was compelled to stay behind for his work. When he came up at odd weekends by train, which took hours, she had begged that, with the monsoon letting up a little, she be allowed to go back with him, that the wives were even more awful to her here without him to act as a buffer. All he had done was tell her she was being silly again.

225

'You've been almost a year in this country, Annie. I'd have thought you'd have got used to everyone by now.'

'I don't know how to explain,' she'd pleaded as they lay in the wide canopied bed in the little house he'd got for her that overlooked other steep-roofed little houses to the main street with its very English frontages. It looked like a slice of some East Sussex village except for being surrounded by mountain peaks. 'I don't know what it is. The young people new out from England always seem to get such a welcome. I never did, and still feel out of it all.'

'They did welcome you,' he had told her as he had done so many times before in every argument over this. 'They couldn't have done more for you or been more welcoming. But you wouldn't have it. You've never mixed.'

'Because I've never felt that I fitted in.'

'Because you never give it a try. No wonder no one comes up to talk to you unless you go up to them. And you don't do that either, do you? It's your own fault, Annie. When are you going to start mixing and not expect me to hold your hand?'

'And have to put up with the funny looks, the way they either pore over me as if they are doing me a favour, or turn their backs on me to talk among themselves.'

'That's your imagination. If you joined in they'd take more notice of you. You make yourself excluded. I've watched you, Annie. You just turn away and walk off. Some of them look quite surprised and bewildered when they turn back and find you gone. They are nice people, Annie.'

'To you maybe. To me they're just a stuck-up lot of hypocrites, making out they're something they're not.'

'You can't blame them, darling. They need to put on an act, here. It's their way of sticking together against this country, as they see it. Doesn't it ever occur to you that some of them would sooner be in England, would like to be with the families they left behind, just as you would?'

'No, it doesn't. From what I hear, they'd sooner be dead than go back to England, having to fend for themselves without any native servants toadying around them. Here they live the life of Riley, mix with the Viceroy and the Maharaja, and they feel like kings, above everyone else, even the Maharaja himself. Or feel themselves at least on a par with him, a ruler in his own right. They are the Raj! Back in England they'd be nothing.'

226

When their argument reached that stage, as she seethed from her own words, hating herself for the sneering tone of her own voice, he would let it drop, suddenly, turning his back on her, leaving her miserable, knowing it was she who'd started the argument, but petulantly blaming him for it.

They had always seemed to argue there when they should have been making the most of their time together. Not during the day when there was so much to do and she and Alex, her hand in his for protection, mixed with the others at the Simla Club, going to dances or the home-produced plays and musicals the groups here delighted in putting on; when the air like sparkling wine made the wooded peaks of the Himalayan foothills stand out so clear it felt one could reach out and touch them; when she and Alex would shop in the main street with its European shop fronts and its English signs or wander arm in arm up and down the steep little roads with their very western houses – little echoes of the homes the Anglo-Indians had left behind. But at night when the world fell silent and they lay in each other's arms after making love, trying to cram the weeks of emptiness, at least for her, all into one brief night, and sometimes even before they made love, so ruining what joy Annie had of him, the argument always came round to the same topic. 'I hate it here. I want to come back with you.'

'You'd hate it even more down on the plain.'

'I want to be with you.'

'You are with me.'

'One weekend out of three?'

'Every other weekend.'

'Not always. I'm so lonely without you. When you miss two weekends I begin to feel you can do without me all the time and have stopped loving me. Out of sight, out of mind, they say.'

And then he'd tell her again not to be silly, that he had never stopped loving her, and one occasion had reminded her what he had given up so they could be together. She had come dangerously near to tears, her arms around his naked body, wanting to push him from her but making those arms tighten in case her misery might, like some tugging rope, pull her from him. 'I know I've spoiled your life,' she recalled saying on that occasion. 'I know I'm the cause of the rift between you and your parents.'

He had written to them in early July while she had been in Simla, at last confessing to this marriage to her. 'Why couldn't

227

you have waited until I was back in Jalapur?' she had condemned him. 'It would have given us a little more time before your father's reply arrived to upset you.' For the letter had been full of wrath and acrimony, informing his son that he would see to it that Alex would be staying in India indefinitely; that he wished he could arrange for him and that *person* he'd taken up with utterly against his and his mother's wills to be sent even further away; that if Alex ever wished to return he would be expected to look for a position other than in the family business, and that as far as he and his mother were concerned, he had made his own bed and must lie in it; he'd receive his salary – would not be cut off, would not starve, blood thicker than water despite how he had abused it – would receive his share of profits – no intention of his status being lowered – but if he ever came home he would find things a darn sight altered. He'd sat very silent for a long time afterwards then had slowly torn the letter in half and put it away. He only wrote his father business letters now.

All this lay well behind them now. January had come, a new year, nineteen thirty-one, new hopes, new ideas, for some perhaps. Alex had now adjusted to his father's attitude, and Annie could see herself being here in India to the end of her days. Some went home, new people came out, but the old guard seemed to go on and on, and she grew no nearer becoming integrated into their circles except for the odd gracious invitation. Perhaps Alex was right. Perhaps it was her and not them. But she was always so homesick.

Gazing into the fire while he devoured the last few snippets of news in the paper, she thought of the Christmas Eve dance at the Club. She had let Alex persuade her, torn between reluctance and a need to get out of the house in which, with Alex at his office, she had been languishing all week.

She had quite enjoyed it at first, sharing a table with Mr and Mrs Ansley Burrington, he a magistrate, and Mr and Mrs Oliver Twining – Annie wasn't sure what he did, but he was a quiet and distant sort of man while his fat little wife talked nineteen to the dozen, keeping the conversation going around the table nearly all the evening. Mr and Mrs Twining hadn't danced but Mr and Mrs Burrington did occasionally between talk, and so had she and Alex.

In an evening dress Alex had bought her, the black silk crepe

falling into straight columns when not in motion, the only orna-
ment a diamanté clip on one of the narrow shoulder straps which
had accentuated her tall slim figure, the spray of pink flowers at
her waist not detracting from that slimness one bit, she attracted
the attention of all. This time the attention did not bother her;
she'd even danced two or three times with Ansley Burrington,
ignoring the look his wife had given her. A couple of gin and
tonics made Annie bold though not tipsy.

Ansley Burrington was rather like Alex in a way: tall, lean,
though he sported a Ronald Colman moustache which gave him a
debonair appearance. He tended to rile his wife by declaring
himself sympathetic towards the Indian, perhaps more than he
should, much to her irritation since she saw them in a totally
different light to him. Her rather raw-boned figure drew itself up
with indignation during one conversation about the Indian's
ongoing and recently renewed certainty of his own country's
destiny without British interference.

'*Their* country, yes, but where would they be without us? Most
of them live in abject poverty. You see them everywhere, cripples,
beggars, young boys, always a hand stretched out for a rupee to be
dropped into it. They try to touch you with their fingers, but they
daren't of course. You can't give to *all* of them. Yet their own
wealthy pass them by without a glance. The country does nothing
for them at all. It is quite untouched by them because they have
always been here. It does nothing at all to help them.'

'Quite right,' Mrs Twining put in, for once reduced to mono-
syllables by the unexpected outpouring of the other woman.

But Burrington said, 'We don't help them either.'

'Of course we do. We give them work. Employ them as
servants, as gardeners, cooks, builders, trade with them in the
market. You don't see poverty like that in England.'

'There is now,' Annie had said, still bold. 'The Depression has
put thousands out of work and on to the dole.'

'But they *get* dole. These people are just left by their state to
starve.'

'I think a lot of people in England and in America *are* starving.'

'My dear,' Mrs Burrington turned on her. 'You don't know
what you are talking about.'

'My mother tells me about it in her letters, and then there are the
newspapers, and . . .'

229

But Mrs Burrington had already turned from her, speaking to Alex, suggesting a spot of tennis in the morning. 'It would start Christmas off quite nicely, don't you think? Give us all an appetite for a nice Christmas dinner – as good as these servants of ours can cook. They have no understanding at all of the English palate. But I suppose they do their best. Shall we say ten o'clock then, before it gets too hot?'

Annie had fallen silent. Not only had she been ignored, suddenly, as usual, but she detested tennis. Not when she and Alex played alone, then it was fun and full of laughs. He had taught her to play and she still couldn't play at all well. People like Mrs Burrington, who had been playing it all their lives, saw her as ungainly and inept. She had looked across at Ansley Burrington and seen understanding in his eyes and she had smiled shyly back at him.

In its way it had been quite a successful evening, thanks to him, but now Alex had said yesterday that they had been invited to the New Year's Eve dance on Wednesday. It couldn't happen twice that she'd have Ansley Burrington to help bolster her. It had started the same old argument when she said she didn't feel like going. Alex had asked why not.

'Because . . . because I don't fit in.'

He had verged on irritation. 'You're as good as anyone there. I can afford nice dresses for you. For God's sake, Annie! You were all right last week. It's your attitude towards everyone here that makes you stand out like a sore thumb. You never relax.'

'I can't.'

'*Make* yourself. For my sake. They're English, damn it. Not foreigners. They're our sort.'

'Not mine. I only have to open my mouth for them to look at me as though I came out of a dustbin.'

'That's bloody stupid, Annie, and you know it. Look at Bainbury – a Yorkshireman with a Yorkshire accent. No one takes the slightest notice.'

'Bainbury's in the diplomatic corps,' she'd snapped. 'Most of them are something in the civil service. You're only a merchant, and they just see me as . . .'

'Thank you!' he'd blurted and she had fallen silent, aware of having touched a tender spot in him, an awareness that he too was not as acceptable to the men's snobbish wives as he might wish to be. 'I get on with most of the men well enough,' he protested before he too lapsed into silence. The rest of their evening was strained, with Annie resolved to insist on visiting her family as soon as the hot weather began in April.

Life in India revolved around the weather. The heat and the slow whirring of electric fans or flap of punkahs and the constant round of iced drinks in a sustained effort to keep cool dominated every thought; houses were designed against the heat, their windows unglazed to let through a constant stream of air, and all of them featured the customary shading veranda. The native shops were completely open-fronted. All clothing had to be light-weight, cotton, so men's suits always looked unpressed. From October to March cooling breezes all the way from the Himalayas tempered the heat, but then it would grow hotter and hotter, stifling, and from July to September it just rained and rained. Oh, how she longed for the vagaries of an English summer's day or even a creeping, silent November fog disturbed only by the trilling of a robin or a wren rather than the irritatingly plaintive bell-like calls of birds whose names she didn't know or the harsh squawking of green parakeets.

Well, this summer she'd have none of it. She'd badger Alex blue in the face until he let her go for a visit back home. Far better than languishing in some insular hill station. After two months she'd return happy and contented, and he would soon see the benefits of it. Already she could see herself at home, taking part in the family once more.

Peggy was ironing at the table before the kitchen range, face florid from its heat, where she had a second iron waiting to be taken off its trivet and used as the other became too cool to smooth the sheets and shirts she laid on an old worn sheet, well singed to a mottled brown from endless use as an ironing cloth.

'Reg and Pete didn't seem too happy about us not asking them and their families here for Christmas Day,' she remarked to Dan in his wheelchair by the fire.

'Didn't they? Pity!' was his grunted reply.

'They spoke about it again to Danny on the boat yesterday,' she continued undaunted.

Even if he was mostly silent and morose, he was someone to talk to. It was still strange having him around her feet all day

231

where she had once been on her own, quite often singing to herself in her rather tuneless voice with no one to hear or complain. She didn't sing any more, but talked to him as if she addressed a wall; he made no reply apart from a grunt, maybe a sentence now and again, or sometimes nothing at all as he sat staring out of the window, smoking his everlasting pipe, or into the fire, not even reading a newspaper properly.

'They looked in on New Year's Eve,' he said now.

'Yes, for a short while, for a drop of whisky to see in the New Year and be sociable. Then they went home to bed. You hardly spoke to any of them. You didn't want to hear anything they had to say about the boat or the business. You didn't seem a bit interested. Not like the New Years we used to have, all evening and into next morning, all of us having such a good time and them all going home hardly able to stand, full of drink. That seems to be all over.' Her elbow bent to her ironing. 'All in the past.'

'Waste of money. Ain't got money to throw about no more.'

That was true. Danny was doing his best. On his own with his uncles he brought in as much as Dan once had. But she couldn't take as much off him as she had Dan, knowing Danny was saving like mad to get married. And times were against him too. The Depression hit them all, was hitting them harder and harder with no sign of relenting.

Josie had lost her job at the Cliffs Hotel. With fewer people able to afford to stay there, there was no need for an assistant receptionist. Cleaners, chambermaids, doormen, porters, many of them had also lost their jobs, were now on the dole. But for young people like Josie, there was no dole.

She had gone up to London today to see what she could find, imagining there might be more hope in the city. Peggy hated the thought of her wandering around up there on her own but she had said that her boyfriend, Arthur Monk, would be with her, helping her to search. It seemed that his work in the docks had fallen off badly and there was little work for him. And he had a mother to keep, just as Danny now had.

Connie was still in work, thank goodness, her firm keeping her on as best they could, though it was all so uncertain. Pam's husband had been laid off before Christmas. That made the third job he'd lost, casual labour which could be dispensed with at a moment's notice. She had been to see Pam this week, unbeknown to their father. Pam had said they were just managing on George's tiny bit of dole money. She had left Pam with a couple of shillings – all she dared afford – to help tide her over a few days, and a couple of dresses for Beth which she'd secretly knitted out of bits of wool from a couple of her old jumpers, piecing any severed strands together so that the dresses were multicoloured. But in this cold weather they were much needed. It seemed George's parents were trying to help as best they could. Maybe they weren't all bad, but try telling Dad that. And all the while Danny was working his socks off trying to help make ends met.

There was still a living to be made from cockling. Cockles didn't know there was a depression, so they bred as well as ever. But it was winter, and harder to get out to them with the weather always worsening around January and February. And last summer the holiday trade had gone down noticeably, another aspect of the times. Most who had once found the half-a-crown day return train fare for a Sunday out at Southend now had other uses for the money, which might keep their family for a week on cheap food. The rent probably got paid by hocking something in a pawn shop, the only businesses doing well these days. And there was Danny's Lily going on about grand weddings and honeymoons. Her dad was threatened with being given the push with the firm he worked for slowly going down, so you'd think she'd know better.

Peggy took the iron that had been heating up in front of the range, put the cool one in its place and spat on the smoothing surface of the new one to test its temperature in case it scorched the shirt she was doing. It sizzled fiercely. She put it on the trivet on the table to cool a fraction before applying it to the material.

She thought suddenly of Pam again and spoke vaguely to the wall before stopping to consider. 'Pam's George is out of work.'

Dan had taken his pipe from his mouth. His voice was a growl. 'We don't know no one of that name, so how would you know?'

Peggy's back went up immediately. This was getting bloody stupid. His own daughter. She stopped ironing and turned on him. 'I've been to see her, that's how.'

The walls of the kitchen with some of the finished ironing airing around them resounded to his bellow. 'You been what? Been to see 'er?'

Hers was a show of defiance and assertiveness. 'Yes, Dan,

more than once. I see her once a week, when I go shopping, ever since before you came out of hospital. She's got a baby now – my grandchild, our grandchild. And if you don't want ever to see her, I do.'

She wanted to add, 'So there!' but she merely stood watching him splutter.

When he found his voice again, it was hoarse, querulous, almost self-pitying. 'Just because I'm stuck here in this bleedin' wheelchair, you think you can take advantage – that I can't do nothing to stop you in this . . . bloody thing!' His clenched fist struck the chair's wooden arm, making it shudder. 'You think you can walk roughshod over me. Well, my word still stands for something in this damned house. You don't go round there any more, hear me? You, knowing what that swine did to cripple me.'

'He didn't cripple you,' she rounded on him. 'You fell.'

'I wouldn't of done if he hadn't been there goadin' me.'

Peggy turned back to her ironing, resumed it with nervous energy. 'Well, whatever, Pam's still your daughter . . . *still* your daughter,' she said, her voice lifting above his effort to protest. She had him captive here. There was nowhere he could go, with her between him and the door, and she wasn't going to move. For the first time in all her married life she had power over him although until this second she had never seen herself as his inferior. It had just been marriage, like all marriages. The women's role was to manage the house, feed her husband and their children on what money he gave her, and see to his comforts. The man earned the money. He called the tune. Now things had changed. Suddenly she could tell Dan what to do. She felt strangely frightened. Of course she would run to his call, continue to care for him, fit her life around him, but at this moment she too had a say in her own daughter's welfare, against all his wishes.

She continued ironing without looking at him. 'Now listen here, Dan Bowmaker. Pam . . . yes, I shall say her name. Pam is my daughter, and I've deserted her long enough. Now with a baby and no money coming in, her and her husband living in that squalid little hole – you've not seen it. I have. In our present circumstances I can't help there, no more than her in-laws can, but I can give her my love even if you can't.'

'But that brat – it's half Bryant. The sod what did for me first time and's done for me again – put me in this wheelchair for the rest of me life. And you can forgive all that?' His tone was incredulous. Peggy felt almost sorry for him, but she also felt strong, determined.

'No, Dan, I don't forgive all that. I'm just thinking of Pam and an innocent little baby. It don't matter if you, or even me, don't approve of what she did, going off and marrying the son of that family. Anyway, I'm not going to argue on that score. But Pam's my daughter. I don't care what she did, she's still my daughter. I'm her mother. And if I can do anything for her and our . . . *my* grandchild – and her name's Beth by the way, Elizabeth, after me – I shall do it to my last breath. So there!'

She had said it, 'so there', and he could do about it what he liked.

Chapter Twenty-Two

'I'm sorry miss, but there really isn't anything.'

The blue-eyed, short-haired blonde gave Josie a wan smile through the grill of the office in which she sat, the smile conveying sympathy, fellow feeling, and a message that but for the grace of God there went she too. She had only just procured this job after five months out of work and intended to hang on to it, tooth and nail if necessary, but Josie couldn't know that.

To Josie, the smile was one of smugness and she felt hate rise up inside her against the unsuspecting girl. You're all right, Jack, came the thought which never materialised into words and Josie nodded glumly, offered the girl a wan smile of her own and turned away.

'No luck,' she said to Arthur waiting outside.

'Me neivver.'

He had been waiting around the dock gates since seven this morning, saw the man on the other side pick a lucky few, saw the iron gates open a fraction to take them in, then close again. No one surged forward to squeeze in with the rest. To what purpose? They'd only have been ejected. There *was* no more work and rushing the gates couldn't make work that didn't exist. A few hung around, hopeful of a ship coming in at midday, though they saw not much chance of it. One and only one had come into London dock this morning, for the whole world faced the same plight: business going down, no money, no cargo, no work for men. The rest of the unlucky throng had moved silently away. It was the silence of despair, of hunger, of forlorn hope that tomorrow might, *might* see them get some work, if only for one day. Cloth-capped, greasy-suited, broken-shoed, they moved off, hands in pockets, heads bent, tight-lipped, silent.

'Might be somefink termorrer,' Arthur said as he and Josie walked away from the employment office she had tried. 'But I ain't 'oldin' me breff.'

Josie nodded. It had been a wild goose chase coming up to London, apart from seeing Arthur, and even that was getting harder to do, what little money she had left all going on train fares to see him.

He'd got himself a bike for two and sixpence off a mate down on his uppers and glad of the money. The bike was old, rattled, had more patches than original rubber on the inner tubes, but on this, armed with an Ever Ready puncture outfit, he'd pedal all the way to Leigh to see her once a week because coming all that way on a cranky old bike was no mean feat to be endured more often than that. Three hours' pedalling, at least it didn't cost him anything. But seeing him leave around three o'clock, because it grew dark so early in February, Josie's heart went out to him. Six hours' pedalling for two hours with her, that was proof of his love for her. Hers for him lay in the prayers she said for his safe return home, and the sacrifice of scarce cash on a return train fare once every three weeks to go and see him.

This week it had been for another hopeful search for work in London, erroneously believed to hold more work for a girl who only knew how to be a receptionist, with no typing or shorthand or clerical skills, than did Southend or Leigh itself.

Her feet ached from walking around following the few hopeful adverts in newspapers, each one having gone the minute it appeared, and trudging from private agency to employment office to company offices themselves in case a job might be going. By the end of the day she would have been willing to take anything, even in a garment factory although she was no commercial machinist.

Josie pulled her coat collar tighter about her neck and glanced up at the cold overcast sky squeezed between the grimy buildings of Leadenhall Street. What she could see of it, yellow with London smoke, looked laden with snow. A clock projecting out from an office block showed three thirty.

'It'll be dark by the time I get home,' she said. 'I'd best start off now.'

237

'Yeah, yer best,' Arthur agreed. 'I'll try ter get down on Sunday. If the bike 'olds out, that is.'

'What's wrong with it?' Unreasonable panic gripped. What if the bike, on its last legs anyway, was no longer usable?

'Brakes,' he said succinctly, which spoke of utter despondency. 'Bust.'

'Can't you repair them?'

'I'm 'avin' a go. Can probably patch 'em up, but it's a long way ter Leigh wivout proper brakes.'

'Won't you be able to see me on Sunday?'

'If I can, Jo, I will. I bloody will. Even if it snows . . .' He glanced up at the leaden sky. 'I will.'

'Oh, no, Arthur. Not if it snows hard and settles. Not with bad brakes. I wouldn't want you to.'

They had turned towards Fenchurch Street Station, and he suddenly pulled her into a covered alley between the buildings, dim and quiet. There he kissed her long and hard, his lips cold on hers. Josie returned the kisses with a longing that seemed to come up from the soles of the high heeled shoes she wore for job-hunting to make her look smarter but which played havoc with feet plodding from one possible vacancy to another.

'Oh, Arthur, I wish we were rich,' she said, breaking away finally. 'I wish we could be . . .'

'Be married,' he finished for her as she hesitated over the word. He had never yet proposed. Talked about the number of kids he'd like when he did get married, but never applied it to her. 'I'd like nuffink better than ter be married. An' one day, that's wot I mean ter do, Jo, get married – ter you.'

It had come out in a rush, almost as though it embarrassed him, taking her utterly by surprise. His next words dumbfounded her even more.

'Wot yer say, Jo? Would yer marry me?'

She couldn't speak, couldn't answer. All sorts of questions rushed through her head in those few seconds, remarkable how many questions could fill one's head in such a minuscule amount of time: did he mean it or was it just that kiss? What would they live on, with both of them out of work? How could they afford even the cheapest of weddings? Where did he expect them to live? Not at her house? Too crowded. Not at his, a Bethnal Green tenancy with two bedrooms both being used. They couldn't afford rent on even a one-roomed place.

Arthur was already speaking for her. 'We'd 'ave ter wait some time, I know,' as if she had already consented; taking it for granted that she had. 'I wanna give yer a good life, Jo. Not some rotten squalid little 'ole, but somfink really nice. Maybe fings'll change in a year or two – the country get itself ter rights again, and I get proper reg'lar work again. Then I'll 'ave money ter ask yer again . . . if yer'll wait for me.'

The last sounded so sad, it wrenched Josie's heart. She found herself crying, 'Arthur, I'll wait till the world catches fire. I'll wait forever.'

'Yer mean that?'

'Every word, Arthur.' Her voice was trembling. She felt like breaking into tears; felt him clutch at her, draw her near, hold her tight against him.

They stood in the dim alley, holding each other fiercely. Against his chest, Josie murmured, 'I'm going to have to go, darling, unless I want to miss my train.'

'Yeah,' he said softly and kissed her. 'Yer best go. An' I'll see yer Sunday, brakes or no brakes. Snow or no snow.'

'I don't want you to come if it turns dangerous. Please don't take any chances. For my sake.'

But she knew that if he did turn up, pedalling through the elements to reach her, the love she would give to him would excel anything they had so far indulged in. If he turned up, she would seal this promise she and he had just made, seal it properly for the first time ever.

Peggy, popping in to see her as usual after her Friday shopping, came up the stairs that seemed to get longer every time she visited puffing under the load of vegetables, a bit of meat, cooking fat and marge, sugar and tea; milk and bread, thank the Lord, were delivered to the doorstep, and fish got from the fishermen coming off their boats. She was met at the door to the top flat by Pam who had heard her coming, each step slower as it rose higher.

Peggy got easily tired these days. Felt her age as she liked to say, but it wasn't age, it was Dan. He was a burden on her, four months at home and she was feeling it. Shopping in a hurry to make up the time she spent with Pam didn't do her any favours either. She still felt guilty about her visits for all she'd defiantly said 'so what' to him.

'Lord, that is a load to carry. Good job the rest of the way's downhill or I'd be on my knees time I get home.'

'Mum, guess what?'

She hadn't noticed Pam beaming. Now she did. 'Guess what, what?'

'George has got himself a job. A proper job. A foreman in a builder's yard. Long term. Could be forever.'

'How on earth did he come by that?' Peggy put down her two bags. She wouldn't be staying that long, just a quick cuppa and a cheerio kiss. Pam already had the pot filled, anticipating the time of arrival.

'He just walked into the yard. He can't believe his luck. There was no one else there looking for work. The boss was there and the men working. George just went in, asked if there was any work, and the boss asked had he ever worked as a foreman? George said yes, of course. He's not daft, George, he's watched foremen in his other jobs, what they did, how they did it. So of course he said yes. He just kept his fingers crossed and prayed. The chap didn't even ask for credentials or anything. He said he'd been informed half an hour before that his foreman had had a heart attack and died that very morning. He was about to look for someone else but he had a job to get done quickly, materials and things to get, and he couldn't do it all himself because he'd sacked several men lately because the work had fallen off. Now this work had come up and with his foreman just dead, he was in a quandary. Can you believe it?'

Peggy hardly could. There was still some grace in the world, still a God somewhere looking after people like Pam and George.

She went to the cot where little Beth was playing safely with a few spoons Pam had put in there for her. She was clashing them together, obliging her mother to shout her news over the top of the noise.

Peggy lifted the child up into her arms, kissing her little face. It smelled of Sunlight soap. Her little cheeks were scarlet from the soap's harshness. Peggy hoped Pam didn't scrub too hard – a light touch of such soap was enough for tender baby skin.

'She's really bonny,' Peggy remarked, taking in the natural

scent of Beth's skin, burying her nose into the fine fair hair to catch even more of it.

'I try to give her as good food as I can, Mum.'

Probably going without yourself to do it, Peggy thought sadly.

Pam had put two cups of steaming tea on the table. 'How's Dad?'

Peggy placed Beth back into her cot and picking up her cup sat down with it, her face already going tight. 'Driving me up the wall.'

'Don't Connie help, or Josie?'

'Of course they do,' Peggy felt her back go up. 'They all do, in their way. But he wears me down. He's so demanding and he's never happy. Well, who would be in that predicament? It's just that he wants to do more than it's possible for him to do, and when he can't he just flies into a temper with everyone. He keeps talking about having splints put on his legs and getting crutches, but just watching him trying to get into bed or out of it, I know it's too early, if it ever does happen at all. As I see it, only a miracle can get him back on his feet. He can't feel his legs at all, you know.'

She took a sip of her tea. Pam had forgotten to put the sugar in, but she didn't remind her. Pam would probably need that spoonful at some time or another. The packet was three-quarters empty and she guessed it was all she had until George came home with his first week's pay packet. Hopefully they might live better from now on, but it was risky to count chickens before they hatched. For all Pam's high hopes, he could lose this job as quick as he got it. It only needed his lack of knowledge as a foreman to be exposed by one error and he would be out on his ear, a skilled foreman taken on in his place. There were dozens, hundreds ready to jump into his shoes just as he had into those of a dead man. It sounded awful but it was how things were.

'I'm going to have to go after this,' Peggy said, sipping the hot tea. She never did have a cast iron stomach and her tea was usually half cold at home by the time she ever got to it. She was used to it that way.

At least she had a few more minutes finishing it to exchange a little more chat: how Pam was coping; how Beth was progressing; telling Pam in return about her latest letter from India – 'I bet the postman thinks we're real quality getting letters from India. He often gives me a funny look. She sends you her love by the way

241

and I tell her all about you'; how Connie was still plodding off to church every Sunday morning – 'I worry for that girl, you know, she just refuses to get over Ben, it makes my heart go out to her and makes me angry too.'

In the final few moments left she crammed in a bit about Danny and Lily. Danny was still hedging about a day for their marriage – 'he's talking about next year now. I sometimes wonder if he really wants to get married, wants the responsibility, you know how he always liked the girls, liked being fancy-free.'

Josie she had hardly left herself time to talk about. Josie, though still out of work and March was already here, was all right. No housekeeping came in from her. 'Well, you can't take anything off her like that. We manage. Danny's not doing too bad. At last Billingsgate came up trumps this winter, kept us out of Poor Street, and he's working hard. With spring just around the corner, we just hope we get a good bit of holiday trade for Easter. Keep our fingers crossed. Right, I must be off.' She drained her cup, glanced at the battered old alarm clock on the shelf and got up. 'See you next week, dear.'

Going over to bestow a lingering kiss on her grandchild's soft cheek and giving Pam a quick kiss, she gathered up her hat, coat shopping and handbag.

She was behind the door, putting on her coat, when a firm knock sounded. 'Now who can that be?' Pam asked with a smile. Peggy smiled back.

'Whoever it is,' she said as she pulled on her brown woolly hat, 'I'm on my way.'

Peggy prepared herself to murmur apology for having to depart the moment whoever it was – a friend of Pam's probably – turned up. Instead, she uttered a startled gasp. For a second the two women stared at each other, neither able to believe who she saw confronting her.

'What're you doing here?' Peggy's face flamed, her fury flying towards the other woman whose features had also turned instantly red and bloated.

'I might ask the same about you.'

'I came to see my daughter . . .'

'Daughter – huh! That's a laugh. The so-called mother who turns her own daughter out on to the streets, didn't care a bugger

242

where she went or how she could cope. I'd say I've *more* right to be here than you. At least we've tried to help her.'

'Help yourselves, you mean. Always been able to do that, ain't you? Now, if you don't mind, out of my way.'

Peggy made to push past the wife of her husband's hated enemy, but the woman's tall angular frame barred her way. 'Hang on a minute! What d'you mean, help ourselves?'

Peggy had no idea what she had meant; the words had exploded from her in pure anger, without foundation. 'Just let me pass,' she blustered.

It was impossible for Peggy to force her way past the larger woman, who continued to rail. 'I want to know what you meant by that – help ourselves. We've never had any thought of helping ourselves to anything. What's our George got to give us, him been out of work all these months and a wife and baby to look after? And what's his wife brought to her marriage that we can *help ourselves* to? Nothing but trouble, that's what she brought into this marriage. But we ain't complained. We understand the love 'tween them two and no blinking arguments can alter that. So I don't know what you mean, *help ourselves.*'

It would have been proper for Peggy to apologise, her words totally uncalled for, but the old long-festering wounds had broken out afresh as though they had happened yesterday. Peggy could see it as if on a cinema screen: Dan staring desolately at his boat, burned beyond salvage; the bleak days that followed trying vainly to take the culprit to court, unable to pay the cost of a solicitor's fee unless prepared to take a risk with the insurance, which was more needed for a replacement for their livelihood. They'd dared not risk everything on such skimpy evidence. Someone said they'd only *thought* they'd seen someone who they *thought* looked like Bryant running from the fire, though Dan knew all too well who the culprit was and had spent years wishing he had taken that swine to court after all as he fought to make ends meet. But the way Bryant had made himself scarce for months after, it could only have been him. Without proper evidence, or money for solicitors, legal people shrugged their shoulders and left it to the warring parties to settle their own scores. Dan had been all for seeking Bryant out and beating him to a pulp, and who would have blamed him but those very people who had refused to fight his case for him. They would have clapped Dan in jail for assault

243

and battery, maybe manslaughter, whereas Dick Bryant should have been put in jail for what he did.

And here was this woman, Bryant's wife, yelling at her like a fishwife in Pam's flat, Pam now in tears, hurt by what had been said about her and by the way her mother was being yelled at; little Beth screaming and choking and no one going to her aid. Peggy wanted to but when she did, she was barred by her adversary.

'You leave my grandchild alone! I was the one stood by her when she gave birth to that child. Where was you? Don't you bloody touch her!'

'I'll touch my own grandchild whenever I want without your leave.'

'Mum! Mum! Both of you!' Pam was shouting, the argument unreasonable.

'Don't you call *her* Mum,' raged Peggy, not looking at her as she found just enough strength to push the woman back to the still-open door way. 'I'm your mum. Not her. It was her husband, your father-in-law, what put your own father out of business. A deliberate act of wickedness.'

'Wickedness!' Mrs Bryant's voice had risen to a scream. 'It wasn't my Dick's fault. You don't know the half of it. You never wanted to know. He tried to explain when your Dan came round after him, but Dick had to run for his life when he came at him with a great big iron rod or he'd 've been beaten to death.'

Peggy had never heard this part of it. But the woman was lying.

'I don't want to hear none of your excuses,' she yelled. 'Dick Bryant's a snivelling coward, that's all I can say. Now get out of my way, you cow!' The word just came out unbidden, shocking even her.

Footsteps were hurrying up the stairs, light and urgent. Neither of them saw the landlady approaching along the landing as Mrs Bryant's outraged hand landed with a resounding slap upon Peggy's cheek. For a moment the hurt stunned her, but rage gave her strength and she pushed her hands out in front of her, handbag and shopping basket swinging, and thrust past the woman, knocking her against the wall, collided with another figure, in her haste not recognising it as Pam's landlady, not even hearing the gasp the woman gave, and was off down the stairs before anyone

244

could see the tears that had begun to spurt from her eyes; not even turning as Pam called frantically after her: 'Mum! Mum!'

How she got home through the busy Friday streets she had no real idea except that the moment she let herself inside the sanctuary of her own house she burst into tears that had been pent up all the way here.

Josie was there, giving eye to her father. Josie remained out of work and moped around the house a lot. Hearing her mother, she ran from the back room.

'What's wrong? What's happened? You ain't 'ad an accident, have yer?'

No longer a hotel receptionist with nicely controlled diction, some of Arthur's dialect had more and more begun to rub off on to her.

'No. I've not had an accident.' Her mother shrugged away from her consoling cuddle, straightened her back and bore her shopping off to the kitchen. Josie followed at a distance, mystified. 'Where is your father?'

'Having a lie-down. Mum, what's the matter? Why're you crying?'

'I'm not crying, I'm just tired!' The words were terse, sharp, filled with anger. Josie watched her begin to unpack the goods she'd bought, hands trembling over the task, the canvas shopping bag unsteady on the edge of the kitchen table and becoming more floppy and unbalanced as she unpacked the bit of meat, sugar and tea, fats, cabbage. Suddenly the weight of the loose potatoes took it over the table edge as they spilled out and rolled over the floor. 'Oh, God! Oh, sod it! Sod everything! Sod her and everyone!'

It was the final straw. She fell back on to a chair by the table, doubled herself forward over her knees, her face hidden in her hands, her whole body convulsing in a welter of weeping. Josie stared, shocked by the sight, then rushed forward and put her arms about her mother. 'Oh, Mum, don't.'

From the back room, her father's voice called, a deep querulous demand. 'What's going on out there? What's the matter with your mother? Josie, help get me out of this bleeding bed. I want to see what's wrong.'

'It's nothing, Dad,' Josie called back, her mother slumped in her arms. It was something she had never experienced before.

Mum was always so staunchly herself, propping up the family, dealing with their crises, dealing with her own, a pillar of strength when anyone needed it. If she cried at all, no one ever saw her. Now this. 'Mum's a bit upset, that's all.'

It was an understatement. Mum was crumpled, sobbing her heart out. She seemed to possess no strength, weeping like a young uncontrollable girl, great gulping sobs.

'Let me see her,' came the demand from the back room. 'Josie, get me out of this bloody bed. I want to see your mother.'

'Don't . . . don't let him see me . . . like this.' The broken plea came muffled by Josie's consoling arms.

'No I won't, Mum.' Her mother was recovering her composure with amazing speed, lifting her head, dragging the heel of her hands across her wet eyes. She sniffed back the tears, a hard determined sniff, smiled at Josie then turned away, almost herself again. 'Get me a hankie out of me bag. Silly bitch, going on like that – and all over nothing.'

'It don't look like nothing to me, Mum.' Josie eased the handbag off her mother's arm, as Peggy looked at it with surprise to see it still there, fished inside and brought out a clean and folded white handkerchief. Her mother had come through the streets with tears falling down her cheeks, in public, not once thinking to wipe them away. 'What upset you?'

'Just me being silly.'

'It must be something bad ter make you be like this.'

'I said get me out of this sodding bed!' Josie looked imploringly at her mother, torn between her two parents.

She saw the understanding in her mother's face as the swollen eyes turned first to her then down at the still-folded but now wet hankie then at her again. 'Let him wait. I don't want him to see me like this. He'll start asking questions and he's the last one I want to tell.'

'Tell what, Mum?'

Her mother took a deep shuddering breath and got up from the chair to collect the scattered potatoes from the kitchen floor. She was more herself again though still not quite. Suddenly she let the potatoes drop and sat back down on the chair. 'I can't tell your dad, but I can't keep all this to meself.'

As Josie listened, on her haunches before her mother, she told her all that had occurred. 'I've never been smacked round the face

246

before, not in all my life. I feel humiliated. I've always thought I knew how your dad felt about that man, what he did to us, but now I know first-hand. And with our Pam married into that family, I don't know what to do. There's nothing I *can* do, but I can't ever go back to that flat. I couldn't bear coming face to face with that woman again. I feel so humiliated.'

'But you must keep on seeing Pam. Don't you want to see her at least?'

'I do, love. But not there. I couldn't . . .'

A roar from the back room interrupted her. 'Come and get me up!'

'I've got to go, Mum,' Josie implored. Her mother took a deep breath.

'Go and see to him. But don't tell him anything I've told you. Just say I had a fall coming home. He won't ask questions. He's too full of himself.'

Chapter Twenty-Three

'I'm sorry Mrs Bryant, I really can't have this going on in my house.'

Pam stood gazing bleakly at her landlady, her eyes full of tears for all she tried to hold them back. She had wanted to run after Mum, but there was her mother-in-law and her landlady blocking the way, and Beth crying in her cot. She felt as she watched her mother go that she had been a traitor to her. She still felt that as she heard her own abject voice saying, 'I am sorry, Mrs Carper. It's the first time anything like this has happened. We've always tried to be quiet.'

Mrs Carper's face didn't move. 'I know you have, but there is always the thin end of the wedge to think of. It could happen again. And then again and again. I can't risk having my house disrupted in this way.'

Milly Bryant who had been composing herself with the aid of a great deal of huffing and puffing after slapping the face of another, stepped in uninvited. 'Are you telling my daughter-in-law to leave, Mrs um . . . Carper? Because you can't throw her and a baby out on the street like that without proper notice.'

'I'm not throwing your daughter-in-law out on the street, Mrs Bryant.'

'I should damned well think not.'

'I'm merely warning her that I do not enjoy shouting and screaming in my house. This is my home. I have a right to expect peace and quiet within it.'

'Then you shouldn't go letting it out to people, should you, if you want peace and quiet?'

'Mum . . .' Pam came and took her mother-in-law's arm. 'It's all right. Please, you're making things worse.'

'Worse?' Mrs Bryant swung on her. 'How much worse can anyone make it? It was your mother what came here making a scene, so don't start accusing me, Pam. Your family have always started these things. If it hadn't been for your father in the first place . . . I'm only trying to help.'

Pam wanted to tell her she didn't need her help, but that would have made things worse. She kept quiet.

'I understand how you feel, Mrs Bryant.' The landlady had turned her attention to the older woman. 'But I'm not throwing your daughter-in-law out. A girl with a young baby, of course I wouldn't. But I do have a say when trouble like this occurs. Her neighbours downstairs came knocking on my door complaining. I had to come and try to quieten things down a bit, for my other tenants' sakes.'

'Well, you were too late, weren't you?' Mrs Bryant snapped. Pam felt her insides leap and cringe. If anyone was going to get her thrown out it was this woman who thought she could right everything in this world with insults.

Her own voice came strong and sharp and loud and a little desperate. 'I don't want anyone taking my side. I can take my own side. Mum, let me sort this out, please.' She turned to Mrs Carper. 'Look, I'm really dreadfully sorry about all this. I promise it won't happen again . . .'

'Don't apologise,' Mrs Bryant interrupted, her voice high with fighting instinct. It brought an exasperated glance from Mrs Carper and a warning one from Pam who hurried on as if her mother-in-law had become invisible and voiceless.

'Please accept my apologies, Mrs Carper. It won't happen again.'

The woman nodded. 'Very well, I realise it wasn't your fault. But I do feel that if it occurs again and my tenants are disrupted by noise like that, I will really have to recommend you find other accommodation. I wouldn't want to do that of course and I'd give you several weeks' notice.'

'How very very generous.' Mrs Bryant's sarcasm cut through the woman's quiet voice, but Mrs Carper continued to address Pam.

'I know you'll give me your co-operation. You and your

husband have been good tenants, even when things have been bad for him. I'll leave you.'

She wrinkled her nose in a friendly manner and closed the door. Pam heard her light footsteps hurrying down the uncarpeted part of the stairs.

Milly Bryant turned to Pam. 'Who do she think she is, when she's about? Bloody cheek of the woman.'

'She did have a point, Mum.' Her heart still racing, the sick feeling that had arisen in her chest still lurking, Pam turned to pick up a now quieter Beth, who had quickly got over all the shouting. She was a placid child; she took after George. That was why Pam loved him, for his placidness. His father was also like that.

It flickered through Pam's mind as she lifted Beth from her cot, how an even-tempered man like Dick Bryant could ever creep out in the middle of the night and set fire to someone's livelihood. Maybe it was because of his quiet temper that he had done so, the revenge of a timid man who didn't possess the hotheadedness her father had to engage in an honest fist fight. Pam didn't think it commendable at all. Maybe Mrs Bryant's forthright, even annoying manner was more honorable than creeping out in the dead of night to settle a score. Pam just hoped George's placid manner would never go as far as his father's had. She wanted George honourable, always. Perhaps he had sufficient of his mother's blood in him to be so. She prayed he'd never stoop to doing what his father had, or even have need to.

'Stupid bitch,' her mother-in-law was saying. 'You shouldn't have to kowtow to the likes of people like that.'

'I haven't got no option, have I?' Pam said a little sourly, reaching for a nappy from a newly ironed pile of them to change Beth, whose earlier crying had made her soak the one she wore.

'You have got an option. George is in work now, you should be looking for another place, a better place to live than this . . . this hole.'

The eyes roved around the poky little place, the lips dropped into a sneer. Pam felt a little irked.

'We could, but George could lose his job as easily as he found it. You can't bet on anything, these days. Nothing's safe. I'm not going to count my chickens just yet.'

'You can't go on living here forever.'

'It won't be forever. But if we just up and went and found a place that costs more, if we couldn't pay the rent and had to look for a cheaper place again, we might end up in an even worse state.' She fell to changing Beth. 'I'll make you a cup of tea in a minute.'

It was hard to keep the terseness out of her voice. She still seethed inside thinking of the slap Mrs Bryant had given her mother.

She had felt her whole body jump as if she personally had received the slap, and had it not been for the landlady's arrival she'd have leapt to her mother's defence, perhaps making everything worse. Now with all that had intervened, it was too late to pick up on it, or perhaps the courage to confront her with it had dwindled into cowardice that she tried to see as prudence. No point making enemies, but she did balk at the insult to her mother and how she must have felt going home with her face stinging from the slap. At this moment she hated Mrs Bryant with all her heart, could understand how Dick Bryant had become such a small man beneath the woman's thumb, even, she imagined, since the very days of their courting. Milly Bryant was the dominant partner and always would be.

'I'll make it,' Mrs Bryant said now, taking charge. She felt the teapot. 'This is nearly stone cold. I expect you can afford another spoonful of tea, can't you, Pam, with George in work? Nothing like a nice hot cuppa to put things back together.'

And not one word of regret about her mother, not one syllable of apology. Mrs Bryant was the most loathsome overbearing woman she knew.

It couldn't be held off any longer. As with all secrets hugged to the bosom, it erupted in a rush at the most inopportune moment. He and Lily were walking home through the soft April night from the Empire Palace, the fleapit of a cinema in Leigh Broadway that belied its name. Its seats were cheaper than elsewhere and all Danny could afford, still saving up for their wedding.

Lily was being full of it as usual, once again reluctantly adjusted to another wedding delay for lack of funds. They walked slowly, savouring the quiet, unseasonably warm night air, Lily with her head on his shoulder making the two of them meander a little, the lamplight casting their wavering shadows before them, her voice soft and dreamy.

251

'We'll make it an autumn wedding, darling,' she whispered. 'It'll give us a bit more time, I suppose, to look for a really nice house. We should be thinking of getting the wedding booked up definitely, and we really ought to start looking for a suitable house soon.'

'Theres plenty of time to look for a place,' he said, his mind entirely on just how he expected to juggle the two – paying rent on a house and keeping Mum going.

And what would she do trying to manage Dad on her own? Dad remained so obstreperous and was becoming worse, talking about trying to walk again, at one time demanding to be left to get in and out of bed on his own with Mum forced to listen to his grunts and puffs and foul language when it didn't go right, the next demanding her help over some small matter he could well have coped with himself. He had badgered the hospital into fitting his legs with callipers and giving him a pair of crutches. The crutches had been OK but the irons inadequate and he had taken a tumble.

It had used all Mum's strength to try to lift him, his legs in irons impeding her until Danny had firmly removed them in the face of all his protests and had lifted him back into the chair, defying him to try it again. Dad had sworn and blustered and he could under-stand the man's frustration, being treated almost like a baby, but it took another man to handle him and Danny couldn't have him bullying Mum as he did. How would she cope without him?

It came out on that thought as Lily prattled happily on; came out of its own accord. 'Lily, I can't leave Mum alone to deal with Dad.'

She stopped mid-sentence about what curtains she would plan for the windows. 'Darling, I was talking about our new house.'

'I know. And I think it's going to be impossible. The way Dad is, I don't think it'd be the best arrangement for me to move away from home.'

God, he'd said it. She had stopped walking, had broken away from him in alarm. 'Are you trying to tell me you don't want to marry me, Danny? After all this time . . .'

'No, it's not that. The thing I want most in all this world is to marry you. What I'm saying is that we might not be able to think of getting a place of our own for a while after we're married.'

She was staring at him. In the light of a lamp at the foot of the hill leading down to the level crossing, its gates open for them to

252

cross, her eyes seemed to glint like those of a small animal. Her pink-rouged mouth had dropped open. Now it closed almost with a snap.

'You're joking, Danny. Danny, say you're joking. We *have* to have a place of our own. All couples do. I've been dreaming of our own place, our own little house which I can be happy in, decorating and furnishing and making it look nice for everyone to come and see. It's every girl's dream to have her own place to show off.'

Disbelief had spread across her face but he had to go through with it now. He owed it to Mum. 'It's not possible, darling, not yet.'

From one of disbelief, Lily's expression had taken on a look of piqued contempt that held more than just a little fear. 'What d'you take me for Danny? You expect me to come and live in your house, is that it? Have all my friends look down on me, them in their own homes, seeing me, pitying me living in with my husband's family?'

'Wealthy people do – in big country seats.' It was a foolish inept thing to say but all he could think of in defence in that moment. Her sneer of contempt flayed him.

'Yours is hardly a country seat, is it? A poky little end terraced house. All of us stuck in it. And what am I supposed to do, sleep on the floor?'

'I can probably arrange for us to have Mum's room now she sleeps on her own, and she can have mine. It's a nice big bedroom. We can . . .' He knew he was being completely impractical even in expecting this of Lily, but he pushed desperately on.

'I'm virtually the breadwinner now Dad can't work. Mum would probably agree to you having the entire run of the house, as if it was yours. She needs me there. I know she'd agree.'

'And what about me? You haven't asked me whether I agree.'

'I'm just asking if you'd think about it.'

'I don't *need* to think about it, Danny Bowmaker. I've thought about it and wild horses won't get me living in with other people in someone else's house as if we're poverty-stricken. I intend to have my own place to go into as soon as we're married or not at all. We don't get married. That's final.'

Somehow she had moved back from him, or he had from her, for she was standing a little uphill, above him. Tall as he was, he was having to look up at her. 'Lily, sweetheart . . .'

'Don't sweetheart me!' she cried at him. 'If you think you're going to do me out of all I deserve as your wife, then I don't want to be your wife. I've had enough of scrimping and scraping to save for us to get married. And now you jump this on me. Well, you can stick your wedding, and stick your idea of us living in with your family, and you can stick your ring as well.'

All this time she had been fiddling frantically with her ring finger and now the ring came off. She flung it at him. In the silence of the night air it tinkled metallically on the pavement and disappeared beneath some shrubby weeds. It could be anywhere, but Danny wasn't thinking of searching for it. He had his gaze trained on Lily's face.

'You can't mean that.'

'I mean every word of it,' she raged down at him, her voice echoing in the quiet night. 'If you think I'd marry you and put up with being a lackey to your Mum and Dad, you've another think coming.'

'There's nothing to discuss.'

'I think there is.' She hadn't moved or given way for him. She stood leaning on the door jamb, arms crossed protectively over her chest. She had on an old skirt and jumper, her hair in curlers, her face bereft of make-up, yet every part of him ached for her. 'Let me come in just for a moment.'

She stood back for him then, begrudgingly, sullenly, not looking at him but at the floor as if that was the most important thing in her life.

They sat in the front room, the one her parents used for best and for visitors. They sat one each side of the empty grate, on the brown pretend-leather armchairs. The room was cold. Like our love, Danny thought, and then shrugged off the thought. He had come to claim her back if he could. He was sure after all this time of being in love, of making plans for weddings, it couldn't all collapse just like that.

What they talked of, he wasn't sure. The conversation just went round and round, as he pleaded with her to reconsider. She muttered about all the months wasted on him, indicating with despondent shrugs and sighs that it was over between them. He said something about didn't she love him at all, ever, and she said she didn't want to talk about it.

He offered her a cigarette and she took it. He took one himself. Later she offered him one of hers and took one herself. The morning went by in a sort of continuous stalemate, the upshot of those long hours being that she was not prepared to share her life with his family under their roof no matter what, that there were better things in life. Her refusal to be persuaded stunned him and, finally defeated, he came away because there was nothing else he could do.

At the door she asked suddenly, though in a listless tone as if it didn't really matter, 'Did you find the ring?'

'No,' he said.

She shrugged again and without looking at him closed the door, leaving him gazing at it.

The day Mum came home crying Josie had planned to tell her that she and Arthur wanted to get married. But the trauma of seeing Mum in that state put it from her mind and she hadn't the heart to bring it up again as Mum went about her chores with a sort of quiet dignity that was painful to see. It was a month before Josie could bring herself to voice her own selfish wants.

What worried her most was that Sunday after he turned up at her house having ridden through a snowstorm on that decrepit bike of his like a knight on a winded horse, when she had carried out her secret promise to reward him as she had never done before.

He'd had dinner with her family. After dinner the snow had stopped. The sun had come out enough to thaw the pavements though little rounded caps of snow had sat like dabs of ice cream on the shadier bushes. They had gone for a walk, muffled up to the eyebrows against the cold. With his arm around her waist feeling seductive and meaningful even through the fabric of her coat, she'd guided their steps towards an old disused shed that stood near the Strand where boats had been laid up on the beach for the winter, its walls rickety, its door hanging off, its roof holed. She'd led him inside and there had let him make love to her, properly.

Fearful of discovery, they had lain side by side on a pile of dry broken nets. He had kissed her, their kisses growing more urgent. He had fondled her at her instigation, for she intended to reward him for that cold and courageous ride through the snow. As the feel of her warm bared flesh overcame him and he had moved breathlessly on top of her, fumbling, he had paused to ask, comically, if she minded. But she hadn't laughed. Her reply had been to pull him down to her. The end had come quickly, too quickly, the pair of them inexperienced, but he'd had enough sense to withdraw hastily at the moment of his climax, leaving her lying on the pile of nets feeling incomplete, already concerned by the thought that she might discover herself pregnant in a few weeks' time.

They had adjusted their dress with haste, not speaking to each other apart from when he asked if she was all right and she nodded. Emerging from the shed they had walked back home in silence, each intensely aware of the other but the common ground they usually shared missing.

Mum had asked innocently where they had been and they had said together, 'Walking,' and she had turned back to whatever she had been doing.

Soon afterwards, Arthur had left.

The next week, snow lying deep on the outskirts of London, he hadn't been able to make it. His letter that week said he'd had to get his old bike into working order and that he missed her. But without work she'd not had the train fare to see him. When he was eventually able to cycle up to see her they hadn't repeated the episode in the Strand shed, but he had asked her once more to marry him and she had said yes, her thoughts dwelling on the possibility that she could be pregnant from that single act of love.

Almost a month had gone by since and at odd moments Josie found herself counting the days to her next period, knowing it should show itself any day now, each day seemingly a lifetime of waiting. Perhaps tomorrow, she thought, then as nothing appeared, perhaps tomorrow. And again, what if I am pregnant, we've got no money, no one's got any money, and how do I tell Mum and Dad. Dad would roar, tell her she was a slut and to leave, as he had roared at Pam telling her to leave. Then on the third day of anxiety, Josie felt the wetness in her knickers and in a wash of sheer joy and relief raced for a piece of tape, two safety pins and one of those pieces of towelling her mother would cut up from old bath towels to hem into twenty-four inch squares for her daughters' use.

Now she could speak about her and Arthur. There was no need to get married straight away. They could save up for a year, maybe longer. Her mother took the news quietly, but pointed out the obvious.

256

'He's not even in work.'

'It's different work he does, Mum. It's spasmodic. It comes whenever there's a ship in the dock.'

'I know.' Her mother was folding aired linen ready to put away. It was Wednesday. She always put away her airing on a Wednesday, a very methodical woman, even with having to look after Dad. 'I read the papers, love. I've seen the pictures of hundreds of dockers all waiting around dock gates just for a handful of them to be picked. Josie, that's no kind of life for a woman, forever wondering if her husband is going to be in or out of work. I like your Arthur. He's a very nice young man, but I did hope for something better for you.'

Josie felt petulance flood over her. She stopped helping to fold sheets, shirts and pillowcases. 'I can't help it if I'm in love with him.'

'Of course you can't.' Her mother's words were calm, sympathetic. 'But it's going to take years for you two to save up enough to get married on and find a decent place to live. By that time anything can happen.'

'Yes, it will.' Josie resumed her folding, laying the results on the kitchen table ready to be put in various drawers and cupboard. 'Things will get better. By next year all this unemployment will be over and Arthur might be coining it again with lots of ships to unload again.'

'I was going to say, you might meet someone else. Someone who'd be able to provide for you a lot better.'

Josie stopped folding altogether, realisation of what her mother was trying to say catching her unawares. 'I'm not going to give Arthur up for anyone. I know he's not what you'd have liked for me, that he don't speak proper and that he's not a doctor or a lawyer or in some fine-paying profession. But I don't care what you say, Mum. I love him and next year I'll be old enough to marry him without anyone's permission. We're engaged to be married anyway, and that's all that matters.'

'And where's the ring?'

'We thought it wasn't worth spending money on one yet.'

The truth was Arthur couldn't afford an engagement ring, not even a cheap one.

'What do you think you two are going to live on?'

'Pam manages.'

'Pam's older. You can afford to wait. At twenty you still don't know your own mind and what this world is all about. I think you should wait at least two more years before thinking of getting married – to anyone.'

But Josie did know her own mind, no matter what Mum might think. All Josie could see was those two years stretching before her as she waited for that something to come right that might never come right. To a twenty-year-old, a year was a lifetime, much less two. She couldn't wait. But with no money what else was there to do?

'Better not worry your dad about it yet,' her mother said, picking up what she had already folded and bearing it off upstairs to be put away.

Chapter Twenty-Four

'What do I do about our Josie?' her mother asked a week later as she and Connie washed up the dirty cutlery and dinner plates between them. The pots and pans would be left to soak for another half-hour before being tackled.

Connie had already been familiarised twice this week with Josie's ongoing bout of moping since receiving no succour from Mum on the matter of marriage. And now Mum was bringing it up yet again.

'She's driving me potty the way she'd behaving, as if I'm to blame for not saying, "OK, love, you go ahead and get married – you've got no money but that's all right, love, you go ahead!" I can't even tell your Dad about her. You know how he is. He'd just boil up like he always does. And I can't talk to Danny. He seems to have been in a world of his own all this week. I can't discuss it with Pam. I haven't been round there for weeks. I'm almost afraid to.' The truth of that was that she still felt humiliated, unable to face her daughter. 'I feel I'm really on my own with the problems of this family lately.' Mum dipped plates into the sinkful of suds with swift strokes, swishing the cloth around them and pulling them out as if she bore each one a grudge. 'You're the only one I can turn to.'

But Connie wasn't much interested in Josie. She had problems of her own in the shape of Mr Ian Lindsay. She had found out the young curate's name, by devious means – to ask anyone outright would have sounded to her own ears to betray her motives – relieved when it had come up in conversation over the Christmas mince pies and mulled wine given to its parishioners by the church. 'Dear Mr Lindsay, we see so little of you lately. Flitting in and out before anyone can say a word to you, you've become quite an elusive creature.' Then a low friendly aside by the vicar reached Connie's ears: 'Hand round some more mince pies, Ian.'

But the criticism of Ian Lindsay's elusiveness had not been without foundation as Connie saw it. He'd not spoken to her since that declaration of his that foggy morning in November, in fact acted as if he'd never spoken to her that way at all. Whether it was because of that she wasn't sure, but she'd find herself watching him surreptitiously as he went about his duties when she should have been concentrating on the service. She had become conscious too of an excited pounding against her chest wall as she hastily bent her head should he look her way.

She still needed to go to church for it was here that Ben's memory was most keen. Nearly a year had passed since his death but it seemed far less; she almost imagined he might suddenly come into church and kneel beside her. She felt annoyed with herself that Ian Lindsay's presence should so often invade her thoughts of Ben. She dreaded the possibility of his speaking to her again. What to say if he did? To avoid any chance of it, she'd arrive just as the clergy and choir began to gather, often only moments before the organist struck up the progressional hymn, and leave amid the main body of departing parishioners. Never again would he find her lingering behind as he gathered up the hymn books from the empty pews. Yet as she made her way home, it would nag at her that she should be running off like this lest he approach her.

What worried her was that he evoked in her the same involuntary excitement Ben once had. Not only did it make her a traitor to Ben's memory but it caused such turmoil inside her that it wasn't at all comfortable. It would have been far better were she to give up going to church altogether. But, bounced back the convenient excuse, that would have been exposing a weakness within herself.

At such times she'd take a train up to London after Sunday dinner to visit Ben's grave, longer April days giving her more time. In East London Cemetery, she'd work it out of herself, taking out the dead flowers from the blue-glazed pot to place in the nearby bin, refilling the pot with clean water from a tap further along, filling it with flowers bought from the stall by the cemetery gate, meticulously arranging and rearranging them, standing back time and time again to stare at the result until it looked just right.

Finally with a wet cloth she would clean off any mould that had gathered on the small marble headstone with its inscription:

In Loving Memory
of
Benjamin David Watson
1905–1930
A Dear Son Ever In Our Hearts

Her lips thin and tight so that they wouldn't tremble while her eyes glistened and blurred her sight with unshed tears, she would hold little conversations with him as she cleaned and tidied and plucked tiny weeds from between the pansies and primulas his parents had planted in the soil at the foot of the headstone. Still needing to draw out her time with him, she would sit on the bench a few feet away; on warm days she would lift her face to the sun, a sun that no longer warmed him here on earth but, she hoped, did so in heaven; on cold days would huddle into the collar of her coat, the brim of her felt hat pulled down, her gloved hands tucked inside her sleeves, her lyle-stockinged legs in sturdy shoes crossed at the ankles and tucked well back under the seat to conserve warmth. She'd sit and remember the good days with Ben, try not to recall that last day they'd spent together, when happiness turned so suddenly to tragedy; guilt, not being there to help save him.

And always the funeral would creep into her thoughts – a lot of it dim, blanked out, but she knew there had been a vast gathering there: his family, his mates, men of the river sombrely dressed, bareheaded, hushed; tugmen, lightermen, representatives of the firm he'd worked for, people he'd known in the café he'd frequented, neighbours her mother knew, people his dad knew, even some old schoolmates of Ben's with whom he'd kept friends. A huge crowd. Ben had been well liked.

She couldn't recall returning to his parents' flat after the funeral, nor could she remember leaving or getting back home. She knew Mum and Dad had gone with her but she couldn't recall them being there. In fact it seemed during the weeks and months that followed as if she had moved in a dream. She retained little recollection of them as though they insisted on being erased from her mind. Somehow life had come back. She existed now. That's

261

all it was, existing, without thought for the future, without expectations.

Later she'd go on to Ben's parents, as she was doing today, and have Sunday tea with them. Alighting from the bus in Bethnal Green Road she bought a bag of shrimps outside the Salmon and Ball, a small offering for inviting herself. Ben's parents would be in. Creatures of habit, they went to a working man's club every Saturday night and Mr Watson would go there again on Sunday mornings for a pint or two with his mates while his wife got Sunday dinner. In the afternoon they'd sleep a little, then get tea.

Ben's mother was pleased to see her, but Connie detected just a hint of reservation in her welcome. The shrimps she accepted with much more delight even though she gushed, 'Oh, Connie, you shouldn't've.'

Tea consisted of the regulation Sunday ham sandwiches and celery, which never varied, today augmented by the gift of shrimps, with a homemade caraway-seed cake to follow, but the conversation was nothing like it had once been when Ben had been alive. In fact it was getting harder, all the old animation gone out of it. For months she had seemed to reach no real common ground with Ben's parents at all until she often felt it a chore to go, at the same time not sure why she did. The house that had once held Ben, always so lively with him there, had taken on an atmosphere of desolation though both his parents seemed cheerful enough. In a way it had all the feel of entering an empty tomb. She knew that making her way homewards this evening, it would not seem as if she had been doing her duty but penance for the thoughts that had attacked her in church as she tried to block out that small insidious voice inside her head telling her that it was no longer Ben but Ian Lindsay upon whom her mind persisted on dwelling.

Ben's mother echoed that small voice, as they were near to finishing their tea. Tea was always eaten in the best room when they had visitors, what Mrs Watson called the parlour though parlours had gone out with the war. No one called them parlours any more except for the older generation. It was either sitting room or lounge. This room in this second-floor flat, one of Waterlow Buildings' best overlooked the junction of Wilmot and Finnis Streets, gave a good view and let in good light. Mrs Watson's parlour was her pride and joy, stuffed full of statuettes and vases that had been wedding presents around nineteen hundred and two, with pictures of long-gone wooden-faced relatives in Victorian and Edwardian clothes. Thick lace curtains and heavy drapes hung at the bay window, ornaments clustered on the huge mirror-embedded mantel over the fireplace, and on the whatnot in the corner. Here too reposed the overstuffed easy chairs and dining chairs, the large round table reigning in full splendour at the centre of it all.

Little used, it had always possessed that unlived-in feel even when Ben had been alive. Today as Mr Watson got up from the table, replete, and went into the back room in search of his pipe, Connie felt a shiver run down her spine from the desolate air that seemed to envelop her as Mrs Watson surveyed her from across the table.

'Look dear, it is nice ter see you, and we know you want to come and see us. But don't you think it's time you started thinkin' about yerself?'

Connie looked back at the woman who had so nearly become her mother-in-law, unable to think what to say to that. But the woman had no intention of her question being answered.

'You can't go on the rest of yer life holding on to Ben's memory, dear. As much as you think you want to. Nothink's ever going ter bring 'im back. You're still young, Connie. You oughtn't to keep lingerin' in the past. That's for us ter do, not you. We've ain't got no future ter look forward to at our age like you have. But you've got yer whole life ahead of you, and it ain't right for yer ter go wasting it on memories. Leave that to us.'

Connie remained silent as she felt she was expected to. Mrs Watson gnawed uncertainly at her lip. 'Look, dear, we don't mean no disrespect and we don't want ter throw yer good intentions back in yer face. You're a good gel, Connie. Yer 'eart's in the right place. But you've got ter start livin' a new life and not keep comin' 'ere to see us, as much as we like seein' yer. All yer doin' is raking up the past for yerself, and that ain't 'ealthy. Do you understand what I'm tryin' ter say?'

As Mrs Watson's voice faded away in anticipation now of her reply, Connie gazed around the silent parlour. That's what it was, silent, dead, full of the dead, of dead memories. Then she nodded. Through sudden tears, she nodded. The next moment she was up from her chair, hurrying around the table to be gathered into the woman's waiting arms.

'Oh, I'm so sorry. I'm so miserable.' She could hear her own words smothered by Ben's mother's embrace. 'I miss him so.'

'Of course yer do, love.' A hand was gently patting her on the back. 'We all miss 'im. We'll never stop missing 'im. 'E was our eldest son.'

With a firm gesture borne of grief too hard to bear, Mrs Watson put Connie from her, smiling damply into Connie's own damp features. 'Now, dry yer eyes. Silly old fool, me, in tears too. I didn't mean to upset yer. Look, it'll start gettin' dark soon and yer've got all that way to go 'ome. Don't you worry about helpin' me wash up or anythink. You just toddle off 'ome.'

Mr Watson had come back into the room, the aromatic smoke from his pipe instantly tainting the grave-like atmosphere the room held; an atmosphere that would never feel any different now, not this room, not this whole flat, forever bathed with the loss of Ben. Suddenly Connie wanted to get out of it, find the clean, fresh, busy, living air of the outside world, away from the mausoleum this place had become which now, even to enter, provoked an involuntary shudder. It hovered here, like an unseen skull or a total sense of nothingness.

'Connie's goin' now,' Mrs Watson announced.

His thick eyebrows rose in surprise through the haze of smoke he was creating. 'So soon? We've 'ardly finished tea.'

'Well it is only early April and it still do get dark quick, and I did say she ought ter be on 'er way or she won't be 'ome until after dark.'

She turned to Connie with a warm smile, her eyes quite dry now, her husband unaware of the tears that had glistened there just a moment ago. 'Now if you want ter come and see us any time, you're welcome. Don't think you ain't. I expect we will see you some time or other. But remember now.'

It was tantamount to telling her to stay away in the most circumspect way possible, and for her own good. But she wondered if in truth it was for their own peace of mind that they really didn't want to see her again, her visits resurrecting what they needed to lay to rest. It felt like rejection.

As she took leave of them at the door, hurried down the flight of worn stone stairs, the door closed behind her with a note of finality that brought a sob to her throat. From the cobbled street below she turned to wave at them standing at the lace-curtained bay window.

Her heart felt it was spilling over, her eyes misted with moisture.

It was over. Ben's memory must be laid to rest. She didn't want it to be over, wanted to cling to the last shreds of it until she was no longer able to think or feel. Even her visits to his parents remained something to cling to no matter how dismal the visits were becoming. But everything was saying to her that she must let go. Nor would she go to church any more – that half-expecting Ben to kneel beside her, sweeping away an awful nightmare, that too was over. As Mrs Watson said, all the weeping, all the prayers in the world wouldn't bring him back. She must get on with her life. But, oh, dear God, she didn't want to. It was going to be hard, so very hard, letting go.

'Ain't seen your Lily for some time. Not for over a fortnight. You two all right?'

Dad was in his wheelchair drawn up at the breakfast table. He refused to have his breakfast in bed, commendable Danny supposed, but not helpful for Mum who in the middle of getting breakfast must pull and tug him about to get him out of bed and into his chair. Danny was glad to have been home this morning. The tide had dictated no need to go out early, so he'd been able to see to Dad for her. This morning, with Dad being extra awkward, an April drizzle making him stiff and fretful, it hurt Danny to have his father, once so powerful and independent, clinging to him for support as he eased him off the bed. It had brought home once again how much he was needed here. If only Lily could see it that way.

He had tried to contact her, but every day the rift grew wider. He'd sent letters, called on her, but the message was always the same – no replies to his letters, no response to his calls except for her mother, stony-faced from tales of woe Lily had no doubt woven for her, saying sharply, 'Lil's not at home, nor do she want to see you.' It had all ended so abruptly, sometimes he couldn't believe Lily meant it, that she would come back. Sometimes he wondered, had she ever really loved him? It affected him day and night. He tried not to be surly and sharp with everyone, but he was.

'Come on, Dad, bloody move! For God's sake try to help yourself a bit.' Immediately he had wanted to bite his tongue off because Dad, glaring back at him, had been trying to help himself, his upper body wriggling to get the useless rest of him off the bed with its hard, sawdust-filled mattress, his arms reaching out for his son's support, grunting and mumbling in his deep voice, cursing and bemoaning his lot. This was what Mum had to put up with every morning of her life when she was left on her own with him.

'No Dad, we're not all right.' He had blurted it out in reply to his father's enquiry. He wanted to get it all off his chest to someone, and why not his father? 'No, Dad, me and Lily's far from all right. We've split up.'

'Split up?' Dad's mouth, full of bread and jam, sprayed a small fleck of half-masticated food on to the baize cloth that covered the kitchen table around which he, Danny and Josie sat. Josie was still out of work.

Josie's blue-grey eyes were wide. From the kitchen range, Mum spun round towards him. 'You can't 've split up – not you and Lily.'

Danny didn't look at her, didn't look at anyone. 'I'm sorry, Mum, we have.'

'Why?'

'Because she don't want to come and live here with all of us.'

'Did you say she had to?'

Now he looked up. He could feel the imploring in his eyes as he gazed at his mother. 'What else could I say? How can I go off and leave you to look after . . .' He let the rest of that trail off, but knew his father was already ahead of him; heard him grunt, but pride prevented Dad from making any comment. He felt it bad enough without putting voice to it.

'I just feel I'm needed here,' he tried again. 'And you need the money, Mum.' Now it was her turn to feel the embarrassment and withhold a reply. He hurried on, feeling he was digging himself into a hole. 'If me and Lily had got married and got ourselves a place to live, I'd still be cockling, using Dad and his brother's boat. How could I pocket what I made on behalf of Dad and let you two fend for yourselves? I couldn't do it, Mum. Not only that, I'd be paying out rent on my place, keeping the two of us, and trying to help you two out. I thought it'd be a far better idea for me and her to stay here. I thought you understood that, Mum. That you thought it was a foregone conclusion. This is a nice house, it's not all that tiny, on the end of a terrace, and it's got that extra bedroom Grandad built all those years ago, and an outhouse. With

Pam and Annie gone away,' he didn't care at this moment that Pam's name was taboo in this house, 'there's plenty of room for me and Lily. You could have had my old room, Mum, sleeping on your own now, and I could have had yours and Dad's old bedroom in the front, and I know you'd have given Lily the run of the house maybe leaving you free of all the worry while you looked after Dad.'

'Got it all worked out, son,' his father's voice growled, but he was ignored as Danny ploughed on. 'It was that I wanted to be here, to support you. I owe it to you and Dad. I couldn't just move off and wash my hands of everything.'

'Of course you couldn't,' Mum said. Breakfast was forgotten. She came and sat on the empty chair near Danny, and took one of his hands. 'But I wouldn't have asked it of you, love.'

'I thought it was understood.'

'I suppose it was, in a way. We need you, Danny, but I wouldn't have asked it of you.'

'What's going to happen about you and Lily, then?' Josie asked.

'Mind your own bloody business,' her father silenced her.

'Lily refused point blank to come and live here,' Danny continued. 'She'd always set her mind on a nice little house after we were married, but I couldn't, Mum. I couldn't have been happy just waltzing off.'

Dad had pushed his plate of bread and jam away, had awkwardly and noisily manoeuvred his wheelchair a few inches to reach for his pipe from its rack beside the kitchen range and was now filling the kitchen with acrid smoke.

Danny looked at him, slightly and unaccountably peeved. 'That's how it stands, Mum. I've tried for a fortnight to get her to come round, but she won't even see me. Her mum said last time I called, yesterday, that she was out with some boy. It makes it look final if anything could. You know she threw her ring at me? It went into the bushes near the level crossing . . .'

He stopped, seeing a small wincing expression cross his mother's face. Level crossing – it was something everyone avoided saying in this house, the very words bringing back memories of that day little Tony had been killed. Danny hurried on if only to swamp the words with others, his tone now filled with bombast.

267

'I couldn't find it, so it can stay there. Do someone a bit of good if they ever happen to find it. I don't want it. And I'm getting to feel I don't want her – not if she can't find a bit of human kindness in her.'

He did want her, felt he would never stop wanting her, but what could he do if she no longer wanted him? Bind her hand and foot and carry her off? He half grinned at the thought, but it was a bitter grin.

Chapter Twenty-Five

The hot weather had arrived. Thoughts of going up to a hill station had plagued Annie from the very start of the year, remembering last summer with a shudder. She could not again stand being cloistered with the other British wives with their silly, somewhat frantic diversions: giving themselves parts in plays they themselves had written, quite badly, or acting, very badly, in the classics; arranging little picnics, organising bridge parties, playing tennis, bowls, croquet, watching polo; all of them trying so hard to instal a little bit of England in India. Here she had Alex to fall back on, up there she would be alone, seeing him for only the occasional weekend.

In February she had started begging him to let her visit her family for a month or two. After all, he wouldn't miss her. No more than he had last summer when she had gone to Simla. It was rather the same thing, and she did so miss her family. Fourteen months had passed since she'd set eyes on them. Homesickness should have abated by now, but it had in fact grown worse.

Alex's answer was always the same. 'Darling. I've told you. I'm sorry, but we just can't afford it. Maybe next year.' She didn't want to wait until next year.

'If we were to put a little by each week,' she had suggested around February, but it was no good. Things were not easy with them financially.

Alex worked hard for what he earned. His father remained unforgiving, not paying him as much as Annie thought Alex was worth; his father's attitude was that profits must be ploughed back into the business so that it would go to his successor, Alex, when he himself was dead – this had been penned dolefully by his mother on one occasion. She still wrote to her son as mothers were wont to, ready to forgive if not condone her son's actions, even if his father didn't. Alex was a long way from home. She pined for him. Had he been in England it might have been a different tale with her; as it was, he was safely hidden away out here, out of harm's way, and could be assumed to be giving his all to his father's company on the promise of it maybe being his one day.

In Annie's eyes it was little less than Alex being cheated. It hurt to see him trying to keep his end up, much of his salary going to impress those far better off than he. He bought Annie nice dresses, gave her whatever she needed, took pleasure in showing her off before those who asked them to tea or bridge parties (Annie had now become quite a skilled player, and despite what she maintained the other wives thought of her was often invited to make up a rubber) or a round of golf. He behaved as if they too were rolling in money. But she'd rather have gone home to be herself again for a month or two.

She had felt it bitterly every time he told her it couldn't be, adding for good measure what a long journey it was. There had been rows, audible enough for all the servants to hear. Annie often wondered if, for all their unobtrusive loyalty, tales of discord didn't trickle back to other ears ever ready to gather gossip.

But by the end of March despite the first onset of hot weather, she had slowly begun to debate whether she really did feel up to the strain of that three-weeks sea voyage to England and a second three-week voyage back. She had proved herself a poor sailor that first time and wouldn't that detract immensely from the joy of seeing her family?

It wasn't easy to admit that the real cause of this gradual change of mind was Mr Ansley Burrington whom she had danced with at the Christmas Eve party, and again at the New Year's Eve ball which Alex had eventually persuaded her to attend. In Ansley Burrington's arms, she had been glad she'd attended. After that, the women had never again seemed quite so daunting as they'd once been, and strangely enough, had become less and less so, especially when he was present. As he very gently befriended her over these past months, she had begun to see him as an ally amid the still vaguely alien members of the English Club. In him she felt she could confide her woes, receive understanding and sympathy and advice. She had confided in him her urge to go

270

home on a visit. His advice had been to recall others who had similarly gone home for a spell.

'They nearly always come back dejected and dissatisfied. I do wonder if it does one any good at all. After all, in time we all go home, recalled to England or finally sick of India itself, or because of ill health. This isn't really a terribly healthy climate for Europeans. It does one down in the end, some of us.'

It was the evening they'd sat on his veranda two weeks ago while his wife had taken Alex into the garden after tea to see the new tank, the term for the formal pool most gardens had. 'Do come and see it, Mr Willoughby,' she'd urged. 'It's quite beautiful with the peepul trees we've had planted reflected in it. Ansley, you stay here with Mrs Willoughby. She is somewhat weary, I fear.'

It had been a pointed remark. Annie and Alex had had a slight difference of opinion before coming, over what she had seen as Alex's recent inattentiveness towards her, and it had shown on her face.

He had been working so hard lately, and it had been unfair of her, she supposed, but he would come home saying hardly a word to her, his head buried in papers he'd bring home from the office. When it was time for bed he'd be too exhausted to make love. These days they seemed to make love less and less. When they had come out to India he had spoken about children, but to Annie the idea of raising a child here in this climate was a risk, even with an ayah to look after it. Not only that, she had at the time pictured herself, a stranger among these high-minded Anglo-Indians, waddling about with her stomach distended, their eyes on her, discussing her. Mystified and confused by her wish to wait a while, Alex had finally become so bogged down with work that lovemaking had all but taken second place until lately he appeared to have little interest in it, stimulating her own misgivings that she had fostered such delicate thoughts about herself. Yet starting a family still seemed to her to sound a death knell for her ever going back home, as if she would be putting down roots in a land she still disliked, never to return to her own country, her home and family.

It was with alarm then that last week she'd found herself missing a period. How it had happened she was uncertain, but she meant to remedy it. A few days before going to tea with the

271

Burringtons she had secretly taken a series of hot baths and had drunk gin and Epsom salts which she had heard could rid one of a pregnancy if caught early enough. It had all but made her sick, but it must have done the trick. She had a period, but what a period, draining her so that the tea had proved a miserable time. She had been glad to relax on the veranda and not go traipsing around the overstocked garden to see how the new young peepul trees and clouds flecked crimson by the setting sun reflected on the lucid surface of the new tank.

When they had gone out of sight, Ansley had come to sit by her. 'You don't look very robust, my dear. Are you really not feeling too well?'

'Just tired, I think,' she had excused herself.

'It's the weather. It's getting very hot.' She had felt his arm steal across her shoulders as a form of comfort. 'Well, soon you'll be up in the hills and out of it. Fortunate women, leaving us men to perspire down here on our own. You are all very unkind to us.'

She had given a small flirtatious giggle. 'You miss us, do you?'

'I shall miss *you*.'

The way he said it, his voice low, had sent a delightful shiver through her. Why she had leaned towards him she didn't know, but the next thing he had bent his face to hers and kissed her.

For a moment she wanted to draw away, but the kiss was warm, his slim, firm moustache an intimate framework on her upper lip accentuating a suggestive softness of the lips beneath. She didn't draw away. It was he who did, abruptly, as his wife and Alex's voices became audible.

Annie expected him to hurriedly apologise for his audacity, but their eyes met and she felt the message that passed from him to her, and, she knew, from her to him before he lifted his voice to greet the returning pair.

Thinking now of how she'd told Ansley of her loneliness and dislike of Simla, Annie watched the servants moving around packing for the journey.

Mid-morning already felt unbearably hot; a glaring sun blazed from an intensely blue void and would have probed all the rooms with unrelenting heat but for frames of tatty at the windows, the fragrant cuscus grass kept wet to freshen the air. But the doors were open to allow trunks of her belongings to be ushered out to the waiting car that would take her to the station.

272

She sat on a box, limp in her loose cotton dress, and felt perspiration trickle down her temples for all the wafting of the punkah. At first she had overseen the packing, but growing hot and frustrated, had left it to Alex who had more command of their staff than she, exhausted from trying to get them to understand what she wanted packed, with nothing left behind. It seemed to her that they took it all in their stride. If something was missed it would not be the end of the world. Philosophical, she supposed. But she with her anxious English mind found herself wanting to check, then double check, worrying endlessly about mishaps that probably would never occur anyway.

She watched Alex supervising, but she wasn't thinking of him. Taking their leave of the Burringtons that evening, Mrs Burrington had gone to make sure the servants had found Annie's mislaid wrap and Alex had gone to stand on the porch to wait for the tonga they'd ordered. Ansley had seized the opportunity to grip her arm and whisper, 'You won't be lonely in Simla, my dear.'

Watching Alex with the packing, Annie gnawed her lip. She'd more or less sanctioned what Ansley had implied, for she hadn't protested, had she?

George was out of work again. The foreman's job hadn't panned out. Three weeks spent walking a tightrope, lurching from one mistake to another, just managing to scrape one step ahead of his own ignorance. A few of the men under him had been kind enough to cover for him, seeing him an easy touch when they felt like shirking; others were only eager for him to go, each of them considering himself far more competent than this idiot who was getting more money than them, until finally he'd been found out. The boss was sorry for him, but he had a business to run. Had to let him go, as he put it.

'What're we going to do?' Pam asked bleakly, but George was full of optimism. He'd got one foreman's job, he'd get another on the strength of saying he had been a foreman. It wasn't no lie, was it? They didn't have to know he'd made a bugger-up of it. But Pam had long ago lost her optimism.

'They'd want references, George, and you didn't get a reference. You won't be lucky enough a second time to step into some dead man's shoes. You don't get many men dropping dead minutes before you turn up.'

273

'I can get a job anywhere,' he said, peeved at her lack of faith, and had gone looking. This time, however, there wasn't the smell of even a bricklayer's job let alone a foreman's.

Pam, unpicking an old dress got from a church charity stall to make into a dress for Beth as she sat opposite George, who, after weeks of searching, had been too despondent to go out today looking for work, let her gaze roam around the flat. With nothing at all coming in, even the rent for this squalid little place they called home was beyond her means. Two weeks overdue and next week loomed equally hopelessly.

He was staring with vacant eyes into the grate which in early May thankfully needed no fire, but she felt no sympathy for him, only anger, though she knew it to be unfair. He did try. But it didn't put bread into their mouths nor pay the rent. She had come to dread the sound of Mrs Carper coming up the stairs when she had failed to go down to settle up; her landlady's fine-boned face growing stern and tight-lipped as Pam promised to have the full rent in a few days. Soon it would become impossible to pay except by minuscule installment that would never catch up.

In desperation, without telling George or his parents, she had taken several paltry items of clothing and linen to the pawn-broker's, something she had up to now managed to avoid; had crept into the shop, the bundle under her arm, hot with shame, praying not to be seen by anyone who might know her. The man, picking over her stuff as though to touch it too firmly would have given him instant leprosy, had offered her two shillings. She'd had to take it; had come out of the place feeling sick. The thought had crossed her mind of going to a money lender, but when she told George, he'd looked as ashamed as she had been going into the hock-shop.

'They want security on it. What bloody security have we got? And we would only be digging a deeper pit for ourselves.'

In her heart Pam knew he was right. They would just have to learn to survive on what few pence they had from the dole until George got himself another job. Lately Pam often went without in order to feed Beth but she didn't tell him. And all the time this unfair anger of hers kept mounting against him.

She knew it wasn't his fault, kept having to tell herself so. There just seemed no let-up at all in this depression for people like him. It wasn't only here in England with something like three

274

million out of work, but worldwide. America had far more unemployment than here. Europe too. Germany was in a terrible state, and even Australia and Canada had their problems.

One small bit of compensation had come out of it, helping people like her – prices being as low as anyone could remember meant that merchants here could trade on the plight of people even worse off in Britain's colonial countries.

For the rich and comfortably-off, of course, it was perfect. With prices falling they just grew richer. There still seemed to be money around. In this small corner of the world day trippers from London came to Southend in spite of mass unemployment. As the holiday trade began to gain strength people were coming into Leigh for the cockles and shrimps. George's dad had started working his boat again. The weather was growing warmer, shrimp were coming back inshore, the catch improving. It was looking good there.

'I think you ought to ask your dad if you could work with him again?' Pam said suddenly as she stood at the table pinning together the cut-out pattern of the finally unpicked pink dress. It had been a large lady's and with all the threadbare and stained pieces cut away, the finished garment would look lovely on Beth. 'Ask him if he needs help.'

George shrugged. 'It don't make money.'

'Surely it's better than nothing,' she shot at him, her scissors held stiffly, irritated by his defeatism. 'That's what you're bringing in at the moment – nothing!'

In the face of his silence, she put aside the dress pieces, and came to stand aggressively over him. 'I think you'd better go and see your dad.'

'He won't have nothing for me. That's why me and him decided I went and got something else. Wasn't enough to keep both our families going.'

'You can at least ask him,' Pam snapped and going back to the table, all but threw the scissors down on to its already scratched surface. 'I'm off to bed. You go and ask him in the morning.'

She knew he would. A man defeated by events, seeing his wife and child struggling, of course he would. Or he'd have her anger to contend with.

* * *

275

Deep in the Sunday paper her dad had relinquished, Mum having got him to bed for the afternoon so that he and his constant grumbling were out of the way for a while, Connie only half heard the gentle knock at the door, only half noticed Mum go to answer it. She only became aware of it when Mum came back into the kitchen to whisper for fear of waking her father: 'It's someone for you, dear.'

'Someone for me?' She didn't make friends easily, not since Ben's death. All her old friends had fiancés, talked endlessly about weddings and wedding dresses. They bored her. They brought up memories she'd rather forget. They made her want to go home and cry. It was better without them, silly, simpering, excited girls. Sometimes she felt fifteen years older than any of them, with their innocence of what life could do to them. Coming up to the anniversary of Ben's death, she wanted to be alone to observe it.

'It's some man, love.'

'Man?' Mystified, Connie stared up at her.

'A very nice-looking young man.' Unless she was mistaken, her mother's face appeared to be aglow with hopeful anticipation. Touched by faint annoyance with her, Connie got up and went past her to hear the added whisper, 'He's wearing a dog-collar.'

The statement pulled Connie up sharply. An agitated feeling began deep inside her. A nice-looking man certainly wasn't the vicar, an angular-bodied, middle-aged man with large features. With another quick glance at her mother, hoping that what she felt wasn't showing on her face, she hurried out through the front room to the street door.

As she expected, Ian Lindsay stood there. He wore a formal expression, that of a man who had come about business.

'I'm doing a few rounds,' he explained hastily before she could even utter a greeting. 'Visiting a few people. I'm afraid you're one of them, Miss Bowmaker.'

How formal. The last time he'd addressed her it had been Constance, months and months ago.

'It's that you haven't been to Sunday service for a couple of months,' he continued with hardly a pause, 'And we thought you might not be well. Some parishioners have asked after you. This is merely a visit, while I am on my rounds, to see how you are.'

Connie found her voice. 'No, I'm all right, thank you.'

He was rolling his black homburg around in his hands, sliding the stiff curled brim through his fingers. It revealed a certain nervousness for all his formal presentation. 'Not ill or anything?'

'No, I'm fine,' she said, annoyed that her heart had begun to race.

'Oh.' He seemed lost for a reply. Then his deep brown eyes sought hers. He seemed to pluck new courage from the air, his next words bursting out in a rush. 'I miss you . . . I mean, *I've* missed you . . . personally. Why don't you come to church any more?'

'I don't feel the need.' It seemed the moment for a lengthier explanation. 'I think I've come to terms at last with the loss of . . . my fiancé last year. I suppose I found . . . I found . . .'

'Comfort?' he finished for her. 'That is good. I am glad. That is what the church is for, what God is for, to give comfort and succour to those who seek it, who are in need.' It sounded as though he were quoting from a text book, the words stilted.

'I expect so,' she said lamely. 'Thank you for coming, and for your concern.'

She found herself reluctant to close the door, but felt it was what she should be doing. She saw him move forward, the proverbial foot in the door, so to speak, like a stubborn salesman.

'I say, Miss Bowmaker . . . Constance . . . I need to confess – I am not here solely on behalf of St Clement's or our parishioners. I've come on behalf of myself. I hope you're not offended.'

She smiled at him. 'Why should I be offended?'

It had been the wrong thing to say. A look of encouragement spread over his face.

'I'm so glad, Constance. The reason I'm here, first of all, is that I really have missed you. I looked for you every Sunday and when you didn't come, I felt I had somehow driven you away, that I had been too forward, that I had frightened you off. I have been deeply dispirited in not seeing you in church and have wanted to make myself clear to you for so long a time and, but for that one moment of indiscretion, have always held back. That moment has haunted me. I lie awake at night knowing the fool I was and pondering how I could ever attempt to change it and let you see me in a better light. Now it has become too late. I shall be leaving St Clement's in two weeks' time. I am going up country, to the Midlands. I have been given a parish of my own, something I have worked hard

277

towards and longed for, but no longer, for it could be I shall never see you again. I cannot go without attempting a last try at making you see how I feel about you. Constance, this call has absolutely nothing to do with St Clement's, but with me. I lied to you. I hope you're not offended. I think I have made a mess of things again.'

The knock had disturbed her father from his nap. Now came his deep voice demanding to know who it was chattering like some damned monkey at the door. Ian Lindsay heard him.

'I seem to have chosen a wrong time – yet again.'

'No!' The protest seemed to spring out of her. It took some control to moderate her voice. 'No, you haven't. I'm sorry I've not been very welcoming but you startled me.'

'Then will you come to church for the next two Sundays, so that I can say my goodbyes to you in the proper manner?'

'No, I don't want to do that.' Somehow the thought of going back into that church made her shudder. It had become the embodiment of all those accrued days of unhappiness which she now had no wish to resurrect. Ben was dead. Bad enough remembering him, the good times and the time of grief. His mother had said, there was no bringing him back, and she was right. Setting foot in that church would be trying to do just that. Just as Ben's home without him there held an atmosphere of the dead, so the atmosphere of that church struck her now. 'I don't think I could,' she said.

The look on his face told her that he had misconstrued, even though he said quietly, 'I understand.'

But, he didn't understand. She hastened to rectify matters. 'It's not anything to do with you. It's how I feel about the whole place. It's a year since I lost Ben, and I can't go on forever mourning him. That place would only bring it all back, and I don't want that. Not any more.'

It was a joy to see his expression clear, become full of hope. Yet he looked sad. 'I shall be leaving in two weeks,' he repeated, this time a strong connotation that he assumed she found him acceptable but that he might have left it too late for anything between them to develop.

'You could perhaps leave me a forwarding address.' She couldn't believe she was saying this. Something inside her was crying out, 'Don't let him go!'

'May I?' It was wonderful to see the light come into his dark eyes.

278

'If you want to.'

She was flirting. Again. It had been so long since she had flirted with anyone. A fleeting memory came to her of the day she had given Ben an invitation with her eyes as he'd looked over at her in that dancehall in Southend where he had gone with his mates on a day trip. She had been with a couple of friends from work. Her heart had suddenly raced at the sight of him, had raced even faster as he'd come over. He had been so good-looking, so . . .

Hurriedly she pushed the memories out of her head, concentrated on Ian Lindsay's nicely cultured voice, so different to Ben's London one. Dear, dear Ben – you must go – you must leave – forgive me for feeling like a young girl again . . .

'Then I shall write. Constance, I will give you my address.' He was fiddling in his breast pocket, dragging out a short pencil and a small black notebook. 'This will do.' Furiously he wrote, tore out the small ruled sheet. 'Could I call on you next Sunday afternoon? We have a christening, and then I'll be free until evening service. May I call?'

From the back room where Dad lay, came the bellow: 'What the bloody hell's going on out there? Peggy, get me out of this bloody bed. How can I sleep with all that bloody row going on?'

Connie felt her cheeks grow hot. But Ian Lindsay was smiling. A man of the church he certainly was. A man knowledgeable about people in general he also was. He shook his head at her glowing cheeks. 'May I call?' he repeated.

All Connie could do was nod wordlessly. He moved back from the doorstep. 'Tell your father I came to say that he has been mentioned in our prayers for the well-being of all our parishioners, and I pray he may one day be back on his feet.'

His quiet manner put Connie at her ease. She laughed. 'Oh, I can see him doing just that one day. He's the most determined, stubborn man I know. He's already talking of getting those calliper things. It could be quite possible, though he'll never walk properly, to swing his weight between crutches with them on. Oh yes, he does mean to be back on his feet again – to the bane of us all at times.'

He smiled and nodded. 'And I will see you next week, Constance.'

'Yes,' she said, sobering, and as he moved off down the road, carefully closed the door.

279

Chapter Twenty-Six

She had been expecting it. Now it had arrived. As she opened her door to the knock, seeing her landlady standing there, her face grim, she already knew what she was going to say.

'I have come up to see if you have the rent on you, Mrs Bryant.'

'Can you give me another day or two? My George has gone out looking for a job. I'm sure he'll get something today.'

Mrs Carper's expression remained unmoved. 'You said that last week, and the week before. Your rent is three weeks overdue. If you don't pay this week it will be four.'

'I know, I'm sorry, Mrs Carper. But it will be paid.'

'Last week I told you that if nothing was paid by this week I should have to ask you to find other accommodation.'

Pam clutched Beth to her a little more firmly. 'I did give you a bit last week on account.'

Her mother had been by and hearing her plight had left two florins by the loaf on the table before leaving. She had grabbed the money up, rushed out and down the stairs with it and catching Mum up at the front door, embarrassed, tried to press it back into her hand. There had been a short amicable squabble, which Pam had lost through her mother's downright refusal to take it back. In tears, Pam had retained the two-shilling pieces, hidden in her fist like two stolen jewels, her hand slowly warming them, out of sight to diminish the humiliation of acceptance.

'A bit.' Mrs Carper's handsome face came close to twisting into a disparaging sneer. 'A drop in the ocean compared with what you own me. You must understand, Mrs Bryant, I can't go on like this. I could let out this room several times over, and I'm not getting a penny while you can't find the wherewithal to pay me.

I'm sorry, Mrs Bryant, I know you've got a kiddie and a husband out of work, but I can't afford to run my business like it was a charity. I have to live as well.'

'Just another week,' Pam heard herself plead, hating the sound of degradation. 'I know George will get some work. Then we'll be able to pay you in full. If you can wait just one more week. Please.'

'I'm sorry, Mrs Bryant.' The woman was backing away, concluding the interview. 'I can't risk it. I am going to have to ask you to leave. If you cannot come up with at least the three weeks' rent you already owe by this weekend, you must go on Monday. I give you the weekend to pack up.'

'But where are we going to go?' The woman seemed to be receding even further away, melting into the dimness of the landing as if in a nightmare. 'What are we going to do?'

'I don't know.' She sounded as if she could visualise the plight stretching before her lodger. 'But I think I'm being generous giving you the two days. I'd be within my rights to ask you to leave today, me getting nothing from you, but I wouldn't do that. Not to someone with a kiddie. So it's understood, Mrs Bryant, you must settle up, or you must find other accommodation in two days.'

The final words dropped, weighty as an object flung down a precipice. There was no retrieving them. Her mind and body utterly numbed, Pam held Beth to her, the child unruffled, wide-eyed and pleasurably distracted by what was going on around her, and watched Mrs Carper go back down the stairs to her own ground-floor quarters.

When George returned home, it was on him that Pam vented all her pent-up fear in an explosion of rage.

'I suppose you've not found any work. Out all day and nothing I suppose. I suppose you've been sitting on your backside in the library with the rest of the down-and-outs, or hanging around on street corners with 'em waiting for work to come to you.'

It was cruel. It was unfair. She saw him sink down on the rickety fireside chair, his body bent forward, his hands limp between his knees. A thousand words cramming her brain to berate him with, and she could only fall silent, seeing him hunched forward in the chair, all the stuffing knocked out of him, too tired in mind and body even to retaliate.

She knew he hadn't been hanging around any street corner or in the local library. Friday – he'd been trudging all the way into Southend for what was laughingly termed public assistance, the dole. It was there on the table, eight paltry shillings with which to buy a week's food for himself, his wife and his child. The weekly rent for this place in which they lived took seven shillings of it, leaving them a shilling to get by on. No unemployment insurance for George, who hadn't been in work for any long enough stretch to draw it. Government handouts allowed for no extras, certainly not for rent it seemed. Last week George had told her that the chap in front of him in the queue had been turned away because he'd been carrying that morning's newspaper under his arm, told that if he could afford newspapers he most likely had enough to live on and obviously didn't warrant dole money. That was how it was. Cold charity.

Pam found her voice, this time as spiritless as he looked.

'We're being slung out,' she said softly. 'Evicted. Mrs Carper came up this morning when I was feeding Beth and told us, no more rent, no more roof over our heads. She's given us two days to get out. We got two days to find . . .'

It was impossible to say any more. Pam bent her head where she stood and began to cry silently, her shoulders shuddering.

Without saying anything, he got up, took off the cloth cap he hadn't even bothered to remove to sit down, so low-spirited was he, and put an arm quietly around her. The whole gesture was purely automatic, and equally automatically she let her face lie against the dark creased jacket that seemed to be the ubiquitous uniform of the long-term unemployed English working man.

'I don't know what we're going to do,' she at last whispered against his chest.

He still didn't reply and she knew he was recalling the row they'd had last week when she'd asked him if he had spoken to his father about going back with him on the boat and when he had said, 'Not yet,' she had turned on him calling him the most spineless twerp she'd ever met.

The row had developed into screams of accusation and cries of protest and he had almost hit her. Almost. Drawing back his arm, he had instantly let it fall as she yelled, 'Go one then, hit me! You can't get a job and you want to hit *me* – it's my fault you're not working.' But of course, the aim that had never landed had been a reflection of his frustration. She knew that, but she'd railed on, working out her own frustrations.

Now the time for that was past. Now it was crisis, and what was needed was an answer to it, an answer neither of them had. So what ensued was only silent acceptance of the fate being ladled out to them.

'We've got to find somewhere to live,' she muttered, sniffing back the grief that had consumed her, rationality returning. 'We'll have to go out tomorrow morning and start looking.'

'What d'you mean, gone?' Connie stared at her mother in disbelief.

She had come home from work a few moments ago, every evening offering up a small prayer of thanks that she still had work to come home from when so many had none. These days she did all sorts of humble tasks at Fenner's Engineering other than the one for which she had first been employed. It was the small firm's show of appreciation of a good worker whose once invaluable services now teetered on the edge of extinction as business dropped away. In truth it was their goodness of heart that Connie gave up her prayers of thanks for, even though her wages had been of necessity all but halved.

'That's it.' Her mother's voice was bleak. 'I popped in this morning to see her and her landlady said they'd gone. They couldn't pay their rent. I had a damned great row with her, told her she should be ashamed of herself turning them out, but that one just kept saying she had her own livelihood to think on and as Pam hadn't paid her rent for weeks . . .'

From his wheelchair, Dad broke in hoarsely. 'Will you shut up about her! I said I won't have her name mentioned in my house.'

'You shut up too!' she snapped at him. 'She's my daughter – I'll say her name whenever I care to. I'm at my wits' end.' She spoke to the air now, moving back and forth between the range and the kitchen table, not really doing anything constructive, taking a stewpan off the heat and bearing it to the waiting plates only to put it back on to the range again. 'It's beyond me . . . Oh, look at me – I don't know what I'm doing.'

Retrieving the stewpan she began spooning out the contents on to two plates more than were needed, her mind abstracted. 'What on earth could've happened to her, where've they gone? Why didn't they come here? We'd have helped them if they were in that mess.'

283

'Like bloody hell I would! I wouldn't have that slut under my roof if she was . . .'

'Not now, Dan!' She turned and put back the pan, stood looking at it, her shoulders drooping. 'I can't understand why she never said she was getting so deep into a mess. I know she said she was behind with the rent. I know I couldn't afford to pay it for her but I often left a couple of bob on the table to help her out.'

'You never told me that. Where'd *you* get a couple of bob from?'

Again she turned on him, her tone defiant, daring him to argue. 'Out of me housekeeping money. And if you're going to say I'm keeping everyone short, I ain't. I know how to juggle with what we've got. No one's going short. I've juggled with money all me life.'

'Should have accrued a little nest egg by now then.'

'Don't be silly. It's all only ever gone on the house and for the winter when money ain't coming in. It's how we've always managed. Didn't you know?'

'I've sometimes left her a couple of shillings when I could spare it,' Connie butted in, seeing another of the far too frequent arguments this past year beginning to foment. Her father glared at her.

'You too? All going behind me back now I can't do nothing. I don't count for nothing no more in this house. Me son doing the work I should be doing, making me feel it's my fault him and that Lily he was engaged to broke up over it. Now me own daughters go against me.'

'It's not that, Dad. I can't see my own sister poverty-stricken.'

It had been unexpectedly difficult to leave the couple of shillings at odd times, embarrassing to be the giver, her sister the taker, the abject way it was accepted, desperation pushing humiliation aside. She'd have liked to give her more, but that would have felt she was bordering on ostentation, and anyway, since her wages had gone down quite considerably – the price of being kept in work – she had to be practical.

Her mother was talking almost to herself and she pushed a plate of stew towards Dad, forgetting to add the cutlery to eat it with. 'I tried to help her, and then she goes off without even telling me. When I saw her Friday morning she never said a word. She could have said.'

'Perhaps she didn't know then,' Connie offered. 'Perhaps she was given quick notice.'

Seeing her mother distracted by it all, Connie went to the kitchen door and called to Josie, languishing in her room, to come down and eat. When she came back, her mother was still with her own thoughts. 'You'd've thought the woman would've given Pam decent time to get out. To turn her out like that, over a weekend. You can't go looking for digs on a Sunday. Where would they have gone, and why didn't she get in touch with us – her own flesh and blood?' A look from her froze an angry rebuke on her husband's lips. 'After all I've tried to do, you'd think she'd've got in touch with me to tell me what happened.'

'Perhaps she felt ashamed, Mum. We hadn't exactly been nice to her, until after the baby was born. I must say, we can't talk!'

Josie came into the kitchen, glancing from one parent to the other and, getting the message instantly, without a word sat down to the plate of stew her mother pushed in front of her.

As Connie distributed cutlery, their mother having totally over-looked it, a thought struck her. 'I wonder if they might have gone to her husband's people.' It was better to refer to George as Pam's husband, to utter his name in this house a worse crime in her father's eyes than the mention of Pam's.

He took a noisy spoonful of stew. 'Typical, her running to that lot instead on us. We don't count. Chance for Bryant to score one over on me again, ain't it? Never misses a chance, him. If I had me legs, I'd be over there now throttling the bloody life out on him.'

He was ignored as Danny was heard coming in at the back door from a day's cockling. Mum caught up with Connie's new thought; her expression grew less stressed, replaced by new hope that Pam and her baby might not be out wandering the streets looking for a roof over her head.

'I'm going to have to go and see.'

'No you won't!' Dan looked as though he was about to leap out of his wheelchair. 'You go round that damned place and I'll . . . I'll . . .'

'You'll what, Dan? Turn me out of doors like you did Pam?'

It still hurt to hark back to that day when she, torn between love of her daughter and bitter memories of how they had struggled after what had been done to Dan by the very family Pam was marrying into, had turned her face away from her. She had suffered over that ever since. At night while he lay snoring away downstairs she'd lie awake, darkness accentuating all that had transpired, guilt and shame driving sleep away as she went over

285

and over the things she should have done and said that she hadn't and her efforts to make up for it since that never seemed enough. Now this. It almost felt as if it had been she and Dan who had reduced her daughter to this. A nice wedding, harmony in the family, surely Pam's start in life would have been different? There had to be an end to all this anger. There was only her to end it. Losing Pam had been almost as bad as the loss of little Tony. Quickly she put that thought from her.

'I am going to see if she is there, and that's that. I'll go round there as soon as we've eaten. It'll still be light and it's only a few minutes' walk.'

'I'll come with you, Mum.' Danny's voice held the ring of the strong ready to protect the weak. 'In case there's any trouble.'

'There won't *be* any trouble,' she said firmly as she placed Danny's dinner in front of him, and the finality of her words silenced him, silenced them all.

Pam had felt George's arm grow suddenly strong about her shoulders as they stood in the humble little place they had called home. His voice too had become strong and resolute.

'We'll go to me mum and dad tomorrow. I've had enough of keeping up appearances, pretending we're making ends meet. *Someone*'s got to help us and not with handouts every now and again. We need proper help. Me mum and dad owe us. So do yours. It's them what's brought us to this – them and their bloody argument what's been going on all our lives. Let them do something for us for a change.'

She couldn't see her parents welcoming them, but George was certain his would. Meekly, Beth in the shabby pram, she followed him to their house off Church Hill. She felt like one of those destitute girls in a Dickens novel. Homeless, it had a dreadful ring to it, unreal, but it was happening to her.

Wordlessly, she stood aside in the pleasant if tiny front room. Beth was deposited on the sofa, while George, for once taking charge, firmly reminded his parents of their responsibilities, so to speak. The way he spoke to them, not pleading, a totally new man to the one she knew, shocked even her, sure that their natural reaction would be to order him out of the house.

Instead, Mr Bryant had nodded and said, 'Yes, I s'pose one on us should pay for what we've done to our kids.'

286

Mrs Bryant had pulled herself up to her full height, a good inch taller than him, with a display of injured dignity. 'You're not the one at fault, Dick. You never were. Why should you take all the blame for what was an accident? Creeping about all them years ago like you'd done it purposely. If you'd stood up for yourself, but not you – just crept around like a criminal, taking all that swine dished out on you. He nearly landed you in court, remember? If anything, it should be them taking their daughter in.'

George had stepped forward. 'Stop it, Mum. If it hadn't been for you, Dad would never have gone near that bloody boat. You're my parents and it's me what's asking for help, on behalf of my wife and child. As my parents I think you've a bit of a duty to help me out, don't you think?'

Standing aside, Pam had pleaded silently for him to consider who he was speaking to, wondering how he could talk like that to his own mother and expect to get away with it. As well, she'd been confused by this talk of accidents. She'd heard it said before, but the mortification of having to stand by while he begged for a roof over their heads – that was what it amounted to – was such that everything else was pushed out of mind.

With his son to bolster him up, Dick Bryant had taken the initiative. 'All right, we don't want to start up any blessed rows, do we? Bad enough other people's. What's important is you two. I say you can move in today. Milly, we can clear out the spare bedroom for them, can't we?'

So it was done. All Saturday was taken up trundling a handcart with her and George's few belongings out of what Mrs Carper had grandly termed a furnished flat to his parents' house. Some of their stuff was installed in the bedroom they'd been given in the two bedroomed house, the rest, what there was of it, stacked up in the Bryant's small smelly shed in the yard.

Sunday had possessed a dream-like quality, Sunday dinner with his parents made Pam feel they would depart for home afterwards as they had done on occasions, very rare occasions, because she'd never enjoyed going round there for Sunday dinner. Now she was here for good, or at least for a pretty good while by the look of it.

George, however, had no trouble settling in. Pam envied him, felt a little out on the perimeter. But one good thing was coming out of it. Mr Bryant had agreed to his son going back with him on

287

the boat, for all the profits would hardly go to keeping two families.

Mr Bryant's bawley had once been a fine craft twenty years ago, one of the old clench-built types, heavily timbered and able to stand up to the fiercest gale. It now had a sad look about it and stank of rotten fish from years of the catch cooked on board as shrimp had to be; left for even a short while uncooked it became unfit for market.

George was to have one third of any profit. 'Better than me without a job at all,' he said when Pam pointed out how little money would be coming in. 'And we won't be paying out rent, just for our food. That's all they'll take.'

It was better than nothing, and it was generous of his dad, especially now. No one had money to throw around any more. A few with half a crown to spend on a day return ticket from London or a couple of shillings on a charabanc did come, but gone was the thronging of Southend's promenade and Kursal and the swarm of people making for Leigh for its cockles and shrimps and whelks and mussels.

'We'll manage, son,' Dick Bryant said over the Sunday dinner, his small lips beneath the bristly moustache curling into a grin, glad to see his son back with him. 'You won't go short, either of you, and our little Beth'll be much better off with us all to look out for her. She's a dear little thing, ain't she, our first little grandchild.' His small age-faded blue eyes turned to Pam as he chewed stubbornly on a piece of stewing beef that these days took the place of a Sunday roast. 'You've done well by her, love, in spite on the times. Let's just hope we'll be seeing a little brother or sister for her afore long, eh?'

He no doubt meant nothing by it, but the remark somehow didn't sit right with her, him talking of more babies, to her ears alluding to the sexual side of the procedure. Dick Bryant was a pleasant enough man, but Pam felt her flesh creep a little as he smiled across at her. She couldn't forget how he had kissed Beth those times when she'd had her at her breast. She could still recall the light prickle of the tip of that moustache against her exposed flesh. She told herself it had been done in all innocence, a grandfather taken by the sight of his tiny granddaughter, but the embarrassment remained in her mind no matter how nice and kind Mr Bryant was.

288

She had a great need that night to hug a little reality to her. Putting Beth to bed in the bedroom they'd been given, its double bed and the cot almost crowding out the single wardrobe, dressing table, and the two fireside chairs they had managed to cram in, she waited for Beth to gradually fall asleep while she sat trying to capture this sense of reality.

Alone for a moment, she quietly tore a scrap of paper from an old notebook George had. She'd find an envelope later. In the rush there had been no time to let Mum know what had happened. Now in these precious moments alone, she would write to her, just a short note explaining, and tomorrow morning post it – if she could find an envelope.

The door bursting open made her start guiltily. George stood there, his expression one of concern. 'You all right, love? You've been up here so long I wondered if everything was OK. You've not been crying have you?'

'No.' In a reflex action, she had dropped the book on the bed, the letter hidden underneath it. She didn't know why she'd needed to hide it, but just felt she had to. 'I was making sure Beth was well asleep. It's a strange house and I thought she might wake up and feel frightened.'

George peeped over the cot. 'She looks well away. Come on, come down. Don't sit up here all alone.'

It wasn't until Wednesday, Mrs Bryant senior in her domineering way making quite sure she didn't have a quiet moment to grieve the loss of her home, that she had a moment to finish her letter in peace.

By that time, as the letter was being sorted for sending by the next morning's post to the address on the tatty envelope Pam had found, her mother was making her way through the still-light streets to the Bryant houshold. Danny's help had been thrust aside. She felt more than capable of having things out with her daughter if she was there, the Bryants if they thought her intrusive, or anyone else who might attempt to do battle with her.

She had not forgotten Mrs Bryant's slap on her face. She had not forgotten that she'd tried to do her best by Pam. She had not forgotten that if Pam had fled to the hated Bryants, it had been rather than come to her in her hour of need. Peggy Bowmaker was getting herself into a right old lather as her small chubby figure strode onward towards Church Street.

Chapter Twenty-Seven

The knock on the door was answered by Mrs Bryant. Pam, busy feeding Beth in a chair which Mr Bryant had hurriedly converted into a baby chair complete with a small table, took little notice of the knock until she heard women's voices raised.

George and his father were off in the estuary most probably chasing shrimp halfway to Harwich, these last days of May having turned chilly enough to send them off into deep water.

Putting the small bowl of mashed potato and gravy back on the table, Pam went to see what was going on. Mrs Bryant was one to raise her voice over any little thing not to her liking. She was amazed and shocked to see her own mother at the door.

'Good Lord, Mum, what're you doing here?' The spoon she still held dripped gravy on to the passage lino, but she didn't notice, her startled gaze trained on the small figure of her mother.

Peggy looked beyond the large woman to her daughter. 'I might ask the same about you, my gel. Why didn't you let me know you was coming here? I had to get all the news from your landlady. I felt a real fool standing there listening to what she had to say. Why couldn't you have come and told us what had happened?'

'She didn't fancy being slung out a second time,' Milly Bryant put in, her voice carrying up the street. Pam leapt to the rescue, forgetting this wasn't her house.

'Come inside, Mum. We need to talk properly.'

'We certainly do,' Milly Bryant added.

'And not out on the street doorstep.'

She watched her mother-in-law step aside to allow Mum in, who, taking a deep breath, moved on past her. Pam conducted her into the back room where she had been feeding Beth. Beth, with some of her food adhering around her mouth, was now playing with a spilled drop of mashed potato, her little fingers erratically brushing it back and forth over the wooden surface of the feeding tray into a smeared mess.

Pam saw her mother's gaze settle upon the child as though longing to pick her up and cuddle her, but Mrs Bryant, a little taken aback by Pam asking her mother in whether she objected or not, began to speak.

'Now you're here, what is it you want?'

'What I said on the doorstep.' Peggy did not flinch. Her hurt angry eyes now trained themselves on her daughter. 'Pam, why didn't you come to us, love?'

'Because I thought Dad would turn me . . . us away, like he did me.'

'*I* wouldn't have turned you away. Your dad don't have any say in the matter but to bluster and grumble. Since his trouble, it's me what needs to sort things out in our house as much as is needed. I wouldn't have turned you away. Ain't I been coming regular to see you, sometimes twice a week like I would have done this week?'

'I didn't think, Mum.' The impact of what she had done by coming here filled Pam with misery. She could hardly say she wished she had.

'Well, if I'm allowed to speak in my own house,' Mrs Bryant said, still standing in the living room doorway as though about to usher the intruder out, 'I say you've got a cheek coming round here after all these years of you lot putting our family down. We don't want nothing to do with you. And now you've found Pam and my son taking up lodgings with us for want of *any other help*, you *want* to help. Well, she don't need it. Now you can leave.'

For a moment it looked as though her mother was about to comply, but she stood firm. 'Not till I've had my say, now I'm here. I suppose it was you what persuaded my daughter not to let me know. I don't know what you've got in mind, but it looks like you're too eager to always rub our noses in it, even to getting our own daughter on your side.'

'It's not like that, Mum,' Pam cried, growing angry. This feud would never stop. 'There's a letter in the post for you about it. I meant to write sooner but it all happened so quickly and there was

291

the moving as well. I started writing on Sunday but I didn't have an envelope. It went off this afternoon.'

Beth, forgotten, was reaching out with open hands, burbling for the rest of her supper. Peggy stood silent, a little chastened by her daughter's explanation. They all fell silent, none knowing what to say. In the end it was Peggy who spoke.

'So you're all right here, then?'

'Yes, Mum.'

'No thanks to you!' Mrs Bryant added vehemently.

Pam saw her mother turn to face the woman, just as she herself did. She felt merely taken aback, but her mother was calm and reproachful.

'That was no more than I expected of you, Mrs Bryant. You're intent on us remaining enemies, aren't you?'

'What else do you expect? It was your man as started this in the first place, belting in to mine like he did, and him miles bigger than mine.'

Beth was starting to whimper with tiredness, rubbing mashed potato into her eyes with her little fists, but no one noticed.

'No, Mrs Bryant,' Peggy was saying. 'Who was it threw that clod of earth at my Dan – I ask you that? That was what started it.'

'That was a sheer accident,' the other woman blazed at her. 'But your bullying husband belted into him without even stopping to see it was. Just as the fire on his boat was an accident, but he wouldn't have had that, would he? Wanted to believe the worst.'

'Don't give me that.' Peggy's voice was beginning to rise, her calm melting away as all the old wounds began to tear open one after the other. 'That pathetic thing you call your husband went creeping off in the dead of night with the sole idea on having his own back, the coward he is. He knew what he was doing, all right.'

Mrs Bryant was blustering, her own wounds opening, wounds she had never been able to share because of the accusations, the threat of court action, her husband's freedom and livelihood threatened if she had made anything of it. It had been better to keep quiet and let the matter subside legally than drag it all out in the open and be branded a liar on top of everything else if the court had found for the injured party. All this she blurted out.

'We never said nothing because we knew we'd never be able to prove it, that my Dick had no intention on setting fire to that boat.'

292

'I don't believe you.'

'There, you see? And you never will. I don't deny my Dick crept off in the dark to get his own back. And why not? Him a smaller man than your man what knocked him around, his nose broke and his eyes all blacked, just because of a bit of mud thrown in a lark happened to land on your husband. How could he, his size, fight back? He'd have been half killed, almost was half killed. When I saw him come home that day, a mate having to help him to walk, I nearly died. And I went on at him, said he shouldn't stand for it. That was when I told him to hit that big bully where it hurt, and that night he went out to make a mess of your boat. That's what he intended to do. Make a mess, pull everything about so that in the morning your man would miss the tide trying to tidy everything up.'

'I don't believe you.' But Peggy Bowmaker's tone had become noticeably less truculent.

Milly Bryant seemed hardly to hear her. 'He slung all the stuff about, and for good measure he went and spilt oil all over the deck so it'd have to be all scrubbed before anyone could walk on it. But in his hurry to get everything done before he was seen, Dick backed into the lamp he had to see with and knocked it over. Before he knew where he was it caught the oil alight and then the ropes, and he didn't know what to do and just ran off. He was in a terrible state when he got home, but there wasn't nothing we could do about it. We just watched the blaze.'

'And you said nothing,' Peggy said in a low voice. She didn't even appear shocked, merely accepting. 'You stood and watched it go up and you didn't raise a warning.'

'We was both frightened. Dick heard someone shout at him as he ran off, and he thought he'd get the blame.'

'He did, didn't he?'

'It was an accident.' The larger woman had become oddly and visibly distressed. She leaned forward. 'Mrs Bowmaker, I've never said this before, but telling you on it now, I wish to God we'd done something about it. All these years . . . I wish we had. It's wrecked our kids' lives. Look at your Pam and our George. What've they got? Nothing. And it's . . . it's . . .'

Our fault. The two women, remembering a day all those years ago, the ensuing hatred, saw in each other's eyes the truth in those lost years. Not that it concerned them any more, that they could endure, but it had all to do with their children, and that seared into them.

Pam, watching, knew that little would change, the two woman would never become friends, too much having flowed under the bridge for that, but something had been laid to rest. How their menfolk would react was anyone's guess – not so well, she imagined – but Pam began to feel sanity was at last descending on them all. She became aware of Beth whimpering and turned to take her up in her arms.

'I'm sorry. Beth's tired, and she hasn't had all her food. I've got to get on.' She didn't realise she had spoken sharply, authoritatively. They both turned and looked at her as if she were a stranger in their midst.

'I suppose I'd better go,' Peggy said haltingly. The other woman gave a small nod and stood by as Peggy planted a little kiss on Beth's smeared cheek. 'Come and see us, Pam,' she reminded her simply, and followed Mrs Bryant out.

Wishing she'd replied to her mother, Pam turned her attention back to Beth, picking up the little bowl of food and began feeding her with what was left in it, her actions automatic as she thought of her mother coming here and the invitation she had offered, knew that something had happened, good or bad she couldn't tell, but she felt no emotion except to feel drained. Only that night, lying next to George in the cramped little bedroom with Beth in her cot beside them did she give way to silent tears; even then not knowing why she cried.

It was a chastened Peggy Bowmaker who returned home. Dan sat silent, his eyes closed as she related what had been said. His silence should have been a warning – the ominous silence of a stalking lion, and only as she finished with, 'It could be we've been wrong about him all these years,' did he pounce with a roar.

'Wrong, is that what you think? Me, wrong all these years to blame that snivelling little sod for putting me out of business? You trying to tell me I should say I'm *sorry* for hating him, I'm supposed to thank him for not exactly *intending* to burn up me boat but only messing it up? What if I'd slipped on that oil he's supposed only to've smeared all over me deck and I'd broken me neck and died, would you still say we'd been wrong all these years? No you bloody wouldn't. It makes no difference if it was an accident or not. He mucked up my livelihood and it was me what got this family through them years. Stupid bitch, you let them dupe you into believing their lies? And you coming home telling me maybe I was wrong?'

His bellowing brought Josie down from the bedroom where she'd been reading out of Dad's way, and Connie from the back room where she had been preparing his bed for him when he wished to retire. They burst into the kitchen together as Peggy was shouting back at him to lower his voice or all the neighbours would hear.

Josie stood in the centre of the room not knowing what to do while Connie ran to her father.

'Dad, calm down. You'll give yourself a heart attack.'

'And you can blame him for that too.' One strong arm thrust her aside with such force that she staggered and nearly fell. 'Still getting at me through my own wife and family now. But I'll see him dead before I am. An' I'll be there to laugh. On me own two feet I'll be there. I won't have him put me in a wheelchair for the rest of me life. I've got him to thank for that too. Well, we'll bloody see about that.'

Before they could get to him, those strong arms had hoisted him up out of the seat, supporting him as though suspended in mid-air. One furious movement of those arms flung him forward, but their strength was not matched by the useless legs. His heavy body tumbled headlong to the floor, sending two kitchen chairs flying against the wall, the table jolted enough to send clattering cups and saucers and plates and cutlery set out ready for the morning.

His head struck the brass fender around the kitchen range; he lay gasping, blood beginning to ooze from a cut on his forehead. Both girls ran to him and between them managed to drag him back to the wheelchair if not into it, for the brake was not on and it kept moving away, leaving them both grunting and sighing under their father's awkward bulk. Their mother ran to the sink for a wet flannel and came back to place it over the wound on his forehead, blood flowing freely enough to make his cheek look as if it had been sliced in two.

'It always looks worse than it is,' Connie said at her cry of alarm. 'Just his head. I don't think it's that bad.' Her father seemed dazed. Connie spoke to her sister. 'Put the brake on, we'll all have to heave him back in.' But it was virtually impossible.

'Why couldn't Danny have been here?' Josie complained as they struggled.

'He's working down the sheds.'

'Your dad'll have to stay where he is till Danny comes,' Peggy told them. 'Josie, run and get him.'

Josie must have gone like the wind for within ten minutes she was back. 'I told him all about it. He's coming. He's left Uncle Pete and Uncle Reg getting on with things.'

Moments later he was there, lifting his father bodily to the man's utter indignation, Danny saying, 'I'm getting you into bed, Dad. It's safer.'

Installed in bed, all but Danny barred from the room, Dan gripped his son's forearm hard. 'Enough of this. I'm goin' to walk, son. If it kills me, I'm goin' to walk. That'll show the lot on 'em. And I want you to help me. Hear me?'

'Yes, Dad.' Danny's eyes met those of his father. Stopping the others coming into the room, it was as if he had known what his father was going to say. 'I hear you.' The look that passed between them said it all.

The following day, Danny was down at the hospital demanding proper splints, crutches and anything else that would be needed. If his father would never *walk* again, as he was repeatedly told by an irritated doctor, he would be upright enough to propel himself along in his own fashion. That at least, Danny swore to himself, would come about.

'Letter for you, Connie.' Her mother held it out to her with a knowing smile. Connie took it from her with cheeks blushing rosy not only from the August weather, already hot in the early morning.

It had been a stuffy, breathless Sunday night, making people hot and restless in their beds; windows stood open all along the street, holidaymakers – those who could still afford holidays – strolled the High Street until late into the night talking and laughing to the annoyance of locals trying to sleep, who uttered many a prayer that autumn would soon come round and the visitors go home to leave them in peace.

Connie had slept as fitfully as anyone. Josie tossing and turning next to her, getting up for drinks of water, had kept her awake, her head full of thoughts night time always managed to magnify.

She'd written to Ian last week and was already wondering if he would reply in the same vein as ever.

Her fourth letter to him, his third to her, had all so far been friendly and cautious. She suspected he, like herself, felt unsure who should be the first to broaden the scope of this relationship a little. Many times she had been tempted to start with a daring Dearest Ian, or even, tempering it a little, My Dear Ian. But it wasn't her place to assume, and so far all she had put was, Dear Ian. She liked to hope he might also be resisting that same temptation while all the time longing to be bolder. There was no way of telling.

Connie opened the letter her mother handed her and unfolded it with the usual hopeful anticipation. The Market Harborough postmark had told her it was from him. The first words she read sent her spirits soaring: My Dearest Constance. Avidly she skipped the usual news of his management of his parish: he'd had a summer cold which had hindered his work somewhat but that he was well now; he was being kept very busy, with his parish in a largish and fast-growing village whose only places of worship other than St Michael's were the Methodist hall just off the high street, and the small Roman Catholic church at the other end of the village; he seldom had time to go visiting his parents in Cheshunt, but – here Connie's spirits soared way out of bounds – he had a short vacation coming up and would she care to meet him there – eleven o'clock by the bus station at Cheshunt, on Saturday the fifteenth of August?

Thrown into a panic, Connie saw the notepaper shake beneath her fingers. Vaguely she heard her mother asking, 'Anything wrong, love?' and came to herself sufficiently to shake her head.

'Ian Lindsay is asking me to meet him in two Saturdays' time.'

Her eyes had detected the next few lines of the letter as she looked up at her mother: 'I would very much like you to meet my parents, if you feel you would care to . . .' and something about them being very kind and warm people, but she had got no further as her mother's voice penetrated her panic.

'Oh, that *is* nice, Connie.' There was relief and excitement in her mother's tone, then anxiety. 'You will be going, won't you?'

'I've only just read it, Mum. I don't know.'

'Oh, but you must. Connie, don't dwell in the . . .'

'I'm not, Mum,' she cut in, anticipating the end of the advice.

'All I'm trying to say is that the past is past, all over and done with. I know you won't ever forget . . .'

'I don't want to talk about that, Mum. As you say, it is past.'

She saw the small, plump features broaden into a beaming smile. 'Will you go?'

Connie made up her mind. She had been missing Ian since he'd left, more than she dared admit to herself, still harking back to Ben whose slowly dimming image she had hung on to out of a warped sense of loyalty, always with a feeling that he was looking down at her, his face sad and lost. She didn't even feel that he expected her to get on with her life, just that she *felt* she should hold fast to him. But the half-acknowledged sense that she had missed Ian's presence had begun to erase Ben's image. It had promoted guilt that it had, but that too no longer seemed of any consequence. Her heart raced.

Meeting his parents held only one connotation – that Ian was thinking of her as his future partner in life. As an honest man of the cloth he would not dream of messing about with a girl's emotions. And as she read on, so she saw that she was right.

I have been cautious because you might not have the same feelings for me as those I have been very conscious of growing for you. But if we meet, and please say we may, these will be the things we can speak of without the barrier of notepaper. Am looking forward with such excitement to seeing you. My very fondest love, Ian.

'Yes, Mum, I think I will go and meet him,' she said, suddenly aware of the thumping of her heart against her ribs.

Chapter Twenty-Eight

What a wonderful summer it was turning out to be. Not at all as she had anticipated, having at first viewed it with dread after last year. Now Annie didn't want it to end.

Alex, as usual, preoccupied by the gem business, didn't visit her for two weeks after installing her in the cool hill station along with all the other wives, who were already planning activities to take them round to September. Then she had been at her most miserable. He had shaken his head when it was time for him to leave after their happy weekend together getting her sorted out in the sweet little residence, her home for the next three months.

'I know you'll miss me, darling. I shall miss you. But I can't just stop work.'

'I know,' she had told him miserably, perched on a coffee table in the elegant sitting room whose wide window gave a panoramic view of distant snowy Himalayan peaks. 'But once you're back in Jalapur you'll get carried away with your business and it'll be weeks before you think of coming up here.'

'I'll be writing to you, darling. You know, you wouldn't be so lonely if we had a family.'

'I've told you, Alex, I don't want to bring up children in this country.'

'And I've told you, Annie ...' Growing annoyed, his tone sharp. 'It'll be a long time before we go back to England.'

But the tone moderated immediately. 'Darling, it isn't as if this is the first hot weather you've spent up here. Once you mingle with everyone else and start taking part in things, you'll enjoy yourself.' He gave a small chuckle. 'Like the rest of them, you'll forget me until I appear on the scene again. You've come to know a lot of the wives and you said yourself a couple of months back, they're not all ogres. I said you'd get used to them, and you have made several friends.'

'It's not that. I just miss you.'

'All the wives miss their husbands. They make the best of it, that's all.' He had kissed her, and she had seen him off, his departing words: 'I'll see you next week. I promise.'

But he didn't visit the next week; a letter said he had been kept by work but that he would be up the following weekend. Then another letter arrived saying he couldn't make it that week either. His mother had written to say his father was ill. Not seriously. He was having a slight heart problem and his doctor had said all he needed was to take things a little easier. His mother asked if he could sort out some extra accountancy work from his end to save his father worrying about it. So another week was to go by for Annie before she would see Alex.

Who she did see was Ansley Burrington. She was sitting on the veranda of the British Club that Sunday with some others, most of the women older than she except for one young person not long arrived from England making Annie feel at last quite an old hand, watching a game of cricket being played when the Burringtons came in to join them.

Mrs Burrington immediately fell into conversation with Mrs Christobel Chauncey whose husband was in the medical profession, surgeon or a consultant of some sort – Annie had never bothered to find out.

Ansley beamed around the small company of ladies, said how-do-you-do to them, and settled his eye upon her. 'Ah, Mrs Willoughby – Anne.' He persisted in calling her Anne rather than Annie. It sounded nice. 'How cool and handsome you are looking. And may I say extremely well? The last time I saw you, you appeared just a tiny bit under the weather.'

'It was the heat,' she excused herself, hoping she hadn't blushed.

'Yes, the heat. Moved up here just in time. It's unnaturally hot down there this summer. Everywhere becoming already scorched and brown. Let us only hope that the monsoon will arrive at its usual time, else we will have a drought on our hands again as we had a few years back. But of course, you wouldn't remember that.

You and your husband came out only a couple of years ago. It is only a couple of years, isn't it?'

Annie nodded. 'Yes, it is.' It was less than that but it didn't matter.

'Time does go by. It seems only yesterday when you arrived all fresh from England with your new husband.'

Tiring of the one-sided conversation, one by one the group turned to each other and then as the cricket finished drifted off in twos and threes to take up some other recreation. Mrs Chauncey and Mrs Burrington got up too. 'We'll be in the card room,' she told him briskly and he indicated that he'd heard, his eyes still appraising Annie, but he didn't speak until his wife was out of hearing.

'I take it your husband didn't come up this weekend?'

She shook her head very slightly. 'No.'

'So what are you doing with yourself today?'

'Well, I'm here at the moment, as you see,' she answered.

'And this evening?'

Annie shrugged and saw him smile understandingly.

'It is so awkward for a young woman alone. Is there no little gathering here on this Sunday night of young women in a similar plight?'

'I'm not sure.' She fiddled with the catch on her small cream handbag. 'I haven't bothered to find out. I'll probably have an early night.'

'As far as I know, my wife and I will be here. There is a bit of a social dance this evening, if you'd care to be our guest. Can't see you all alone in your room while we're having good fun. Would you join us?'

'I'd – like to.' The prospect of people having fun while she went early to bed brought a weight to lie in her chest. 'It's very good of you.'

'Nonsense, my dear. It would be my greatest desire to be your host. We will call for you around eight. We know your address.' He got up quickly as his wife came back out on to the veranda alone. His voice came jovially loud. 'No cards, then?'

'All the tables were taken. I left Mrs Chauncey talking to a boring woman whose sole delight appears to be home affairs and the state of the government at home. I need to go and write some letters. Are you coming, dear?'

She had seemed a little put out, huffy, and perhaps that was why

301

he hadn't immediately mentioned his invitation to her. So Annie was a little taken aback when he presented himself at her door earlier than she had expected, and on his own.

'I'm afraid my wife has developed a headache,' he explained as she invited him in. 'So I thought it only polite to come and apologise that we will not be going to the club. I didn't want you to sit here worrying yourself that we hadn't turned up.'

It seemed only polite to offer him a drink. He had whisky and soda. To be sociable she had a vermouth, Ranji, her servant here, pouring them and then withdrawing with a small salaam.

'Please convey my sympathies to Mrs Burrington,' she said as she sat opposite Ansley on the settee to sip her drink.

It was disappointing not to be going out; she had dressed for the evening in a long sleek gown of midnight blue crêpe de chine that Alex had bought her. It had narrow shoulder straps to which she had clipped a sapphire brooch. Her hair, much longer now that fashion dictated that, curled softly about her ears and the sapphire earrings touched her bare neck with soft brushing sensations when she moved her head. Her face had been made up but she had not yet put on her perfume and somehow that made it seem to her as though she'd been caught still in her dressing gown. A woman should meet her visitors fully ready when called on.

'I'm sorry, I should have been ready,' she apologised inadequately, mainly for something to say. He smiled at her.

'I was early. It should be I apologising. Unforgivable, calling on a lady before she is ready.'

It sounded almost as though he were her date. They fell quiet, sipping their drinks. Annie began to fidget. He immediately interpreted it.

'I should go, I suppose.' But he sat, gazing at his glass, still with a drain of whisky in it. She hadn't answered either way. It was nice him being here, someone taking away the sense of loneliness. When he spoke again his voice was low. 'I don't want to go.'

He looked up, and she, caught out staring at him, lowered her eyes. 'It's nice here,' she heard him say. 'Very quiet. Very . . . relaxing.'

Still she didn't reply, unable to find anything to say. She didn't want him to go either.

'I don't have to leave immediately, Anne, if you don't want me to.'

Now she found her voice, looked across at him. 'Won't your wife be wondering where you are, why you're so long?'

It held a note of inverted invitation if ever there was one. I should not have sounded that way, she reproached herself, but it was too late to amend it. One shouldn't be caught blustering, trying to dig one's way out of a hole. So she fell silent.

The trouble was, there was a racing deep inside her; she felt certain that he'd read something into those words, taken them to heart. And sure enough, he got up slowly from his chair and, placing his glass down on the coffee table between them, came to sit beside her. Before she could find the presence of mind to move away or do anything, he had put his arm about her shoulders and had drawn her gently towards him, bending his face towards hers in order to kiss her softly. The worst of it was that she let him. His lips, tender against hers, the thin moustache harsh against her cheek, raised a whole host of sensations and she found herself wanting that kiss, at the same time panicking a little as to where this might lead.

In her mind came visions of his hand slipping the narrow straps of her dress down over her shoulders, of his lifting her up in his arms and bearing her to the bedroom, laying her down on the soft yielding surface . . . He did none of those things.

He broke away slowly and his arm left her shoulders. 'That was despicable of me. I should apologise.' He paused, then looking into her face said, 'But I don't think I will. I think you need a friend to talk to. I shall be your friend, Anne. Talk to me.'

Suddenly she was lying against him, his arm once more around her shoulders, his hand warm against the skin. She was whispering all the small unhappinesses that surrounded her here.

'Coming out here seemed so promising, a new life, a new husband. But none of it was as I expected. I know this must sound trivial, but it's important to me. Do you understand what I mean?'

His arm tightened about her shoulder. 'It's not at all trivial. But it's not unique, my dear. Many young women, and young men, fresh out from England feel as you do.'

'But not for as long. Alex adjusted well.'

'He has his work.'

'And I'm supposed to have the social life, make friends, but I don't seem to have adjusted at all. It's me, I know. But every-thing's been such a huge disappointment. And it's not just the

Anglo-Indians.' She used the old colonial words for the British in India. 'I've been here a while now and I've met no Indians beyond the servants and they only try to ape us. Everything is so false, everyone pretending they're part of India. But they're not. The truth of it is, I've seen nothing of the real India beyond gazing out of a railway carriage or from a tonga. I see it passing by but I'm not part of it, and I thought I would be.'

'You haven't missed much,' he said.

'I think I have. In a way I feel a little cheated. I don't feel I belong anywhere. I'm so lonely, even with the friends I have made. Alex just doesn't see it. He doesn't understand. I miss him. I miss his company, not just his, but any company. We go to friends and have tea. I meet them in the club. I play bridge and golf and bowls – I'm no good at tennis – but I never seem to have company. I don't know if you understand what I'm trying to say.'

He did understand. The firmness with which he held her told her so. There'd been no need to say as much in words, but he said it nevertheless.

'May I be your company?'

Made desolate by all she had said, Annie nodded. She so desperately wanted someone close and Alex was never there; when he did come, apart from making love in bed, he treated her casually, his mind taken up with other things around him, his work, his enjoyment of the social life. Annie needed a closeness of companionship and she wasn't getting it and it was slowly destroying her. Automatically she let Ansley kiss her again, let him slip the straps of her dress, his hand gentle against her breast, and this time no panic came rushing into her head at all, not even thoughts.

It had gone on from there. And now when Alex did not appear, it was Ansley who visited her, became her lover, and it did not matter any more that she and Alex lay together in their bed only to sleep those odd weekends when he could find time to come up to Simla. He said often how pleased and relieved he was to see her so cheerful and independent and went back to his office in Jalapur with good heart, leaving her to long for the next weekend of his non-appearance when Ansley would take over his role of lover. And so clever was he at visiting her that no one knew about it.

Now the heat down on the plain was beginning to slacken its fierce grip and up here in Simla the nights were getting chillier.

304

Monsoon clouds were gathering to the south and before long it would be time to pack up and leave for another year. A few more weeks yet with Ansley. She didn't want it to end, felt the heaviness of losing him, for she couldn't imagine this carrying on with Alex home every night, nor did she want clandestine meetings and shabby intrigue, yet she felt she was in love with Ansley, who was so kind and gentle and understanding, not at all like Alex. What would she do back in Jalapur without Ansley to visit her? But it had been a wonderful summer.

All summer Danny's thoughts had been on nothing but Lily – all to no good.

All the while he stood at the window at the rear of the dilapidated wooden cockle shed, leaning on the little counter with its basins of cockles and its string of cotton bags and its salt and pepper pots and its vinegar bottle and little saucers to hold a portion of cockles for eating on the spot, he looked among the Sunday summer visitors for her in case she might come by. He lay awake at nights pining for her. He should have married her, found a nice little house for themselves and let Mum and Dad get on their own way. It needn't have been far away so he'd have been within shouting distance if they'd needed him. Then common sense would raise its merciless head: him trying to keep himself and Lily *and* them? He could never have done both. His marriage would have descended into arguments, disruption. But she shouldn't have walked out on him. If that's what she was like . . .

Yet still he pined for her, cursed the fate that had parted them, traced that fate right back to the night of his father's boat going up in flames, and, like reading a book, followed its progress forward to the day Dick Bryant appeared on that mound of cockle shells as Dad was traversing the springy board with his load of cockles on his shoulders. And as with his dad, Danny felt the hatred rise up inside him against Dick Bryant. But for him he would have Lily for his wife and a nice little house and even a family on the way, his and Lily's child.

Word had come to him that she was seeing some other chap, going steady with him. It hurt. All the time he went out with his mates to dances, cinemas, playing football on Sunday mornings if the tide was in and he wasn't working, it hurt. He not so much as glanced at any other girl these days. Because a lot of his mates

305

were going out with girls, one seriously, the rest on casual dates, he was urged to snap out of it, ribbed, even downright derided. 'All this once-bit-twice-shy, lark,' he was teased jovially, but he'd grin and let it slide like water off a duck's back. It wasn't easy to find another girl after Lily. He didn't want a girl anyway. Girls! They weren't worth it. Throw you over soon as look at you!

Sunday marked the end of the schools' summer break. The kids were all going back tomorrow and London families were coming down for a last glimpse of the sea on the cheap. Special cheap trains were scheduled to catch the last end-of-season punters, and he was having his work cut out selling cockles as fast as he could. All the sheds were doing a good trade, but in a month's time there'd be hardly anything.

Connie was helping, home for once instead of visiting with her young man the vicar – Ian something-or-other – as she had been doing every other Sunday. She'd finally got over Ben.

Today Josie too was helping behind the counter, her pretty face and flying fair hair helping to drum up trade from the young lads who came to ogle her. Her Arthur ought to have been here to see it but he was laid up with an attack of summer flu, otherwise no boys would have been allowed to whistle and ogle Josie. Still, she was making a bit of money for herself. She'd had a casual job this summer waitressing in a seafront café in Southend, but that had finished, and nothing else seemed in the offing. Danny hoped she'd get a job soon. With hundreds of girls all after the same ones if they came up, no one stood much of a chance.

'I'll take a sixpenny bag, please.' He hardly glanced at his customer as he measured the pint of cockles into a bag for her. It was only her lively voice that made him look up as she added. 'Thank you very much,' as though it only just hid a merry laugh.

Blue eyes dark as a tropical summer ocean met his, half querying his gaze, then looked away as she took the bag he passed to her, dropping her money into the palm of his hard hand.

'Thank you,' she said again and the lightness of her tone prompted a small leaping sensation in the depth of his chest. But she was already on her way, moving with a swift springy walk.

Danny moved on an impulse that he himself did not quite understand nor pause to interpret.

'Look after this lot,' he called to Connie, leaving her standing as he sprinted after the retreating figure. He caught her up several

306

yards along the path that ran beside other sheds, all surrounded by people.

'I say!' She turned. He came to a stop beside her, swallowed hard to catch his breath. 'You forgot your change.'

How he'd thought of that one he had no idea. They were the first words to spring to his lips, and it was only then that he realised she had given him the right money. Now he had to bluster his way out of that.

'I . . . I thought . . . I thought you'd given me a shilling.'

'No, I gave you sixpence.'

'Oh, did you?'

'Yes.'

She wasn't pretty. Why had he thought she was? In fact she had quite a plain face, square, no make-up, straight mousy hair pulled severely back. What was the matter with him? But no, it was those eyes, large, wide-spaced and an incredible dark blue. They held his gaze.

'It was specially nice of you to run after me like that.' And that voice, as though laughter had been caught up in it. 'But I assure you it was six . . .'

'I've not seen you here before,' he blurted. The pounding against his ribs hadn't ceased. Yet there was nothing about her to inspire. She was thin rather than slim, of average height, her complexion showing the pallor of one whose work was predominantly indoors. Her clothes were far from fashionable or even alluring: severe white blouse, burgundy skirt and – despite the warm day – cardigan, serviceable flat shoes, and now he noticed the rimless spectacles that hung from her neck by a slim black cord, obviously used only for reading.

She was smiling. 'I expect there are quite a few people you don't see more than once.'

'Maybe not,' he said, then hurried on without thinking, 'but I don't always notice other people. I mean . . .' What did he mean? 'I s'pose it was your eyes. I've never seen eyes so dark blue before.'

She dropped her gaze, coyly it seemed. One hand came up to worry the spectacles lying against her chest, a small chest he noticed, which three years ago would have been all the rage but which now merely looked prim.

'If that's a compliment, thank you,' she said quietly.

307

'No, I meant it.'

'Still, thank you.' Her voice was light. She seemed to say 'thank you' an awful lot.

'I really am serious.' He was fumbling for words, wondering at this inane urge to keep her here talking. 'I was just wondering, now you've been here, will you be coming here again?'

She shook her head. 'I'm afraid I seldom have the time to come this far. I teach, you see. A primary school in Prittlewell.'

'Prittlewell's not all that far away.'

'Most days I get off are spent marking school work and preparing work for the next day. It often takes up much of my weekend as well, and when I do get time for myself, I just spend it quietly reading and relaxing.'

It sounded bloody boring. Danny felt himself squirm at her idea of a life. 'Don't you ever take a holiday? Like a summer holiday?'

'Not really.' They had begun to walk on, side by side, dawdling. 'I'm only a primary school teacher. I don't earn enough for holidays. Now and again I go to London, to an art gallery or the museums, and treat myself to lunch somewhere.'

'Where d'you live?' He was beginning to grow sorry for her. Not much of a life. Yet she seemed happy enough.

'I've a furnished room not far from the school.'

He was surprised. 'I thought you might live with your parents.'

'I'm an orphan.' She gave a small smile. 'If you can call someone my age an orphan.'

He had judged her to be around twenty-five, but the way she voiced that afterthought made her sound as if she saw herself more as forty though he guessed she was really trying to mask the impact of being without parents. 'I'm sorry,' he said hurriedly, trying to sound sympathetic.

'No, not at all. I've never had parents. At least, I don't know who my father was. My mother died when I was born. I was put in an orphanage.'

'I'm sorry,' he said again. It sounded as repetitive as her thank-yous.

'It's all right.' She shrugged and smiled. 'I've a good job – something to be grateful for these days. And I have somewhere to live.'

'Do you have a boyfriend?'

'I get little time for meeting anyone, and all my fellow teachers, the male teachers, are married.'

'I was wondering . . . if you like . . .' Danny broke off abruptly, an inexplicable eagerness mingling quite unannounced with his pity for her sort of life. But he felt compelled to finish what he'd begun to say, though now he was stammering. 'Could I . . . if you like . . . I mean . . . do you have any time for yourself to be, well, taken out for an evening?' She had stopped walking, was gazing up at him. 'I mean, would you like me to take you out?' The last came out in a frantic gabble. He almost wanted to add, I'm sorry, again, but he merely stood looking down at her, seeing the sunlight shining in her eyes making the blue much lighter.

Her lips came together as she contemplated him. He saw her lower her eyes. And then she said slowly, 'Yes, I'd like that. Thank you.'

'I don't know your name.' He felt suddenly bolder, self-assured.

'Holly.' She gave another of her light laughs. 'The orphanage – I was born a week before Christmas, you see. Orphanages are like that, all for the appropriate name.'

He laughed with her. 'Mine's Daniel. But my dad's Daniel as well. The father's name is usually passed on in Leighman's families like ours. I'm known as Danny, but my dad's known as Dan. He was a cockler – a cockle picker. But he don't work now. He can't. He had an accident.'

Before he knew it he was relating half his family history. He also realised all at once that he was gabbling too much about his family and she had none. He stopped, reverting to his first enquiry. 'When can I take you out? What about next Saturday, say around three o'clock?' His fisherman's mind had already calculated the tides a week ahead, when the Saturday afternoon would be no good for his work and the cockles all boiled and bagged.

'I could meet you here, on this spot.' He looked around. Talking as they walked, they'd left the cockle sheds well behind, and had already reached the High Street the small square building of Leigh Station looming. His house was at the other end. He didn't want to go further.

'That would be very nice,' she said. Her eyes held an eager look. 'I'll be here, I promise. I must go now. My train for Southend, you see. And then I get a bus. Goodbye then.'

309

He watched her go. She walked quite briskly. His heart felt light as her cheerful goodbye repeated itself over and over in his head. Summer had taken on a brightness he hadn't noticed all season and he found himself already longing for Saturday to arrive.

Saturday found him waiting at the appointed place in a fever of panic. Would she turn up? It had occurred to him sometime during the week how well spoken she had been, how far above him in education, and now he cringed. She had probably thought herself above the likes of him and had decided he wasn't worth turning up for. But he hadn't taken her for that kind of girl, she hadn't been at all offended by his rushing after her; not at all stuck up. But a person couldn't always go on first impressions . . .

'Hello! It is Danny, isn't it?'

He spun round to the voice, such relief taking hold of him that it was hard to resist an impulse to grab her to him. Instead he stood there politely smiling and resisting a second impulse to reply that she had turned up then.

'I'm glad you came,' he managed.

She was smiling too, 'I promised to, Danny. Besides, I wanted to.'

'Yes,' he said inadequately, then lapsed into silence.

He saw her look down at the gloves she wore. They were white. They matched her sandals. She was wearing a blue summer dress with white flowers on it. Her handbag and her small cloche were white as well. She looked trim and efficient, her glasses dangling on their thin cord. He was beginning to feel just slightly intimidated as the hiatus began to extend itself. A little desperately he searched for something to say.

'How was school?' It struck him as a stupid question, but she tilted her head a fraction, a little wearily he thought, leaving him wondering if she really liked her job.

'It went quite well,' she replied. As though by some unspoken mutual decision, they'd begun to wander in the direction of Benfleet. 'The first week is always a bit of an anxiety,' she continued. 'New term, new faces, the new class trying to assess how far they can go in playing their teacher up. One has to walk quite a tightrope for the first few weeks.' She spoke so easily.

Having started, she was proving to be a good conversationalist

310

to the relief of Danny, who'd imagined it becoming something of a strain getting to know each other. He'd even had visions of them saying goodbye at the end of their day, going off in their own direction never to meet again. It wasn't at all like that. By the end of the day, she'd told him all about herself, and he about his life as a cockle picker and almost all of his family history.

When the time came to take her to her bus stop, he felt he had known her all his life. It was almost a foregone conclusion to meet the next Sunday, and again after that. In fact, it was she who suggested popping on a bus to see him on odd evenings after school. 'It's only a hop,' she'd said lightly.

So the month went by. Of course there was a distinct difference in their education, her diction way above his own local one, yet she seemed not to notice, or if she did, it didn't appear to concern her. It was obvious that she derived pleasure telling him things he'd not known before, but he didn't mind. It was funny to watch her eyelids blink rapidly in the joy of imparting these snippets. He in turn entertained her with knowledge of marine shore life, the set of tides, wind directions and weather signs. She'd listen avidly as though storing it all away in that filing cabinet of her teacher's brain.

It did occur to him how much they did converse, hardly stopping for breath, often cutting across each other's words, neither of them being put out by it. It was a common bond; one, it went through his mind, that would hold a marriage together where most couples only ever had anything to say if it had to do with what the kids had said, how naughty they'd been, what he wanted for dinner, or she needed more money for housekeeping.

Danny smiled as he imagined he and Holly married, talking on a much higher level, maybe even while they were engaged in something far more urgent, such as making love . . .

He stopped thinking suddenly to realise that his mind had actually formed the words, marriage and making love. On the strength of that, on their next date he had kissed her as they parted company, the first time he'd ever ventured to do so. She had kissed him back, her arm coming up about his neck to hold his lips against hers that much longer. And Danny knew that the word, marriage, that had crept into his head had real substance after all.

311

Chapter Twenty-Nine

The monsoon had departed, leaving the air fresh and sweet. Everything was green and the streets colourful with people and vehicles and animals, and full of noise.

Inside the humble little shop that sold foodstuffs, open-fronted as were all those along the side street off the busy main thoroughfare, sat four men: the shop owner himself, Mr Syed Hamed; his cousin Mr Mahmud who was a policeman; Ranjit Sandhu, servant to Mrs Alexander Willoughby, and his friend of many years, Panna Chand, servant to Mrs Ansley Burrington, both men well known to Syed Hamed in that they always came to buy food from his shop counter on their day off.

Syed Hamed, eager to show off the new upright chairs he had just bought, had invited the three in to sit on them and as it was nearing time for tiffin had given them a drink of tea, a little food from his counter and some sweetmeats in which he often mixed the tiniest morsel of bhang, the dried leaf of the hemp known as cannabis which had loosened their tongues a little after they had admired the chairs.

They spoke in English as Mr Mahmud was originally from another part of India, his native language being Urdu, and Panna Chand's language was Gujarati. And anyway English was the official language of India.

'It is a good thing the British will be leaving to return to the plains in two weeks. The monsoon will be over. I have had enough of them demanding my attention for this and that as though I am mud under their feet.'

Ranjit Sandhu waggled his head at the speaker. 'It is all very well for you to say that, Mr Mahmud, but the British are my bread and butter.'

Very well for Mr Mahmud. Mr Mahmud, being a policeman, would still have his job when the British began to flock back to the plains in a week or two's time.

'When they leave Simla, then I am having to look for work unless Mrs Willoughby finds me invaluable enough to take back with her to Jalapur. I am looking to that with all my heart.'

'But that, it seems to me, doesn't stop you gossiping about her,' Syed Hamed put in, engaged in smoothing a proud hand over the seat of his new chair.

'Forgive me, Mr Hamed, I assure you, I do not gossip.' Ranjit was hard put to remain this polite, but as a guest in Mr Hamed's shop and also with Mr Hamed being Muslim and he Hindu, it wasn't polite to row with one's host, nor seemly for a Hindu to show himself up in appearing impolite to one of another religion.

'I merely happened to mention, Mr Hamed, that Mrs Willoughby seems to me a far happier woman now that Mr Burrington is keeping her company,' he went on. 'More so that her husband is so seldom with her which makes her very lonely.'

'I do not understand these people,' Syed Hamed said. 'I am afraid I find them most arrogant. Especially the women. I for one breathe a sigh of relief when they leave.' Syed Hamed was a mere shopkeeper and in that lowly station, lowly in the eyes of the British, he had cause to complain. 'They ignore us, they are rude and think themselves far above our own ladies who are the most modest of all women, even consider themselves equal with, if not exalted above, the Begum herself. They put on airs. Yet do they not all behave most atrociously.'

Ranjit was in agreement. 'Yes indeed. Most atrociously,' he echoed, then leaned forward on his chair, his voice dropping confidentially. 'My own mistress, Mrs Alexander Willoughby, speaks most sweetly. As the British say, butter would not melt in her mouth, though I cannot see the reasoning behind that state-ment because butter melts in everyone's mouth, good and bad. She is very pleasant to me, I must say. But, I ask you all, is it right for a woman like that to be having a debatable association with the husband of another woman?'

'Is that what is happening?' queried Panna Chand. 'And who is the wronged lady?'

313

Ranjit waggled his head again, but a cunning look came into his dark eyes. 'It is not for me to say. I do not spread gossip. That is left adequately enough to the wives of the British to do. You, my dear Panna, can think what you will, you being the lady in question's servant.'

There came a long, low, slow gasp. 'Oh me! Oh my! Not Mrs Burrington you say?'

'I am saying nothing, my friend. I have said nothing. As I regretfully appear to some to be a gossip, I am vindicating myself. So now I am saying nothing.'

An awkward silence descended over the group, then Mahmud struck up heartily. 'I offer up a great prayer when the British leave Simla. How quiet it is when they go. As near to heaven as can be.'

The shopkeeper inclined his head in agreement and took a sweetmeat from a dish with its tiniest morsel of bhang, enough to lighten one's head and spirits and make one's words a little more eloquent. 'They should quit India altogether, I say. But mark my words, the day will come when they will – I am sure of it. For too long have we been under the heel of the British. For long we have striven to drive them out. But the day will come.'

Mahmud smiled sagaciously. 'Then you will miss them. And sadly, so shall I, for all my grumbling. Why, as arrogant as they are, they spend good money in our shops. They keep the peace most adequately. Without them I think India would dissolve into chaos. Though I have no love for them, we will all be the poorer once they go. I am thinking India herself will be the poorer when they go altogether.'

'I disagree. India will be the richer. We will be ruling ourselves again. For the first time in three hundred years. No longer under the British heel, we will hold up our head high as a nation in the world.'

The spouting going over their heads, Ranjit and his friend Panna fell to talking together, their voices low. 'Are you sure of what you said?' asked Panna. 'My mistress is a very shrewd woman. In such a small community how is it she cannot know of her husband's infidelity with your mistress?'

'For one thing,' Ranjit said, 'Mr Burrington does not visit my mistress all that often, but only when Mrs Willoughby's husband has not been to see her for two weeks or more. Her husband visits so rarely, being busy with his work in Jalapur. Your master has not visited my mistress above four times in all.'

'Ah . . .' The sound carried wisdom. 'So he is not head over heels in love with her, or he would manage many more times.'

'Indeed.' Ranjit drew deeply on his cigarette, and picked himself a pink sweet. 'It is my opinion he is dallying with her, but she does not see that and looks forward eagerly to his visits far more than she does her own husband's.'

The conversation began to blend as the other two included them once more into theirs and the matter was forgotten in the ensuing debate on their country's state of health, the spasmodic uprisings here and there and the hope that one day India would come into her own again and all the British with their overbearing, puffed-up opinions of themselves go home for ever.

Panna Chand, merely a temporary servant to his mistress while at Simla, had no loyalty towards her and far less opinion of her than Mrs Willoughby's servant had for his employer's wife. It amused him to know that he held in his hands the key to the haughty Mrs Burrington's plunge from arrogance. She had been harsh to him, short with him, had accused him of insolence and if time were not getting short before her departure would have sacked him without reference. So it profited him in a way to see her brought down. And he might still get a reference if he went about it carefully so as not to put himself in any bad light. It took him five days to rehearse what he was going to say.

'Will I put out port for master?' he asked innocuously an hour prior to Mr Burrington's return from his round of golf at the club.

Mrs Burrington cast him an exasperated look as if regarding a backward child. 'Panny . . .' She insisted on calling him that, preferring something more English-sounding than Panna. He hated it. 'After all this time, you know the port is only put out for guests. Master prefers a brandy when he comes home. He does not drink port. And I prefer vermouth. Have you got that?'

'Yes, mistress. It is that I was told by Mrs Willoughby's servant that he has port there.'

She was staring at him, her brittle blue eyes hard. Panna Chand felt his insides tremble. Had he gone too far? He fought with himself to look innocent.

'*Who* was it told you that?' she was asking.

315

'Mrs Willoughby's servant, mistress. When Mr Burrington is there.'

'*When* is Mr Burrington ever there?'

'Mrs Willoughby's servant said to me, often.'

'*How* often?'

'I do not know. But many times . . . he has said.'

'What time is he there?'

'In the evenings. I do not know. I am only told this. I am told he is going as a friend when Mrs Willoughby's husband cannot come to see her. I am told it is to keep her company.'

Mrs Burrington's face had paled. Her tone had dropped. 'How long does he stay?'

Panna found himself beginning to falter, stammer. He was getting himself into deep water and he was frightened.

'I asked you a question, Panny. How – long – does – he – stay?'

'I have not been told that.' But this would defeat the object. 'Mrs Willoughby's servant did mention that it was many hours.'

He could see by the working of Mrs Burrington's face that she was doing calculations as to when her husband came home at odd times, the lateness of those times, and he debated whether he should dare further his information or leave cats to find their own way home. Then he made his mistake.

'Mrs Willoughby's servant says he is very kind to her, kissing away her tears when Mr Willoughby does not come . . .'

'Stop! How dare you! How dare you people discuss our affairs. Who do you think you are? Get out of my sight! You're dismissed. Do you understand? Dismissed!'

Carefully Panna put the bottle of port he'd been holding down on to the little drinks trolley and made a brief, begrudging salaam. It was obvious he had gone too far and would get no reference to give his next employer if ever he found one. Dismay consumed him but there was little he could do. It was back to his family who farmed locally, working the soil, a poor living, until luck came his way again. He prayed to the Divine Will to give him luck.

'And take that with you!'

Quickly Panna snatched up the offending port, salaamed again and withdrew.

'God, Annie – you've been an utter damned fool. What made you think you could get away with it?'

She watched Alex pace the floor in their Jalapur residence as she packed her belongings. They had returned here in virtual silence. What she had done had become common knowledge among all the British at Simla, and it had followed her all the way back to Jalapur. And even here in Jalapur no one was receiving her.

'You've made me look an utter fool too.'

'Is that all that matters to you, Alex?' She found her voice, but it came in a tremulous whisper, a pathetic attempt at rebellion. 'That I've made you look a fool?'

Of course it wasn't all that mattered to him. He had been stunned, then disbelieving, then outraged and wounded, the painful realisation sinking in slowly that with another man she had made a mockery of their marriage. Yet still his disbelief lingered and it was this disbelief that hurt her most.

'Why?' he had queried, like a child not knowing for what it was being scolded. 'When did you stop loving me?'

Annie had been in tears, blubbering that she didn't know what had possessed her but that she had been so lonely, had looked on Ansley Burrington as no more than a source of companionship, then comfort, and that he'd taken advantage of her loneliness, and she, idiot that she was had let him seduce her. She hadn't realised what she had been doing, how she would hurt Alex, and if only Alex had visited her more often none of it would have happened. It all sounded so weak and unconvincing. Alex had been withdrawn, civilised, had said that their marriage was over, that he couldn't look her in the face any more. Here, in Jalapur, he remained so, even when she, as she had a moment ago, came again to him to beg his understanding, his forgiveness, saying that she still loved him, asking if they couldn't try again. But she had hurt him too much for that. She knew now, their marriage was wrecked.

How her silly affair with Ansley had come to his wife's ears was still hazy. But of course she knew how it had spread – servants' gossip. Mrs Burrington would have wanted it kept quiet. But out of hand she had dismissed the servant carrying the tale and most likely out of spite he had let the story travel on until the whole station knew about it. Of course, affairs abounded in these often lonely circumstances, people looking for a little diversion in a tight and unnatural community. Gossip helped to make their

317

world go round more excitedly. A little tittle-tattle in the club could sometimes be brushed under the carpet before too much harm was done. But she hadn't been liked from the beginning. They had pounced on her, ostracised her, or she had ostracised herself keeping away from them all, Annie wasn't sure which. But her life these past two weeks had been spent in isolation and misery with Alex having found out, or having been told. Annie suspected the latter.

He was being very civilised about it, but she knew that beneath the stiff exterior he was devastated, terribly hurt. She heard it in his voice when he had whispered, 'I really thought you loved me, Annie.'

'I do love you,' she had implored in a torrent of wailing. 'It was all a ghastly, silly mistake, I was so lonely, he took advantage of me. If only you'd been with me more.'

Now she was packing to go home; the home she had yearned for so long to return to for a visit was to be her final destination. Alex had bought her a single ticket. He would stay here. There was to be no reconciliation. She hated seeing the look on his face, the hidden tears giving him a stricken, grey look. And there was nothing she could do about it.

Closing the lid of her last trunk, Annie straightened up, looked beseechingly across at him, but he turned his face away, and she looked instead out of the open door to the veranda, the garden beyond fresh and vivid after the monsoon. This would be the last time she'd see it, this scramble of shrubbery, trees, vines, brilliant tropical flowers, a harsh blue sky reflected in the tank. So many times she'd yearned to look out upon the subdued tones of a soft English scene, now oddly she felt sad that she'd never see this one again.

A servant came in to say that the car was here to take them to the railway station. Alex was going with her. There he would see her settled into her compartment and go outside to stand and watch the train leave. Would he kiss her before he left? Would he wave her goodbye? Or would he walk away without a backward glance?

The drive to the station was made in silence. Only once did he speak. 'Have you got enough money?'

'Yes, adequate,' she replied and occupied herself in gazing at the passing scene, unbelievably pink buildings, open-fronted

318

shops, the thronging thoroughfares, the hordes of bicycles, tongas and colourfully painted motor trucks; the camel-drawn carts, the odd elephant pulling some heavier cart, goats, dogs, and of course the sacred cows that wandered at will, fed by anyone as a matter of course, thin only because, like India's human population, the overwhelming heat itself discouraged any tendency towards sleekness.

She concentrated her mind on the noise about her, the constant tinkle of bicycle bells, the squeak of cart wheels and rumble of the lorries, the babble of people, the cries of vendors and the occasional thin sound of a snake charmer's flute, the cobra weaving in a drugged figure-of-eight to the charmer's own movements.

Moving slowly through the traffic, Annie even welcomed the several faces that peered in at the window, the hands extended for alms, the bric-à-brac waved in her face in hopeful exchange for a few rupees. She welcomed anything so as not to have to think of what was happening to her. The only time Alex spoke was to order the vendors and beggars away and to tell the driver to try and move faster – impossible in this day-time traffic.

At the station it was quieter. The train stood gently puffing; she boarded, had Alex get her baggage loaded on, watched him tip the porter who salaamed deeply and many times at the generous amount, the money gripped between his cupped palms.

'Are you all right?' Alex said as he came back. She nodded. The train smelled of warm oil, the carriage faintly of sweat and more pungently of perfume meant to erase any other smells. It made her feel sick. Her last smell of India. Yet she had no longing now for the fresh, newly-cut-grass smell of England, its sweet chill air and the salt tang of Leigh. All she wanted to do was cling to these powerful odours to which she had become acclimatised. It tore at her with hands that did not want to let her go and she in turn mentally held those invisible hands.

'I don't want to leave you,' she heard herself say to him. Her hands touched and held his sleeve momentarily but he had already turned away, whether to hide his own misery or his rejection of her, she didn't know.

She had said this so many times these past two weeks, begging forgiveness, pleading to stay with him, promising to make amends. It was all to no avail. And this was the last plea she gave or was allowed to give as he stepped out of the carriage and off the train. He stood silent as the engine gave a small jerk, then another stronger one, began to move, sounded its whistle. He stood with his eyes lowered and she willed him to lift them.

Briefly he looked up as the train gathered speed 'Take care of yourself.'

That was all. She wanted to cry out, 'I love you, Alex.' But it was too late and they were too civilised. She let the train carry her away knowing it was the last she would ever see of him. There would be a divorce. He was staying on in India, putting his life together. Well, his parents had had their wish. The marriage hadn't lasted. They had their son back. In time he would come home to England, but not to her.

Annie sat back on the hard wooden bench that would be her seat, or another like it, all the way to Bombay, to the ship that would take her home.

She had forgotten how cold England could be. October was only just beginning to produce a chill in the air, but Annie, newly arrived, shivered desperately as she moved down the gangway on to English soil.

It had been strange sailing back home. Leaving Bombay in the damp debilitating heat, they had sailed up from the Indian Ocean to the still hot but by then arid climate. The ship had called in at Aden, and moved on into the Red Sea, still hot and dry, passing Alexandria and Cyprus. Then an imperceptible change had set in as they neared Marseilles though the weather remained warm. Even the passengers seemed to change too – a brisker attitude perhaps, more alert. Reaching Gibraltar the weather had taken a dramatic turn. Within a day, fresh progressed to cold as the ship sailed northward, the Bay of Biscay heaving, making her stomach heave with it, though not as much as it had going out. Perhaps she'd been too dull of spirit to care.

Now in the quiet chill of an English October, Annie stepped down the gangway to await the unloading of her several trunks, and heard an eager shout from the waiting crowd: 'Annie! Annie, over here!'

The next thing she knew she was being held in the welcoming arms of her brother. The young lady with him stood back, smiling serenely, watching them reunite. It was the young lady's presence that kept Annie tears at bay, but she would have loved to weep in Danny's arms, and almost resented the woman's intrusion.

'Welcome home, Annie. How was the journey? We got your letter saying you was coming home. It said you'd tell us about things when you got here.' Tucking her arm through his, holding it protectively, Danny gabbled on, conducting her through the main barriers, the young woman following behind. 'The porters are bringing up your stuff. Mum couldn't come – she had Dad to keep an eye on.' Pausing, he turned to hold out a hand to the woman with him. 'Annie, this is my . . . my fiancée. Yes you are, Holly. My fiancée. Annie, this is Holly. I wrote to you about her. We met six weeks ago. It seems longer, but it was at the beginning of September.'

Now he put an arm about the woman and drew her close. 'I've asked her to marry me and she's said yes, bless her. She's all the things I never expected any woman to be. Loving and kind, honest and dependable and . . .'

'Stop it,' the girl scolded affably, her pale cheeks colouring, and he laughed.

'She's willing to come and live with us all once we're married. Holly's a school teacher. She's got no family of her own and she lives in a furnished room at the moment in Prittlewell. We met just by accident and I instantly fell head over heels for her.'

Not a word about how she, Annie, was. But then, she hadn't told anyone the reason why she was home. Holly was still protesting at the praise of her attributes, Danny laughing, planting a kiss on the flaming cheeks.

The trunks arrived on a trolley, were trundled to a waiting taxi and loaded on to it as the three of them got into the passenger seats.

'This isn't taking us all the way home, is it?' Annie asked.

She was beginning to feel better, the cosiness of home beginning already to surround her, at least until she let her thoughts wander to Alex and her broken marriage again. Then the lump she had come to recognise as grief would lie within her breast squeezing the tears that hovered there up into her throat and to her eyes. But she must not cry now she was home.

'No expense spared,' Danny joked, and continued chattering all the way from Tilbury to Leigh. It was only as they got within a mile of home that Annie cut harshly through the light-heartedness.

'Danny. There's something I must tell you. I'm going to tell the whole family, but I need to tell you first, before we get home. I think I might need your support and you might understand better than the others.'

Danny, sobered, took his arm from around Holly's shoulders. He sat quiet and so did she as Annie told the whole story behind her homecoming. She found herself not resenting the girl's presence now, understanding exuding from her without her ever needing to say a word.

'So you see,' she finished glumly. 'I can't blame Alex. I'm to blame. I was lonely, out of my depth and Ansley Burrington was a straw to clutch at. He was so kind, but now I know he was only using me for his own pleasure. But I'm to blame for the break up of my marriage. I wrote and said Alex was sending me home for a visit, but this is for good. He doesn't ever want to see me again. I don't know how I'm going to tell everyone. I feel so ashamed. And they're going to be so angry and hurt. I don't know how I'm going to face them, especially Dad. You know how he is.'

'You leave Dad to me,' Danny said grimly. 'But you're going to have to tell Mum yourself. I suggest telling her on her own. Don't make a public thing of it. Just her on her own. Let everything else sort itself out slowly.'

Danny was as good as his word. Annie sat with her mother and Holly, now privy to all of Annie's guilty secrets, listening to her father's roars from the downstairs bedroom they had made for him; Danny's voice sounded strong and commandingly pacifying.

Mum, who'd had a little cry over Annie's news, now sat quietly. Annie, waiting, felt Holly touch her hand and hold it firmly, as if she had known her all her life. For the first time Annie felt she had found a real friend.

In the taxi, Danny had extolled Holly's virtues as the girl blushed, openly announcing that she was all the things his former girlfriend wasn't. He explained proudly how Holly and Mum had got on famously from the start; how she had even gained his father's high opinion. In the taxi, full of assurance about his own future, Danny had even spoken of how he was in a frame of mind to more or less forgive the Bryants for Dad's accident, though not altogether, because that family would always spell trouble.

He'd told her that Pam was now living with the Bryants but

322

occasionally came to see Mum, because Mum wasn't inclined to set foot in the Bryant household even to see her own daughter. Dad still remained totally against her setting foot in his home, still refused to speak to her, but Danny had told Mum to ignore him, that he would sort him out, as he was sorting out this present business. It seemed to Annie, listening to his voice in the other room, that he'd taken complete charge of this family since their father's accident and what he said, went. And when Danny finally came back to them he was smiling. 'I've sorted him out,' he stated, as if it was no more than expected.

Chapter Thirty

Christmas would arrive in a few weeks' time and not a word had come from Alex.

'I'm not going to say put it all behind you,' Connie told her and Connie should know. It had taken her eighteen months to put her loss of Ben behind her and Annie suspected her sister still pined after his memory even though she now had her vicar with talk of their getting engaged. Connie a vicar's wife – it sounded strange.

'Losing someone you love is what you could call a two-year disease,' Connie said. 'You can do your utmost to put it behind you but it's no good.'

Maybe it was of some help to have someone who understood. Mum understood too. She'd lost Tony all those years ago and sometimes she still had a faraway, sad look in her eyes when she thought she was alone. And there was Danny, losing his girl-friend. Lily, that was her name. That must have hurt him very much. All three knew what it was like to lose someone, or be alone again. Yet none of it made her own heartache less. It seemed to break afresh the moment she woke up to a new day, seeming to get worse with time rather than better.

It was all she could do not to weep and make a nuisance of herself; all she could do to try not to harp on it and get on everyone's nerves, and at least look interested in what went on around her, just as she tried to look interested and pleased when Josie came rushing home on the first Monday afternoon in December to say she had got a job as an assistant receptionist. At the Grand Hotel in Southend of all places.

'It's supposed to be over the Christmas period,' Josie gushed as

324

she danced around the kitchen in joy. 'But if I prove suitable they'll keep me on afterwards.'

The kitchen smelled of spice. The table was covered with bits of bread from making breadcrumbs, with flour, dried fruit, suet and all the other ingredients for Christmas pudding. Her mother, reigning supreme over it all, smiled at her daughter. 'If you prove suitable.'

'I know I will,' Josie exclaimed. 'I was always a good receptionist at the Cliffs Hotel, and I am presentable. I know one thing, good looks stand you in good stead when it comes to getting a job. Oh, Mum, I'm so thrilled.'

Ceasing to skip around the small kitchen, she flung herself at her mother and hugged her, ignoring the danger to her best coat from the large sticky wooden spoon with which Mum was blending the Christmas pudding mixture together. 'There were crowds of girls there all hoping for the job. But I got it! I'll have money for Christmas!'

Her mother, knowing where she had gone that morning and praying all day that she might get the job but holding out little hope for it, said she knew all along she would get it.

Annie, the only one at home besides Mum and Dad, and busy stoning raisins, gave her sister a bleak smile and tried not to let her voice break.

'Congratulations, Josie.'

Josie sobered sufficiently to look at her and murmur a thank you, for a few seconds seeing the despondency that lurked in her sister's eyes. But soberness didn't last beyond those few seconds.

Her respect for her sister's broken marriage forgotten, Josie swept on. 'Not only that, but you remember that letter I got from Arthur this morning, Mum? Well, I couldn't read it straight away, because I was in a hurry to get to Southend for the interviews before too many applicants arrived, and I was too nervous to read it on the way there and while I was waiting. But I read it on the way home. And guess what? Arthur's got himself a job too.'

'He's already got a job – in the docks,' her mother said, mystified. 'If you can call it a job – more out of them than in, all the good jobs according to him going to men who know-what's-about, as he puts it.'

Arthur when he came to the house was always on about the docks, and they had all become familiar with the jargon he used: words like gangers, and phrases like on the stones, shaping-up, call-on, and so on.

325

'He's always been a floater,' Josie said, another of his words for men operating alone. She took a deep breath, preparing herself for what would be a long explanation 'He wouldn't get in with other gangers after his dad died – felt like he was taking advantage of his dad's name – Arthur's funny like that, wants to do things his own way, and his dad getting killed in the docks upset him a lot – but I told him, he ought to look to the main chance or he'd never get anywhere, more so now times are hard. Well, Arthur took my advice at last, Mum, and a ganger who knew his dad offered to take him into his gang when some chap or other left, and now he's realised what he's been missing, and this chap's apparently a real whiz and puts himself about so his gang get more call-ons than a lot do, and now Arthur won't be left waiting on the stones on his own any more.'

She finished practically breathless after this enthusiastic surge of information, taking another deep breath to end, 'So with us both in work, we'll be able to get engaged properly, with a ring an' all, and next year we can get married, and I'll be twenty-one and just the right age, won't I?'

Her mother, smiling gently, went on mixing the initial ingredients for the Christmas pudding. The rest of the ingredients waited, already prepared. Only the raisins were still to be stoned: Annie was working far too slowly with them.

'Is that what was in your Arthur's letter?' Peggy asked calmly.

Josie made a face. 'Well, not exactly, Mum, but we've talked about it a lot, so it goes without saying, once we get some money around us, we can get married, and we'll be saving hard, and that's what we talk about all the time, and . . .'

'Yes, dear,' her mother sighed. 'But I've got to get on with this pudding and put it aside to rest or it'll never get boiled.'

'Are we all getting a stir and a wish?' Josie asked, coming to a full stop mid-sentence.

'I expect so. We usually do. And I'll put in the threepenny bits too.'

Annie, still busy stoning raisins, knew what her wish would be but held no hope of it ever coming true. Her marriage was over, wrecked.

'I'm going to wish for me and Arthur to get enough money to get married on next year,' Josie cried. 'And for dad to walk again as well.'

'You only get one wish,' her mother said, her face down as she mixed.

'You can do it, Dad.' Tense and anxious, Danny watched his father struggle to get the crutches under his arms. He dared not help him. Danny made himself appear calm, confident of his father's eventual triumph. Not in a million years would he betray the fear that lay inside him. If Dad were to fall . . .

'You're all right. Just take it steady.'

For months Dad had been going on about getting back on his feet. But getting back on his feet would not be walking in the sense that others would recognise – his feet would never feel the ground beneath them, his dead legs would never move independently of each other. His whole weight leaning on the broad heavy crutches, he would only ever be able to propel his body forward on the crutches and swing his iron-callipered legs forward together until his weight settled on top of them and brought him upright a foot or two further towards whatever destination he was aiming for. But if it worked he'd be mobile, no longer a burden to others.

Only Danny and Holly had been allowed to see him struggle to stand on those lifeless legs, more like tree trunks supporting a too-heavy branch, his wife and the rest of his family were permitted nowhere near. Danny because he was his son, another man with whom he need not feel a lesser man; Holly because there was something about her that instilled confidence, a certain neutrality. Danny felt proud that Dad had taken her to his bosom. He couldn't have wished for a better person than Holly to be his future wife, and Dad approving of her as he did had made it all the better.

'Come on, Dad. You can do it.'

Peggy stared at her daughter, the light from the room piercing the December evening to pick out the man standing immediately behind her with Beth in his arms.

'Pam.' The shock seeing her husband standing there bold as brass made Peggy's head reel, and she could find no other words to convey that while Pam was welcome, her husband was not.

Pam was smiling as if nothing untoward was occurring. She'd been here several times since moving in with the Bryants, she and little Beth, but always on her own.

'We've come to wish you happy Christmas, Mum.'

327

'Christmas's still three weeks away. Bit early ain't you?' She couldn't help the sharpness of her tone.

'Well, we'll be spending it with George's people, Mum. Dad wouldn't want us here, so we thought we'd come ... Can we come inside for a bit? It's cold out here and Beth's already got a bit of a sniffle.'

She made to step forward but Peggy barred her way. 'No! No, you can't, Pam.' Almost immediately she felt remorse for her abruptness, tried to modify it, but it was hard with George standing there. Still, he had to understand she couldn't welcome him here. Pam, her own daughter, was one thing. George was another entirely. Old wounds did not heal as many might think. Natural instinct made him obnoxious in her eyes, for all she knew he was guilty only of being a son of the Bryants. Nevertheless, she moderated her tone, tried to sound civil as she spoke to him directly. 'I'm sorry, I just can't ask you in. I don't want to be the cause of disrupting our family. Bad enough getting Pam's father to accept her back, but not you. I'm sorry.'

The pair looked at each other, then came to an unspoken decision, and George handed the baby over to his wife. 'You go in, love. I'll stay here. I don't suppose you'll be long.' It sounded pointed. She saw Pam wince.

'I can't leave you out here in this cold wind. You'll catch your death.'

He gave a small chuckle, one that unreasonably grated on Peggy ears. The nerve of him coming here expecting to be asked in.

'I'm out in all weathers, love,' he said evenly as if the wife of his father's adversary wasn't there. 'A bit of cold wind won't hurt me.'

'Are you coming in or not, Pam?' There was no Christmas spirit in her voice, not even premature Christmas spirit.

Without a word Pam followed her in, Peggy starting to close the door on the intruding husband, saying as she did so, 'Your dad's asleep. I don't want him woken up.'

She had the door only half closed when Danny came into the room. He had full view of the man at the street door.

'What's he doing here?'

'Shh! You'll wake your dad.' But Danny had already brushed past her. Chin jutting belligerently, his eyes glaring at the other man, he reached him before Peggy could stop him.

328

'Bugger off, you!'

George stood his ground. 'I'm with my wife to keep her company.'

Danny narrowed his eyes. 'I tell you this. If you wasn't my sister's husband I'd send you on with a thick ear, standin' here as if you own the bloody place. We tolerate you, at a distance, because you're Pam's husband. You've not done us any harm. It's your family what has. But that don't give you no cause to come here to our doorstep as if you own the bloody place.'

George appeared ready to shape up to him, his body tensing. A larger man than his father had ever been, and Danny not as big as *his* father, they were more or less well matched.

'You'd rather me let me wife and kid out alone on a night like this then?' George growled.

'I'd better go, Mum,' Pam said hurriedly. 'We only came because of the season of good will.'

'It's a bit too early for that,' Peggy said again, but this time more gently. She put a hand on Pam's arm. 'I don't mean to be rotten, dear, but look, it's difficult for us to take to your husband. Give it time.'

The soft words brought the two men into line, the wind going out of their sails. 'He oughtn't to be round here,' Danny said.

'Did you want me to leave me wife and child . . .'

'Yes, like you said,' Danny cut in roughly, dismissing him. 'Didn't mean to interfere, Mum.'

She smiled at him, then at Pam, leaning forward to plant a kiss on her granddaughter's wind-chilled forehead, taking in the special perfume the child's hair possessed. 'Merry Christmas, love. But pop in a few days before Christmas, Pam. During the day.' It was a pointed indication that she did not expect George to be with her. 'And bring Beth to see me. I ain't even got her little Christmas present wrapped up yet. It's a doll, not much, but I've knitted the clothes for it and it do look pretty.'

'Thanks Mum.' Pam leaned forward and laid a kiss on Peggy's cheek. There was a stirring from the downstairs rear bedroom, Dan coughing. Pam moved back. 'I'd better go. See you nearer Christmas, Mum.'

She passed Danny with a glare towards him. 'You an' George,' she hissed, her eyes narrowing. 'You've got nothing to quarrel about. It's not our argument. But you want to keep it going, don't you?'

329

To which Danny said nothing as she went out into the early darkness of the cold winter evening.

The weekend before Christmas, Connie went up to Market Harborough. Ian was buying her engagement ring. Before she went, she paid a visit to East London Cemetery and stood awhile beside Ben's grave.

In the cold wind, the black bare branches of trees shuddering before it, everything else had a grey look about it, the scudding clouds, the monotonous tarmac paths, the lines of headstones poking though a colourless earth, the lacklustre lawns. Even the vases of flowers to the memory of loved ones departed displayed hardly any colour to speak of, their blossoms bleached and drooping.

She hadn't brought flowers. Somehow it seemed wrong after all this time. But she'd brought a strip of red ribbon on some nameless whim. This she wound around the pot of stiff rain-splattered white chrysanthemums, no doubt brought here last weekend by his parents, their petals already falling in the chill wind. Better to have left them living and bright on their roots until nature saw fit to let them die. For no apparent reason, Connie felt tears sting her eyes and brushed them quickly away. Silly. The time for weeping was over. Why had she brought this piece of red ribbon? Symbol of love? That too had been silly.

There came an urge to speak the words: 'I did love you, Ben. I'll never forget you.' But it would have been sentimental and melodramatic. To wish for it all back would have been hypocrisy because what was gone was gone. Coming here had been a mistake. Her love for him had been buried with him and now she was only sad, not for herself, not for the past, merely that a young life had ended. But that young life was no longer part of her.

In turning away it went through her mind, to go and see his parents, but that too was over. It would be unfair, to her and to them, appearing on their doorstep. She'd write a letter instead, telling them about herself. Then she thought not. She'd always remember him with fondness, maybe with a tear, but best the past be left to itself. She wouldn't come again to this grave.

Turning one last time halfway along the tarmac path, she saw that the piece of red ribbon shone through all the greyness, the one bit of brightness, it seemed, in all this place of the dead. Then the wind caught her hat so that she had to lift a hand to stop it blowing

330

from her head and she hurried away, in her mind's eye still seeing that scrap of bright red fluttering madly.

It would come loose in the wind and blow away shortly, get caught up in a tree. Her original gesture would be wasted. But by then she'd be on her way. Her new life lay with Ian. So why was a warm tear still on her cheek?

The weekend gales had died. The weather had warmed somewhat. The following weekend had brought a fine drizzle of rain. Now with an overcast sky and a mild south westerly breeze, one or two more needy shrimpers had been tempted out to see what could be caught before the year's end. Danny too thought it worth his while.

London's Billingsgate fish market would take anything. Christmas loomed a week away and people still looked for whatever would help make an East End Christmas tea table jolly on the cheap. Shrimps and winkles, jellied eels, whelks and cockles could be had from stalls outside all the pubs. Billingsgate did a pretty decent trade despite the unemployment that abounded.

Danny knew George Bryant and his father had gone out. He'd seen their boat leave. Idiotically he felt instantly prompted to try his luck, as if the idea of the Bryants making a bit of cash while the Bowmakers sat around on their arses was something not to be countenanced.

Foley, a shrimper Danny was acquainted with, was preparing his boat in readiness to set off too. Danny watched him awhile, then said, 'Going out, then?'

The man nodded without looking up from what he was doing. 'Might as well. Heard shrimp are around not far off – this warm spell brings 'em in closer to shore.'

'Chance of dropping me off on Mush End?' Mush End, derived from Marsh End, officially known as Chapman Sands, lay near the entrance to Leigh Ray just off the end of Canvey Island. Not too far and a good ground for cockles.

'On your own?' The man still hadn't looked up, but his words were a small warning. 'We'll be out some while, I reckon, and you could get fog come up later out on this weather.'

'Might get my uncles to come along,' Danny said chattily, but the man, intent on his preparations, had still not paused to look at him.

331

'We'll be ready for off in half hour.'

'Right!' Danny headed off to find his uncles.

'What about it?' he coaxed his Uncle Pete after explaining the offer. It meant not having to get their own bawley ready. Merely be dropped off on Chapman Sands with their baskets, lavanets and rakes, spending the time raking cockles until Foley's shrimp barley came back to pick them up as the tide turned.

Pete shook his head, taking stock of the debatable weather signs. 'Ain't worth it, lad. Not really. If fog comes up we could be in trouble there.'

His Uncle Reg had already settled himself in for an easy weekend at home. 'Not much point sloshing about out there for a few cockles this time o' the year,' he'd said. 'I need a bit of a rest sometime. Help your aunt get things ready for Christmas.'

Danny didn't argue. All very well for him, but he needed the money if Uncle Reg didn't. Every little bit helped towards his and Holly's wedding, he hoped next year, but not if he didn't take the chance to make whatever bit of cash he could.

They'd known each other for such a short while but all he wanted, more than anything in the world, was for Holly to be his wife. The days they were apart, he on the boat or in the sheds and she teaching, felt endless.

Danny returned to his other uncle's house. Something told him that he'd be foolish to be out there on Chapman Sands all on his own. Safer with two people. Pleading in his tone, he told Pete of his need to make what money he could, spoke of his wedding, of the cost, all the time seeing the precious half hour to Foley's departure ticking away. To his delight, Pete finally relented.

'All right. But we wrap up warm despite it bein' on the mild side, take a flask and a bite to eat. Could be a long wait for ole man Foley to pick us up again, comin' back in with the tide.'

'Well, he do know he's got to pick us up so he won't leave it late,' Danny said, cheered up no end at seeing a bit more added to the coffer.

Ten minutes later they were clambering on board the *Juniper*, old Foley muttering he'd thought they'd changed their mind, and that with the tide going out fast he had to be making headway. Soon they were standing beside their gear on the newly exposed sand and mud under a weak sun watching the boat chugging off into the distance, the putt-putt-putt of its engines dying away to leave silence hovering over the mud flats except for the gurgling of the mud itself and the far-off squeal of a gull.

In the silence the pair got to work, raking a bounty of cockles into the lavanets, tipping them in turn into the wicker baskets.

'Bloody hell!' Danny heard his uncle swear.

He straightened up, rake in hand. 'What?'

'Didn't bring any stakes.' Stakes were used to mark out a guide for direction should fog shut in as it could do in the estuary, with alarming suddenness.

Danny cocked an eye at the hazy sun, discarded a vague twinge of anxiety and laughed. 'Don't matter. We're all right. No sign of any fog.' His own words helped ease the brief concern he had felt and he bent again to raking.

At midday, the weak low winter sun already dipping to the horizon, they rested for a few moments, laying down their rakes in the traditional way, points downward and trodden into the sand to prevent accidents by being stepped on. Anxious to get going again, they devoured their couple of thick cheese sandwiches, washed down with stewed tea. Then, rescuing their rakes, they carried on.

They would spend this evening boiling the cockles ready for a lorry to take the cooked meat to Billingsgate in the morning. It would mean Danny not seeing Holly this evening. He was missing her already. But Christmas would compensate for all that. She would be spending Christmas with his family. With no home of her own but a furnished room, his home was already becoming hers, his family hers. Weekends she was more with them than in that room which for all its pokiness she had done up prettily, made to look so bright. She'd do the same to his home. In fact by just being there she brightened it up. Mum loved her already. Dad too had taken to her. And she got on well with everyone she met, with Connie and even Josie whose head was forever in the clouds and as woolly.

Without glancing up, Pete with the instinct of the old cockler alert to the subtle change in the air that would escape other men observed quietly, 'Tide's on the turn.' Today it would come in fast having been held back by a stiffening southwest breeze, but there was nothing to be alarmed about.

'Plenty of time,' Danny muttered. The cockles were plentiful, the baskets were filling; thoughts of the profit they'd bring in

333

made him headstrong. He continued raking. 'We'll see old Foley back any time now.'

To confirm it, he straightened up and broadened his gaze out to the horizon, hitherto much too preoccupied to look. Now what he saw brought a small crawling sensation of alarm along his backbone. He could not see the horizon. What was more, the sky had grown yellow, obscuring what little sunshine there had been. The Kent side of the estuary was no longer visible and a bank of mist was creeping in rolling tendrils to blot out the whole of the nearer shore. Even Canvey, low-lying, had disappeared.

The mud had begun to stir as if coming alive. Tiny rivulets of water were not so much flowing through the shallow grooves and depressions as filling them quietly. A while remained before the tide came in properly, but this with the now rapidly descending fog was its first sign. Danny recalled his earlier smirk at his uncle having worried about a few sticks. Put in at intervals they assured that if fog rolled in, the men wouldn't lose touch with each other as they gathered the last of their harvest into their separate baskets. But where was Foley? No chance seeing his boat from a distance now. In a swiftly thickening fog, would he spot them? Anxiety, if not yet fear, was becoming real. Raking for cockles forgotten, Danny stared about him. This was becoming no joke.

With the fog had come a chill and he was glad of his heavy doubleknit sweater and the equally heavy oilskin coat, which he had laid across his basket as he had warmed up, but now quickly put back on.

Turning round, he realised he could no longer see his uncle. He could not be far away. 'I'm over here,' he called and heard the man's answering call. 'Here!' But the now seemingly solid fog, having come up so fast, muffled the voice and he wasn't certain from which direction it had come.

'Where are you?'

'Here. Where are you?'

'Here.'

Stupid. Who could tell where 'here' was? 'Just stay where you are,' came the disembodied voice which no longer sounded like his uncle's. 'Don't go wandering about and gettin' y'self lost now.'

In the chill clinging shrouds, Danny did as he was told. His basket when he had last tipped his net of cockles into it had been some three or four yards away, to his left, or was it to his right?

334

Had he turned without realising it? 'Pete – you still there?' he called again.

'Stay where you are,' The reply sharpened his idea of making towards it.

'Keep shouting,' he cried. 'I'll find you.'

'No, you'll miss me. You could miss me by yards.'

He well knew what that could mean. Lost with an incoming tide. Even so, he couldn't just stand here. He must have been standing still for quite a while because the water had reached him, moving around the soles of his thigh boots, softening the mud enough to cause his feet to sink into it if he dare move a few inches off. Normally there was nothing hazardous. One knew where the firm parts were and where the soft parts. It was no problem. Now it was. But he had to get nearer that hailing voice. He began to move.

Seconds later he seemed to have gone downhill sharply, water around his knees. He let out an exclamation, heard his uncle call, 'What's up?'

'Nothing,' he called back, his own voice a lonely sound, surrounded by nothing but whiteness. 'Just gone into a gully.'

'I said don't move, you bloody idiot!'

'I've got to get back on to solid ground.' But he had turned somehow, and stepping back on to what he expected to be solid footing, he slithered even more deeply into water that came instantly up to his thighs. Now which way? Panic was taking hold. Mindlessly he began to struggle. The tide had been coming in fast, but surely not this fast. Where was he?

'Pete! Help me! I'm gettin' out of me depth.'

Whether the voice answered or not, he didn't know as, slipping, he found himself floundering. A white blanket seemed to have been wrapped around his head. He was all alone, isolated, unable to keep his footing, his thigh boots, his sodden heavy jumper and the oil-skin coat all weighing him down. With the incoming tide driven before the stiff chilling breeze, the sea had become choppy. He choked as, losing his footing, water slapped into his mouth. God, the sea was cold. Beneath the water-logged jumper it chilled his flesh to the bone; his brain too in his panic had begun to feel frozen, totally incapable of conveying to him what he must do next.

Seconds later a figure appeared at his side, it too slithering, sliding, hands under his armpits, endeavouring vainly to hold him

335

up. 'I got yer.' Pete's voice. 'You silly young bugger! Lucky I found . . .' He stopped talking suddenly. 'Listen!'

Out of the silence that surrounded them came a faint putt-putt-putt of a boat's engine.

'It's him. It's Foley. Thank Christ for that. Shout, Danny! Help! Over here. Help!'

Together they bawled into the fog, unable to tell which way to shout, just bellowing at the top of their lungs. Came another voice, hollow through a megaphone.

'Hoy there! This is the *Millicent*. Who are you? Are you in trouble? What boat are you?'

Filling his lungs, Danny bellowed back. 'We're stranded on the mud, out of our depth.' A wave spilled into his open mouth, entering his lungs like a deluge. He broke off, gasping for breath as another wave caught him.

'Stay where you are,' came back the voice. It was of course an utterly inane piece of advice. Where else would they go? But this time, Danny was sure he had got the direction of it. To his uncle he managed to splutter, 'Swim for it. That way.'

'I can't,' came the splutter. 'Never could.'

Danny tried to hold his face above the splash of waves, finding it a losing battle. He couldn't swim either, had never seen the point. Thanks to that oversight, came the odd thought, he was now on the point of drowning.

Visions of Connie's Ben drowning off the gaswork's jetty filled his mind. He heard himself yelling in panic. Then a voice came from somewhere above him. 'We're puttin' down a skiff to look for you. Hold on.'

For a moment a partial break in the swirling fog revealed the boat to be a shrimper, no boom to her mainsail to make easier trawling. Then the shape vanished as fog closed in again.

But, chilled to the bone, the two men in the water felt hope rise as they strained for their feet to touch bottom, still not out of reach, though by now both were becoming desperate as the swiftly deepening water splashed their faces continuously, the sweep of the incoming tide threatening to take their feet from under them. If the skiff failed to find them in time . . .

Danny was yelling his lungs out, his uncle, finding the chill water overpowering, merely croaking and gasping. He in his state could go under before Danny did.

336

There came sounds of a skiff being lowered, the splash as it hit the water, voices, scraping sounds as men got themselves into the craft. A strange distracted thought entered Danny's head as though in a dream. Why hadn't he and Pete thought of bringing their own skip with them? Old Foley would have taken it on board. And where was he? The boat here wasn't his. And all the time Danny could hear himself yelling, 'Over here! F'Christ sake! Over here!' As if it wasn't him at all who called, but someone else. He himself seemed to have no life left in him to yell.

Hands grasped him. Others hoisted his uncle. A voice, somehow familiar, was shouting. 'Get a line to him! We'll have to haul him up.' But Danny could hear nothing as he was yelled at to catch the rope thrown to him, much less help himself. It floated uselessly by him; he had too much water in his body now to reach out and grab it, was totally frozen, incapable of doing anything constructive. 'It's no good,' someone was shouting. 'I'm going in to help him.'

Someone had leapt into the water beside him. A face came close to his, the words choking and spluttering. 'Christ, I forgot, I'm no bloody great swimmer.' Very few fishermen were, oddly enough. 'But there weren't no other way to get this rope to you.' Forced to plunge several times beneath the surface, his rescuer, finally got a rope around him. Just hang on to me, Bowmaker. Right, there, haul away!'

The person knew his name? In all the flurry about him, Danny found himself wondering why. And why he should even think this with water going into his mouth, into his nose, swallowing it by the gallon so it felt. Maybe he *was* drowning. That too came as a distracted thought. Maybe Ben hadn't felt anything either, just this helpless swallowing of water while thoughts floated across his brain.

He didn't know how they got him into the skip, when the *Millicent*'s crew pulled him up into the shrimper in the manner of bringing in a catch: as the vessel leaned into the sea to slacken the line, they were grasping the rope to wrap it around a baling pin, pulling on the backward lean, again and again, then as Danny's body came within grabbing distance dragging it over the side until it lay in the scuppers like some dead cod.

337

Chapter Thirty-One

Seawater was being urgently pumped out of his body, and it hadn't taken long to regain consciousness.

Danny came to, face down on a moving deck, water spilling from his mouth with every downward pressure on his back from the man kneeling above him. A wrinkled, weather-beaten face came down level with his and he found himself gazing at a pair of anxious, faded blue eyes.

'He's awake,' a voice buzzed in his waterlogged ears. 'Y'can stop now. Don't seem t'be any more in them there lungs. Reckon he's all right.'

'Let's sit 'im up!'

Danny felt himself turned over and carefully brought to a sitting position. Beneath him the boat was heaving forward gently. Shivering with shock and cold, his soaked clothing icy on his flesh, he stared witlessly around him, vaguely recognised Pete, and . . .

A blanket draped unceremoniously around his shoulders shut out the faces for a second, then, with a mug of hot tea thrust into his shaking hands to add to the warming process, he gathered his wits enough to recognise the owner of the weather-beaten face as Dick Bryant, and behind him, his son George. He recalled the voice beside him in the water, recalled seeing the figure dive down again and again to secure the rope beneath his armpits and pull the heavy oil-skin coat off him as he spluttered and took half the estuary into his lungs; this was the owner of the voice who had shouted: 'get a line to 'im!'

George now studied him closely. 'You feel all right?' Danny nodded, a vague animosity rising inside him. 'We thought you was a goner for a minute.'

'Was it him that got me out?' he asked, still finding a need for confirmation from this ring of faces, the crew of the *Millicent*, he assumed.

George Bryant was silent, but all eyes had turned to him. 'It was 'im as jumped in,' said Dick Bryant, his voice trembling with pride. 'And 'im a poor swimmer. Thought we'd niver get you out, what with them boots and that bloody oil-skin weighin' you down. My George had to risk his life getting you out on 'em and a line around you, an' you danglin' on it like a dead thing when we hoisted you up. We thought you *was* dead. It was 'im what saved you.'

'Thanks,' Danny said inadequately, self-consciously.

'We thought him was goin't'go too, tide making in so quick like, an' him takin' in water and choking. His wife could a' bin made a widow, easily. And her pregnant too.'

Danny looked directly at George, hardly his enemy any more. How could he be, a man who'd leapt into icy water to rescue him?

'Pam and you – another little'un?' was all he could say.

'Seems so,' George muttered.

His father had come forward, bent to look at the rescued man, his expression strained, his lips pale behind the bristly grey moustache. 'You feel all right now, son?'

Danny nodded, finished his mug of tea and handed it to someone. With help he got shakily to his feet. His uncle who seemed in better shape than himself, was already up on his feet, a blanket around his shoulders as he sipped at the scalding hot liquid handed to him.

Danny's knees weak beneath him threatened to let him down and he locked them so as not to fall back onto the deck and look a fool before these two. Beneath his feet, the jerk and roll of the boat making her way slowly through the fog, her thin tinny foghorn sounding at intervals, didn't help.

'We'll have you ashore as soon as we can,' George said, noticing the way the other shook and trembled, his face ashen, his lips white as chalk.

Hesitantly, he reached out and pulled the blanket closer around Danny's shoulders. Then the hand, still extended, moved towards Danny in an unmistakable gesture.

'For Pam's sake,' he said simply.

For a moment Danny regarded the outstretched hand, then knowing exactly what he meant, slowly took it.

George's father, looking on, appeared speechless, but as far as Danny was concerned, the old feud that had gone on for so long would not carry on into any other generation. What George's mother would make of it he had no idea but he was sure Mum would understand, and Connie and Josie and Annie. There was still Dad, but it didn't matter. Dad was in the minority in this, and it was right that his hatred should be his alone with no one but him feeding on it.

His legs becoming even weaker, Danny let them unlock, let men carry him into the wheelhouse to take off his soaked clothing and ply him with another mug of steaming tea on which to warm his still chilled hands.

Two days to go to Christmas. While everyone was making a fuss of Danny, Annie felt nothing but that low throb of loneliness this particular festive season could inflict upon some.

Josie's excitement at having her Arthur here on Boxing Day, his pay enabling him to come by train instead of braving the weather on his bike, jarred in Annie's head.

There was Connie all aglow and flashing her ring about. Her new fiancé, Ian Lindsay, would be managing a few hours with them on that same day, Boxing Day allowing him a little respite from his round of church services.

There was Pam carrying her second child, glowing with pride and happiness, her position in this household restored, she and her husband due to pop in after Christmas Day and hopeful that her father would accept her husband, if only grudgingly.

Mum, caught up in final preparations for Christmas, her puddings and her cake sitting waiting to be eaten, the turkey to be bought at the last minute in the market at half price; she was too busy to take note of her daughter's unhappiness.

And Dad, almost himself again, upright, everyone remembering again how large a man he was as he paraded his new-found mobility around on his two crutches, swinging his paralysed legs forward on them with an aggressive defiance; he too had not stopped to see how unhappy she was.

Only she had nothing to celebrate. Couldn't they see it?

'Annie, love, stop staring at the fire. Kettle's boiling. Fill the teapot.'

'Yes, Mum.'

'See what I've got for Arthur?' Josie was saying. 'It's a tie. Pity I can't give it to him until Boxing Day. But it's still his Christmas present. What do you think of it?'

'Nice, Josie.'

'Is that all? *Nice*? I paid a good bit for that.'

'It is nice. He'll love it.'

'When Ian and I are married next year,' Connie said, 'I expect I'll be spending all my time in church coming up to Christmas. Any other time come to that. Lots to do as a vicar's wife, seeing to this, seeing to that, organising things, meeting people.' Connie spoke with such joy it wrung Annie's heart.

Only Danny seemed quiet, but there was little he could say. And he still hadn't quite recovered from his ordeal. He had a nasty cold which was affecting him, but Mum's hot drinks and endless Beecham's powders would keep it from turning any nastier. There was no cough, so pneumonia had no say in it. And Danny was strong and basically healthy. Allowed to do little, he sat by the fire most of the time, a perfect place for watching her.

And Holly when she was here, which seemed to be most of the time with school Christmas holidays, was quiet too around her; when she spoke to her it was in low tones as though she saw it as wrong to enthuse noisily while Annie suffered. That Holly knew she suffered was a comfort of sorts to Annie and she silently thanked her, aware that Holly even seemed by some sixth sense to know she thanked her though nothing was said.

Dad was having a little sleep, Danny was resting up in his room, Holly was helping her make coloured paper chains to hang up around the small tree Uncle Reg had brought in for them. Danny had not been well enough to go out and get one. Reg and his brother and their families would be here on Christmas Day and Boxing Day, as would Mum's side. It was Mum's turn to have them, having missed last year out altogether for many reasons.

'How you're going to get them all in this house I can't imagine,' Holly remarked as she and Annie worked. 'If it gets too noisy, maybe you and I can go for a quiet little walk – if the weather lets us.'

She glanced through the window where outside the warm air had departed, the wind veering right round to the southeast bearing raw cold and a threat of snow on it. 'That's if you want. Though I expect you'd like to be on your own.'

341

'No, honestly,' Annie said, not looking up from her task. 'I'd like to have you with me.'

Of all people she wanted Holly with her. Perhaps to Holly she could explain more the cause of her marriage breaking up. No one had really listened. Mum had cuddled her, told her to try and put it behind her, but she had bitten her lip and moved away or changed the subject when Annie had tried to explain how lonely it had been with Alex too preoccupied to see how his absences had affected her. The mere mention of her giving her body to another man brought a sick look to Mum's face. Dad, of course, was out of the question. The others had too many of their own worries or pleasures for her to even begin imparting confidential secrets to ease her heart.

Holly would listen, she knew that instinctively, but would confession really ease her conscience? Nothing would ever do that, but she was paying the price.

'If only I could see Alex again, speak to him, tell him why it all happened.' She said this to herself a dozen times a day and often aloud, to the exasperation of everyone around her. But Holly was different, patient.

'Would he listen?'

'I don't suppose so.' They had their heads lowered, both apparently absorbed in what they were doing.

'He wouldn't listen before,' Annie went on. 'He just behaved hurt and bewildered and then said it would be better if I went home. He might as well have said he didn't love me any more. If he'd loved me, he would have forgiven me. I'm sure he would.'

'Forgiving can be the hardest thing in the world to do, even though you still love that person you can't forgive. You can't turn love off that easily. I'm sure he still loves you.'

'I don't think so.' Annie sniffed back the ready tears, seeing the futility of hoping her marriage would ever mend. One day the postman would bring a long heavy envelope with a solicitor's seal on it and she'd know without having to open it what would lie inside, the commencement to the end of her marriage, paid for by Alex's wealthy family, only too glad to get rid of her.

Annie bent her head even lower, hoping the tears stinging her eyes wouldn't fall on to the strip of yellow paper she was looping around a blue one.

At a knock on the door, Mum ceased painting milk on to the

342

pastry tops of the second batch of mince pies to make them shine before going into the oven – the cooked ones lay on the table, their tops all glistening, the cosy kitchen filled with their warm sweet aroma. Wiping her hands on her apron, she went to answer it.

Probably Mum's sister, Anne, after whom she herself had been named. The last thing she wanted was to smile at visitors. She heard her mother exclaim, then a voice sounded in the front room, a man's voice – not Aunt Anne, probably Uncle Bill. Annie didn't look up as the two came into the kitchen.

'Annie?'

At her mother's voice she lifted up her head and an anguished cry burst from her, the cry itself seeming to propel her out of her chair.

'Alex! Oh! I can't believe it!' The next second she was in his arms, not pausing to think whether he wished this or not, was here with good news or bad, all the pent-up guilt stored up inside her pouring out in a gush of words, muffled as she buried her face against his chest, the coat he wore cold and rough against her cheeks. 'Oh, Alex, please . . . forgive me! I did such a terrible, wicked thing. I'm so sorry. I've missed you so much.'

For a moment he held her tightly, then gently eased her from him to gaze into her face. His was solemn, but she read the message in his eyes and immediately threw herself back into his arms which closed, oh so gloriously, around her.

Behind her, her mother signalled to Holly, and easing themselves past the pair without touching them, they went out of the room. On the table the mince pies ready for the oven lay in their tray, the brushed milk slowly seeping into the pastry.

Sitting before the kitchen fire, the rest of the family keeping out of the way in the front room, Alex spoke in low sombre tones of how things had been since her leaving while she wept intermittently, unable to discern from those flat tones whether he still blamed her and merely felt he should forgive her, or whether he saw her as the gullible innocent party in that affair. Not once did he say he still loved her.

In this way he told how the whole club had proclaimed their support and sorrow for him, telling him they were all on his side; how he'd felt when everyone had spoken her name in defamatory terms; the revulsion he'd had for himself at not being strong enough to defend her, taking it all in silence.

343

Worse, it appeared that the Burringtons had made up, Mrs Burrington loudly accusing Annie of leading her husband on, saying she'd practically thrown herself at him, a man powerless in the hands of such a scheming brazen hussy whom he had merely been trying to comfort and whose clutches he hadn't known how to escape, even that she had blackmailed him once she had him in her claws with the threat that she would tell his wife all if he didn't do all she wished.

'That was a lie,' Annie wept. 'It was all lies. It was him. I thought he was being kind. And I needed someone to be kind to me, to be with me. He made me feel you didn't care, that you never bothered to come and see me. And I was so lonely up there in Simla and you down in Jalapur. No one else ever seemed to understand. He was the only one who seemed to.'

She came at last to a hiccuping stop, knowing Alex would see no point in her efforts to vindicate herself. Telling him the truth didn't lessen her part in ruining their marriage. It had happened no matter who was to blame. His forgiving her could never turn back the clock. So why had he come here?

This she asked him, stemming her tears sufficiently to ask.

'I came,' he said slowly, 'to tell you I had to return to England. My father passed away two weeks ago. I wrote and told him our marriage had broken down and he called me home immediately. I was just in time to be there when he died. It was all very sudden.'

Annie listened bleakly. She couldn't even say she was sorry for his father's death. She didn't know him, and she had long blamed him for his attitude towards her and his son. The way Alex spoke, he didn't seem all that grieved either, merely stating the facts. But it was obvious Alex hadn't come back to pick up the threads of their marriage. As far as he was concerned she had been unfaithful, had been the one who'd broken up their marriage. He was only exercising good manners in letting her know he was back in the country. No doubt also he'd inherited from his father. What better reason to come back to England?

Embittered, she became aware he was still talking. 'The funeral was last week, but I would have had to come home, even if my father hadn't asked for me. I couldn't stand it out there after you left. I'd wander around the house. It seemed so empty, seemed so deserted. I couldn't put my mind to my work. I felt completely . . . I felt lost.'

344

He turned to her. 'Annie, please forgive me for the way I treated you. I never thought. I know how discontented you were out there, but I was so wrapped up trying to prove to my parents I could make our marriage work. I wanted to prove to them it didn't matter if we were from opposite ends of what they like to call the social scale. But instead all I did was to wreck what we had. Annie, I want to start again. Come back to me?'

He had been speaking so fast she was left hardly able to fit together what he was really saying. It was only as she looked up and saw the beseeching glow in his eyes that she realised he had been asking that their marriage be rescued, and from somewhere deep inside her a voice cried: 'Oh, Alex, yes.'

Seconds later he was kissing her, his breath harsh on her cheek. And, oh, the joy that consumed Annie as she kissed him in return. All the obvious problems of their future together seemed of no importance: the turbulence that being the wife of a wealthy

businessman would inflict on her; the social life she would be expected to lead; the people she would be asked to meet and mingle with, she with no grounding for it. That wasn't entirely true – she'd had good grounding in India. The second time around she would know the pitfalls, and in England perhaps be able to meet them on her own terms. It would be difficult even here, she knew, as she kissed Alex, but she would surmount them, the foolish mistake she had made in India forgiven as she in turn silently forgave him for having been partly the cause.

The lingering aroma of Christmas cooking still filled the house this Boxing Day. The turkey now was a carcass from which people picked little bits as they went by it, the debris of yesterday's celebration still lay uncleared, everyone sat about, full to the gills from eating too much, stupefied from too little sleep, having played cards into the night and dozed where they could.

Daniel Bowmaker looked around at his family as he leaned heavily on his crutches in the doorway, his paralysed legs supported by the hefty iron callipers. Boxing Day as it used to be. Everyone was here. His brothers and their families, Peggy's people, Connie and her new fiancé, Josie and hers, Pam . . .

Daniel looked at Pam and his heart swelled with affection despite all that had happened. As for her husband – George was responsible for Danny's being here today with nothing worse than

345

a stinking cold where he could have been a drowned man – he supposed he could put up with George if he put his mind to it. But the boy's father he would never forgive, though for Pam's sake he would never refer to it again in her hearing. So the burning of his boat had been an accident. But Dick Bryant, low coward that he was, intending merely to cause a bit of vandalism to get his own back, had still burned down his entire livelihood.

He smiled as little Beth toddled over to him to show him the dolly Father Christmas had brought her, unaware it was he who had given it. He stood now on his crutches, and looked around at the rest of his family.

Annie, reunited with Alex, would go away again, perhaps only to the other side of London, but socially it would be to another land. He wondered if she would come home sometimes and not forget her humble roots. He hoped so. They would all go away, Annie with her wealthy husband; Connie to Market Harborough, a vicar's wife, her role in his parish keeping her away from her family for weeks on end; Josie, going to live in East London with her Arthur once they were married.

That left Danny, at the moment sitting in the corner, blowing his nose noisily in a sheet of a handkerchief. And beside him, Holly, attentive to him, a sweet, contented soul – not a beauty, but what was beauty? Said she was happy to come and live with them when she and Danny married. She'd look after her husband and help her future mother-in-law; she who had no one else in the world saw her future here as a gift from God.

Yes, Danny would make out. His new blood would bring prosperity to them. In time this seemingly endless world depression would come to an end – as everything did. Life never stood still. Things would change. For the better he hoped. A week from now would see in a new year. And ten years from now, he was certain, life would be happy and peaceful and full of hope again, the hard years forgotten.

'Dear Lord,' Daniel Bowmaker prayed silently as he watched his family on Boxing Day, 'let nineteen thirty-two bring 'em all joy. And let 'em have peace and prosperity for the rest on their lives. They all deserve it. Amen.'

And though he wasn't normally a praying man, he was sure the Lord would answer that one.